A Passing Splendor...

Jared's merriment subsided and, of its own volition, his hand touched the knot of hair resting against her neck. She raised her eyes to his and they held only briefly before she was in his arms. It happened quietly, naturally, instinctively. He held her to him and whispered her name repeatedly against her ear, his breath sending shivers of pleasure down her spine.

He drew back and searched her eyes for some sign of rejection, but saw only invitation. His mouth took hers in a telling kiss. Their lips sought and found and celebrated each other. The kiss was tender, but held promise of restrained passion. It was committing, but left room for reservation, for caution. It was a kiss for the moment. For now. Only now.

Dear Reader:

We trust you will enjoy this Richard Gallen romance. We plan to bring you more of the best in both contemporary and historical romantic fiction with four exciting new titles each month.

We'd like your help.

We value your suggestions and opinions. They will help us to publish the kind of romances you want to read. Please send us your comments, or just let us know which Richard Gallen romances you have especially enjoyed. Write to the address below. We're looking forward to hearing from you!

Happy reading!

The Editors of
Richard Gallen Books
8-10 West 36th St.
New York, N.Y. 10018

Hidden Fires

LAURA JORDAN

Q

PUBLISHED BY RICHARD GALLEN BOOKS
Distributed by POCKET BOOKS

A RICHARD GALLEN BOOKS *Original* publication

Distributed by
POCKET BOOKS, a Simon & Schuster division of
GULF & WESTERN CORPORATION
1230 Avenue of the Americas, New York, N.Y. 10020

ISBN: 0-671-45147-2

First Pocket Books printing July, 1982

10 9 8 7 6 5 4 3 2 1

RICHARD GALLEN and colophon are trademarks
of Simon & Schuster and Richard Gallen & Co., Inc.

Printed in the U.S.A.

To Michael,
a wellspring of patience

Hidden Fires

Chapter 1

The heat from the September sun was like a physical assault to the young woman who stepped down from the train at the Austin depot. Her ivory cheeks were slightly flushed, and a few vagrant tendrils of raven-black hair escaped the chignon under her hat. She fanned a lacy handkerchief in front of her face as she eagerly scanned the crowd for a familiar brown Stetson, and the tall, white-haired man who would be wearing it.

A sizable throng had gathered at the depot for the arrival of the noon train from Fort Worth. Families embraced returning prodigals, while others waved goodbye to passengers boarding the train. Commissions to write soon and be careful were issued in a cacophonous blend of English and Spanish, with the train's hissing white steam and sharp whistle providing the percussion for this discordant orchestra. With amazing alacrity, porters wheeled long, flatbed carts loaded with luggage, managing to skirt old ladies, businessmen, and young children.

Mexican women dressed in bright, full skirts strolled the platform hawking homemade candy, flowers, and Texas souvenirs. *Vaqueros* leaned lazily against the depot wall, toying with lariats, rolling cigarettes, or squinting at the train they were reluctant to board, for they preferred open spaces and the cerulean ceiling of the Texas sky to the narrow confines of a railroad car.

Many of these cowboys noticed the young woman who watched each approaching carriage expectantly. Her gray eyes, which had been so full of excitement only minutes ago, became clouded with anxiety as the crowd began to diminish. The folds of her skirt swished behind her enticingly as she walked the length of the platform and back again. Dainty, high-button shoes tapped on the smooth boards with each step.

One by one, the *vaqueros* sauntered toward the train bound back to Fort Worth. Most cast one last, longing look at the girl who, despite the heat and her obvious agitation, maintained a cool appearance.

With a screech of steel on steel, a geyser of steam, and a long blast of the whistle, the train slowly inched away from the depot, gained momentum, and finally chugged out of sight.

The platform emptied of people. The Mexican vendors covered the wares in their baskets, and the porters parked their carts in the shade of the building.

The girl in the navy-blue serge suit, white shirtwaist, and tan felt hat stood beside her meager luggage looking forlorn and lonely.

Ed Travers bustled out the depot door, sighted the girl and, tugging his vest over his rotund stomach, hurried toward her.

"Miss Holbrook?" he inquired politely. "Miss Lauren Holbrook?"

The dismayed eyes brightened at the sound of her name and she smiled, parting perfectly formed lips to reveal small white teeth. "Yes," she answered breathlessly. "Yes, I'm Lauren Holbrook. Did Ben . . . uh . . . Mr. Lockett send you for me?"

Ed Travers covered his bafflement with a reassuring smile. "No, Miss Holbrook, not exactly. I'm Ed Travers, the depot manager. I'm sorry I kept you waiting, but the telegraph machine—" He broke off, impatient with himself for bungling what was already a delicate situation. "Forgive me for rambling and forcing you to stand in this heat. Come with me and I'll explain everything." He signaled to a lounging porter, who reluctantly came forward to carry Lauren's luggage.

Mr. Travers indicated the end of the platform by tipping his bowler hat. Still Lauren hesitated. "But Mr. Lockett told me—"

"Mr. Lockett did come for you, Miss Holbrook, but he fell ill and asked—"

"Ben is ill?" she asked quickly, paling and clutching the station manager's arm in alarm.

Her reaction stunned Ed Travers. Why did she keep referring to Ben Lockett? What was this girl to that old buzzard? She was beautiful. No question about that. And Ben had always had an eye for the ladies. Everyone in Texas knew what kind of marriage Ben had with Olivia, but even so, this girl was perplexing. Where did she come from? Why had she come to Texas to see Ben Lockett? She could be no more than twenty, and Ben was in his sixties. Maybe she was a relative. She certainly didn't look like a doxy. And why would Ben be setting up a mistress? He had—

2

"Mr. Travers, please." Lauren was anxiously waiting for an explanation, and the pleasant, kindly man was studying her with an unsettling intensity. Having arrived after an arduous trip from her home in North Carolina only to find that Ben was not here to meet her was disconcerting enough. Of course, he had warned her that if he couldn't leave Coronado, he would send someone else to greet her. "Is Mr. Lockett ill?"

"Ben?" Travers asked distantly. Then, clearing his throat, he said, "No, not Ben. I guess he sent Jared after you, and he's the one who's sick."

He was leading her down the platform with an encouraging hand under her elbow.

"Jared?" she asked.

My God! She didn't even know Jared! But then, it would be distressing to think that this lovely young woman had anything to do with him. It all came back to Ben. What was his game this time? He had a reputation for practical jokes and surprises, usually embarrassing for the recipient. But would Ben's legendary humor extend to victimizing an innocent like Miss Holbrook? In the few moments he had spent with her, Ed Travers had inferred that Lauren Holbrook was trusting and naive to a fault, uncommon as that was in this third year of the twentieth century.

"Jared is Ben's son, Miss Holbrook," he answered patiently. "Didn't Ben ever mention him to you?"

Lauren laughed easily. "Oh, yes. He told me he had a son. I don't recall if he told me his name, though." Her smile faded into an expression of genuine concern. "He's ill?"

"In a manner of speaking," Travers said gruffly, taking her arm more firmly as they descended the steps to the ground below. Lauren saw a long, flatbed wagon parked several yards ahead of them. The green paint on its sideboards was faded and peeling, the wheels mud-splattered. Its two horses were grazing at a tuft of grass under the enormous pecan tree.

Another horse, a palomino of magnificent proportions, was tied to the end of the wagon. Proudly he tossed his blond mane as if protesting the indignity of being hitched to such a lowly vehicle.

"Apparently, Miss Holbrook, Ben sent young Jared for you, and he came from Coronado last night. This morning, when he became incapacitated, he asked me to escort you to his home. I'm afraid the trip won't be very comfortable. I apologize, but this was the best conveyance I could find on short notice."

"I'm sure I'll be fine." She smiled. Ed Travers became dizzy under the radiance of her face and gentle voice. Then he cursed himself for being an old fool and hastened toward the wagon.

The depot manager assisted Lauren onto the rickety seat. As the porter dropped her bags unceremoniously onto the rough floor of the wagon bed, she heard a muffled moan.

She gasped in surprise when she saw the long figure sprawled on his back in the wagon. "Mr. Travers!" she exclaimed. "Is he seriously injured?"

"No," he answered. "Only a little indisposed. He'll live, though he may soon wish he were dead." He mumbled the last few words, and his meaning escaped Lauren.

She settled herself as best she could on the uncomfortable seat. The brown leather was cracked. At intervals where it had ripped open, the stuffing poked through in hard lumps. The rusted springs groaned under her slight weight. She kept her gaze focused on the road ahead.

"I must run back inside for a moment, Miss Holbrook, and speak to my assistant. If you'll indulge me, we'll be on our way without further delays." Ed Travers doffed his hat again and turned back toward the depot. The porter shuffled after him.

Lauren sighed. Well, it's not the greeting I expected, but it's novel, she thought. Then she smiled with the sheer joy of being in Texas and almost at the end of her journey. Had it been only three weeks since she last saw Ben? It seemed like eons. So much had happened since he had visited her guardians and issued the impulsive invitation for her to come to Texas.

They had all been in the parlor of the parsonage. Lauren was pouring tea, which was one of her chores when Reverend Abel Prather and his wife, Sybil, entertained. Guests visited often with the middle-aged couple, who had opened their home to Lauren when her clergyman father died eight years ago. She loved the Prathers, though she realized they were unenlightened about anything outside their sphere. Most of their callers were either other ministers or parishioners.

Their guest on that particular day had been unique. Ben Lockett had served in the Confederate Army with the young Chaplain Prather during the last three years of the war. Their philosophies differed greatly, but the two men enjoyed each other's company and found pleasure in taking opposing sides of any debate, whether over the strength of the Union Army or predestination.

After the war, Ben Lockett had left his native Virginia for

unknown parts of Texas. He was of a breed of ambitious, angry young men who defiantly carved empires out of the vast plains of Texas. In the forty years since the War Between the States, Ben Lockett had become an influential cattle baron.

Lauren was intrigued by the imposing Texan. He stood tall and lean, with only the slightest paunch to indicate his advancing years. His hair was thick and snowy white, brushed back from his wide, deep forehead like a crest. Blue eyes twinkled merrily from under shaggy white eyebrows, as if he were perpetually amused by the world. But Lauren observed that Ben was capable of a piercing, glacial stare if his emotions dictated it.

His voice was deep and mellow when he said to her, "Tell me, Miss Holbrook, what you think of Texas. Like most Texans, I feel that everyone should be as enthralled with my country as I am." He stared at her from under the shaggy brows, but it was a friendly look.

"I . . . I don't know that much about it, Mr. Lockett," she replied honestly. "I've read about the Alamo, and I know that the state was once a republic. The rest of my knowledge is confined to the penny-novel book covers that I see on display at the general store. They depict train robberies, cattle rustling, and saloons. I don't know if that is a true characterization or not."

Ben threw back his head with its shock of white hair and roared with laughter. The booming sound rattled the china figurines that cluttered every conceivable space in Sybil Prather's overdecorated parlor.

"Well, we have our share of train robberies, and I've frequented a few saloons myself, begging your pardon, Abel. I've even chased a few rustlers all the way to Mexico." He paused. "Maybe the pictures you've seen are accurate at that, Miss Holbrook." He studied her for a moment longer, then challenged, "Why don't you come back to Texas with me and see it for yourself?"

There were several startled exclamations.

"Ben, you're joking, of course! I'd forgotten what a tease you are." Abel laughed.

"Let my Lauren go to Texas where Indians live!" Sybil cried. The ruffles covering her ample bosom quivered with distress.

"What an utterly preposterous suggestion!" came from William. William. Yes, William Keller had been there, too.

Lauren shuddered, even in the stifling heat. She pushed the thought of William out of her mind. She wasn't going to let the memory of him ruin her reunion with Ben Lockett.

Another groan, accompanied this time by a mumbled curse, diverted her from her reverie. Hesitantly she swiveled her head to look at the ailing man. Her eyes lighted first on an ornately tooled saddle, with filigreed silver decorations glittering against the black leather. Her bags were at the back of the wagon, near the man's feet.

He must be very tall, Lauren thought as she quickly scanned the length of the prone body. Her initial impression was that he was lean and well proportioned. After that first hasty appraisal, she began at his boots and studied the figure with increasing fascination.

The black boots were of smooth leather and came to just under his knees. Tight black chinos were tucked into the tops of them. Lauren blushed at the perfect fit of the pants, which contoured the long, muscled thighs like a second skin.

Lauren's breath caught in her throat, and she stared as one hypnotized at the bulge between his thighs. The tight pants emphasized and detailed his anatomy. To Lauren, who was raised in deliberate ignorance of the opposite sex, it was a bold display. How could anyone be so flagrantly nonchalant about his . . . person? she wondered.

Her palms grew moist within her gloves.

She forced her eyes to move from his crotch. The buff-colored shirt was shoved sloppily into his belted waistband. Only the last two buttons of the shirt were closed, and the soft fabric fell away from a broad chest that rose and fell with his even breathing. The wide chest tapered to a flat belly and was covered with light brown hair that glinted with golden highlights as the sun filtered through the branches of the pecan tree and shone on him.

Lauren had never seen a man shirtless before. Once a member of Reverend Prather's congregation had caught a deadly fever and she had glimpsed his upper torso as one of the married women in attendance had bathed him. The sufferer was fat; his skin was pink; and his chest was smooth and hairless. No, he had looked nothing like this.

Lauren swallowed hard and pressed her hand against the fluttering in her stomach.

Jared Lockett groaned again, and she held her breath, afraid that he would awaken and find her looking at him with this shameful temerity. But he only sighed, making a deep hollow of his stomach under his rib cage. His hand moved onto his chest, where it stirred restlessly before remaining still. The hand was tanned and large, with strong, slim fingers. The same sun-bleached hair that covered his chest sprinkled the back of his hand.

A strong column of throat extended from the powerful shoulders. Lauren raised her eyes to his face and was crushingly disappointed. His features were covered by a black, flat-crowned, wide-brimmed hat. Her curiosity was piqued by this son of Ben's, and she wanted to view the face that belonged to this long, hard body.

Lauren almost jumped when Ed Travers said briskly, "There. I think we can leave now."

So engrossed was she with Jared Lockett's form that she hadn't noticed the man returning from his errand.

"You are extremely kind to do this, Mr. Travers." Lauren's level voice surprised her. The tickling sensation in her stomach had spread into her chest and throat. These symptoms of "the vapors" were uncharacteristic of the usually serene Lauren Holbrook.

"No problem at all," Travers hastened to assure her.

He clucked to the bedraggled horses and began maneuvering them through the traffic on the streets of the state's capital. They dodged trolleys, buggies, and horseback riders as they made their way through the city. There were no motorcars, which Lauren had seen on recent trips to Raleigh.

She enjoyed looking at the capitol building from the different angles their route afforded her. "I think you're justifiably proud of your capitol building. I've read about it. It's very impressive."

Travers smiled. "The red granite came from a quarry near the Lockett ranch."

"Keypoint," Lauren said. She remembered Ben's proud voice as he told her about the ranch. Her comment on its clever name, which used a play on words with *Lock*ett and *Key*point, caused him to beam at her astuteness. "You'd be surprised at how few people catch that," he said. As he grinned broadly, the furrows on either side of his mouth deepened into facsimiles of dimples.

Lauren smiled at the memory, and Travers glanced at her out of the corner of his eye. So she knew about Keypoint. Did she also know who lived there? Conversationally he asked, "Have you ever been to Texas before, Miss Holbrook?"

"No, I haven't. That's why I was delighted to accept Ben's invitation to come and stay with his family for a while."

The wagon lurched when Travers suddenly jerked on the reins. She was going to stay with them?! In the house in Coronado? Or at Keypoint? Either place was inconceivable. This girl was as innocent as the day was long. Had Ben Lockett gone mad?

They were outside the city now and heading west on the well-traveled road. When Lauren pulled the long pins out of her hat, Travers warned her, "I wouldn't take that off if I were you, Miss Holbrook. Our sun is hot. You might get a burn on that pretty nose."

Lauren agreed and readjusted her hat, but slipped out of her jacket. The slight breeze stirred by the movement of the wagon cooled her damp skin somewhat.

When she was settled again, Travers returned to his thoughts. That wild buck in the back of the wagon was enough reason not to keep any decent woman under the same roof with him.

Jared Lockett was notorious throughout the state for whoring and drinking. When he was younger, his activities had been deemed "sowing wild oats," but since he had passed his thirtieth birthday, they had become a matter of public scorn. When was Jared going to start acting responsibly? No time soon, Travers mused glumly.

Just last month, Jared had caused a big disturbance at the Rosenburg depot. He and some of his feckless cronies had gone into the Harvey House there and had spent the afternoon drinking and gambling. They had made their presence known in the restaurant by behaving like a pack of wild dogs. Jared made an unseemly proposition to one of the more winsome Harvey girls. The girls who worked as waitresses in the restaurant chain that served the Santa Fe Railroad were known for their scrupulous morals. If a man proposed anything to one of those young ladies, it had better be nothing less than marriage and a vine-covered cottage.

When the girl summarily rejected his suggestion, Jared had become more aggressive. The management had ejected him from the place, but not before Jared, fighting like a demon out of hell, had wreaked havoc on furniture, dishes, and a few of the patrons. It had taken six men to subdue him.

Well, sighed Travers mentally, it was probably just as well that this young woman didn't know about Jared Lockett's antics. They would no doubt scare her to death.

"Is it always this hot in September?" Lauren asked, trying to draw the station manager into conversation. She had had years of practice making small talk in the Prathers' parlor. Mr. Travers had been kind to her, but she was made uneasy by the wrinkled brow and the puzzled expression that would cross his face whenever he looked at her. Was she that different from the women in Texas?

"Yeah," he answered, reassuring her with his easy, open smile. "We usually get our first Norther about the end of October. Most years, September is hotter than June or even July. Is it this warm in . . . ?" He let the question trail off suggestively, and she didn't disappoint him.

"North Carolina. I lived—live—in Clayton. It's a small town not too far from Raleigh. And no, it's not this hot there in September."

"Is that where you met Ben?" he asked curiously. At her affirmative nod, he prodded, "And what was Ben doing in Clayton, North Carolina?"

Lauren explained the friendship between her guardian and the rancher. "For years, they corresponded, but the letters had lagged for the past decade or so. Still, on his way home from a business trip to New York, Ben decided to pay his old friend a visit."

"How long have you lived with this guardian?" Was he being too nosy? He didn't want to offend her, and no man in his right mind would cross Ben Lockett. However, she answered him readily enough and without self-consciousness.

"My father was a clergyman, too. Abel Prather was his bishop. I was twelve when my father died. The Prathers gave me a home with them."

"Your mother?" Travers asked quietly.

"I was three when she died giving birth. The baby—a boy—was stillborn." Her voice was suddenly soft and pensive. Travers noted that she touched the brooch watch pinned to her shirtwaist just above the gentle swell of her breast.

The small brooch was all she had of her mother's possessions. That and a picture taken of her parents on their wedding day. She vainly tried to remember moments she had shared with the pretty, petite woman in the picture, but no memories would come. Lauren had no inkling of the personality that had lived behind the shy eyes captured in the photograph. In stressful times, or when she longed for the parent she couldn't remember, she touched the watch with her fingertips as if the action brought her in contact with her mother. But this was a habit Lauren wasn't conscious of.

After his young wife's death, Gerald Holbrook had totally dedicated himself to his work. He delved into religious dogma and contemplated theological doctrines in the hours when he wasn't actively serving his congregation or preparing his inspired sermons. If the care of his young daughter fell to his current house-keeper, that was the price one had to pay for absolute commitment to Christ. Lauren knew that, in his way, her father loved her and wasn't bitter over his neglect—though she felt it. She would have welcomed a more demonstrative relationship, but knew her father lived on a higher plane—like God.

She was a well-behaved child, quiet and unobtrusive as she sat near her father when he studied in his library. She learned to read at an early age, and books and the characters in them became her playmates and confidantes. Her classmates weren't particularly inclined to include the "preacher's kid" in their pranks. Out of loneliness, Lauren acquired a talent for creating her own diversions.

When Gerald Holbrook died, Lauren barely missed him. She moved into the Prathers' house and assumed their routine without question. They were kind and, because of their childlessness, welcomed the adolescent girl into their home. Their generosity extended to giving Lauren piano lessons. She was musically gifted, and the piano became a passion along with literature.

No one ever left the Prathers' gaudy, crowded house without knowing their pride in Lauren. She had never betrayed their trust or disappointed them.

Except with William. How unfair was their changed attitude toward her! She was blameless!

"Miss Holbrook?" Ed Travers asked for the third time, and finally succeeded in gaining her attention.

"I'm sorry, Mr. Travers. What did you say?" Lauren flushed under her hat at being caught so deep in her own thoughts.

"I asked if you would like a drink of water," he said, reaching under the seat for a canteen, which he had filled before leaving the depot.

"Oh, yes, thank you." Lauren reached for the canteen. Never having drunk from one, she felt like a pioneer as she tipped it back and took a tentative, ladylike sip.

Just then, the wagon hit a deep rut in the road, and some of the water sloshed onto her shirtwaist. She wiped her dripping chin and laughed delightedly. Her merriment was checked when the figure in the back of the wagon groaned and cursed vehemently.

"Sonofabitch!"

Chapter 2

Lauren whirled her head around so quickly that the motion hurt her neck. Jared's hand came up and clamped the hat more firmly over his face. He adjusted his long body to another position, contracting and relaxing muscles that Lauren didn't know existed. But then, she had never seen a masculine physique like this before. His languid movements were repelling and thrilling at the same time. It was like watching some pagan god who was beautiful even in his decadence.

She looked at Ed Travers, who was blushing furiously. "I'm sorry about that, Miss Holbrook. Don't pay any attention to his language. He—"

She interrupted with a question. "What's the matter with him?" She was afraid that Ben's son was seriously ill.

"He . . . uh . . . must've tied one on last night." When Travers realized her total lack of comprehension, he reluctantly explained. She might as well learn about Jared now. "He drank too much, don't you see," he said anxiously, "and got—"

"Drunk?" she asked incredulously. "He's got a hangover?" She stared with fixed horror at the prone figure. Never in her twenty years had she witnessed intoxication. A cordial glass of sherry and wine with Thanksgiving and Christmas dinners were the extent of alcohol consumption in the parsonage.

Jared had apparently slipped back into unconsciousness. Gentle snores were coming from under the black hat.

"Yes. Please don't fret about it, Miss Holbrook. It happens all the time. We're just lucky the sheriff didn't pick him up and take him to jail to sleep it off. Fortunately he made it to my office early this morning and asked me to meet your train and drive the two of you to Coronado. He passed out about an hour before you arrived."

"Ben told me that if he couldn't come to Austin himself, he'd send someone else. I imagine that Jared wasn't too happy over being appointed the emissary," Lauren commented.

"Whether he liked it or not, he knew he'd better do what his daddy told him to. Despite their differences, Jared respects his father."

Lauren sniffed as she cast one last reproachful glance over her shoulder. "I can't see that Jared Lockett has much respect for anyone or anything."

Ed Travers chuckled as he diverted the wagon around another collection of deep ruts. "You're probably right, Miss Holbrook."

He turned his attention to private musings, and conversation between them waned. Lauren gazed at the landscape around her.

Ben had told her he lived in the hill country, and her eyes could testify to that. Gently rolling hills covered with grass turning brown in the last days of summer surrounded them. They were driving west out of Austin, and on the right a cypress treelined river cheerfully wended its way through the rocky ground. Cattle grazed among small cedar trees.

As the sun slipped lower on the horizon, it became hotter. Lauren could feel rivulets of perspiration coursing down her scalp. She longed to whisk off her hat, release her heavy hair from its restricting pins, and allow what little breeze there was to blow through it.

Her hair had been the scourge of every housekeeper who had worked for Gerald Holbrook. Its washing and combing had been a constant source of muttered grumblings. Mrs. Dorothea Harris, an embittered widow who had been housekeeper from the time Lauren was seven until her father died, had declared that the girl had enough hair for six children. Each morning, she roughly pulled it into braids that were so tight they brought tears to Lauren's eyes. Lauren's father had said in a rare compliment that her thick black hair was like her mother's. In this Lauren took secret pride.

Of course, it was out of the question to take her hair down now. It wouldn't do at all to arrive at the Locketts' house without a hat, let alone with unbound hair.

Dismally she looked at the fine layer of dust on her navy skirt and agonized over the disheveled appearance she would present when she arrived at her destination. What would Ben think? Would he be ashamed of her and regret his invitation? Lauren wanted so badly to impress his family.

She flicked away what she could of the settling dust. It was instantly replaced, and she sighed resignedly.

Ed Travers said, "It does get a mite dry and dusty. Ben must have done quite a sales job to get you to leave the green hills of North Carolina and come all the way out here." His curiosity over Lauren Holbrook's future status in the Lockett household hadn't yet been satisfied.

Lauren laughed. "He did sell me on Texas, and I haven't been disappointed. It's wonderful."

"How long will you be here?" He couldn't help asking.

She averted her head quickly and clenched her hands into fists. "I . . . I'm not sure." She managed to control her initial agitation and go on. "It will depend on Mrs. Lockett. You see, I'm to be her secretary."

Ed Travers almost fell off his seat. Olivia Lockett with a secretary? What was old Ben trying to pull?

He swallowed hard before he asked squeakily, "What are you going to do for her?"

"I've spent years helping my guardians entertain. Ben thought that I might relieve Mrs. Lockett of some of those responsibilities. I can help her with her correspondence, for instance. The length of my visit will depend on how well we get along and whether she likes me or not," Lauren answered. As she explained her future to him, she tried to assimilate it in her own mind.

Poor lass, thought Travers. If it were a case of Olivia Lockett liking a young, pretty girl living under her roof, then the innocent Lauren Holbrook would be on the next train out of Austin heading anywhere. Olivia could freeze the balls off any man with one icy blast from those hard, green Creole eyes of hers. What would she do to this poor child?

Intuitively Lauren sensed Travers's bewilderment. She had felt that same incredulity at Ben's offer. It had come so suddenly, and she was completely unprepared for it.

They had dined on overdone lamb and bland vegetables, the typical fare that came out of the Prathers' kitchen. Lauren was always painfully aware of the unpalatable meals that Sybil Prather served her guests. She was grateful to Ben Lockett for doing justice to his plate, though he graciously declined a refill.

After dinner, Lauren played the piano for the guests at the persistent urgings of her guardians. The recital was well received but, as usual, the Prathers' gushing praise embarrassed their ward.

Sybil, her plump figure swathed in pink ruffles, sat beside her husband on a garishly upholstered settee. Unfortunately Sybil's taste in clothes extended to her house as well. Her motto was: "More is better." The house was dark and heavy with brocades and velvets. Chandeliers and vases of dark-colored glass added to the gloom. Wallpaper in overgrown prints and a maroon carpet splashed with large orange and yellow flowers vied for supremacy.

The pastor's wife simpered as Abel boasted of her prizewinning roses. Much to their surprise, Lauren's relief, and William Keller's aggravation, Ben asked Lauren to show him this noteworthy garden.

The evening had been warm and still, and cicadas serenaded them as Lauren led Ben to the small rose garden and sat down on a low bench.

"Do you grow roses in Texas, Mr. Lockett?"

"Indeed we do. I have a Mexican gardener who tends to the grounds around the house in Coronado, and he grows them much sweeter and much larger than these prizewinning flowers of Sybil's. I think his secret is horse manure."

There was a momentary pause. Lauren wasn't sure what her reaction should be. Then they both laughed spontaneously. She chided herself for condoning his indelicacy but, somehow, it didn't seem to matter.

"Thank you for inviting me out here with you," she said. "Abel and Sybil usually contrive for me to be alone with William."

"And you don't want to be alone with William?"

She shuddered and said, "No. I don't."

William Keller was a serious, thirty-five-year-old preacher who had accepted the pastorate of a small church on the outskirts of Clayton. Lauren sensed that, beneath the guise of piety, he was ambitious and shrewd. He was continually trying to impress the bishop with the strength of his moral fiber and his undying love for humanity.

Much to Lauren's dismay, the Prathers considered William a superb candidate to relieve her of the state of spinsterhood. They extolled William's virtues to her at least three times a day, and she was forced to take these doses of him much as one is forced to take bad-tasting medicine at regular intervals.

Lauren had only a vague conception of what the intimacies of marriage implied, but the idea of even sharing the same room with the preacher convinced her that spinsterhood would be preferable to a lifetime spent with William Keller.

Normally Lauren's impressions of people were charitable, but she found William physically unattractive, intellectually boring, and socially bigoted. His entire person repulsed her. He had an annoying habit of talking to one's chest rather than one's eyes. Tall and stoop-shouldered, he had thin, lank blond hair which was perpetually falling into colorless eyes fringed by equally colorless lashes. His nose was the most prominent and unfortunate feature of his face. Lauren thought he greatly resembled illustrations of Ichabod Crane, Washington Irving's main character in *The Legend of Sleepy Hollow*.

Ben Lockett had brought her attention back to him with a brusque clearing of his throat. He didn't pursue the subject of William. Instead, he asked her, "What do you do, Miss Holbrook?" Lauren looked at him, puzzled by the question. He clarified, "What keeps you busy around here? Are you happy?"

She answered him frankly. "The Prathers are dear people, and it was kind of them to take me into their home when my father died. I had no relatives. Father had a small annuity, which they have refused to accept for my expenses. I had hoped to teach music or perhaps tutor students in literature or grammar and earn my own money, but the Prathers adamantly reject the idea of my working outside the house."

"So you entertain their guests. That's all?" He smiled at her kindly, and she didn't take offense.

"It's not a very ambitious undertaking, is it?" she asked ruefully. "Oh, I do charity work in the church, sit with shut-ins and sick people, help new mothers with the rest of their families while they're in confinement. I play the organ for the Sunday services and teach a children's Sunday school class." Even to her own ears, these accomplishments sounded dreary.

"Did you ever think of having a family of your own? Marrying?" He fixed her with a blue gaze that was penetrating and compelling.

"I . . . well, not really," she said shyly, and shifted her eyes away from him.

"When I'm trying to make some decision and sort things out, I ride the line for a few days by myself. I like being alone with no company except my horse and Mother Nature."

"'Ride the line'?" she asked with quickening interest.

"Yes. We ride along the fences to make sure none have been knocked down or cut down. Sometimes rustlers try to steal Lockett cows, or maybe a sheep farmer wants to water his flock and not pay for it, so the sheep just make themselves at home on Lockett land."

Lauren drew a deep breath and held it a long time before releasing it. "It sounds . . . oh . . . beautiful, primeval, exciting. I don't know the word to use."

"It's all those things." He studied his knuckles for a moment, then asked, "Why don't you come to Texas with me?" His tone was no longer bantering, as it had been when he made the same offer, publicly, earlier that afternoon.

"You're teasing me about this, Mr. Lockett." The statement contained only a hint of query.

"No, I'm not, Miss Holbrook. I'm just an old cowboy who believes in saving time and getting right to the point."

"But what in the world would I do in Texas?" She had thought at the time that it was an impossibility for her to have such an adventure but hadn't wanted to give up the idea just yet.

"My wife is very active in social and civic affairs in Coronado. That's the town we live in. It's about half a day's ride from Austin. I'm at Keypoint or away on business so often that she can't always count on me. I think she could use someone with your abilities to help her. You've had a lot of experience in arranging social functions. You are an accomplished musician and well read, both of which would be helpful. You could handle her correspondence and such. What do you think?"

When she didn't respond, he pressed his point.

"Of course, we would pay you a salary and give you a room in the house. My son has never married, so we have a lot of space that I was hoping would one day be taken up with grandchildren." He paused for a long moment and, when Lauren looked at him, he was staring unseeingly at the rose bushes. Then he seemed to shake himself loose from the thought and continued, "I want you to feel like one of the family. You would in no way be considered a servant." He grinned engagingly.

"But why are you asking *me?* I'm sure if Mrs. Lockett were looking for a secretary, she could find one."

He shrugged negligently, dismissing her logic. "I'm sure she could, too, but it would probably never occur to her to look for one. My reasons are my own, but I promise you that they are above reproach." He smiled down at her, and his eyes twinkled like blue lights under the bushy white brows.

"Mr. Lockett, I appreciate your liking me enough to invite

me," Lauren said earnestly, "but my place is here. This is where my father wanted me to be."

"Your father is dead. You're alive, but you'll be as good as dead if you don't get out now."

Lauren had been startled when he stood up abruptly, almost angrily, and took several impatient steps away from her. When he turned back, he had looked at her with tenderness and spoke more gently.

"Lauren," she noticed his switch to her first name, "I know you have been taught to obey without questioning. You have a keen sense of duty that is admirable. But I think I see in you a restlessness, an eagerness for life, that needs to be unleashed. You could come to stay a while, and if things didn't work out, or if you hated Texas and the Locketts, I would see that you were sent home right away. No hurt feelings."

What a fool she had been not to accept his invitation right then! Instead, with her head bowed, she had responded softly, "Mr. Lockett, your invitation is overwhelming, and I would love to accept. But I can't go anywhere." She shook her head sadly. "I *have* been taught duty and responsibility, you see. I will probably live with the Prathers for the rest of their lives. They depend on me. It would destroy them for me to leave."

"And what happens to you when they die? If you haven't been pawned off on William or someone like him, what will you do then?"

"I'm sure that some provision will have been made for me."

He sighed heavily and, seeing him so deflated, Lauren was almost prompted to change her mind. He seemed to lose some of his vibrancy. His age was suddenly more apparent on the chiseled features, and there was a mute appeal in the deep blue eyes.

"If there is ever the slightest possibility that you might change your mind, wire me immediately. I mean it. You have a standing invitation."

"Thank you, Mr. Lockett," she replied graciously. She wanted his understanding and she said, "I don't want to be like them." She had been horrified at her admission. "No, no, I don't mean—"

"I know what you meant, Miss Holbrook. I'm sure that you have very few unkind thoughts, but you would like to have a broader horizon than the Prathers do, am I correct?"

"Yes! That's what I was trying to say."

"Remember, if you ever change your mind . . ." he reiterated quietly as they walked back toward the front door.

The sun beat down on the wagon relentlessly. Lauren was becoming weary. The muscles of her back and shoulders ached with fatigue from maintaining her erect posture on the uncomfortable leather seat. Though she had taken numerous sips from the canteen, her throat was parched, and she was covered with dust from the road. Just when she was despairing of ever reaching their destination, Ed Travers nodded his head forward and said, "Coronado."

The wagon topped a hill, allowing Lauren a panoramic view of the small town where Ben lived when he wasn't at his ranch. As the horses picked up their pace on the downward side of the hill, she asked eagerly, "How many people live here?"

"Ummm, about three thousand," Travers replied.

"And how far are we from the ranch? From Keypoint?"

"About a three-hour ride west."

Lauren's disappointment was covered by her interest in Coronado as they drove down the main thoroughfare. She realized that people on the street recognized the large palomino tied to the back of the wagon. Several whispered conjectures were exchanged behind screening hands. Lauren resolutely ignored the man behind her and the persons speculating on his condition.

Her only purposes now were to see Ben again and to meet Mrs. Lockett. Examining her feelings for the man who had come to mean so much to her in such a short space of time, Lauren concluded that Ben Lockett represented the father she had never had. He was merry while her own father had been austere; he was big and robust while the pastor had been slight and less than hearty; he was warm while Gerald Holbrook had been reserved, even toward his own daughter. Ben's deep voice and sharp sense of humor had attracted her to him, and she was breathless with excitement to see him in his own element.

Travers turned the wagon onto a wide, tree-shaded avenue that led south from the center of town. Through the trees, Lauren glimpsed the large house long before Mr. Travers directed the horses up the shell lane.

The house was a credit to whomever had designed it. It was Victorian in design, but not overly ornate, with only a minimum amount of trim. Graceful but sturdy railings outlined the porch that surrounded the house on three sides. On each of the front corners of the second floor were circular rooms domed by onion-shaped cupolas. The tall windows, three on each side of the front porch, were framed in brick-red shutters which contrasted beautifully with the cream-colored frame house. The front door was the same brownish-red and flanked by urns which sported a profusion of red geraniums. The lateness of the summer season didn't hinder the zinnias, petunias, and roses from blooming in the lush beds that lined the front porch. The grass inside the iron picket-fenced yard was still green and clipped to perfection.

"Oh, how lovely," Lauren whispered as she gazed at the house in awe. She sat for several moments relishing the fact that she was finally here at Ben's house.

Travers eased his aching body out of the wagon and went toward the rear of it. He lifted out Lauren's bags and set them at the end of the sidewalk that led up to the steps in front of the house. He then returned to the back of the wagon and, none too gently, nudged Jared Lockett with his fist. "Come on, Jared, wake up. You're home."

Lauren barely noticed the disgruntled groan that issued from under the black hat. She was distracted from her joy over the house only by Ed Travers coming to her side of the wagon and offering his assistance as she alighted. She straightened her hat as best she could without a mirror, shook some of the dust from her navy skirt, and was about to pull on her jacket when the body in the back of the wagon finally climbed down.

She stopped to stare at the rumpled figure. It leaned against the sideboards of the wagon and held its head as if in an effort to keep the head on its shoulders.

Impatient fingers were raked haphazardly through sun-bleached brown hair that disobediently fell back into wavy disarray. The man bent from the waist and supported his upper body by placing his hands on his knees as he drew in several long, shuddering breaths. Lauren was fearful of seeing him plunged into the throes of nausea, but he slowly straightened up to his full height. Only then did he turn and see the young woman who was staring at him in fascination.

The deepening afternoon shadows prevented Lauren from having a clear look at his face. She thought his eyes must be dark, but his constant blinking to focus them made their color impossible to discern.

A sardonic smirk lifted one corner of his sensual mouth before he straightened his shoulders a trifle and took three stumbling steps. He stood within an arm's length of her. She was entranced by this man and his barbaric behavior, and couldn't find it within herself to move away from him.

Jared placed a hand over the left side of his chest, which lay bare under the loose, unbuttoned shirt, and said with a slur, "Your servant, Miss Ho . . . Hol . . . Holberk."

He bent from the waist again, this time in a travesty of a courtly bow. Executing the gesture was beyond him in his present state. To Lauren's horror, he continued on his way downward until he grasped her around the waist with two strong hands and leaned upon her bosom to break his fall. She gasped in mortification as he found what he considered to be a haven of repose. His head nestled between her breasts and he sighed contentedly, not knowing or caring what a comical picture he made. Instinctively his hands slid around her narrow waist to her back, and he pressed her closer.

His breath was warm on her skin through the thin linen of her shirt. For an instant, when his nose nuzzled the inside curve of her breast, Lauren felt certain she would faint. Even more staggering to her was a fleeting, overpowering urge to clasp his head into the soft depth of her cleavage.

Suddenly Mr. Travers circled the wagon, angrily grabbed Jared by the shoulders, and hauled him off her.

"Lockett! My God, man, you're an animal."

The animal seemed oblivious to the insult as he slumped once more against the wagon, a stupid grin on his face.

A Mexican man came running from the back of the house to lend his assistance as the front door opened and a woman stepped onto the porch.

Lauren's head was spinning. Things were happening too quickly, and she couldn't take them all in. She wanted to see Ben and rely on his sturdy presence to restore some measure of sanity to this situation. Hurriedly she shrugged into her jacket before facing the woman who stood on the edge of the porch looking down at her.

Lauren smiled shyly and walked through the iron gate and up the sidewalk. She halted in front of the bottom step and looked up at the woman. Instinct warned her she should go no further. The figure at the top of the steps had the aspect of a sentinel protecting an inviolable domain.

"Mrs. Lockett, I've brought—"

"Yes, thank you, Mr. Travers," Olivia Lockett sharply interrupted the man. "Can you find accommodations for the night? We will compensate you, of course, for your time and trouble."

Ed Travers was being dismissed, and he knew it. He nodded his silent acquiescence but didn't leave Lauren's side.

"You are Miss Holbrook," Olivia said.

The statement was clipped, and Lauren answered with like brevity, "Yes, Lauren Holbrook."

The woman appeared to be slightly taller than Lauren. Her hair was dark but, around her face, it was streaked most attractively with silver. She was slender, but held herself straight and rigid. This militant stance made her seem larger than she was. Her face was unlined; her complexion was olive. It was impossible to see the color of her eyes in the poor light, but Lauren was uncomfortably aware of their hawklike penetration.

She wore a green dress of some stiff fabric, and it would have been incongruous with her character to see one wrinkle, one piece of lint, any flaw that would mar her impeccability. Because of her disheveled appearance, Lauren felt at a distinct disadvantage. The woman's face betrayed neither approval nor disapproval of her guest.

"I'm Olivia Lockett. I trust your trip was uneventful." She didn't wait for a reply but continued in the same crisp tone, "I think you may have made the trip in vain, Miss Holbrook. I cannot conceive what my husband had in mind when he invited you here."

Lauren was stunned by Olivia Lockett's harsh words. Where was Ben? Obviously Mrs. Lockett had expected her. So why this instant hostility? She stammered, "I . . . I'm sure that if we could all sit down and talk about it, Ben would explain—"

"Is Jared all right, Pepe?" Olivia interrupted Lauren imperiously.

"*Sí*, Señora Lockett," the man who had come to Jared's aid answered her quickly, still supporting the younger man, who slumped against him unconsciously.

"He really got drunk last night, I guess," Olivia said. Lauren thought she saw the hint of a smile in the corners of Olivia's mouth, but then it was gone, and she was sure she had imagined it. What mother would be pleased to see her son in such a condition?

Continuing to ignore Lauren, Olivia addressed Pepe again. "Take Jared to the stable and sober him up." Her tone was caustic. "Miss Holbrook, I'll send someone out for your bags."

Lauren took that to be the only invitation to enter the house she was likely to get. Where was Ben—at Keypoint? Why had he deserted her this way?

She lifted her skirt and climbed the steps until she was level with Olivia. The woman looked at her coldly, and a premonition of disaster coiled in Lauren's stomach. She found the courage to say, "If you would summon Mr. Lockett, I'm sure—"

"That's impossible, Miss Holbrook. My husband died early this morning."

Chapter 3

Lauren was struck dumb. Was Olivia Lockett mad? The aristocratic face looking back at her with implacable eyes conveyed no emotion.

"That's impossible," Lauren breathed. The words were barely audible.

"I'm afraid it's true, Miss Holbrook. He hasn't been well for some time. He told me upon his return from New York that he had gone there to consult with a heart specialist." She paused for a moment and looked toward her son who, still supported by Pepe, was disappearing around the corner of the house. "Last night, Ben and Jared argued. After Jared left, Ben had a seizure. He died this morning," she repeated.

Lauren's eyes filled with tears. "I'm sorry," she said. What was she going to do now? "I didn't know anything about his illness. You must believe that, Mrs. Lockett."

Olivia looked at Lauren closely and then said in the same brisk tones she had used to address Pepe, "We can discuss this another time. For the next few days, make yourself comfortable in your room. Elena will be assigned to you. I must ask you to stay to yourself as much as possible. It would be awkward to explain your being here at this difficult time. Do you understand?"

Lauren simply nodded.

Turning, she looked down at Ed Travers, who remained standing at the iron gate, holding his hat at his chest. His slack mouth and wide eyes revealed his astonishment at the news of Ben Lockett's death.

"Thank you for your help, Mr. Travers. You have been most kind," Lauren called down to him.

The depot manager said humbly, "I'm always at your service, Miss Holbrook. If there's ever anything I can do for you, you have only to ask." Travers raised his hands expressively as he spoke.

"Thank you," Lauren mumbled.

"Mrs. Lockett, with your permission, I'll help notify the public of Be—Mr. Lockett's demise."

"The funeral will be the day after tomorrow at two o'clock. Your help is always appreciated, Mr. Travers. As is your discretion."

Her last words sounded almost like a threat. Ed Travers nodded and, replacing his bowler hat on his head, returned to the wagon.

Lauren followed Olivia into the house.

The impressions she drew from what brief glances of Ben's home she was allowed were delightful ones. A wide foyer with rooms leading off either side of it ran the length of the house. The staircase was directly opposite the front door and, at the top, hallways extended in three directions.

Lauren and Olivia ascended the stairs, turned right, and passed down a long, well-lit hall with doors, probably opening into bedrooms, on either side. At the end of the hall, Olivia opened a door. Like all of the woodwork in the house, it was painted a pristine white. Lauren followed Olivia into the room and looked around the chamber in which she would be sequestered for the next few days.

Well, if I have to be imprisoned, this is a pleasant cell, she thought. The small room was one of the round ones she had seen from the front of the house. It was beautifully furnished. The floors were stained oak, relieved now and then by small throw rugs. An intricate ecru lace spread covered the full-sized, four-poster bed. The walls were papered with a pale yellow flower print that was subtle and tasteful. There were a dresser and washstand, a bookcase, a rocking chair, a round table next to the chair, and a smaller table at the bedside. Fresh flowers filled several vases scattered around the room and, though the windows were curtained now, Lauren knew the morning sun would flood the room with even more cheerfulness. *Someone* had planned on receiving her graciously.

"It's lovely, Mrs. Lockett. Thank you."

"Then you won't mind staying in here for a few days until the funeral is over."

Lauren wanted to attend the funeral. But something in the woman's manner clearly indicated that she would strenuously object to an appearance by Lauren.

"The bathroom is through there." She indicated a door. "There's a door on the other side of it, but it remains locked. You needn't worry about anyone disturbing you."

Or me disturbing anyone, Lauren thought.

"Elena will be here soon with your supper. If you need anything, ask her. She is solely responsible to you." She was about to leave the room when Lauren halted her.

"Mrs. Lockett, I'm sorry about your husband. He was—"

"Yes," Olivia broke in. "Goodnight, Miss Holbrook."

Lauren sat down in the rocking chair and tried to absorb the events that had taken place since her arrival.

Ben Lockett dead? It wasn't possible. For weeks, she had envisioned his kind face and heard his voice compelling her to come here. Now, he was dead, and her future was, at best, uncertain.

Having sat down, she realized how tired she was. The endless days and cramped nights on the trains, the rough, dusty drive from Austin, that horrible man sprawled in a drunken stupor even as his own father lay dead, and then the confrontation with Olivia. It was all too much. Lauren rested her head on the small pillow attached to the back of the rocking chair and fell into a deep sleep.

She was awakened by a persistent voice and someone shaking her arm. Go away, she thought. I don't want to wake up, because something terrible has happened. I don't want to remember.

The pest wouldn't go away. Lauren awakened to meet the blackest, most liquid eyes she had ever seen. She took in the rest of the face. It was dark, smooth, unblemished, and beautiful. The smile was gentle and warm. The voice was soothing and sympathetic.

"Poor *señorita*. You are so tired that you fall asleep in the chair. With your hat on! No supper? No bath? Elena will help you, *sí?*"

"Elena? I'm Lauren. How do you do?" Lauren grasped the girl's friendliness like a lifeline.

"You're so beautiful, *señorita*. I think you be prettier and feel better after a bath. I run the water for you. You get undressed, *sí?*"

Elena stood back from the chair, and Lauren saw her protruding stomach, announcing the late stages of pregnancy. Was Olivia hiding Elena by "assigning" the maid to her? Her condition would no doubt be an embarrassment to the family and their expected callers.

Elena couldn't be more than sixteen or seventeen, and seemed unaffected by being seen when her confinement was so near. Her breasts, the dark nipples readily apparent, were almost as large as her stomach, and hung unrestrained under an embroidered white blouse.

She waddled into the bathroom, keeping up lively chatter in a mixture of English and Spanish. The topics of conversation she chose switched as quickly as her languages. When she returned to the bedroom and saw that Lauren had not moved, she scolded her.

"*Señorita*, your water will get cold, not to mention your supper. Come, let Elena help you."

Lauren was shocked when Elena turned her around and began undoing her buttons with deft fingers. She wanted to object but was too tired to force the words through her lips. Swiftly Elena divested her of her clothes.

When all that remained were Lauren's pantalets, corset, and camisole, Elena shook her head from side to side and made a "tsk"ing sound.

"A corset! And you are so slim. You can't even breathe." She loosened the laces, and soon the offending garment was lying in the heap of soiled clothes at Lauren's feet.

Lauren caught Elena's hands when the maid tried to remove her other underwear. Hastily she stepped into the bathroom, which was decorated as tastefully as the bedroom. She looked gratefully at the bathtub of scented water, stepped into it, and eased her tired, sore body into the steamy water. She finished bathing, and was luxuriating in the first relaxation she had known for days, when Elena bustled in. Lauren gasped in surprise for, since early adolescence, no one had seen her naked.

"*La señorita* is ready for me to wash her hair, *sí?*"

"No!" Lauren protested, desperately trying to cover herself. When she saw the hurt expression on Elena's face, she added hurriedly, "I can do it myself."

"But why should you? I'm here," Elena said with happy logic. "Señor Lockett say, 'Take care of the young lady,' and so I do." She made the sign of the cross across her enormous breasts at her mention of Ben.

Elena had already begun to take the pins from Lauren's hair, which needed no encouragement to cascade down her back to her waist. The Mexican girl continued to chatter as she poured pitcher after pitcher of warm water over Lauren's head. She lathered the thick tresses in a massage that was hypnotic. Lauren felt her nerves dissipating under Elena's capable hands.

"Señor Lockett look so forward to you coming. He tell all of us about the pretty lady who come to live with us. He order the room be made ready. He check it himself to make sure everything okay." Before Lauren could protest, Elena pulled her out of the tub.

Lauren's efforts to cover herself were ineffectual, but Elena didn't seem to notice her embarrassment. The bright pink blush that suffused Lauren's body was due only in part to her warm bath.

It was necessary for her to change the subject away from herself and Ben. She couldn't think of him now. Her grief would be saved for a more private time. She asked companionably, "When is your baby coming?"

"*Quién sabe?*" Elena shrugged. "When he get ready to come, he come." She smiled.

"What does your husband do?"

"Oh, he one one fine *vaquero* on the Lockett ranch. His name is Carlos. He one fine man." She rolled her expressive eyes at Lauren, who blushed instinctively. She didn't want Elena to elaborate.

"Isn't it late for you to still be working? Feel free to go anytime."

Elena's laughter bubbled forth again. "*Señorita,* I live here. Carlos stay at the ranch, and I stay here. We get together when we can at his mamma's house in Pueblo."

Lauren was aghast. "But surely you would rather have your own home and live together!"

"*Sí,* but we would also like to eat. With no money, we could do neither." She giggled.

"I see," Lauren murmured, although she didn't see at all. Thus far, she understood nothing of this alien land and its people.

They were back in the bedroom. Elena took a nightgown out of one of Lauren's bags and slipped it over her head. Lauren stood in the middle of the room feeling lost and helpless as Elena arranged dishes on a large tray. Apparently she had carried it up with her and deposited it on the table before she had awakened Lauren. Delicious aromas filled the room as Elena lifted the lids of the dishes, and Lauren's mouth began to water. She hadn't eaten since . . . when?

Elena set the tray on Lauren's lap. On it were a beautifully grilled steak, potatoes, a salad, and two kinds of bread. One was a yeast roll, and the other was a flat, round bread that was totally foreign to Lauren. There was also a bowl of beans with a tomato sauce ladled over them.

"What is this?" she asked, pointing to the bread.

"Tortilla. Bread made of corn," Elena explained.

Lauren took a bite and found that it had very little flavor. Then Elena scooped some butter on it, salted it lightly, and rolled it like a cigar. It was delicious. *"Tortilla?"* Lauren repeated the word, and Elena nodded, clapping her hands.

Lauren then pointed to the bowl of beans.

"Frijoles," Elena said. "With *picante."*

Lauren had lost her timidity now, and took a generous mouthful. She knew instantly that she had made a grave error. Her mouth was on fire! She quickly swallowed what she couldn't manage to spit out, appalled that she could do such an unladylike thing. Elena was laughing so hard that her breasts and stomach were bouncing.

"Water," Lauren croaked. She gulped the glass that Elena gave her and asked for more. Finally the fire was out, but she tentatively tasted the other foods before taking any more big bites. The rest of the meal was delicious, and she finished everything—except the *frijoles.*

Despite Lauren's objections, Elena braided her hair into one long plait. The maid then hurried to pull down the bedcovers.

"Go to bed now, *señorita,* and rest. It has been a hard day, *sí?"*

"Yes, it has." She climbed into the bed as Elena quietly loaded the tray and went around the room turning off the gas lamps.

"Buenas noches, señorita," she whispered as she left the room.

"Goodnight, Elena."

Lauren burrowed between the sheets. The house was quiet, though she could pick up muted and indistinguishable voices that wafted up the stairs.

"Ben Lockett, how could you do this to me?" she asked into her pillow, and was immediately ashamed of her thoughts.

After the dreadful scenes she'd been subjected to before leaving North Carolina, Ben's strength, affection, and warmth had been her salvation. She had hoped to start a new life with Ben's family.

Now, all those hopes were dashed. Ben was dead. This splendid house seemed to swallow her. And what of the cold, formidable woman who dominated it?

It occurred to Lauren then that Ben's widow hadn't shown any signs of emotion. Maybe Olivia was one of those people who expressed her grief privately. Maybe. The thought was disturbing.

What would Jared Lockett think when he learned of his father's death? Why would a man who had money and position get blind drunk and make a public spectacle of himself? Ed Travers had intimated that it wasn't at all unusual to see Jared in such a condition.

Well, it's none of my concern, Lauren thought as she resolutely closed her eyes. She wouldn't have any dealings with *him*.

He was very tall, wasn't he? She wished she could forget the tremors that had coursed through her when his hands had closed around her waist and caressed her back. The heavy pressure of his head against her breasts hadn't been an altogether unpleasant sensation. His hair was light brown. Did sunlight bring out streaks of gold as she knew it did in the down on his chest?

Lauren awoke languidly, after ten hours of sleep. The room was awash with sunlight, which filtered through the airy, yellow drapes in the east windows.

She flung off the covers and padded into the bathroom. Desolation over Ben's death and uncertainty over her future still weighed heavily on her mind. She couldn't stay here now. And she definitely couldn't return to North Carolina, either.

Elena came in just as Lauren finished dressing.

"Buenos días, señorita," she greeted her cheerfully.

"Good morning, Elena," said Lauren, continuing to brush her thick, black hair.

"Did you sleep well?" Elena asked conversationally as she spread the covers smoothly over the bed. She busied herself with straightening the spotless room, watering the plants and flowers, and arranging the breakfast dishes on the same tray that had held Lauren's dinner the previous night.

"Yes, very well." Lauren swallowed uncomfortably when she recalled some of her dreams. They had been unsettling. Tall men stalked her. One man had white hair and Ben's smiling face. The other's face was shadowed by a large black hat, but she recognized the physique. It was imprinted on her mind with indelible clarity.

After eating the large dinner last night, she didn't think she could be hungry. But the fresh melon slices were delicious and juicy. She drank the hot coffee, though she would have preferred tea. Timidly she asked Elena if she could have tea from now on.

"Oh, *sí, sí*. My mamma, she is the cook." She laughed at the startled expression on Lauren's face. "She work for the Locketts since before I was born. You call her Rosa."

"I hate to think of you carrying that heavy tray upstairs for my meals, Elena, but Mrs. Lockett made it clear that I am to stay as close to this room as possible during the funeral preparations and while they're receiving callers." Her gaze drifted to the open windows as another wave of sadness ebbed over her. "Is the funeral still scheduled for tomorrow?"

"*Sí*," Elena answered softly. "Lots of people coming from places far away."

"Well, I guess I shall busy myself somehow," Lauren sighed.

She managed to while away the long hours reading and embroidering a sampler she had brought with her from Clayton. She was denied Elena's company; the girl explained that she was needed to help her mother in the kitchen.

The day passed slowly. To Lauren, who was accustomed to activity and would seek out chores if none were apparent, it seemed interminable.

Late in the afternoon, she paused in her reading when she heard a heavy tread in the hallway. Whoever it was entered a room before reaching the end of the hall where her room was located. Slipping off her eyeglasses to rest her eyes, she listened closely to the sounds of drawers opening and shutting, of wardrobe doors swinging back, of heavy shoes or boots dropping with a thud onto the floor. Stockinged footsteps shuffled back and forth.

Lauren heard the clink of glass on glass, water splashing, a few low mumbled words, the scraping of furniture against wood floors, the rustle of clothing.

Some minutes later, the person was finished with his toilette and left the room. A door closed quietly and footsteps receded down the hall. Someone occupied the room on the other side of the bathroom. Lauren hadn't been aware of anyone being in there since she had moved in.

That evening, Lauren was embroidering as Elena gathered up the dinner tray and said goodnight.

"Elena," Lauren asked, "who occupies that room through the bathroom?"

"Ah! That is Señor Jared's room." Elena's eyes widened expressively. "My Carlos threaten me never to go near it." She giggled as she adjusted the tray around her expanded belly. "He say Señor Jared can please any woman." She winked broadly as she closed the door.

Lauren's gray eyes stared unseeingly at the bright bead of blood on her pricked finger.

Chapter 4

The sun refused to shine on the day of Ben Lockett's funeral. It, too, seemed to be mourning the man who had spent long hours under its hot rays, worshiping the land and its elements.

For two days, Lauren had watched from her window as all types of people came to pay tribute to Ben. There were wealthy visitors, their affluence evidenced by their clothes and their conveyances. Others looked to be farmers or ranchers wearing clean but worn clothes. Their wives tagged after them staring at the beautiful house in awe. *Vaqueros* in dusty leather chaps rode up to the house on trail-weary horses. The mourners came singly, in pairs, or in groups, but there was a continuous parade of them. Lauren couldn't imagine the woman who had greeted her with such hostility graciously welcoming the humblest of these visitors.

The hearse came down the shell lane, glistening blackly. With its tassel-trimmed, fringed drapes, plumed horses, and driver who wore a cutaway coat and top hat; it looked like some sort of circus vehicle. Ben would hardly have chosen such an ostentatious, frivolous conveyance to carry him to his grave, Lauren thought, feeling another pang of grief for the rugged, virile man.

Lauren watched from her window as Olivia was escorted down the front walk by a man no taller than she. From Lauren's perspective, his bald head seemed on a level with Olivia's veiled black hat. His black coat fit snugly across a portly torso. Shyly he touched Olivia's elbow as he assisted her. It was hard to tell if his hesitancy in touching her was in deference to her grief or in fear that she would turn on him. His attitude toward her seemed to be almost subservient.

Lauren inhaled sharply when she saw the figure behind the other two. His height and the breadth of his shoulders gave away his identity, though she still couldn't see his face under the wide-brimmed black hat. His black suit bore no distinguishing details. He appeared to be withdrawn, oblivious to the sympathetic friends who watched him with pity as he followed his mother and the other man to the covered carriage which waited behind the hearse.

The coffin was ceremoniously lifted into the hearse. Lauren thought Ben would have scoffed at all this pomp and circumstance. She was sure he was somewhere watching all of them, his blue eyes twinkling in amusement. She offered a prayer for his soul as the hearse led the procession away from the house.

As the family's carriage rolled by, she noticed a strong, lean, tanned hand dangling negligently against the door.

The summons came so suddenly that Lauren was unprepared for it. Elena had flung open the door to the room and, with colorful skirts swirling around her bare legs, and breasts bobbing like lanterns suspended on a wire, she sputtered the message.

"*La señora* wants to see you *pronto, señorita*. Quickly she say. Quickly. She is with Señor Wells in Señor Lockett's office."

She was a flurry of motion as she helped Lauren button her shirtwaist, which had been discarded when she had prepared for a nap. Her hair was hastily pulled into its usual bun. Elena knelt down to button her shoes. Lauren would have thought it impossible for Elena to fold herself into that position, but didn't have time to wonder about it now. She was breathing rapidly, her heart was pounding, and her palms were sweating. In all her life, she had never been this nervous.

They left the room after Lauren grabbed a lace handkerchief. Whether it was to dry her hands or to have something to hold onto, she didn't know. Elena also seemed jittery as she led Lauren down the hall to the wide staircase. They descended quickly and walked toward a large sliding door. Elena gave Lauren a quick nod of encouragement and pulled aside one panel of the door. Lauren drew a deep breath.

She stepped into the room and was again surprised at the simple beauty of the house. There were floor-to-ceiling bookshelves on one side of the room. Other shelves flanked a large fireplace. The mantel was intricately and masterfully carved. Wide, full-length windows composed the fourth wall.

An Aubusson rug covered most of the hardwood floor. Leather chairs and small tables, strategically placed, lent themselves to private conversations. There was a long sideboard loaded with decanters and glasses of cut crystal. The window drapes had been completely opened, allowing the afternoon sun to stream in and reflect on the glass surfaces.

In front of the windows was a massive desk littered with ledgers and papers of various shapes, sizes, and colors. Olivia sat in the high-backed leather chair behind the desk. The short, stout man Lauren had seen with her as she left for the funeral was seated in a chair in front of the desk. He stood and walked toward her.

"Miss Holbrook, this is indeed a pleasure. I'm sorry that circumstances have prevented me from meeting you before now. I hope you haven't been too uncomfortable since your arrival." He seemed to expect no answer as he continued, "I am Carson Wells, an old friend of Ben's and Olivia's, and also their lawyer. How do you do?"

"How do you do, Mr. Wells." Lauren's nerves were calmed by his graciousness. She replied steadily, "I have been most comfortable. I'm only sorry that I was an intruder at an unhappy time."

"No one blames you." He spoke to her gently, and she was glad for his presence in the room. He was bald except for a skimpy fringe of nondescript brown hair which adorned the back of his head. As if to compensate for his bald-headedness, bushy sideburns grew, in an outdated fashion, to within inches of his fleshy nose. His eyes were kind and smiling, and he seemed aware of her awkward situation.

Olivia had not uttered a sound. Now, she said in level tones, "Mr. Wells and I wish to speak to you, Miss Holbrook. Will you sit down? Would you care for some sherry?"

Lauren accepted the chair Mr. Wells held for her and declined the sherry. Olivia's position in front of the glare of the windows outlined her frame, but kept her features dark and inscrutable. Lauren wondered if Ben had thought how advantageous this placement of his desk would be to the person sitting behind it. She almost had to squint to see Olivia clearly.

"I will get directly to the point of this discussion, Miss Holbrook. I'm ignorant of my husband's reasons for inviting you here. I had construed some, though upon meeting you, I realize that they were wrong." She didn't explain and her meaning eluded Lauren. Olivia continued, "In any case, he was determined that you stay for at least two months. The night he had his seizure, as ill as he was, he asked me to allow you to stay for that length of time. Your being here was obviously important to him."

Lauren moistened her lips nervously with her tongue. She wasn't sure she could speak. "Your husband told me that you might find me helpful in handling your correspondence, entertaining, things like that. I envisioned myself as a sort of secretary."

Lauren's heart was pounding so loudly that she could barely hear her own words.

Olivia came the closest to smiling that Lauren had ever seen. Carson Wells reached over and patted her hand as he said quietly, "Miss Holbrook, Ben liked to surprise folks and joke with them. Olivia is an astute businesswoman and has a number of clerks at the bank at her disposal. Ben may have told you his wife needed a secretary, but he had an ulterior motive, I assure you."

Bank? She didn't know anything about a bank. She was grasping at straws and she knew it, but she stammered, "I . . . I play the piano quite well. Maybe he thought I could give small concerts for your guests or something."

Olivia lifted a derisive eyebrow. "That would be lovely, I'm sure, but we don't even own a piano."

Lauren was stunned, and had nothing else to say. She looked first at one and then the other. Humiliated beyond endurance, she bowed her head and stared at the soggy, twisted handkerchief clenched in her lap by white, trembling fingers. "I'm sorry. I didn't know any of this. You must think . . . I was so sure . . . He didn't tell me . . ." The tears that had been clouding her vision finally flooded her eyes and spilled onto her cheeks.

"Now, now, no need for that," Carson said quickly. "I'm afraid old Ben was just playing one of his notorious tricks on someone at your expense, and didn't live to see it through. You can stay for a while. Olivia and I will try to make this an enjoyable visit for you. Come now, stop crying." Carson sounded genuinely distressed and was patting her hand so vigorously that it stung.

"Will you join us in the dining room at seven-thirty for dinner, Miss Holbrook?" Olivia sounded annoyed at this display of emotion.

Lauren took her cue of dismissal and stood as she said, "Yes, thank you, Mrs. Lockett."

She summoned all of her poise as she nodded to them in turn and then glided to the heavy panels of the door. Olivia called her name sharply. "Miss Holbrook."

"Yes?" Lauren said tremulously as she turned back to face them.

"There's something I must know."

"Olivia, please—" Carson interjected. He was ignored.

"Were you my husband's mistress?"

Mistress! The word screamed at her, echoing in her head and ricocheting off the walls of the room. Had Olivia thrown stones

35

at her, Lauren couldn't have felt more abused. Her cheeks flamed with color, but her whole body had turned cold.

"No!" she gasped. "Whatever . . . ? No, no." She was too astonished by the question to deny the allegation more eloquently.

"I didn't think so," was Olivia's only reply. "We'll see you at dinner."

Retracing her way to her room, Lauren barely held onto a tenuous thread of composure. When she was in her room, she collapsed on the bed and cried. She felt mortification for her naivete and Olivia's surmise. All too recently similar words had been flung at her, and had been equally unjust. Why was she suspect?

She grieved for a man whom she had trusted and who had deceived her. Trepidation for an ominous future consumed her.

Two months! What had Ben expected to happen in that time? And at the end of those sixty days, what was she to do?

She dressed carefully for dinner, wearing one of the two nice dresses in her wardrobe. It was made of soft lilac voile. Slender pleats and tiny pearl buttons adorned the bodice, and a high, lace-lined collar reached to just under her jaw. The skirt fell in soft folds to the instep of her white leather slippers.

Elena assisted her with her toilette. It seemed almost natural now for the Mexican girl to help her bathe and dress. Lauren had always been more or less alone, but these last few days seemed the loneliest of her life, and she was grateful for her new companion.

The dining room was decorated with the same elegant understated taste evident in the rest of the house. If either Carson or Olivia noticed Lauren's reddened eyes, they didn't mention them as they took their seats.

The meal was served by an obese Mexican woman whom Lauren supposed was Rosa, Elena's mother. Each time she carried in a platter of food, she looked at Lauren and smiled with open friendliness. Lauren smiled back thankfully.

The food was sumptuous and she ate everything except the beans and *picante* sauce, which seemed to be a staple at every meal except breakfast.

The conversation was limited to trivial, everyday topics, and since Lauren had supervised many dinners similar to this in the Prathers' parsonage, she was at ease. She wondered at the absence of Jared Lockett, and started violently the first time Carson made reference to him. His not being there seemed of no concern to them. Olivia mentioned to Carson in passing that Jared would be at Keypoint for several days.

Olivia was relieved to see that Lauren Holbrook exhibited good manners at least. If someone came to call, she wouldn't have to explain a gauche, stupid strumpet, which was how she had pictured the girl when Ben had first told her about Lauren. She was obviously well read, and maintained her composure this afternoon even when she resorted to that weak, feminine trait of crying. How sweet, how captivating, thought Olivia sarcastically. Carson had naturally succumbed to the tears, as all men did. They couldn't resist a vulnerable woman.

Carson Wells had indeed felt compassion for Lauren's pitiful state this afternoon. She wasn't the scheming, devious woman he had feared she would be. He had expected a floozy who would drop a baby on the Lockett's doorstep, declaring Ben's paternity and demanding a sizable purse.

Lauren Holbrook was an innocent, a victim of circumstances. Olivia could have spared the girl the question about her relationship to Ben. He hadn't wanted her for a lover, Carson was certain of that. Ben had liked them lusty, naughty, and buxom. This fragile, doe-eyed young woman could melt a man's heart with her delicate beauty, but she would never have stirred the loins of Ben Lockett.

As for Carson, there was only one woman for him. Always had been. But no man was ever going to possess her. No man. Still, Carson loved Olivia Lockett. After all this time, after all the pain she had put him through, after having to bear the guilt of betraying his best friend, Carson loved her.

The talk turned to business, and Lauren listened distractedly, not really grasping or caring about the subject. Instead, she speculated on which chair Jared sat in when he ate in this dining room.

A few facts did manage to arrest her attention. The Locketts owned the Coronado Bank. They were trying to get a railroad trunk to Coronado, though there were some obstacles involved. Keypoint was managed by someone named Mendez, though the Locketts were apprised of the profits and liabilities to the penny.

Carson was speaking in an emphatic voice. "We've got to get Vandiver out here and wine and dine him, Olivia. He's the power behind it. Without him, we don't get the railroad. Now that Ben . . . well, now is the time to approach him again."

"We'll have to come to terms with the water rights, you know," Olivia said coolly.

"That's something we'll face when the time comes. The important thing now is for us to let them know we're interested. What about Jared, Olivia? Do you think he'll object?"

"Jared will do whatever we tell him to," she snapped. "There may be some resistance but he knew that Ben wanted the railroad. I think that's the point to stress to him."

They were quiet for a moment, and Lauren looked timidly at their faces. Both were wearing expressions of deep concentration.

Jared was tired, dirty, and in dire need of a drink as he trudged up the stairs. The ride from the ranch had been hot even on this early October day. The trails were dusty, choking off a man's breath. It hadn't rained since the day of the funeral. He stopped abruptly in mid-stride and forcibly thrust that thought from his mind.

As he reached the top of the stairs, he noticed that the door at the end of the hall was slightly ajar. For some reason he couldn't name, he stepped lightly as he approached his room. So stealthy were his footsteps that his spurs didn't even jingle. Thorn would be proud of him, he thought with a smile.

He stopped outside his room and put his hand on the doorknob, but an overwhelming curiosity compelled him to continue down the hall until he stood in front of the door to the guest bedroom.

Why not open it? She probably wasn't in there. And if she were, what the hell? This was *his* house, wasn't it?

He pushed open the door. Thanks to its well-oiled hinges, it opened silently. Lauren sat at a small desk. She was writing acknowledgments to letters of condolence. She had insisted on a project, and Olivia had grudgingly, and with a secret respect for the girl, assigned her this tedious job.

Well, well. The old boy hadn't done so badly for himself, Jared thought. All he could see was her back, but Lauren turned her head slightly as she bent over the letter she was composing.

It was completely silent in the room except for her pen scratching across the paper and a small clock ticking on the bedside table. Dust motes danced in the warm afternoon sunlight that projected into the room at slanted angles.

Lauren straightened her shoulders slightly and sighed deeply as she dipped her pen in the inkwell. Jared held his breath lest he be discovered, but she bent over the paper once again. From his position at the door, Jared had only a partial view of her face—a smooth ivory complexion with a hint of blush at the cheekbone, and a pair of small eyeglasses perched on the straight, slender nose.

Her clothes were too proper to be true, he thought. The white, high-necked shirtwaist and the maroon skirt could have belonged to a schoolmarm. It was fetching the way the buttons on her blouse followed her spine as if inviting a man to trace his fingers along that graceful back up to a slim column of neck above which was piled a luxuriant mass of hair. God, what hair! It was coal-black with dark blue highlights that added to its richness. A few tendrils had escaped the heavy bun on the top of her head and lay coyly on her neck. Jared wondered what those curls would feel like between his fingers.

She was slender. Maybe too slender. Skinny.

Moving slowly, hoping not to attract her attention until just the right moment, he reached into his breast pocket and took out a cheroot and a match. He clamped the cheroot between his teeth and, putting on the face he showed the world, struck the match against the doorjamb.

The sound was like a cannon shot in the small, quiet room, and Lauren bolted out of her chair. She drew herself up sharply against the desk when she saw Jared, and clutched a dainty, tight fist to her breast.

Jared's eyes flitted to her chest, and he amended his first speculation. No. She wasn't skinny.

She looked at him in terror from over the top of her spectacles, and Jared was momentarily taken aback by his first full look at Lauren's face. What in hell color eyes were those? Blue? No, gray. Goddam. He had to hand it to his old man. She wasn't bad at all.

Lauren felt like a cornered animal as she leaned against the desk for support. Jared lit the cigar, his eyes never leaving her. The smoke wreathed his face as he lazily pushed the flat-crowned hat back off his head with his thumb. It caught on a thin leather cord tied around his neck and hung against his shoulders.

He squinted at her through narrowed eyes in an insolent and lascivious fashion, raking her body up and down until her cheeks were on fire with embarrassment.

Lauren did not move or speak as she returned Jared's scrutiny. His hair was brown, with sun-bleached strands giving it the golden highlights she had expected. His complexion was dark, a combination of heredity and long hours in the sun. His eyes, though brown, were light, amber-colored. Like two perfect topazes.

There was a lot of Ben in him, particularly in his physique, but his face showed none of Ben's merriment. The stance, the face, the expression communicated arrogance, conceit, and contempt.

He leaned negligently against the doorframe, ankles crossed, dressed in much the same manner as the first time she had seen him in the back of the wagon, except this time there was a colorful bandana around his throat. The silver spurs on his boots fascinated her, and she stared at them for a moment before her eyes traveled up the long body to catch his amber eyes, which were still fixed on her in an unsettling appraisal.

"Miss Holbrook, I came to offer my humblest apologies. I understand that on our first meeting, I was somewhat indisposed and behaved abominably." His voice was Ben's. It held the same soft timbre and low pitch, but was full of sarcasm. Lauren wondered what she had done to earn this disdain. *He* was the one who deserved ridicule. "What can I do to redeem myself?"

"You might start by apologizing for entering my room without invitation," she commented.

He was surprised at her aplomb and cocked a skeptical eyebrow. He recovered quickly, however, and said in soft, conspiratorial tones, *"Would* you invite me into your room, *Miss* Holbrook?"

She flushed at his emphasis on the "miss." Realizing that she still held her fist against her chest, she lowered it quickly, touching her watch fleetingly. At the same time, she took off her eyeglasses with the other hand. Smiling wickedly at her discomfiture, Jared watched her hands, particularly the one that fondled the watch.

"It's still there," he said quietly. "I'm not a thief."

She was furious at having drawn attention to her body.

He pushed himself away from the doorjamb with a shove of his shoulder and crossed the room with the slow, predatory gait of a stalking cat. His spurs jingled on the hardwood floor.

Lauren's throat closed completely when he stood only inches in front of her. He towered over her, and she had to tilt her head back to look into his face. It required a tremendous amount of courage to do so, but she instinctively knew that it would be to her disadvantage if he thought she were afraid of him.

Her false bravado evaporated as he raised his hand and extended it toward her. The long fingers reached out and, by an act of will, she didn't recoil.

"What is this, anyway?" he asked softly. His fingers closed around the watch pinned to her shirtwaist. His breath stirred the fine hairs that framed her face, and she caught the pungent fragrance of tobacco.

He held the watch in the palm of his hand and stared at it in a silent pensiveness that contrasted with the fierce emotional explosions that erupted from deep within Lauren's body.

She was on fire. Every cell burned with an unnamed compulsion to move even closer to this man who tormented her with his nearness.

The brooch was laid back in its original position, but not without the firm pressure of Jared's hand on her breast to assure its security.

For long moments, time ceased to exist. Amber eyes locked with gray, and the cynicism in the amber ones was replaced by wonderment. Jared's head descended toward Lauren's with imperceptible motion. For one heartbeat, she thought he was about to kiss her. Her moist lips parted of their own volition.

She didn't know that it was that involuntary gesture of welcome which jerked him back into the shell of scorn he used for protection. Mockery cooled the eyes that had been clouded with warmth, and Lauren was sensitive to the change. The pressure on her breast increased, but without the former tenderness.

She swatted his hand in a lightning reaction.

He chuckled deep in his throat. "What's the matter, Miss Holbrook? I was only checking the time of day," he sneered.

She ignored his sardonic words and tried desperately to restore balance to the spinning world. Still, she was gasping when she said, "Please, Mr. Lockett, I have a lot of work to do." Why was her heart thumping this way? Her whole chest was hurting and congested. She could no longer look directly into his handsome face or those brown-gold eyes. Why didn't he leave? Why didn't she want him to?

He stepped away from her and took a long draw on the cheroot which he had been holding at his side in his inactive hand. "I'll see you at dinner, I guess," he drawled.

He never looked back as he sauntered down the hall to his room. Lauren walked, entranced, to her door, and closed it.

Chapter 5

They were all in the formal parlor adjacent to the dining room. Lauren could hear their muffled voices as she descended the wide staircase. Not only would she have to endure her first dinner with Jared Lockett at the table, but Elena had informed her there were three guests tonight. One was Mr. Wells, whom she felt moderately comfortable with. She had shared most dinners with him at Olivia's table. The other two guests were important men from Austin.

Lauren's dress rustled against her legs as she walked across the wide foyer. She dreaded entering the dining room. Meeting these powerful men from the state capital would be intimidating enough, but the real cause of her consternation was having to face Jared Lockett. Her private introduction to him in her room this afternoon had left her flustered.

She wore her best dress, a peacock-blue crepe. The high collar and straight, tight sleeves were trimmed with cream-colored lace. The cummerbund was of the same cream color and adorned with one pink silk rose that was pinned to the left side of her waist.

Nervously she stood framed in the doorway, watching the others.

Olivia and Carson were bent in concentration over some charts that the two men from the capital had spread before them on a low table. All four were poring over the diagrams with rapt attention.

Jared was slouched in a chair, his long legs stretched out in front of him with booted ankles crossed. He was examining the contents of a crystal tumbler with the exactitude of a chemist. The amber liquid matched the color of his eyes.

The room was another expression of Olivia's perfect taste. It was softly lit by glass lamps shaded with frosted globes. The sofas and chairs, arranged in harmonious order, were upholstered in pastel damasks and blended beautifully with the drapes that were drawn across the large windows. A Persian rug woven with the same muted greens, golds, and beiges evidenced in the furniture covered a large portion of the floor.

Each vase, ashtray, and picture had been chosen and positioned with utmost care. It was a peaceful room. But, like the woman who had decorated it, it lacked warmth and cheer.

Carson Wells was the first to notice Lauren, and he immediately jumped up from his chair and came toward her, both hands extended.

"Miss Holbrook, you are indeed looking beautiful tonight." He always met her with chivalry that was as overdone and outdated as his muttonchop sideburns, but Lauren appreciated his welcoming smile and returned it tremulously.

"Good evening, Mr. Wells."

"Come and let me introduce you to our guests." He took her arm and escorted her toward the two men standing near the table where they had previously been involved in their discussion.

"Miss Lauren Holbrook, may I present Mr. Parker Vandiver and his son, Kurt. Gentlemen, Miss Holbrook."

Lauren nodded to each of them as they acknowledged the introduction. Kurt Vandiver took her hand in his, raised it, and kissed the air inches above it.

"It is indeed an honor to meet so lovely a woman here in Coronado. An honor and a surprise," said Kurt, his blue eyes glinting in the soft light.

A rude, derisive sound came from across the room. Everyone chose to ignore it, but the embarrassed tint in Lauren's cheeks deepened.

"We're proud of our beautiful Texas women, Miss Holbrook, but it seems they've all been transplanted from places like North Carolina. I believe Carson said that was your home?" The younger Vandiver hadn't released her hand and, as he spoke the flowery compliment, Lauren gently pulled it away from his firm grasp.

"Yes. Clayton, North Carolina. I thank you, Mr. Vandiver."

"Good evening, Lauren. Would you care for some sherry?" Olivia spoke to her for the first time. She was dressed in black, the first evidence of mourning Lauren had seen her display since the funeral. Jet earrings dropped from her ears and matching beads glittered darkly from the bodice of her dress. She was beautiful, but in a dangerous sort of way. Lauren looked at her much as one would look at a deadly beast—with admiration, but caution.

"Yes, thank you. I'll get it myself," Lauren replied to Olivia's question.

"No, allow me please, Miss Holbrook. Sit down and I'll bring it to you." Kurt lightly took her elbow, guided her to one of the small sofas, and went to the sideboard that was well stocked with liquor and glasses.

Lauren's eyes moved involuntarily to the silent man lounging in the chair and she was disconcerted when they locked into his golden gaze. He had not even stood when she came into the room. How very rude! His stare was almost menacing.

She held her breath, afraid that he would make reference to that afternoon, but he only held his glass to the light and studied it carefully as he said in a bored fashion, "Good evening, Miss Holbrook." He made her name sound like an insult.

Kurt handed her the sherry, and she took a quick sip, determined to divert her attention from Jared. Kurt sat next to her on the sofa and began asking questions about her visit to Texas. She kept her responses as general and vague as she could. Kurt's interest made her uneasy. His heavy body took up much of the space on the sofa, and she had to make an effort to avoid touching him. Deftly she steered the conversation away from herself.

"What line of business are you in, Mr. Vandiver?" Hadn't Olivia and Carson referred to the Vandivers one evening at dinner? She couldn't remember what had been said.

"Investments." She looked puzzled, and he laughed slightly. "All kinds of investments—railroads, lumber, cattle. Currently we're interested in getting electricity into these smaller towns."

"I see," murmured Lauren, although she didn't see at all.

Carson picked up the conversation by launching into what he considered a humorous tale. Out of the corner of her eye, Lauren watched Jared get up from the chair, saunter to the sideboard, and pour himself another neat whiskey. Abruptly Olivia suggested they all go into dinner. To Lauren, the suggestion sounded like a command. Or a threat.

Lauren looked toward Olivia quickly and saw her gimlet eyes boring into her son. As if to be deliberately provoking, Jared gulped his drink and poured another, which he carried into the dining room along with the crystal decanter. If anyone but Lauren had noted this hostile exchange between mother and son, they didn't show it. The Vandivers laughed heartily at Carson's story as they crossed to the dining room.

Olivia and Carson sat at opposite ends of the table, with Lauren and Kurt on one side, and Jared and Parker on the other. Jared was directly across from Lauren. He gave her a slow appraisal as he took his seat, but his face was expressionless.

As dinner was served by Rosa, who had forsaken her bright skirts and loose blouse for a starched white uniform, Lauren studied the Vandivers.

Parker had a pugnacious face, almost brutal in its strength of feature. His piercing blue eyes darted around the room in quick movements, as if looking for hidden secrets. His voice and manner were polite and conversational, though Lauren suspected that he absorbed only the facts he considered pertinent and sloughed off the rest of what was said as inconsequential. His body was thick and solid. His fat hands, with fingers like tight, pink sausages, rested folded on his stomach whenever he was not using them. This relaxed posture was contradicted by his busy eyes.

Kurt was taller, though built in the same solid way. His eyes were as aggressive as his father's, but he had deep dimples which appeared and disappeared at will, relieving the belligerence of his face. The cropped blond hair, also like his father's, was crisp and wiry, fitting his head like a snug cap. His ruddy complexion made his eyebrows look white against his beefy forehead.

Though the Teutonic-featured Vandivers had exhibited perfect manners toward her, Lauren was instinctively wary of them. Their etiquette was too polished, their conversation too eloquent, their attitude too humble. Their entire demeanor seemed too rehearsed to be sincere. When she caught Kurt's eyes on her, she shivered involuntarily. His rapacious expression was reminiscent of William's.

Jared spoke very little, ate almost nothing, drank quite a lot. He responded in low, disinterested mumbles when anyone directed a question to him, and initiated no conversation himself. Lauren was uneasy at his careful, persistent scrutiny of her. It seemed that his implacable eyes never left her face for the hour they were at the table.

If Lauren found the meal tedious, to Jared it was interminable. He despised the Vandivers and the grasping ambition that they unsuccessfully tried to camouflage with sleek conversation and courtly manners. Jared hated all forms of deception and pretense. And this China doll opposite me is an expert at it, he thought cynically.

He tried to ignore Lauren, but finally gave up the effort and studied her, wanting to figure her out. He admitted to himself that she wasn't what he had expected. Not at all. And Jared didn't like surprises. That's why he had been furious with Ben the night before he died.

No, I refuse to think of that, he told himself.

Lauren handled her cutlery with graceful ease, and Jared was intrigued by her hands. They looked soft and smooth. The fingers were long and slim and tapered to pink oval nails that were well kept. What had he expected to see? Red nail lacquer?

What had Ben said? Oh, yes. She was a pianist. Jared chuckled to himself and thought ribaldly of a more pleasant activity for those hands. Then he wondered fleetingly if this woman even knew about things like that, and quickly decided that she didn't. He had seen the fearful caution in her eyes this afternoon when he had touched her. It was genuine. That was the rub.

She raised the velvety lashes that hid her eyes and glanced in his direction. For a moment, she returned his steady gaze, then rapidly shifted her eyes away from him. He could see why Ben had been hoodwinked by the little tart. A man could drown in those dove-colored eyes before he even knew he was sinking. She knew how to use them, too. You were never graced with a full look, only an elusive glance. It was enough to make you go crazy if she didn't look at you directly.

She had too much hair, he decided. It was too heavy for her finely boned face and figure. Yet the knot on top of her head was softened by the bouffant fullness around her face. She didn't need any "rats" like other women used to achieve this style. The wispy tendrils that framed her temples seemed more translucent than the china from which they ate.

His eyes moved to the gold watch pinned to her breast. He shifted in his chair uncomfortably and unconsciously moistened his lips with his tongue when he looked at the gentle rise and fall of her bosom. Whatever else was fake about her—her quiet voice, circumspect manners, her reasons for trailing Ben halfway across the country—one thing was real. He could still feel the firm cushion of her breast against his palm. His hand trembled slightly as he poured another glass of whiskey, and his manhood refused to relax.

He should leave now. He should mount Charger and go into Pueblo for a nice, uncomplicated toss in the hay with a whore. But he didn't really want to. He knew his constant staring was making Lauren ill at ease. If it weren't such a damned entertaining exercise in itself, her discomfort was incentive enough for him to stay.

As they returned to the parlor after the meal, Carson commented, "It's a pity that you don't have a piano, Olivia. Lauren could play for us."

"That is a pity. I would love to hear you play," Kurt said at Lauren's elbow.

"What brings you to Texas, Miss Holbrook?" Parker Vandiver asked bluntly as they took seats.

Lauren was momentarily at a loss for words. The cold, incisive blue eyes seemed to challenge her.

"Lauren is the sister of one of Jared's friends at Harvard. Jared had visited the Holbrooks on some of his holidays from school, and we wanted to repay their hospitality. Since her brother has married, we issued the invitation to Lauren. Ben brought her back with him on his way home from New York."

Lauren stared incredulously as Olivia lied so glibly. The older woman smiled radiantly at the stunned girl as she continued, "She has been such a comfort to me since Ben passed away. I don't know how I could have managed without her."

Lauren's astonishment turned to anger. How dare Olivia lie about her that way! She had nothing to be ashamed of or to apologize for!

"I don't recall seeing her at the funeral," Parker observed shrewdly.

"She was overcome with grief. She and Ben had become quite attached on their trip. I wouldn't allow her to go through such a public ordeal," Olivia said simply.

"That's perfectly understandable. I felt that way when my mother died," Kurt whispered as he reached out to pat Lauren's hand. She pulled it back quickly.

Carson redirected the conversation. "Tell us about this power plant you envision, Parker."

"It's no vision, Carson. We intend to build it, one way or another. Of course, we would like to have the help of the Locketts."

"What will happen to the electric company that's already here?" inquired Olivia, all business now. She referred to a small power plant owned and operated by Orville Kendrick. Lauren had heard Olivia and Carson discussing it. The plant provided electric power to the citizens of Coronado each evening from six until ten. Oddly enough, the Lockett house was not yet wired for electric power.

"It will no doubt go out of business," Parker answered Olivia's question brusquely. "We will provide twenty-four-hour service. Kendrick won't be able to survive the competition. One day soon, everything will be powered by electricity."

Kurt leaned toward Lauren and asked, "What do you think of electric lighting, Miss Holbrook?"

All eyes turned to her, and she hesitated before timidly stating, "I think it's ugly." At their shocked expressions, she hastened to explain. "I see the need for it, and I agree with Mr. Vandiver that we'll become more reliant on it, but I do think it's ugly. I prefer the softness of gas lighting."

"Spoken like a true romantic," Kurt said, and nodded his approval.

"Hear, hear."

The two caustic words fell like stones into the room. Everyone looked at Jared, who had resumed his slouching position in the chair. This was his first utterance since dinner.

"I'm interested in your opinions on all of this, Jared," Parker broke the silence.

"My opinion," Jared snarled, "is that we cut all the bull and get to the heart of the matter, Mr. Vandiver." His voice was hard and quiet.

"And what do you perceive to be the 'heart of the matter'?" Parker fired back.

Jared unfolded himself and stood up slowly, strolled to the sideboard, poured a full glass of whiskey, and only then turned to face Parker. Lauren noted the impeccable fit of the black wool suit on his trim frame. His white shirt collar was a startling contrast to his dark face, which had hardened into a sinister scowl.

"The heart of the matter is that you want to build a power plant that will destroy another man's business. In order to generate that power plant, you must have water. The most accessible source of water is on Lockett land. Am I right so far?"

"Your assessment of the facts is somewhat distorted, but it conveys the gist of the plan." Parker spoke calmly, though his face was flushed once again, and his fat fingers were furiously working with the gold watch fob stretched across his stomach.

"What happens to all of the people who depend on that water for their livelihood when you come along and dam it all up? The Locketts have prided themselves on being generous with their water. It's a source of revenue, yes, but sometimes my father took a lamb or two as payment, sometimes as little as a basket of corn from a farmer who'd had a bad crop. Even before the land acts were effected several years ago, Ben allowed cattle or sheep ranchers with smaller herds to water their stock on our land. What will happen to those people when the water is no longer available?"

Lauren listened avidly. Jared's speech was eloquent. The thick brows that reminded her so much of Ben were drawn together in determination. There was no insolence in his manner now.

"Mr. Lockett . . . Jared," Parker said with condescending patience, "perhaps I understand the business world better than you do. After all, I've got about thirty years more experience. In every business venture, there are those who gain and those who lose. It's a basic fact of economics."

"I'm not an idiot, Vandiver, so you needn't talk to me as if I were," Jared cut in. "I have a business degree from Harvard of which my mother is very proud. Please continue. I think I can keep up with you." Jared mocked the other man with a salute of his glass.

"Very well, I'll be blunt," Parker said. "You want something, and we want something. We make a trade. Your railroad for our power plant. We both stand to profit tremendously."

"Parker, I don't think it's necess—"

"Carson, don't interrupt him," Jared commanded sharply. Lauren was surprised when Carson obeyed without question. "We're getting to the good part. Mr. Vandiver and *son*," he said the last word with a sneer, "have come all the way from Austin bringing a detailed TransPlains Railroad diagram showing a straight track into Coronado." Jared paused and took a long drink of the whiskey. "I'd hate to think they've wasted their time."

Lauren viewed this whole scene with fascination. The man became more of an enigma every time he opened his mouth. Cowboy, Harvard graduate, businessman?

"Vandiver," Jared continued, "the railroad has been in Kerrville for several years. Comfort and Fredericksburg are in the process of negotiating one. With Lockett cattle, the granite quarries, and the cedar posts business, why do you imagine we need your help in obtaining a railroad?"

"Shut up, Jared. You're drunk and you're offending our guests," Olivia barked. Her face was a mask of fury.

"Quite all right, Olivia. He asked a simple question, to which I will give a simple answer." Parker bowed to her slightly before facing Jared again. "Ben Lockett was a respected man in this state. A very powerful man. I don't have to tell you that. Yet for years he was unable to secure a railroad into Coronado."

"That's because he wasn't going to exploit the people who respected him!" Jared shouted.

"Whatever the reasons for his failure, you still have no railroad. I happen to have many friends on the Railroad Commission. If I tell them that Coronado is a bad risk . . ." He shrugged expressively. "On the other hand, if I say that it's a potential money maker, they'll jump at the chance to build train tracks here. If a man as influential as your father failed to achieve this goal without my help, how do *you* propose to do it?"

Some of the arrogance and fire went out of Jared then. He placed his glass on a small table and faced Parker, staring at him for several long, silent moments. Parker stared back levelly, clearly evaluating a foe.

Calmly, hardly above a whisper, Jared pronounced, "You *are* a sonofabitch."

"Yes, I am," Parker agreed grimly.

Jared turned his alcohol-brightened eyes on Kurt, who had remained silent throughout the exchange. "I wonder what that makes you," Jared said contemptuously. Then his eyes swept across Lauren to his mother and Carson. His face registered disgust and resignation before he turned and strode from the room, the heels of his polished black boots emphasizing his anger with each long, hurried step on the parqueted floor. A few seconds later, the front door slammed.

Always the diplomat, Carson conciliated, "Parker, Kurt, you must be patient with the boy. He just lost his father. Ben's death hit him hard."

"If he were a boy, I could tolerate his behavior," Parker said. "As it is, he's a thirty-year-old man acting like a boy. Olivia, you'd better get things straight with him. If he can't be counted on for his support in this venture, then the deal is off. Your son is Ben's heir, and everyone will be watching to see how he handles himself. If word gets around that he can't control his temper and his personal habits," he paused and looked significantly toward the liquor cabinet, "then I couldn't endorse a joint venture for fear of losing my own credibility."

"I understand, Parker." Olivia's green eyes were as cold and hard as emeralds. "Jared will come around to our way of thinking. He always does."

Lauren was unaccountably irritated by Olivia's self-assured guarantee. Jared was a grown man who had made some astute observations of his own. She felt a compulsion to defend him but, of course, she could not.

"He has a terrible reputation for activities that are unmentionable in Miss Holbrook's presence," Kurt contributed sanctimoniously.

"I don't need you to tell me my son's virtues or vices, Mr. Vandiver," Olivia snapped.

"No, Mrs. Lockett. I only meant—"

"I think it's time for us to take our leave," Parker interrupted his son. "We've had a thorough discussion. We should give the proposal some further study and weigh all the elements involved." He stood, walked over to Olivia, took her hand, and held it in both of his. "Thank you for a lovely evening, Olivia. The dinner was excellent. That Lockett beef can't be beat."

"I'm sure we can look forward to working together in the future, Parker. Your plans will proceed without interference, I assure you."

"I hope so."

Kurt murmured a personal goodnight to Lauren. This time when he raised her hand, his fleshy lips brushed across the back of it. It took all her composure not to jerk her hand away. She was grateful when the wide oak door with the etched and beveled glass closed behind the Vandivers.

Carson, Olivia, and Lauren stood in the foyer. The rest of the house was silent. Lauren turned to Olivia and faced her squarely. "Mrs. Lockett, why did you lie to them about me? You made me an unwilling accomplice in that lie." She was astounded at her own temerity, but honesty was an integral part of her nature.

"Unwilling?" Olivia asked. Her brows arched over her eyes like two black wings. "You could have denied it right then and told them the truth. But you didn't. I think you saw, as I did, that my story was more plausible and less . . . compromising."

Lauren looked at Carson, who was staring at his shoes and offering no help. She clenched her hands tightly at her waist and gnawed on her bottom lip. Her initial instinct was to deny again the insinuation that she and Ben Lockett had meant anything more than friends to each other, but she refrained.

Two months. She must stay at least two months. Then . . .

Quickly she excused herself and went upstairs.

* * *

Carson lay in the tester bed and watched Olivia as she stepped from behind the decorative screen and walked naked across her bedroom.

She never ceased to amaze him. He knew her to be in her mid-fifties, but her excellent body belied her age. As she took down her hair, he could see her high, firm, full breasts reflected in the cheval glass. Her stomach was flat, and her thighs were without the heaviness that cursed most middle-aged women. Her hips were slender and taut. The skin on her buttocks was smooth and un-wrinkled.

Each time he saw her thus, he was made painfully aware of his own unattractive physique. Out of the confines of his tight vest, his chest and stomach sagged, and his short legs had thickened with age. Carson had always envied his friend Ben his lithe, tall body. That powerful build and thick white hair had turned the heads of many women even as his years advanced.

Unperturbed by his careful observance of her, Olivia walked to the bedside and turned down the gas lamp. She sighed tiredly as she lay down and rested her head against the scented pillowcase.

"You were marvelous with them tonight, darling. I'm sure the evening was exhausting for you," Carson said as he reached over to stroke Olivia's luxuriant hair with his stubby fingers.

"Those bastards," she hissed. "They know they have us over a barrel, and they're making full use of our position to kick us while we're down. If I didn't want that railroad so desperately, I'd never give that goddam German sonofabitch the time of day." Carson was used to her explicit language. He was gratified that she spoke this candidly only with him. He saw it as an indication of trust.

"I know, my dear. We'll just have to play their game for a while. We've had to make sacrifices like this before, but they've always worked in our favor."

"Yes. But this time it's particularly galling."

"Forget them for now and try to relax." Carson moved closer and settled his stocky body along hers. He stroked her cheek before raising himself to kiss her briefly on the mouth; he knew she didn't enjoy ardent kisses.

Laying his head as close to Olivia's as space would allow, Carson trailed his hand down her throat and chest to cup her breast. Her one pregnancy hadn't darkened her nipples, and they were almost as pink as a young girl's. He continued to enjoy the feel of her warm flesh and the tender peaks of her breasts until she shifted impatiently. Her restlessness was his signal to go about his business.

He mounted her and met no resistance when he entered her quickly. His passion rose and climaxed in a matter of minutes. He never tried to sustain the pleasure. Olivia had been taught by the nuns at the Ursuline Academy in her native New Orleans that ladies didn't enjoy the sexual act, but tolerated it out of love. Carson understood. If he ever wished he could coax a warmer response from Olivia, it was a fleeting fancy. His own cries of ecstasy were muzzled by the thick pillow in which he buried his face.

He was treated to a brief caress on his shoulder and a brush of her lips across his before she extricated herself from his embrace. Since that day over twenty years ago when she had unemotionally invited him to be her lover, he had never been allowed to linger inside her or enjoy her nakedness afterward.

Tonight, as usual, she left the bed and went directly into her bathroom. He heard the sounds of her washing. When she came back into the room, she was clad in a nightgown and robe.

"Carson, I have an idea." She paced the expensive rug at the foot of the bed. He was never allowed to spend the entire night with her, and he begrudged the time she spent out of bed.

"Yes, dear?" he asked resignedly. He could tell by her agitated posture and the intent expression on her lovely face that she was enmeshed in thought. Tonight he would have to content himself with what lovemaking she had already permitted.

He listened with unconcealed astonishment as she related her plan. It was audacious and dangerous, clever and manipulative, impossible yet feasible. He objected to her motives, protested her means, but, as he always did, he agreed to her scheme.

Chapter 6

While Olivia outlined the plan that would have a dramatic impact on Lauren's life, the girl was in her own bed trying vainly to sleep. She tossed restlessly, myriad thoughts darting through her mind and upsetting the modicum of serenity she had managed to preserve since her arrival at the Lockett household.

Olivia and Carson were a puzzle she couldn't decipher. One moment she felt they accepted her for what she was, and the next moment she felt they posed a threat to her. Carson treated her kindly, but he was Olivia's chattel. And Olivia's attitude toward Lauren was reserved and cool to say the least.

The Vandivers had frightened Lauren. She was unaccustomed to hearing business deals discussed, and Parker's callousness had appalled her. And Kurt was no doubt as greedy and ambitious as his father.

Thoughts of that young man made Lauren shiver even under the warmth of her bedcovers. He was handsome in a brutal sort of way, but his thick, powerful body repelled her, and his unctuous voice and conciliatory manner made her uneasy. She felt threatened by him, but it was a different kind of alarm than she felt when she looked at Jared Lockett.

Jared. Ben's son was a rake and scoundrel, a drunkard and a womanizer, so why did she continue to dwell on him? Why did Jared's long, lean body intrigue her so? Why did she feel a compulsion to touch him?

Since she had been initiated into the rites of womanhood at age eleven and given a very rudimentary explanation of her body's workings by the embittered Dorothea Harris, Lauren's education on the subject of sexuality had been sadly deficient.

She was fifteen before she realized something mysterious, some strange chemistry, attracted the bodies of men and women to each other. She was at a picnic held in the city park in honor of the veterans returning home from the Spanish-American War in Cuba. As she sat under a shade tree, her attention was diverted from her book to a young soldier and his pretty young wife. Lauren knew them both. They had been married only a few weeks before he joined the army.

They were sitting close together under another tree. They weren't talking, but were nonetheless communicating. They gazed steadfastly into each other's eyes. The young woman rested her hand on her husband's thigh and lightly caressed it with her fingertips. Lauren watched covertly from behind her eyeglasses as he raised her hand to his lips and kissed the palm ardently. He then returned her hand to his thigh, pressing it gently.

For some inexplicable reason, Lauren's heart started pounding, and she felt hot and flushed all over. She noticed a strange sensation in the lower part of her body. Her breasts were tingling, and the nipples became taut and pointed under her camisole. She was uncomfortable and ashamed to have such distinct physical reactions in these private parts of her body.

The man leaned down and whispered into his wife's ear. She smiled, nodded. He stood, extending his hand to help pull her to her feet, then kissed her fervently on the mouth. Lauren was finding it difficult to draw a full breath.

They smiled at each other and, glancing around, clandestinely left the picnic. They said goodbye to no one, and apparently Lauren was the only one to witness their leaving.

Those disturbing but exquisite sensations she had experienced years ago when she watched the intimacy between the young couple had almost been forgotten. They had come back to her with stunning clarity when she saw Jared Lockett leaning negligently against her doorjamb that afternoon. Why?

She read his scorn for her in the amber lights of his eyes, and was deeply hurt. What had she done to evoke such disdain? Not even the hateful, ugly words William had flung at her had pierced her like that knowing, twisted smirk on Jared's sensuous mouth.

He had stared at her all during dinner. Kurt had watched her, too. But his stare was cold and calculating, while Jared's eyes had burned into her like tongues of golden flame.

Her whole body trembled under her nightgown. She closed her eyes, but Jared's image was imprinted on the back of her lids.

Once again, she relived the moment when his hand had pressed against her breast. She felt his breath on her face, and tried to imagine how his lips would feel against hers. A long, shuddering sigh escaped her and she moaned into the pillow. She wanted to know what it was like.

And she knew that finding out would bring her perilously close to the brink of hell . . . or heaven.

The pendulum wall clock in the office chimed the hour of eight. It was the morning following the dinner with the Vandivers. To Lauren's ears, the tolling chimes sounded ominous as she sat in silence with Carson and Olivia, waiting for Jared to join them.

Olivia looked full of resolve and purpose as she sat upright and grim in her chair behind the desk. Carson was nervous and uneasy, periodically wiping his forehead with a linen handkerchief. Lauren daintily sipped a cup of tea.

She had awakened early after her restless night. Her heavy maroon skirt and ecru shirtwaist were donned hurriedly, and without Elena's help. Lauren had pinned her hair into a haphazard chignon at the nape of her neck and left her room. Her haste in making an appearance at breakfast was probably unnecessary, but she didn't want her hostess to think her lazy.

Before she entered the dining room, Carson intercepted her and asked if she would please join him and Olivia in the office where they had interviewed her previously. She would always think of it as Ben's office, for an aura of the man still clung to the atmosphere.

Lauren went in behind Carson and quickly poured a cup of tea, sweetening it liberally, intuitively guessing she would need some sustenance during this mysterious meeting. Carson's full cheeks reddened considerably, and he wouldn't look her fully in the eyes when he extended the invitation, which Lauren knew was not an invitation at all, but a command. Carson's jitters were communicated to her.

Something was in the wind. And it obviously affected her. But how? She couldn't imagine. Maybe in light of the events of last evening, they were going to ask her politely to leave. They would have their hands full for a while with the business of the railroad, and she couldn't blame them for not wanting an outsider cluttering up their lives.

Why was it necessary for Jared to hear her fate? She'd prefer that he didn't witness the interview. He, however, would undoubtedly relish any misfortune that befell her, she thought dismally.

Lauren started as she heard his boots echoing on the parquet floor in the hall. He stomped into the room and looked darkly at his mother.

"This better be damned important for you to root me out of bed this early when I got in late and feel as godawful as I do. I'm going to get some coffee." He strode out of the room and no one spoke until he returned a few moments later carrying a steaming mug of coffee. He sipped it and cursed under his breath when it burned his tongue.

In contrast to Olivia's military neatness, Jared was disheveled—his brown hair mussed, the wrinkled shirt hastily and sloppily stuffed into rumpled pants, the boots which had shone last night now scuffed and dull. He slouched in a chair in a posture Lauren was coming to know. He ignored her and Carson completely.

"If it weren't important, Jared, I would not have disturbed you." Olivia spoke as if no time had elapsed since he first came in and rudely addressed her. "Carson and I had a long talk last night after the Vandivers left. We have arrived at some conclusions and want to tell you our course of action that will resolve our problems with Parker."

Carson once again mopped his perspiring brow, and licked his lips nervously as he watched Jared from across the room. If they were going to rehash the same argument, Lauren would prefer to return to her room and the correspondence she was doing for Olivia. Or start packing her bags.

"Why do I suspect that I'm not going to like our 'course of action'?" Jared asked stonily. "You know how I feel about those jackasses. I don't want them on one square inch of Lockett land."

"I don't particularly like them, either, and I trust them less; but I want that railroad, Jared. Carson does, too, and so did your father."

"Ben didn't want it bad enough to let a thief like Vandiver make the deals for him."

"Jared, what your mother is trying to say is that we've got to give a little in order to gain a lot." Carson looked at the younger man almost pleadingly. "I know why you hesitate about damming up even a small tributary of Rio Caballo. Some of the smaller farmers and ranchers will suffer setbacks, but we'll work with them all we can. We're not going to leave them high and dry." He laughed skittishly at his own play on words, but Jared didn't even smile.

Lauren had watched Jared since the discussion began and saw

the same expression of conviction that he had shown last night. His jaw worked convulsively as he clenched his teeth.

Then he hung his head and swirled the coffee around in his mug. He studied it hard, a deep groove forming between the thick brows. When he looked up again, his face had completely changed. He looked at his mother with accusation, at Carson with disgust, and then assumed an attitude of complete indifference.

He shrugged insolently. "Do whatever you like. I don't give a damn. The two of you will make great partners with Vandiver."

He set the mug on the table in front of him and stood to leave, but Olivia checked him. "Jared, wait. I'm afraid it's not as simple as that. Sit down." Impatience was written on his surly face, but he slumped into the chair again and restlessly propped one ankle on the other knee.

"It seems, Jared, that some of the investors in this railroad of ours are concerned about your attitude. After word of your behavior last night gets around, I'm sure it will confirm their low opinion of you. You must be, or at least appear to be, behind this project one hundred percent. The power plant, as well as the railroad, needs your public endorsement now that you are taking over your father's businesses."

"Taking over? That's a laugh," he muttered caustically.

Olivia ignored the interruption. "Of course, Carson and I will be running things for you until you feel ready to assume responsibility. But to the world, you must present a credible air of authority and maturity." She let all of that sink in, pausing dramatically before she said, "That's why we feel you should marry as soon as possible. Marry Miss Holbrook."

The words hung in the air, suspended on the palpable currents of differing emotions evoked in those who had heard them.

Rivers of blood rushed to Lauren's head, causing a great roaring, and a fire consumed her eyes and ears even as perspiration covered her body in a chilling film.

Olivia remained unperturbed. She sat calmly and regally, waiting for her subjects to do her bidding so she could get on with the affairs of state.

Carson's eyes darted from Lauren to Jared to Olivia, and then back to Lauren. He had no idea what the girl was thinking. She stared in front of her as if she had lost all her senses.

Jared's reaction surprised them all. He burst out laughing. He stood and stumbled around the room holding his sides until, completely spent, he collapsed against the windowsill. Drawing in several gulps of air, he said with total incredulity, "You can't be serious! Marry Miss Holbrook! That's the best laugh I've had in weeks." He wiped tears of mirth from his eyes and Lauren was poignantly reminded of Ben. Only that memory penetrated her shocked brain.

Olivia stated quietly, "I'm not joking, Jared. I'm serious, and I think you'll see why if you let me explain it to you."

"I don't need any explanations, Mother. It's absurd," Jared cried. He pointed a finger at Lauren. "She's still wet behind the ears."

"Miss Holbrook is twenty. Ben told me."

"I wasn't referring to her age, dammit, I was refer—"

"I know what you meant," Olivia said. "It's a far cry from your earlier opinion of her. I remember your accusing Ben of bringing his 'southern belle whore' into the house when he told us about her."

Lauren swelled with anger at Jared's unjust and unwarranted comment. He hadn't even met her! Before she could fill her constricted lungs with enough air to protest, Olivia continued, "We made a plausible story of her being a classmate's sister. We'll embellish it and say that you fell in love on one of your visits with her family. Your father surprised you by bringing her here, and you can't bear for her to go back. You'll be married right away." She held up a palm to stave off the objection she saw coming. "We expect you to be more discreet in your . . . other interests, Jared, but you need not change your lifestyle. Lauren is educated and refined and will add a convincing touch to your new, responsible image."

Jared leaned against the wall, crossed his ankles, and folded his arms across his chest. He sounded amused when he drawled, "We weren't exactly a loving couple last night. How the hell do you expect those shrewd Vandivers to fall for your little farce?"

"We'll say Lauren thought it improper to marry so soon after Ben's death and that you had quarreled about it. You were having a lover's spat." Then, dismissing any further arguments, she said, "You will marry immediately. Have I made myself clear?"

Jared looked at his mother levelly for a few moments. When he spoke, all traces of humor were gone. His voice was low and menacing. "Every goddam decision in my life, you have made for me. I'll go along with your scheme for the railroad, but there's no way you'll saddle me with an unwanted wife. No way in hell."

Olivia smiled smugly. "I think there is, Jared. I happened to overhear your argument with Ben the night before he died. Do you wish to tell Miss Holbrook why Ben arranged for her to come here?" Jared's face paled alarmingly, even considering his hungover pallor. His eyes looked pained. He stood up straight and balled his hands into fists at his side, but he didn't speak. "No?" Olivia turned to Lauren. "Well, Lauren, it seems that Ben picked you out for Jared. He was bringing you here in the hopes that before he died, he would see his son married and settled down with you."

She faced her son again. "It's ironic that for once my objectives are the same as your father's, isn't it, Jared? And it was your vehement objection to his matchmaking and your promise to make Lauren's visit as abominable as possible that caused your father's heart attack. I think you owe him his last wish, don't you?" She leaned back in her chair and smiled dangerously. "Yes, I think you owe him this."

Jared's jaw had turned to iron. His teeth clenched and unclenched; his hands worked at his sides. He turned and faced the window, looking out with eyes blinded by impotent rage.

Had Lauren not been so stunned by the events of the past few minutes, she would have resented being discussed as if she were deaf and mute, an object rather than a person. Ben had invited her here for that wastrel to marry! How could he have been so callous? And Olivia and Jared had known all along, probably Carson had, too. They had conspired to deceive her, had even humiliated her with spurious doubts of her virtue.

Olivia turned a hard, green stare on her and said, "Lauren, we've not heard your opinion." Clearly her statement was a mere formality. Olivia would brook no opposition.

At Lauren's obvious inability to speak, Carson hesitantly cautioned, "Olivia, maybe we're being unrealistic. Let's give them time—"

"No," Olivia said. "The sooner the better, Carson. I'm sure when Lauren hears the rest of our proposal, she'll agree fast enough."

Lauren met Olivia's eyes again and felt a spurt of courage. This woman could never force her into marriage. Never.

Before Lauren could tell Ben's widow exactly what she thought of the entire family, Olivia said, "Lauren, we don't expect you to do this without compensation. We're only asking that you stay married until the railroad is complete and running to our satisfaction. Then, when all the fireworks are over, you may go wherever you wish. For your time and trouble, we'll give you twenty thousand dollars in cash when you leave."

"I don't want any money from you, Olivia!" Lauren declared. She wasn't even aware of having used Olivia's first name. This final insult was too humiliating. Olivia had actually offered her money to marry Jared!

She ignored the derisive snort that came from the direction of the window. Her eyes were riveted on Olivia as she whispered hoarsely, "This is impossible. Surely you are joking?" Olivia only stared back at her stoically. Lauren looked toward Carson, who was wiping his moist hands with his handkerchief. The man at the window remained motionless, brooding. He was leaving her to fight this battle alone, when they should have been allies. Anger made her brave.

"I won't marry anyone. I don't want to marry anyone," she declared with a defiant lift of her small, pointed chin.

Olivia laughed indulgently. "My dear Lauren, I'm not suggesting that you marry in the biblical sense of the word. The marriage need never be consummated." Again Lauren heard a scoffing sound from near the window. "I would think our offer would be attractive. You don't want to return to that dismal parsonage right away, do you? When you leave here, you'll be a woman of independent means."

"I would also be a married woman," Lauren protested.

With a hint of impatience in her voice, Olivia replied, "An unconsummated marriage can be annulled expeditiously. Don't worry about that now. As Jared's wife, things will be very pleasant for you here."

The green eyes narrowed on Lauren and Olivia asked pointedly, "Was there someone you were involved with in North Carolina? Perhaps a former love is the reason for your resistance."

"No," Lauren rasped. She shuddered when William's gloating face invaded her thoughts. "No," she said with finality. Feeling bolder now, she challenged, "If you've known all along why Ben brought me here, why didn't you say so?"

"That's a lesson for you to learn, Lauren. Gather what information you can, and then save it until just the right moment. Had this occasion for us to use you not arisen, you would have been sent away after two months none the wiser." She smiled tightly. "No doubt Ben's romantic soul hoped you and Jared would develop an affection for each other during your visit. Ben was always a fool about such things."

Lauren was shocked by the hatred in Olivia's voice, and could only stare at the woman in lieu of a response.

Olivia stood up and briskly crossed the room. "Then if there is no further discussion, I need to start making preparations." She looked at Jared, then at Lauren. When no one made an objection, she motioned for Carson to follow. He patted Lauren quickly on the shoulder before he left the room in the wake of Olivia's stiff, rustling skirts.

Lauren's mind was in turmoil. Why was she still sitting here? She should be upstairs furiously packing. She should run away from this house at once. She stared vacantly as her thoughts ran rampant.

What were her options? She couldn't go back to North Carolina and face William and her former guardians. She had closed that chapter of her life. Or rather, it had been closed for her.

She would live with a loveless marriage to a stranger. But not forever. She would have the means to start over when she left the Locketts and she would somehow survive the stigma of divorce. Maybe she could even pass herself off as a widow if she moved far enough away from Texas. In the meantime, she would live comfortably.

What else could she do? Briefly she thought of Ed Travers and his kind offer to help her. Maybe he could secure her a position as a Harvey House girl. Swiftly Lauren rejected the idea. Her experience at entertaining parlor guests would not have prepared her for the dining room of a restaurant where she would have to serve food from heavily laden trays. And she would despise living in a dormitory where moments of privacy were scarce, if they existed at all.

The pros and cons paraded back and forth in her head, but the basis of her decision was the same one that Olivia had so cleverly used on Jared. Ben had wanted it.

It always came back to that. Ben had chosen her for his son. *Why?* It was an agonizing thought that she would never know his reasons.

Lauren had been so engrossed in her own musings that she didn't remember until now that Jared was still in the room. He stood rigidly at the window in the same position as before, with his back to her. Why hadn't he said anything?

She looked at the man and tried to analyze what he must be feeling. Would marriage to him be so terrible? Olivia made it clear that his bride would be only a figurehead. She would remain a bride, and never become a wife. For the marriage was not to be consummated. Lauren's heart skipped a beat and fluttered in her breast. The mechanics of such intimacy still eluded her, but she knew that the word implied a physical avowal of the marriage.

They must speak to each other. Before she consented to this preposterous action, she must know his feelings. Timorously she vacated her chair and approached him. She cleared her throat. "Mr. Lockett?"

At the sound of her voice, his body tensed automatically. When the tremor passed, he straightened his shoulders and pivoted slowly on the heels of his boots until he faced her. He didn't say anything, only looked at her with an aloof, cold expression in his eyes. The full, sensuous lips were set in a grim, hard line.

"I . . . I want to know—" she stammered before he interrupted her.

"You took their bait, hook, line, and sinker, didn't you? You couldn't wait for this chance, could you? All that money! And a husband! My, my, the old maid preacher's kid has come a long way up the ladder today."

His words were cruel and vicious and delivered with intention to hurt. Is that what he thought of her? Did he think she had known about Ben's plans for her? Anger and shame forced unwanted tears to gather in the corners of her eyes, and she looked at him imploringly. "Mr. Lockett, you must—"

He lunged, grabbing her shoulders with his strong hands. Her head snapped back painfully and the bun at her nape began to uncoil.

Through clenched teeth, but with a voice oozing feigned charm, he growled, "I think that under the circumstances, we can dispense with the Mr. and Miss. My name is Jared. Say it!" he commanded.

His hands were unrelentingly tight on her arms, and her teeth chattered in fright, but she managed to gasp, "Jared," before one huge tear escaped her lower lid and rolled like a sparkling gem down her cheek.

That one tear infuriated Jared further and he hissed, "I don't know how you so completely hoodwinked and bewitched a man as smart as my father, but don't think you can resort to tears and vapors to get to *me*. Those fathomless gray eyes won't work on me, understand?" He gave her a little shake. "We're in this together. Just stay out of my way, and possibly we'll be able to stand it. Old Ben was famous for his clever tricks, and he seems to have played his last big joke on me. He sure found a willing partner in you."

"No!" she cried. "I didn't know what he intended. He only mentioned you once in passing. I didn't—"

"Then you're more of a fool than I thought. Did you think Ben wanted you for himself? Well, then, the joke's on you, too, isn't it? Were you after a nice, rich, elderly husband who would more than likely make you a rich widow very soon. *Were you?*" He shouted the last two words, his face inches from hers. He held her tight against him, each muscle straining and pressing into her.

His amber eyes flickered for an instant when he looked down at her appealing face. His surprised expression mirrored hers as they simultaneously realized that their bodies were touching chest to toes. It was softness against hardness, weakness against strength, femininity against masculinity. The contrast was too compelling to ignore.

Jared hadn't planned it, had never even thought about it, but he couldn't control taking complete possession of her mouth with a bruising kiss. He wanted to insult her, to further humiliate her, to shatter her damned poise. But her body was so female, her lips so soft, warm, virginal, that what had been hurtful and brutal became tender, seeking, questioning.

His arms went around her slowly, drawing her into an even closer embrace. He disregarded the heels of her hands on his shoulders making a weak, futile attempt to push him away. One hand went to the back of her head and held it immobile until her lips parted under the increased pressure of his. His fingers unconsciously entwined in the thick strands of hair that tumbled further down her neck.

Sweetly his tongue plundered the hollows of her mouth, unique in taste and feel from any other he had kissed. His arms tightened around her until her breasts were flattened against his chest. The feel of her taut nipples through the soft linen of her blouse clouded his judgment, and his mouth became even more avaricious.

Lauren's mind fed on the new sensations—the scratching stubble of his beard, the coffee taste in his mouth, the faint aroma of tobacco, the feel of his lips, teeth, and tongue as they explored, the sound of a moan that came from . . . where?

Jared pushed her away from him so suddenly that she almost fell backward. She regained her balance and tried to assimilate what had happened. Both her hands came up and covered her mouth. Over her trembling fingertips, she looked at Jared, who appeared none too composed himself.

He stared at her, breathing rapidly, then swallowed convulsively. When he was moderately restored, he dropped the mask of indifference over his features and sneered contemptuously, "Very nice, Lauren, but I told you it wouldn't work on me." His lips curled cruelly and his thick-fringed eyelids lowered speculatively over the cynical eyes. "You were no doubt comparing my sexual prowess to Ben's." He barked a short laugh. "Well, I'll be damned before I'll have any of my father's leftovers!"

It seemed that every blood vessel in her head had burst, for her whole world was washed in red fury. She advanced on him like a warrior bent on vengeance and slapped him smartly on the cheek.

Chapter 7

Jared was too astonished to react. She glared up at him, eyes wide and dark, chest heaving with agitation. At any other time, he would have found her anger ludicrous and would have been greatly amused. Now he stood statuelike as she said scathingly, "You are insufferable, Jared Lockett. Never, *never*," she stamped a small foot for emphasis, "insult me as you just have." She spun around and marched from the room, leaving Jared nonplussed.

As soon as she closed the door of the office behind her, Lauren ran toward the staircase and, quite unladylike, raised her skirt above her ankles and sped up the stairs. By the time she reached her room, her face was bathed with tears. "I hate him!" she professed in a grating whisper. "He's abominable. They all are," she cried. The pillows caught her when she fell across the bed. They absorbed her tears and muffled sounds of frustration and anger.

Why!? Why had he thought such a thing about her? What had she done in innocence that made them all suspect her of something evil? Olivia and Carson had been half-convinced that she and Ben had been lovers. Jared must have thought the same thing, and even attributed mercenary motives to her.

Even Abel and Sybil, who had loved her like a daughter, were ready to accept William's vicious lies about her. Their first expressions of shocked disbelief when William had told his tale had turned to the same contemptuous frown that Jared had worn moments before. She had done nothing to warrant their severe judgment.

William. Even now, when his memory was beginning to fade from her mind, the pain he had inflicted came back with terrific force.

The day Ben Lockett left early after breakfast, the Prathers had decided on the spur of the moment to travel to Raleigh for the day. Abel had invited Lauren to accompany them, but the prospect of spending the day in close company with the parson and his wife, much as she loved them, was unappealing. Lauren gave the excuse of a headache and begged them not to change their plans on her account. Indeed, Sybil was already enumerating the stores she wished to visit and naming possible places for a late luncheon.

Lauren waved to the Prathers cheerfully when they finally departed. She was immensely grateful for the day she could spend alone. She needed to nurse her feelings about having given up the opportunity to seek a new life for herself.

The day passed too quickly. She became involved in a new piece of music and spent hours practicing until she played it to her satisfaction. She spent a quiet hour lying on her bed with a novel, but found her thoughts kept drifting back to Ben Lockett. She would never see him again, but he would forever be in her mind. He had been so kind. How she wished her father had been like that.

Resolutely, she shoved Ben to the further reaches of her mind as she cooked an omelet for her dinner. Since Abel and Sybil were to stay the night in Raleigh, she viewed the privacy as an unexpected but welcome gift.

After her light and, for once, well-seasoned meal, she was on her way upstairs when the bell at the front door rang. Accustomed to people calling at all hours seeking Abel for one emergency or another, she opened the door without hesitation.

William Keller stood on the porch.

She was tempted to slam the door in his pale face, but her innate good manners made such an action impossible.

Hoping to rid herself of his company, she said, "Hello, William. Abel isn't at home." She barred the door with her body and purposely didn't ask him in.

The Prathers' absence was no news to William. Abel had called him about a hospital patient who needed visiting before they left for Raleigh, casually mentioning that Lauren was staying home.

He looked at Lauren smugly and took a step through the door. She was forced to move aside or have her body come into contact with his, and that she would avoid at all costs.

"Good," William oozed. "I'm glad that I'll have a chance to speak to you frankly and privately."

He deposited his hat and coat on the hall tree and proceeded into the parlor, unaffected by Lauren's cool greeting.

Lauren hadn't been in this room all day. Apparently neither had anyone else, for the drapes remained unopened and only narrow slits of violet dusk outlined them. The parlor was dim, stuffy, and close, and William's presence made the atmosphere seem even more stifling.

"What do you want to speak to me about, William? I'm very busy," she said in a shaky voice. She knew then that the one emotion William had always stimulated in her was fear.

That was ridiculous! What did she have to fear from him? She tilted her chin higher, determined that he would not see her nervousness at being alone with him in an empty house.

William stood in the middle of the room with his hands at his back as he faced her. "Abel has given me permission to ask for your hand in marriage," he stated pedantically. "Before you find yourself unable to resist the advances of men like this recent visiting cowboy. I have decided that we should marry as soon as possible."

She was aghast at his words, and her nervousness gave way to anger. "Ben Lockett did not make *advances* to me. But whether he did or not is of no concern to you, William, for I have no intention of marrying you." She paused to draw in a ragged breath and clasped her hands together at her waist. "This discussion is over. I'll see you out."

She turned and walked toward the portiere. Before she reached it, William's cold hand gripped her arm above the elbow and whirled her around to face him. She was so surprised at his accosting her in this manner that she didn't try to extricate herself, but only stared at him incredulously.

"Not so fast, Miss Priss," he snarled. "I'm not finished with you yet." His voice was a feral growl, and she leaned away from him in revulsion. "You may have everyone else fooled, but not me. What kind of proposition did Lockett make you out there in the rose garden?"

She tried to jerk her arm away, but his grip became painfully more restricting and she winced. "I don't know what you're talking about. He asked me to go to Texas for a visit, that's all."

"Oh, I just bet he did." William smirked. "The only visits you'd be paying him would be to his bedroom."

Lauren gasped. "I . . . I have *no* idea what you're talking about." This was true. She had only a vague notion of what his words implied, but she knew instinctively that the implication was ugly.

William squinted at her carefully. "Maybe you don't. Well,

then, I'm going to be the one to teach you. Not some old, overgrown oaf."

Terror gave Lauren the strength to free her arm and, turning, she tried to run from him. He was right behind her and grabbed her again before she had taken two steps. His arms went around her in a viselike grip and pulled her around to face him. His fleshy, wet lips mashed against hers.

Lauren couldn't believe this was happening. Her mind screamed silently while his mouth over hers made actual screaming impossible. He held her even closer, his legs straddling hers as he bent over her. Then, placing his wet mouth against her ear, he muttered, "Don't fight it, Lauren. I've watched you move in that maddening way of yours. I'm not fooled by the perfect lady act." All this time, she could feel his cold hands working with the buttons on the back of her shirtwaist. She did scream when she felt his bloodless fingers against her flesh.

He stopped the scream with his mouth again and, as Lauren's mouth was open, he thrust his tongue into it deeply. She fought even harder, scratching his face, pulling his hair, kicking his bony shins. An instinct of self-preservation drove her to do things she would never have thought herself capable of.

She was horrified to think about what all this awful pawing and slobbering culminated in, and she knew she could not allow it. Repulsion and fear gave her one last surge of strength, and she shoved against his chest with all her might. He staggered and fell backward over a petit-point cushioned footstool in front of Sybil's easy chair. While he made an ungainly attempt to stand, Lauren lunged toward the fireplace and seized the iron poker, brandishing it in front of her.

"Get out of here," she managed to croak between gulping breaths. "If you try to touch me again, I'll kill you."

Standing there with bleeding scratches on his face, his thin hair sticking out at varying angles, his clothes in disarray, William bore little resemblance to the stiff, circumspect minister who delivered hair-raising sermons to his congregation on the consequences of pursuing the lusts of the flesh.

"What would you tell everyone, Lauren darling, when they came in and found my skull crushed if, in fact, you succeeded? Your reputation would be irreparably damaged. People would believe that you'd invited me here while your watchdogs were out of town." He took a tentative step toward her.

He stopped when she raised the poker higher. "I would never have thought myself capable of murder, but so help me, I will do it, William," she threatened. "You're a hypocrite and a parody of a man. Now get out of my sight. At once!"

He snickered nastily. "I'm not giving up. You probably delivered the goods to Lockett, anyway." Having flung this final insult at her, he walked past her warily and paused in the hall only long enough to straighten his clothing and slip on his coat and hat. Lauren heard the front door open and close softly. She stood with the poker raised and only when the weight of it began to make her arms ache did she lower it.

She moved with stunned, dreamlike slowness. After climbing the stairs as if she wore lead shoes, she opened the door to her room and then locked it behind her. She crossed to her dresser and looked with dismay at her reflection in the mirror.

Her chin was still shiny with William's saliva. Her hair hung in tangled knots down her back.

She removed her clothing as she drew water into the deep tub. She rinsed her mouth out several times with antiseptic, and then stepped into the hot water to soak away the degradation. The bruises on her upper arms were painful.

Lauren had awakened the next morning still shattered from the experience of the night before. Pacing the floor, she tried to arrange her thoughts. How was she going to tell the guileless Prathers what had happened? Their disillusionment with the young pastor would be shocking. Certainly Abel would have to relieve him of his position and forbid him to ever enter this house again. Lauren wished she could spare them this hurt, but she couldn't remain silent. William Keller was a menace.

It never occurred to her that her guardians wouldn't believe her.

When they came home, she welcomed them happily. Sybil's chattering helped dispel the gloom in the house, which had seemed to become even more oppressive since last evening. Lauren was presented with a box of lace handkerchiefs. She thanked the Prathers profusely while consciously ushering them into the parlor.

They had just sat down when the doorbell rang. Lauren was astounded to hear William's voice when Abel answered it. They spoke quietly for a few moments before a perplexed Abel stood under the portiere and said, "If you ladies will excuse us, William has an urgent matter to discuss with me. We'll no doubt join you shortly."

He disappeared in the direction of his study and a nameless premonition pricked Lauren's mind. She was nervous and apprehensive as she listened to Sybil's detailed account of the trip. Lauren's mouth went dry and her agitation grew as the interview in the study stretched into a half-hour.

Her heart lurched when she heard the study door opening and the two men came into the parlor. Abel's face was an alarming red. He shook his head as he looked disbelievingly at Lauren. William stood several humble steps behind him. He seemed contrite, but Lauren caught a victorious gleam in his reptilian eyes when they lighted on her.

"Abel, what—" Sybil's voice quivered when she saw her husband's obvious distress.

"My dear, I wish I could spare you this, but I'm afraid you'll have to know of our shame sooner or later."

Abel crossed the room with a heavy tread and sat down beside his wife, taking her hand. William stood just inside the doorway and studied the ugly carpet under his serviceable shoes.

Was it possible William thought she had told the Prathers about his shameful behavior last night and had come to apologize? Her surmise was rejected when she saw the expression on Abel's face as he turned toward her. It was sad. It was censoring. It was sanctimonious.

He sighed before he said, "Fornication is a grievous sin, Lauren." Her lips parted in astonishment. Sybil gasped and crammed a handkerchief against her lips.

"What—" Lauren started to speak, but Abel continued.

"It is an abomination unto the Lord. William has come to me like a man and confessed that the two of you have for several months yielded to your lusts."

Sybil collapsed against the back of the sofa, and tiny sobs escaped from her trembling lips. Lauren opened her mouth to protest, but again Abel anticipated her.

"A man's drives are stronger than a woman's. Even a man of God like William isn't free from the cravings of his flesh. However," here his voice became more stern, "it is up to the woman to keep a tight rein on those cravings. William told me that you enticed him to the point where he succumbed."

Sybil cried out loud now, the tears flowing copiously down her fat cheeks. All the blood drained from Lauren's face. The wild pounding of her heart seemed to stop. I must be dreaming, she told herself.

"Somehow we, who loved you as our own, have failed. You were entrusted into our care by your sainted father. We have betrayed that trust just as surely as you have betrayed our love."

Lauren's heart ached at seeing her guardians suffer so, but she made no effort to speak then. She glanced at William, who continued to stare at the floor in abject repentance.

Abel closed his eyes for a moment, then said, "Lauren, William told me that he couldn't live with himself another day without arranging for an immediate wedding. He offers you marriage, not out of guilt, but out of deep and abiding love. I, for one, am grateful—" He broke off and buried his face in his hands.

Witnessing his misery spurred Lauren into action. She flew out of her chair and crouched beside Abel. She placed both hands on his and waited until he raised his head to look at her before she spoke.

"He's lying, Abel," she stated simply. "The only time I have been alone with William was last night. He came her while you were gone and tried to kiss and . . . touch me." Tears rolled down her face as she recounted the indignities she had experienced.

When she finished her story, she felt William's hands on her shoulders as he pulled her conciliatorily to her feet. "Lauren, dear, we don't have to hide anymore. Don't you see? We will be married and live together. We have sinned. But I've confessed my sin to God and Man. If you confess your transgression, you, too, will feel the peace that now suffuses my spirit."

She jumped away from him, her eyes flashing. "Are you mad? The only thing I'll confess to is my loathing of you."

William smiled sweetly at Abel. "I'm afraid she's overwrought. She wanted to prevent you from finding out about our illicit relations. She wanted to spare you that."

"Of course," Abel agreed, staring at Lauren as if he'd never seen her before. "I think the wedding should take place as quickly as possible. Lauren, I appreciate your charity in trying to spare Sybil and me. I will bless this marriage. You will be restored to my family and to the family of God."

William had won. With satanic subtlety, he had conceived this counterattack, and the Prathers believed him. Abel had spoken of betrayal, but he couldn't know how deeply she felt betrayed.

She could show them the purple bruises on her arms, but why should she? If William's seeds of deception had found such fertile soil in the minds of those who should know her and love her better than to suspect her of such depravity, then she wasn't going to plead her case. Abel was God's servant, but he wasn't God. And her conscience was clear.

"I'm not going to marry William. He is lying. And even if he weren't, I would never marry William Keller."

Sybil shrieked, and fell back against the cushions once again.

"Lauren, do you wish to heap burning coals of shame upon our heads? Child, please consider us if you don't consider your immortal soul," Abel pleaded.

"I have done nothing. I will not be condemned to a life of unhappiness with a man I despise," Lauren said firmly. "But you needn't dread the shame my continued presence in your house will bring you. I intend to leave."

And she had. She left within the week, taking out of the bank what small funds belonged to her.

Her telegram to Ben Lockett sent the morning after William's conference with Abel caught the cattle baron just as he was arriving in Austin. He hastily replied, and his evident joy at her imminent visit restored her high hopes. She left the Prathers' parsonage several days later, unforgiven, an anathema. But she was on her way to Texas, and a new life with the family of Ben Lockett.

The family of Ben Lockett. She was about to become a member of that family. Was she doing the right thing?

Yes, she told herself. She was doing the only thing she could do, short of leaving penniless and without direction. Yes. Her best course was to marry Jared.

His kiss had stunned her, offended her. But where was the disgust she should be feeling? Nausea had kept her awake the night William had kissed her. Why hadn't she been sickened by Jared's mouth? All she could recall of his kiss was the sensuous persuasion of his lips and tongue and the protective warmth of his firm embrace.

She rolled on to her back on the bed and covered her face with her hands against the shame she felt. She had enjoyed that kiss.

And she would never forget it. Could she marry the man, live with him, and constantly be reminded of that one fleeting moment of passion? Added to all his other insults, could she tolerate that final humiliation, knowing that he would remember that kiss, too?

On the other hand, she had not yet thought of a palatable alternative. At least by marrying Jared, she would have a goal to accomplish, an obligation to fulfill.

The money seemed insignificant now, but in two years, it could be extremely important. The twenty thousand dollars could mean the difference between living comfortably and destitution. Looking at it strictly from a financial point of view, did she dare pass up an opportunity like this?

And then there was the man, Jared Lockett. No! She wouldn't think about him, for thoughts of him clouded her ability to reason logically. Somehow they would learn to coexist peaceably. That would be a major accomplishment, but she would take it a step at a time.

She made her decision.

For the remainder of the day, Lauren stayed in her room, trying to still the turbulence of her mind. At dinnertime, she changed her shirtwaist and recombed her hair, securing it better than she had that morning. A cool, damp cloth pressed to her eyes had relieved them of the redness and puffiness of weeping. She felt restored, but her heart pounded painfully as she descended the stairs.

At the dinner table, Olivia stated, almost as an afterthought, "Lauren, the wedding will take place here a week from tomorrow. There will be a select number of invited guests."

"Very well," Lauren answered.

Jared wasn't at dinner. His absence was never mentioned or explained to his fiancée.

Chapter 8

For the next few days, Lauren was thrust into such a beehive of activity that she had little time for introspection. The sheer importance of the transpiring events prevented her from examining them too closely. It was far easier to be swept along on the tide. So busy were the days, that at night she fell into bed exhausted, hoping for rapid and complete oblivion. But her brain refused to slumber, and she was forced to dwell on what she was about to do until her mind finally relinquished its control over her body, and her burning, gritty eyes closed in restless sleep.

Elena and Rosa were at first surprised that Señor Jared was marrying the lovely Miss Holbrook. But soon they were riding the crest of excitement and got caught up in the flurry of activity. They nearly drove Lauren to distraction with their petting and fawning over her.

Jared's reaction to their upcoming marriage was one of cool acceptance. He neither feigned affection, nor treated her with the resentment she knew he must feel. Each time they were together, he regarded her with the same aloof indifference that he did everyone else. He was polite, but not effusively so. He conversed with her when necessary, but didn't initiate any private dialogues between them. He could have loved her passionately or despised her with equal fervor. His remote expression gave away nothing.

Olivia organized the wedding in the brief span of time allotted. Lauren was consulted on little in regard to the arrangements. She was told it would be a private civil ceremony held in the large parlor. There would be a small reception afterward for the few invited guests. The following day, Lauren and Jared would go to Keypoint for a "honeymoon."

Lauren was fitted several times a day for the trousseau which Olivia insisted on despite Lauren's protests to the contrary. Olivia's gesture wasn't motivated by generosity or any blossoming maternal affection for Lauren, but by concern that everything appear proper and above suspicion.

She had spread the word of Lauren's background through several famed gossips. The story was that Lauren's parents couldn't attend the wedding because her father was suffering from a heart condition that made travel impossible. Lauren's dear mother had far too many responsibilities to oversee the wedding, so Olivia had graciously offered to handle it. If anyone was suspicious, they feared the indomitable Olivia too much to say so.

Mrs. Gibbons, the seamstress who had been commissioned to provide Lauren with a complete wardrobe in an impossible amount of time, reflected the general shock and thrill that Texas's most eligible bachelor, Jared Lockett, had finally been snared.

Lauren was amazed at the quantity and quality of clothes being made for her. There were skirts and shirtwaists of the finest fabrics. All of the blouses were trimmed in delicate, weblike lace. Dresses for daytime and evening, cloaks, coats, hats, gloves were strewn around her room in varying stages of completion. Mrs. Gibbons worked around Lauren like a sculptor around a masterpiece, measuring, twisting, pulling, turning, lifting, pinching, all the time murmuring to herself in appreciation of her subject. She made undergarments of the finest linen trimmed with blue satin ribbons and fine lace.

Lauren stood with flushed cheeks as Mrs. Gibbons deftly pinned a new chemise onto her. "They are very . . . sheer, aren't they?" Lauren asked shyly, glancing down at her breasts so clearly revealed through the fabric.

Mrs. Gibbons chuckled softly. "Mr. Lockett will love these underthings, but he'll be impatient to see you out of them, too. You have a beautiful body, Lauren. After he sees you without your clothes, he may never let you dress again!"

Lauren was appalled at such a thought. She was still alarmed over her reaction to Jared's kiss. Though she had fought William with all her strength, she hadn't resisted Jared, at least not strenuously. Of course, one couldn't compare the two men. William was repulsive, while Jared was handsome and virile, and his eyes . . .

No! She wasn't going to think about him. He obviously didn't think of her. Where before he had stared at her relentlessly, now he studiously ignored her. Of the two, Lauren couldn't have said which disturbed her most.

To Olivia's credit, everything was completed in time. Lauren's new wardrobe hung in her closet except for the clothes Elena had packed for her to take to Keypoint.

Rosa and several extra helpers had been cooking and baking for days in preparation for the "small reception." The house was bedecked with flowers and potted ferns. How Olivia had managed to have them transported from Austin without their wilting would remain a mystery to the bride.

She watched the dawn of her wedding day from the upstairs window where only weeks before she had watched Ben Lockett's funeral cortège commence.

"Are you pleased, Ben?" Lauren asked in a whisper just as the sun broke over the horizon. She tried to convince herself that the timely sunrise was a good omen.

Elena arrived with a breakfast tray. Anticipation glowed in her liquid eyes and she chattered cheerfully. When Lauren had eaten all her nervous stomach would tolerate, she bathed leisurely and Elena began helping her dress.

Lauren's wedding gown spurned tradition and was beautiful in its uniqueness. Ecru lace was lined with a silk slip of the same color. The leg-of-mutton sleeves and the bodice, to the top curve of her breasts, were left unlined. The collar stood high and flared slightly at her jaw. One deep flounce accented the bottom of the slim skirt and barely brushed the vamp of her bone kid slippers. She pinned a nosegay of deep purple violets at her waist. Her brooch watch was invisibly secured to her petticoat.

Her hair was pulled up in its usual pompadour, but Elena insisted on curling a few loose tendrils to hang around her face and on her neck. Lauren looked back at the girl in the mirror and wondered if that vision in the costly gown, with the pale face and cautious eyes, could really be she.

Elena stared at her idol with reverence. "Señorita Lauren, you are beautiful," she whispered. "Like the Blessed Virgin Mary." Shyly she kissed Lauren on the cheek, her huge eyes filled with tears.

"Thank you, Elena. I wish you could be there during the ceremony. You're my best friend."

"I would like that, but . . . ." Elena gave a characteristic shrug. Then she giggled and said mischievously, "I would rather be a witness to the wedding night and see if all the stories about Señor Jared are true. They say he is as big as a stallion. You are very lucky, no?" Still giggling, she pushed Lauren toward the stairs. The bride's face had whitened significantly.

It was prearranged that Carson would escort her down the aisle. As she met him at the foot of the grand staircase, Lauren was terrified that her knees wouldn't be able to support her much longer. Carson spoke to her softly, smiled, patted her arm reassuringly, and led her toward the formal parlor.

They stood under the portiere while the fifty or more guests who had been whispering animatedly suddenly ceased all conversation. The organ, borrowed for the afternoon from the Methodist church, filled the room with soft, slightly wheezing strains.

This was the first time anyone except Parker and Kurt Vandiver had seen the mysterious Miss Holbrook, and all were instantly captivated by her breathtaking beauty. It was easy to see how she had lassoed the mustang heart of Jared Lockett.

Had the groom not had years of experience in keeping the rigid muscles of his face from showing any emotion, he might very well have gasped in pleasure at the sight of his bride. He was adamantly against this farce of a marriage, but how could any red-blooded man remain indifferent to the woman who would soon bear his name?

Dammit, under different circumstances he might even . . . That kind of thinking won't do, ol' boy, he cautioned himself. However, it didn't hurt to look, did it? Isn't that what bridegrooms were supposed to do? The woman walking toward him on Carson's arm was exquisite. She was like, like . . . what? . . . whom? No one he'd ever seen.

He studied her as she moved closer, her gray eyes chastely downcast. Quite different from a few days ago, when she had slapped him. Then her eyes had been a dark blue-gray, like the most ominous of stormclouds that gathered over the plains. And they had been just as threatening, just as exciting, just as electric.

Lauren's slim figure was accentuated by the perfectly fitted gown. Her full bust was noticeably defined above the narrow waist encircled by the high cummerbund. Jared imagined he saw faint shadows where the crowns of those high, proud breasts would be, but told himself it was a foolish fantasy and clenched his fingers, which longed to touch those shadows. Swallowing hard, he dragged his gaze away from her chest to her face.

She raised her eyes, and the fear in them was evident. Had he been the devil incarnate, she could not have looked more apprehensive. Why did he feel a sudden urge to reassure her?

Carson delivered Lauren to Jared, and she graced the older man with a timid smile before he left her and took a seat next to Olivia on the front row of chairs temporarily set up for the ceremony.

Jared extended his arm and Lauren slipped her hand through the crook of his elbow as they faced the judge. Jared hadn't planned to, and Lauren certainly hadn't expected it, but his opposite hand closed over hers. The warm strength of his flesh contrasted with the cold fragility of hers. Her fingers were firmly pressed against the fabric of his sleeve. She risked looking at him through her lashes, keeping her eyes lowered. Her heart turned over when she met glowing amber eyes filled with an emotion she had never seen in them before. Was it understanding? Approval? Even admiration? She could almost imagine that his lips softened into the semblance of a smile. She wanted to continue looking at this transformed Jared, but the judge was speaking. Reluctantly she freed her eyes from her bridegroom's possession.

The ceremony was brief and to the point, not like any of the weddings Lauren had attended. She felt a twinge of disappointment. In the ceremonies he performed, Abel had talked about the sanctity of marriage and God's blessing on the institution, about Jesus performing his first public miracle during the celebration of a wedding feast. Of course, this was the service for a civil ceremony. Yet when the judge said, "I now pronounce you man and wife," the words rang hollow and held no meaning for her.

Judge Andrews beamed his congratulations on the attractive couple in front of him.

"You may kiss your bride, Jared." He smiled.

Jared arranged his features into a detached expression. He prepared to face Lauren perfunctorily, to place his hands on her shoulders, and to kiss her coolly on the cheek. His plan went awry. His composure slipped when his eyes riveted on her pink, trembling mouth.

He remembered that other kiss. The kiss that had shaken him to the core. The kiss that had been earthshattering in its violence and enlightenment. The kiss whose impact on him had not yet been diminished.

The recollection that came unbidden to his mind brought with it both intolerable pain and immense pleasure. A now-familiar heat radiated from the center of his body to its every extremity. He longed to taste those lips again and either quench the fire in his veins or increase it to a pitch where he could not be held accountable for seeking its source and extinguishing it. He called upon every particle of self-restraint when he drew her to him and woodenly placed his lips against those that promised such sweetness.

He was rescued from further torment when Olivia and Carson and their friends, who were eager to meet Lauren, surrounded him with hearty congratulations. He surprised himself by possessively tucking Lauren's hand under his arm.

For the rest of the afternoon, the Locketts entertained their guests with an abundance of food and drink. Only a month ago, many of these guests had been here to pay their respects to Ben Lockett, who had lain in state in this very room. All gloom was now dispelled. A festive mood prevailed.

Carson made a flowery wedding toast, and glasses of champagne were lifted in salute. As Lauren raised her glass to her lips, her eyes met Jared's over the crystal rim. The lights in his eyes shone with golden effervescence and were much more intoxicating than the wine. Her sip was more frugal and daintier than his, but when she would have lowered her glass, he reached out and tipped it again to her mouth. The champagne trickled down her throat and heightened the fluttering in her stomach. *They say he is as big as a stallion!* The exact meaning of Elena's words escaped Lauren. All she knew was that as she looked at Jared, thoughts of his physique shocked and thrilled her.

Just as he was lowering his glass, someone jostled his elbow and champagne dribbled down his chin and onto his lapel.

"Oh!" Lauren exclaimed, then couldn't help the laugh that bubbled out of her throat.

"You think it's funny, do you? Having a soggy bridegroom?" He was smiling, too, as he set down his glass and shook off his wet hand.

Acting instinctively, Lauren whisked away the droplets on his lapel. Obeying a subconscious command, her fingers settled under his chin and her thumb gently removed the drops of wine from beneath his lips. "There, that's better," she said smiling, and raised her eyes to his. She recoiled from the bitterness she read there.

Jared's body had betrayed him. At the moment her fingers made contact with his face, he felt himself swell and harden with arousal. He had begun to think that her innocence was real. Hell.

No woman could touch a man, look at a man the way she did and not know exactly what she was doing. Ben should have been smarter than to fall for her act. Jared was determined not to fall for it himself.

"Jared . . . ?" she asked waveringly.

"We'd better mingle with our guests, Mrs. Lockett," he said curtly as he gripped her elbow and guided her toward a group of well-wishers.

Lauren's heart sank. Just when she thought she was making headway, Jared's true feelings for her surfaced. How could they possibly survive the next two years? Inwardly she sighed. It was too late now to dwell on that. She would have to cope with the future later.

Today she could concentrate on nothing except the man beside her. His charisma made him almost impossible to ignore. Indeed, Jared looked exceptionally handsome in his black suit and white shirt. His eyes sparkled with amber lights and brilliant teeth flashed a dazzling smile on his tanned face. He won the confidence of everyone present. He charmed the women shamelessly as their approving husbands looked on. He drank only the two traditional glasses of champagne, and used affectionate terms and gestures when introducing Lauren to people whom he had known all his life, accepting with aplomb their jibes on his cunning in finding such a delightful bride.

There was a noticeable pause in his effusiveness when the Vandivers came over to express their congratulations. Lauren saw a tightening around Jared's mouth and felt his body, ever near hers, grow tense. He was coolly polite, but his voice lacked conviction when he thanked them for attending the wedding.

"You sure pulled a fast one, Jared." Parker patted him on the shoulder and Lauren detected the tension under the black broadcloth. "We had no idea that you and Lauren were planning to marry."

Jared met Parker's piercing stare without flinching. "I'm afraid you caught us in the midst of a tiff. She thought it was improper to have the wedding so soon after my father's death. Fortunately, I was able to talk her out of her scruples."

He put a possessive arm around Lauren's shoulders and looked deeply into her eyes as he pulled her closer to him. He was playing his part well, she thought. This proximity to his body and that probing gaze made breathing difficult for her.

"Mrs. Lockett, may I wish you much happiness." Kurt looked at Jared with a challenge on his smug face. "I *do* have your permission to kiss the bride, don't I?"

Without waiting for an answer, Kurt leaned toward her and pressed thick, hard lips against hers. She recoiled even as Jared's fingers gripped her shoulder so hard that she almost cried out from the pressure.

Kurt smiled a slow, provoking smile and moved away.

Jared watched with a deadly glint in his eyes as Kurt sat down beside one of the local girls who was heartbroken over this sudden marriage. The ever-watchful eyes of Parker Vandiver saw the animosity on Jared's face. He chuckled to himself and thought how stimulating the next few months would be. He relished dissension.

Jared was unaware that he still held Lauren in a deathlike grip until she shifted her weight uncomfortably. He withdrew his arm quickly and muttered under his breath, "No one can resist your charms, can they, Mrs. Lockett?" In the same undertone he warned her, "Smile, Lauren. You're the radiant bride and don't you forget it."

One of the other guests came over then and Jared resumed his character of loving bridegroom with the ease of an experienced actor. Lauren's head spun with the effects of the champagne and the emotional clamor of the past week. She longed to excuse herself and seek the cool serenity of her room. But, of course, that was out of the question.

Ben's widow reigned over the reception with her customary regal bearing. She looked beautiful today, Lauren noted. The silver streaks in her dark hair caught the afternoon sunlight, and her smooth face was flushed with excitement. Lauren suspected that this was as close as Olivia could ever come to being happy. She wore a dress of sea-green georgette, and it floated around her tall, imposing figure like a mist.

Carson paid court to her in his pitiful, humble way. Lauren felt great tenderness and sorrow for this man. He had never shown her anything but kindness, obviously a rare sentiment in this house. He was pathetic in his devotion to Olivia, who either ignored, patronized, or berated him with equal aptitude.

Lauren's glance around the crowded room chanced to fall on Kurt Vandiver. His blue eyes were penetrating under the white-blond brows, and she felt unnerved by his stare. Instinctively, and totally unaware that she did so, she moved closer to Jared, welcoming the protection his large physique intimated.

He looked down at her quickly, distracted by her touch from his conversation with one of the bank directors' wives. He followed Lauren's anguished gaze across the room to Vandiver, who was lounging against the wall. Impulsively Jared slid his arm around Lauren's slender waist and rested his hand just under her breast.

The movement wasn't lost on Kurt. Like a voyeur wandering through a bordello, he licked his lips lasciviously. Lauren shuddered, but didn't know if she were reacting to the lewd expression on Kurt's face or the warm pressure of Jared's hand seemingly burning through the fabric of her dress. Kurt winked at Jared, pushed away from the wall, and strolled through a door leading to the wide porch outside.

Jared and Lauren didn't move. The banker's wife gushed and simpered, totally unaware of the drama being played out beside her.

Lauren could smell the starch that kept Jared's shirtfront crisp, which blended intoxicatingly with tobacco and champagne. When he spoke in confidential tones to the silly woman, Lauren could feel the vibration of his voice in his chest. The bank director's wife moved away, and still Jared retained his possessive hold on her. His hand trembled slightly as his thumb moved upward and lightly stroked the side of her breast. Or did she only imagine it? Lauren thought she would die from the constriction in her chest that pounded up into her throat and sought release in a small moan.

Another guest walked toward them. Slowly, reluctantly, the strong fingers were withdrawn, leaving behind an imprint on Lauren's skin as scorching as a brand.

The afternoon had waned into an indigo twilight. The guests were gone. Carson and Olivia sat together on one of the sofas. They were weary and relieved that, at last, the ordeal was over.

"Well, we pulled it off beautifully. Everyone was convinced that it was a marriage made in heaven. And word will get around," Olivia gloated.

"We owe it all to Lauren," Carson said generously. "You are a beautiful bride, my dear."

"Yes. She's the perfect little wife, all right." Jared smirked at Lauren, who was helping Rosa load dishes onto a large tray. He tossed down a tumbler of whiskey.

Olivia coughed to cover a malicious smile that rose unbidden to her lips. Obviously her son disliked his wife. That could be most advantageous in the future. "You performed your part well, too, Jared," she said. "Treat Lauren courteously in public, and no one will be the wiser."

Lauren kept her eyes lowered. She was still no part of them, and they cared nothing for her feelings.

"You can stay at Keypoint for as long as you like. We'll pass that off as your honeymoon. Not very glamorous, but if anyone inquires, we'll say that Lauren was eager to see the ranch," Olivia remarked, stifling a yawn.

"Good," Jared said. "I can't wait to get back. When I left—"

"We know your unwarranted enthusiasm for the ranch, Jared. Please don't bore us with it now," Olivia said curtly. Her laziness of the moment before was gone.

Jared's lips pressed together in a hard line before he said brusquely, "Lauren, we'll leave first thing in the morning. And I mean first thing. You can ride, can't you?" The question sounded almost like a dare.

"Yes, I can ride, Jared," she said. He scowled at her. Had he wished she couldn't? Would he have liked to find another flaw to ridicule?

"Then we'll go on horseback," he said impatiently. "Pepe'll bring our bags in a flatbed." Then, looking at her, he said sharply, "We're traveling light, so don't pack everything you own."

"I hadn't intended to," she shot back, her own ire rising under his imperiousness. She continued in spite of his dark look, "Since we are to leave early, I think I'll go upstairs. Goodnight Carson. Goodnight, Olivia." Her head was held high and her back was straight as she crossed the room. At the doorway, she paused and looked at her mother-in-law. She found it difficult to say what she knew she should. "I know you went to tremendous effort and expense, Olivia. Though it wasn't for my sake, I appreciate your doing it just the same. The flowers, the food, the clothes, everything was lovely. Thank you."

The other three didn't say anything for several moments after Lauren left them.

Then Carson coughed uneasily and said quietly, "Jared, treat her kindly. We have our ulterior motives, but she is an innocent party in all this. Be gentle with her."

Jared resented being instructed on how to treat a woman. Intending to make a retort to that effect, he turned away from the liquor cabinet where he was getting a large bottle of whiskey. Carson's face was guileless. He hadn't issued a directive; he had made a plea. Jared stifled the rejoinder already on his lips, mumbled his goodnights, and plodded up the stairs.

For an hour, he had been in his room drinking steadily and listening to the light taps that small slippers made on the floor next door.

"To my wedding night," he scornfully saluted himself in the mirror over his dresser. He was shocked by the reflection. He didn't remember discarding his vest and coat, but a swift glance over his shoulder revealed them to be carelessly draped over the back of a chair. When had he taken out his cuff links and unbuttoned his shirt? In a characteristic gesture, he raked his fingers through his hair.

His bride was undoubtedly just as immaculate and cool as she had been when she met him at the altar. Or maybe she was already dressed for bed. What did she sleep in? Nothing provocative, he scoffed silently. Something chaste and . . .

Why not? Why not see for himself? Why should he be the only one to suffer through this hellish night? He was her husband after all and, by God, he had some rights!

He didn't consciously decide to disturb her but, propelled by some mystical and obsessive force, he found himself before the door that connected their rooms through the bathroom.

He knocked sharply. No answer, but the movements in the adjoining room halted abruptly. He knocked again, this time saying her name. It came out as a tremulous sigh. He cleared his throat, shook his head, and repeated it with more force. Silence.

"Yes?" Apprehensive. Tentative.

"Open the door." It was a command. He hoped.

Long pause.

Finally, calmly, "What do you want, Jared?"

He laughed mirthlessly, muttered a few unintelligible obscenities, and raised his voice another decibel. "Open this door!"

He heard her footsteps and the rustle of her clothing coming closer until he knew she was in the bathroom just beyond the door.

"We can talk from here, Jared."

"If you don't open this goddam door," he growled, "I'll kick it down. Do you want a ruckus? It won't embarrass me, because I don't give a damn."

There was a momentary hesitation, then the key was turning in the lock made rusty by disuse. The knob rattled as she pulled the door open.

Her hair was down, framing her face in a black cloud and cascading down her back in heavy waves to her waist. She wore a rose-colored dressing gown cut in a deep V in the front and buttoning from her breast to her knees. Lace spilled over her delicate hands at the end of the wide sleeves. Her trembling lips were parted to allow agitated, quick breaths to escape. She tried unsuccessfully to mask her fear.

The sight of her stupefied him, and her flowery scent filled his head with a greater vertigo than had the vast amount of alcohol he had consumed. He longed to taste the smooth skin at the base of her throat, which fluttered with the frantic beating of her pulse. He wanted to investigate what treasures lay beyond that first button of her dressing gown.

By an act of will, he regained his self-control and said thickly, "You needn't look so frightened, Mrs. Lockett. I have no intention of forcing you to give me my conjugal rights."

Her only response was to moisten her lips with a dainty pink tongue. Jared swallowed hard, stifling an animal groan, and said, "I demand only one thing. There will be no locked doors. Separate bedrooms are not that uncommon, but a locked door invites speculation. Maids gossip, you know. One locked door between us and this whole farce is shot to hell. So no locked doors. Is that understood?"

"Yes, Jared," she answered levelly.

Dammit! Why didn't she scream or swoon or something? She was so damned composed, while he stood here like an adolescent idiot with his sweating palms and pounding heart and aching loins.

Not trusting himself any longer, he reached for the door and closed it quickly. He didn't hear the key turn in the lock before her footsteps receded into the bedroom beyond, but he lacked the nerve to turn the knob and test her obedience.

"I guess I showed her who's boss," he boasted as he flung himself upon the bed, wondering why he felt no satisfaction in his victory. All he felt was a deep longing which he tried to obliterate with sleep.

Chapter 9

Elena gently shook Lauren's shoulder and whispered, "Señora Lockett, wake up. It's time to get ready for your trip."

Lauren opened her eyes. She was greeted by a dark room and mumbled a protest into her pillow. She didn't want to give up the sleep that had been so long in coming. Elena's persistent needling finally penetrated her slumberousness, and with sudden clarity she remembered where she was going today. She threw back the covers and rolled out of bed. Soon she was wide awake and, in spite of her misgivings toward Jared, was excited about seeing Keypoint for the first time.

As she performed her toilette, Elena chattered about how lovely the wedding had been, how beautiful Lauren looked in her bride's dress, how handsome Jared was, and how lucky Lauren was to have such a husband.

The maid had been surprised only minutes earlier when she had knocked on Jared's door to awaken him.

"Señor Jared, are you awake? Time to get ready for your trip. Señora Lauren, do you hear me?"

Only silence greeted her until Jared mumbled a sleepy, "I'm awake."

"Señora Lauren, do you want me to help you?" Elena twittered, thinking that the new husband would probably take over some of her former duties.

There was a rustle of bedcovers, a muttered curse, and then Jared said, "She's in her room. Go wake her up."

Elena had stood outside the door staring at it in a puzzled fashion. "But, señor—"

"She's in her room," he growled.

Now, as she packed last minute additions to Lauren's bags, Elena shrugged. Why wasn't Lauren sleeping with her new husband? The ways of the *gringos* had always been a mystery to her.

The one possession that Lauren had that kept her from coming to Jared as a pauper bride was her riding habit. It had been a gift to her from the Prathers, who had insisted that she attend a riding academy. The blue velvet habit with its long, trailing skirt and tightly tailored jacket fit her figure to perfection. It had taken up an exorbitant amount of space in one of her valises, but she couldn't bear to part with the finest garment she owned when she left North Carolina.

Elena eyed the riding habit dubiously and asked Lauren tentatively if she wouldn't prefer wearing one of the split skirts that Mrs. Gibbons had made for her.

"No," Lauren adamantly refused as she thrust long pins into the smart matching hat with its decorative veil. "I want Jared to see me in something of my own. Something his mother didn't buy for me."

The two young women were snapping shut the fastenings of her bags when Pepe tapped lightly on the door. Elena opened it and he bowed swiftly and said, "Señor Jared, he is waiting." Pepe picked up Lauren's bags and preceded the women down the stairs. He looked at her attire skeptically and muttered to himself in Spanish, shaking his head in bewilderment.

He carried her valises through the large front door. Stubbornly Lauren detoured into Rosa's kitchen for a quick cup of tea. The morning was chilly, and the tea warmed her body, but nothing could warm the chill in her heart. She had not yet seen Jared, and after their confrontation at the bathroom door, she dreaded facing him again. What would his mood be today?

Rosa was bustling around the kitchen even at this early hour. As Lauren was eating fresh, hot *tortillas* dripping with butter, Rose saw the sadness on the young *gringas'* face. Rosa knew everything that went on in the house, and she wasn't fooled into thinking this sudden marriage was based on love. Maternally she reached out and patted Lauren's arm. "Señora Lockett, everything will be all right. Señor Jared, he . . . he hurt inside. Here." She placed a plump hand over her enormous breasts. "But he is a good man. He like you very much." Lauren moved to protest, but Rosa went on quickly, "Rosa knows the boy since he is born. I can tell." She smiled radiantly, reassuringly, and squeezed Lauren's hand. *"Vaya con Dios,"* she whispered.

Pepe poked his head through the kitchen door, cleared his throat, and said apologetically, "Señor Jared, he . . ." and indicated with his head that Lauren should follow him without delay.

Before she left the kitchen, Lauren turned to Rosa and hugged her, her arms barely encompassing the woman's girth. Elena was standing by the front door, tears glistening in her eyes. Lauren hugged her as close as her protuberant stomach would allow.

"I'll be upset if the baby comes while I'm away. Can you send word to me? I hope you'll be all right."

"I will let you know, but don't concern yourself. The *niño*, he will be born fine." Elena laughed.

"Goodbye, Elena." The two women clung to each other for a few seconds, then Lauren stepped through the door.

Jared was sitting on the large palomino that had been tied to the back of the wagon the day Lauren arrived. He was a *vaquero* again. He wore tall black boots, the customary tight black pants tucked into the tops of them. A leather jacket protected him against the coolness of the October morning. A blue shirt was under that, and a red bandana had been tied negligently around his throat. The black hat was pulled down low over his brows, and he was casually smoking one of his thin cigars.

Jared looked her up and down, only his eyes moving, and in the early morning darkness his expression was inscrutable. Pepe held the reins of a saddled mare. Both the mare and Jared's stallion pranced skittishly when Jared's deep laugh roared through the still morning.

"Where the hell do you think you're going in that getup?"

Lauren was stunned. She thought she looked quite fetching in the riding habit with its rich fabric and matching bonnet. "Th-this is a riding habit," she stuttered lamely.

"I know what it is," Jared said witheringly. "It's just going to be entertaining as hell to see how you get up on that horse in it, that's all." He chuckled.

Lauren looked at the beautiful sorrel mare. She seemed to be placid enough. Then she saw the saddle and swallowed convulsively.

"I would prefer a sidesaddle, Jared," she said with all the poise she could muster.

"You would?" he drawled, securing the cheroot in the corner of his lips. "Well, that's too bad, because all we have are western saddles. Can't you ride astride?"

Again the gauntlet was thrown down. "Of course I can," she retorted.

"Then go change into some of those new clothes you have and get your . . . rear . . . out here quick. We're wasting time." As she turned back to the front door, he added, "And do something with your hair. You can't wear a proper hat over that . . ." He made a descriptive motion with his hands around his own head. "And if you don't wear a hat, you'll scorch that buttermilk complexion of yours," he said scathingly.

Lauren lifted her heavy skirt and stumbled back into the house. Elena, who had been standing inside the door and had heard everything, sympathetically took Lauren's arm and led her back upstairs.

Silently the Mexican girl divested Lauren of her habit and redressed her in a brown split skirt which Lauren thought disgracefully tight across her hips and much too short. A white cotton shirt that buttoned down the front much like a man's went on next. Elena ignored the tears Lauren sniffed back and the quivering shoulders over which she slipped a soft leather jacket. Brown kid boots molded to Lauren's calves, and she was modestly grateful that they covered her legs to just below the knee where they met the bottom of the culottes.

The tears began to roll down her cheeks as Lauren thought of the humiliation Jared had subjected her to. He had stripped her of all dignity in front of the servants, her friends, and he had enjoyed it.

In silent sympathy, Elena removed Lauren's hat, took the pins out of the heavy black hair, and brushed it hurriedly. She braided the ebony tresses into one long plait that hung to Lauren's waist like a silken rope. Then she handed Lauren a brown, flat-crowned hat that looked like the one Jared wore, and Lauren placed it on her head, securing the thin leather cord under her chin. Finally Elena handed her a pair of brown kid gloves.

They had been in the room no more than ten minutes, but the transformation was astounding.

As they went down the broad stairs, Elena whispered, "Lauren, can you ride astride?" In the crisis, all formality was dropped.

Lauren swallowed hard. "I don't know. I've never tried." Elena looked at her compassionately, but saw only determination on Lauren's face. The tears had vanished.

Lauren strode out the front door without so much as a glance in Jared's direction. Expectantly she stood beside the sorrel mare. She placed one small, booted foot in the stirrup and grasped the pommel. Pepe cupped his hands and boosted her up by her other foot. She landed in the saddle with a plop, almost crying out in shock as her tender thighs slapped against the leather. She immediately composed her face and took the reins Pepe offered up to her.

Jared watched her with interest and smiled a sardonic, knowing smile. This was going to be some ride!

They didn't speak as they rode out the lane to the house and followed a road leading west out of town. Lauren scanned the countryside.

The sun was only now rising behind them, and its rays gradually illuminated the breathtaking scenery. Tall cypress trees lined the bends of the Rio Caballo, which paralleled the road on the right. On the left were gently rolling hills glistening with frost, which sparkled like a mantle of diamonds as the sun reflected off of it. Oak and elm trees were tinged with the russet tones of fall, and the cedars provided a dark evergreen contrast. White limestone formations jutting out of the hillside caught the morning sun and dazzled the eye.

They rode side by side, Lauren guiding her horse away from Jared's any time it came within a few feet of the larger animal. Her hat fell back against her shoulders, and Jared looked at the top of her head as the sun crowned it with highlights.

In spite of her declaration to the contrary, he knew she had never ridden astride before. She's got some spunk, he conceded silently. She was riding well, but God, she was going to hurt later on.

He broke the silence. "You don't look quite so comical now. Isn't that outfit more comfortable than that contraption you had on before?" he goaded.

"I'm fine, thank you, Jared."

Damn! Always so cool. I'll just bet she's comfortable, he thought snidely. That cute little butt he'd noticed as she mounted the horse was probably screaming in pain. Why didn't she complain?

He deliberately spurred his horse and increased their pace.

Lauren did likewise in order to keep up with him, and the throbbing in her thighs and bottom was almost unbearable. But she would rather die than reveal her discomfort to that superior, arrogant, hateful man!

In spite of her mounting anger, she couldn't keep her eyes away from Jared. She wanted to hate him, but that was hard in light of his handsomeness. No picture she had ever seen of the dashing western men depicted anyone as exciting as Jared Lockett.

Try as she might, she couldn't forget how the sight of him last night with his chest bare and his hair mussed had caused her heart to pound. She had been terrified of opening that door, but it wasn't only his threat to break it down and rouse the house that had constrained her to obey. She had to admit that she was curious about what would happen when she did. Tremors had coursed through her body, setting up strange sensations as the topaz eyes traveled over her. Lauren almost imagined that Jared had been unnerved himself, but that would be out of character for him.

Objectively she studied horse and rider now. They moved together as one being. The stallion's honey-gold coat was almost the same color as the sun-gilded hair that covered Jared's chest.

The sun rose higher behind them, and they continued at a canter. Finally, when Lauren thought she couldn't keep from crying in pain much longer, Jared slowed down and led her off the road toward the swiftly running river. They reined in under the enormous cypress trees.

"I'm ready for a break," he said as he lithely dismounted. He led his horse to the stream and the palomino lowered his head to drink.

Lauren still sat on her horse. She had done exceptionally well in riding, she thought, but she was unsure about mounting and dismounting without a block to stand on.

Jared looked back, then walked over and offered his hands up to her. Painfully she pulled her leg from the far side of the saddle and timidly placed a hand on each of his broad shoulders. His hands encircled her waist, and he lifted her gently to the ground. She didn't look at him, but kept her head lowered until he released her. She felt his breath against her cheek. It was warm.

The mare needed no encouragement to join Jared's mount at the river. Taking a canteen from his saddlebag, Jared uncapped it and handed it to Lauren. She took a few swallows and gave it back to him. "Are you hungry?" he asked.

"Yes, a little." She was trying not to wince as she slowly and stiffly lowered herself onto a large, flat rock.

He pulled a few wrapped sandwiches out of the saddlebag and offered her one. "I made these this morning, and I can't vouch for their quality."

"It's fine," Lauren said, biting into the thick, dry ham sandwich.

"I know how to cook over a campfire, but a kitchen makes me nervous." His mouth quirked in the semblance of a smile.

She had never made small talk with him before. Since he had initiated the conversation, she was eager to continue it. Strained though it was, it was a beginning. "I like to cook. My guardians in Clayton had a cook/housekeeper who ruled her kitchen like a despot, but sometimes she would let me experiment with a recipe."

"Maybe Gloria will let you putter around in her kitchen. If you can stand all the kids underfoot."

"Who's Gloria?" she asked with interest.

"She's Rudy's wife." He saw her eyebrows raise in another question. "Rudy's my . . . uh . . . he's the foreman at the ranch. He and Gloria live there with . . . his mother. They have a baby every year or so." He smiled, and Lauren noticed that his eyes crinkled at the corners. She had glimpsed only a few unguarded genuine smiles at their wedding reception. They made him appear younger.

"Ben . . ." she hesitated over that name. Why should she? She continued doggedly, "Ben told me that one of your *vaqueros* is an Indian."

Jared laughed. "You'd better believe it. Right down to his boots—which he usually forsakes for moccasins. Thorn is a Comanche. My father found him when he and a few Rangers raided a village to rescue some white captives. Thorn was half-dead with a gunshot wound and starvation, either of which should have killed him."

He swallowed the last bite of his sandwich and dusted his hands free of breadcrumbs. "Anyway, Ben brought him back to Keypoint. Thorn was about eleven or twelve, I guess. It was long before I was born. He's been there ever since and is one of our best hands. He and Ben were very attached to each other. Thorn used to take us—Rudy and me—out on the plains. He taught us to stalk deer, read the stars, the weather, things like that."

Lauren was amazed, not only at the story, but at Jared's telling it. He had never been so loquacious. "Then you and Rudy grew up together?" she asked.

He was made uneasy by the question and answered laconically, "Yeah."

She tried again. "I think your land is beautiful, Jared. I really do." She said it impulsively, but emphatically.

He looked at her strangely, then away. He squinted his eyes against the late morning sun's glare as they swept the panorama before them. "Yes, it is beautiful." He seemed entranced with the view for long, silent minutes, then stood up abruptly as if embarrassed by having spoken so freely. "If you need some privacy, go behind those rocks over there."

It took her a few seconds to comprehend his meaning. Then

she lowered her head in confusion and stammered, "No, I
. . . I'm fine."

"Then if you'll excuse me," he said with exaggerated gallantry.
He loomed over her with characteristic impudence, and she blushed
to the roots of her hair. He laughed out loud as he sauntered off,
his spurs jingling against the small rocks lining the riverbank.

Lauren rewrapped the remainder of her sandwich and put it
back into Jared's saddlebag, standing warily beside the huge palomino. A rifle was sheathed in a scabbard strapped to the back
of his saddle. She had noted earlier that Jared was wearing a
holstered pistol. Never in her life had she been around firearms,
and they terrified her. Yet her husband seemed not to think anything at all about having them so close at hand.

When he had come back and gathered the reins of the horses,
she commented, "I noticed some uprooted trees over there. Is
someone clearing that land?"

"No, that's what the Rio Caballo can do if it gets angry enough.
That happened two years ago and was one of the worst flash floods
in recent history. Trees, cattle, houses, even bridges, were washed
away."

"But the river seems so tranquil."

"Most of the time, it is. But if it rains hard enough and fills
up the streams in the hills, the river can become an entity to reckon
with. It takes back some of what it's given to the land." It was
a poetic philosophy for this usually taciturn man.

Mechanically he gave her a boost up to her horse. She couldn't
contain a gasp as she resumed that torturous position. To cover
it, she asked, "What is my horse's name?"

"Name? I think the *vaqueros* call her Flame because of her
color."

"And yours?"

"This is Charger," he said proudly, patting the beautiful stallion's neck. "He's not his usual self this morning. I think
. . .Flame has got him excited." The golden-brown eyes slanted
toward Lauren and were rewarded with a high blush that stained
her cheeks. Involuntarily her eyes were drawn to the part of the
stallion that manifested his maleness.

They say he is as big as a stallion! Lauren nearly choked when
Elena's words once again came back to her.

Jared roared with laughter. "Don't worry, Lauren. He's too
much of a gentleman to mount her *in public*. But I'll keep a tight

rein on him, in case her attraction proves to be too much for him."
When his laughter subsided he said, "He's quite an animal, isn't
he? Ben gave him to me when I came home from Cuba." In an
instant, Lauren's embarrassment vanished and was replaced by
astonishment.

"You fought in the war?" she exclaimed in surprise.

He nodded curtly in affirmation. He obviously didn't appreciate
reminders of the war. His eyes turned as hard and cold as agates.
Distressed that she had spoiled his civil mood, she turned her head
away from him and became intensely interested in the horizon.

They rode for another hour before cresting a hill and reining
in. On the other side, the land spread out like a large, shallow
bowl, creating an incredible vista. A sizable herd of cattle, mostly
Hereford, was grazing in the pasture and standing in the shallows
of the river, which wound through the meadow. A few cattle,
whose curly red coats contrasted with the colors of the verdant
pasture, lazed in the shadows of the cedar trees dotting the valley.

Lauren was so taken by the sight that she wasn't aware of the
thundering hooves approaching her and Jared until the horses were
almost upon them. She screamed when she saw about ten riders,
bandanas pulled up over their noses, hats pulled down low, brandishing pistols and rifles and shouting at the top of their voices.

They rode toward her and Jared pell-mell, leaning forward over
their saddlehorns. She whirled toward Jared in fright, and was
astounded to see him adjusting his red scarf over his nose in the
same manner as the bandits. Faster than she could follow his
movements, he whipped the rifle from the scabbard and cocked
it. Then, spurring Charger, he galloped toward the attackers giving
a bloodcurdling Comanche yell.

The bandits fired their guns into the air and effortlessly surrounded Jared. He reined in on Charger so hard that the horse
reared and pawed the air. Miraculously Jared maintained his seat.

Lauren's heart pounded in her ears in pure terror. Why had
Jared left her? Surely he didn't think he could fight off all of these
desperadoes single-handedly? After they killed him, what would
they do to her? Flame pranced excitedly beneath her. She couldn't
concentrate on holding the horse steady, so fixed was her attention
on the scene being played out before her.

Jared slid off Charger, and the leader of the gang dismounted
his own horse with a similar graceful motion. The others remained

in their saddles and formed a tight circle around their leader and Jared, who faced each other squarely. Everything was deathly quiet.

Lauren was terrified as she realized that Jared and the bandit were going to draw on each other. The men stood a few feet apart, their legs wide, arms loose at their sides, every muscle tense. They were much alike in build and height. They stared at each other over their bandanas. Lauren held her breath.

They moved with lightning speed, and the pistols exploded simultaneously in the silence, the blast echoing off the surrounding hills.

Chapter 10

Either the sudden crack of the pistols or Lauren's kneejerk reaction to it startled Flame. She bolted and raced uncontrolled across the pasture. Lauren was too frightened to scream. Only instinct forced her to hold onto the saddle as the ground rushed under her in a blur. The thudding of Flame's hooves was joined by another's, but Lauren didn't risk turning around for fear of unseating herself and greater fear of what she would see in pursuit.

From the corner of her eye, she saw a flash of blond mane seconds before she felt an iron arm grab her around the waist and drag her from Flame's back. The mare streaked out from under her. Lauren's legs danced in midair like a puppet's as she was held against the heaving sides of the horse. She closed her eyes tightly. Her arms closed around the waist of the man in the saddle as he hauled her up in front of him.

After what seemed like an eternity, they began to slow down, and then were completely still. The heart in the hard chest beneath her head beat loudly against her ear. Lauren raised her head and looked into amber eyes over a red bandana.

"Lauren?"

She recognized the voice and slumped against Jared in relief that they were both still alive. He tightened his arms around her. She was content to leave her head against his chest with her eyes closed. Sounds of approaching horses invaded her serenity. She had forgotten their attackers!

"Is she all right, Jared?"

"I think so. Just a little shaken up." Jared's reassuring voice reverberated in her head. "Lauren," he repeated quietly. Reluctantly she opened her eyes and raised her head.

Jared lowered his bandana and looked down at her. Was it concern she saw in his face? Charger impatiently tossed his head and brought her out of the hypnotic state that this unplanned closeness to Jared had induced.

97

She looked at the other rider. His features were much like Jared's, except he was darker of complexion and hair. He, too, had pulled the bandana from his face and was smiling at her congenially. Shyly her gaze traveled around the semicircle of *vaqueros* nearly surrounding them. They appeared not in the least malevolent, but only curious and a trifle chagrined.

"Lauren, this is Rudy Mendez and these are Keypoint's *vaqueros*—some of them. Did we frighten you?" Jared's tenderness amazed her.

She nodded dumbly; then, remembering the draw contest, said, "But I saw you shoot each other." Her lips trembled.

Rudy laughed and white teeth flashed in his swarthy face. "Sometimes I think Jared needs shooting, but we try to miss when we're only playing." He winked at her. "Rudy Mendez at your service, Mrs. Lockett. Welcome to Keypoint. Jared should have warned you of our rough games. Our welcoming committee got overzealous today. Can you forgive us?"

His smile was so engaging that Lauren smiled tremulously and murmured, "Yes. I'm sorry I caused such a fuss." Suddenly she was conscious that she must look a fright. Her hat had been torn from her head and was resting on her shoulders. Her hair had loosened from the tight braid, and wisps of it blew around her face. Worst of all, she was being held in a most unladylike way across Jared's lap, his strong arms supporting her. When she realized she still had her arms wrapped around him, she withdrew them instantly.

But she hadn't counted on Charger choosing that time to stamp the ground impatiently. She came close to being unbalanced most ignominiously. Grasping desperately for whatever handhold was available, her fingers groped around the tight bulge between Jared's thighs. His expletive echoed in her ear just before he hissed unevenly, "For godsake, don't do that. Put your arms around my waist and keep them there." She obeyed. Luckily Charger had continued his prancing, so no one had witnessed her folly. With a flick of his wrist, Jared brought the horse around. He was unaware of the silly grin on his face that was so obvious to everyone else.

The *vaqueros* and Rudy stared unabashedly at Jared's bride. She was so beautiful! When word had gotten back to the ranch that their Jared was hurriedly marrying a girl from back East, there had been some unflattering speculations on her charms. Now they saw why their boss had been so eager to get this girl into his bed.

Lauren was becoming increasingly uncomfortable under their stares, and Rudy noticed it. "Doesn't anyone have work to do?" he asked the *vaqueros*. They caught his drift and one by one tipped their hats to Lauren and pulled their horses around, heading back toward the herd. "I'll fetch your horse, Mrs. Lockett."

"No, Rudy," Jared said. "I'll take her the rest of the way with me. That mare is probably into her second bag of oats by now."

"No trouble, Jared," Rudy taunted. Jared's preference for the current arrangement wasn't lost on him.

The *vaqueros* whistled and hooted back at them as Jared nudged Charger with his knee and they started across the pasture. "Dammit," Jared muttered close to her ear. Oh, God, he groaned silently as she shifted her hips, looking for a more comfortable position.

Rudy rode up beside them and watched as Lauren eased herself away from Jared's chest. His arms seemed reluctant to relieve their firm hold on her, but Rudy saw the muscles slowly relax. There appeared to be a tangible tension between these two.

Jared had cursed this Lauren Holbrook when he came to Keypoint after Ben's funeral. He insulted her heritage, intelligence, and morality. Rudy had teased him about her then but, to his surprise, Jared informed him he hadn't even seen the girl.

"Then how do you know she's so disreputable? Anyway, I thought you said you had gone to Austin to pick her up."

"I did!" Jared exclaimed angrily. "But I . . . oh, hell. Just drop it, will you?"

Rudy knew better than to press further. Scarcely a week later, Pepe came out to the ranch with supplies and the news that Jared was marrying the very girl he had claimed never to have seen and yet had called a "conniving little tart." Well, Rudy thought, he's seen her now. But good.

Gloria and Mamma were thrilled about the marriage, so Rudy had kept his reservations about its future to himself. If Jared had a brain in his head, which Rudy sometimes doubted, he would keep this woman under lock and key. She was gorgeous, and a lady, and, by the tortured look on Jared's face, he wasn't oblivious to her charms. He chuckled to himself. Good for you, Lauren.

He spoke out loud, "Gloria, my wife, is looking forward to meeting you, Mrs. Lockett. She's been more excited than the kids."

"Please call me Lauren. How many children do you have, Mr. Mendez?"

"I'm Rudy." He grinned. "Well, let's see," he said, silently ticking off names on his fingers. "Jared, help me. Is it six or seven?"

Jared snorted. "I think when I left it was six, with number seven well on the way. Of course, if Gloria has delivered early, I'm sure you've already started number eight."

"Don't be crude in front of your bride," Rudy scolded, but his eyes were twinkling. He looked several years older than Jared, and there was something familiar about him.

Lauren was trying to decide what it was when she saw the ranch house. It was large and sprawling, a one-story building of limestone blocks with a cedar shingle roof. Four cedar posts supported the roof over a wide front porch running the breadth of the house. There were several outbuildings, all built of the same materials. Well-constructed corrals dotted the compound. Laughing, squealing children played about the yard, the only area where grass was growing. The two horses were led into the yard and halted before a hitching post. Rudy dismounted.

Jared and Lauren remained as they were for a moment before Jared looked down at her and said softly, "You were frightened. I'm sorry."

His face was very close to hers. There was no measurable expression on it, but the voice was so unlike any he had formerly used that she was held spellbound. Emotion swelled her throat, but she said, "It's all right. I've recovered." Again she witnessed that quick lifting of the corners of his mouth that might be considered a smile.

He took a firm hold around her waist with one arm and lowered her gently to the ground. On her descent, his hand slid from her waist to her armpit. His fingers lightly grazed her breast.

They were both shaken by the contact. Lauren tried to recover herself by straightening her clothing. Jared swung down from his horse as if irritated. Rudy, who had seen the whole thing and noted the reactions, caught Jared's eye and winked slyly. Jared glowered at him.

The door of the house was flung open and Gloria flew out of it. The children, who had spotted their father and Jared, rushed over to them, grabbing them around the legs, pushing and shoving and vying for their attention.

"Lauren, Lauren, welcome. I'm Gloria."

The uninhibited Gloria hugged Lauren in a warm, encompassing embrace. Lauren laughed at the Mexican woman's exuberance.

She was older than Lauren and, though she lacked the classic beauty of Elena, was very pretty. Her olive complexion glowed with health and happiness, which were also reflected in her dark eyes. Like Elena, she was expecting a child, though her time wasn't as imminent. She wore a dark skirt, with a full but tailored shirtwaist over it in deference to her condition. Her glossy black hair was pulled back from a center part into a chignon at the back of her head.

"Thank you, Gloria. I'm happy to be here. I hope our visit hasn't put you to any trouble."

"No, no. Besides, this is Jared's home. I'm just glad the scoundrel has finally brought a wife to it. I've been after him for years to get married. Now I'm glad he waited. I bet he is, too." She laughed and pinched Jared on both cheeks, having to stand on tiptoe to reach him. He leaned down and kissed her soundly on the mouth, his arms encircling her waist.

"If Rudy would let you out of bed long enough, we'd run off together, wouldn't we, Gloria?" He hugged her tight and patted her bottom. She pushed him away with feigned annoyance.

"You! Here with your bride, hugging a fat, pregnant lady! Shame on you, Jared Lockett." She grinned at him affectionately.

Such familiarity appalled Lauren, but then, what about this culture hadn't shocked her? Rudy shepherded the children toward her.

"Lauren, may I present James, John, Maria, Anna, and Lucy. Who's missing?" he asked.

One of the boys piped, "Consuelo. She's little. She's in the house taking a nap." he explained to Lauren.

"Children, this is Jared's wife, Lauren."

Lauren looked at the faces turned up to her and met five steady, curious stares. One of the girls, five-year-old Anna, whispered reverently, "You're beautiful."

Lauren smiled. Leaning down to the child's level, she said, "I was going to say the same thing about you."

"Lunch is ready. Come on in." Gloria took Lauren's arm and hurried her toward the house. Lauren winced with each painful step as the abused muscles in her thighs and bottom throbbed.

They stepped into a large room that was as wide as the house. At one end was a stone wall with a fireplace large enough for a man to stand in. At the other end was a dining alcove containing a table, sideboard, and china cabinet. In between was a comfortable living area, which exuded an aura of warmth and welcome. There were several long sofas, easy chairs, and ottomans, colorful rugs scattered over the quarry tile floors, paintings depicting Western culture, bookcases filled to capacity, and a roll-top desk. Lauren loved it.

Two hallways led off the big room, and she assumed they led to bedrooms. Another door off the dining area, she knew, must lead to the kitchen. Gloria beamed as Lauren complimented her on the decor.

"I'll show you to Jared's room. I've tried to tidy it up for you, and add a few feminine touches. You know how barren a bachelor's room can look."

Lauren had no idea how a man's bedroom looked. She blanched at the words "Jared's room."

They walked down the hall and Gloria opened the door to a large bedroom with wide windows opening onto a view of rolling hills and the river in the distance. It was magnificent.

The furnishings consisted of a chest of drawers with a shaving mirror on it, an overstuffed chair with an ottoman, and a wardrobe which Gloria opened to show that she had pushed all Jared's clothes to one side.

Jared's clothes!

A double bed dominated the room. A small table stood beside it.

"I moved this in here for you, Lauren," Gloria said. "It was all I could find in the storage shack." She indicated a small vanity table with a washbowl and pitcher on it. The mirror was wavy and cloudy. "Pepe will pick up something else for you and bring it out on his next trip." She took Lauren's dismay for dislike. "Is it all right?" she asked shyly.

"No! . . . I mean yes. Everything is beautiful, Gloria. You have gone to a lot of trouble, and I appreciate it more than you know, but . . ." Her voice trailed off when she didn't know what else to say. She looked helplessly toward her husband. He and Rudy stood in the doorway. Jared seemed as disconcerted as she.

Rudy leaned against the jamb with his arms and ankles crossed. He was enjoying himself immensely. A mischievous light glinted in his eyes as he looked at Jared and said, "Gloria and I will leave you two alone so you can wash up. Then we'll eat. I know you must be starved, but take all the time you want."

"I . . . uh . . . think I'll go out to the bunkhouse and say hello to some of the hands. I'll wash up out there." Before anyone could object, Jared rushed out of the room, leaving in his wake a very surprised Gloria, a mildly surprised Rudy, and a relieved Lauren.

Damn! Jared cursed as he crossed the yard. He hadn't even thought about the bedrooms at the ranch. Rudy and his brood used every goddam one of them except his. He liked his room. He didn't want to give it up, but there was no way he could ask the romantic Gloria to move his wife—his bride—out of his room.

Even more nerve-racking to consider was spending the night in the same room with Lauren. He had made a vow to himself not to touch her. But it would take a blind, feeble ninety-year-old monk to stay the night in such intimate confines with Lauren and not—

He'd have to think of something. Fast.

When, after a short toilette, Lauren went into the large room for lunch, she saw a woman sitting alone at the dining table. She was beautiful and of Mexican heritage, and Lauren was struck by her bearing. She held herself straight and proud, yet serene.

She was small, her figure dainty. Her black hair was streaked with gray and pulled back into a glossy knot on the nape of her neck. She wore a high-necked black dress. There was no jewelry or other adornment to relieve its severity. Her face had cameo perfection. Smooth, well-shaped brows framed dark, sad eyes. Her nose was straight and narrow. Above a delicate chin was a sweet, well-shaped mouth.

Her smile was genuine as Lauren shyly walked toward her. "Lauren Holbrook Lockett. I am Maria Mendez. Welcome to Keypoint."

"Señora Mendez, it is a pleasure to meet you. You are Rudy's mother?"

"Yes," she answered abstractedly as she studied Lauren's face. "You are just as beautiful as he said. He was very eager to have you here. I think he did the right thing."

"You mean Ben?" Lauren was puzzled as to how this woman knew so much about Ben's plans for her.

She nodded. "He told me all about you the last time I saw him."

She seemed about to say more when Jared came through the front door carrying a Mendez offspring under each arm and one on his shoulders. The one on top was holding on for dear life with tight fistfuls of Jared's hair. All were laughing and shouting as the other children ran in behind them.

"Do it to me, Jared!"

"No, to me."

"Please, Jared, me next."

Gloria came through the door that led to the kitchen clapping her hands. "Leave Jared alone. He's just arrived. There will be plenty of time to play later. Come to the table, and I'd better not see any dirty hands."

The children reluctantly released their hold on Jared and took their places at the table. Jared raked his hair with his fingers and tucked in his shirttail, which had come out during the scuffle.

Lauren would never have imagined that Jared could enjoy child's play, but he was laughing as he smoothed the cotton shirt over the muscles of his wide chest. When he sucked in his stomach, in order to shove his shirttail into the front of his pants, Lauren's eyes flickered lower. She tried to swallow the increasingly familiar congestion in her throat.

Jared's head came up with a snap and his eyes locked with hers as if she had called out to him. Her hair had been rebraided. Jacket, gloves, and hat had been discarded. The shirt molded against her breasts, making them look softer, more touchable than ever. The tight fit of the split skirt announced her femininity like a banner. Jared wiped damp palms down his thighs and looked away from that intriguing spot where the legs of her culottes came together. As he moved farther into the room, he cursed his physical susceptibility.

His eyes lit up with affection as he sighted Maria Mendez at the table, and softened as Lauren had never seen them do before. "Maria, how are you?" He came around the table and took the lady in his arms, giving her a big hug. He had never addressed Olivia in such a warm manner.

"Jared, I have just met Lauren, and I think your bride is lovely."

Jared darted a glance at Lauren and muttered under his breath, "Yes . . . well, thank you."

Rudy came in and Gloria carried the last platter from the kitchen and placed it on the table. The meal began. It was a loud, confusing time, but Lauren enjoyed it immensely after all of the lonely meals at her father's house, the stuffy, dull dinners at the Prathers', and the silent, tense meals at Olivia's table.

Everyone chattered, relating things of great importance or no importance. Rudy told them about the incident of the "gunfight." As the children laughed at Lauren's mistake, Gloria and Maria chided the men on their recklessness.

The table was crowded despite its length, and Gloria had assigned Lauren and Jared side-by-side places. Their elbows were constantly touching as one or the other lifted their cutlery or glasses. Several times, their knees or thighs would press together under the table. If anyone noticed two forks suspended motionless en route to two surprised mouths, they didn't mention it.

Rudy noticed, and chuckled each time. They were fighting it, all right. It was going to be interesting to watch this—the downfall of Jared the Great—at the hands of a slip of a girl who barely reached his shoulder.

When the meal was over, the men left to attend to the never-ending work of running a ranch. Lauren watched as they strolled companionably toward one of the corrals. They were dressed almost identically and walked with the same graceful swagger. Each sported broad shoulders, a narrowness of hip, and long, lean legs. Each had buckled on flopping chamois chaps and pulled on leather gloves. "They look alike from the back," Lauren mused aloud.

Gloria was standing at her shoulder. "Yes, I think anyone could tell they are brothers."

Lauren whirled her head around to Gloria in astonishment. "Brothers?" she gasped.

Gloria was nonplussed. "Why, yes. I thought you knew that Rudy is your brother-in-law." She was amazed that Jared hadn't told his wife of the kinship.

"Mrs. Mendez and . . ." whispered Lauren, still trying to fit the puzzle together.

"Maria and Ben," Gloria finished for her. At Lauren's shattered look, Gloria's features closed coldly and she said, "Don't judge them too harshly. They loved each other very much. Maria has lived here with Ben for almost forty years."

"But . . . but Olivia was his wife," Lauren protested weakly. Ben had lived in adultery? *Her* Ben?

"You've been with Olivia," Gloria was saying. "You know what kind of woman she is. Ever since Ben brought her here from New Orleans, she made his life miserable. She insisted on living in Coronado and refused to have anything to do with Keypoint. She assumed the responsibility of the bank. Maria was the daughter of one of the first *vaqueros* Ben hired to help him run the ranch. He fell in love with her on sight, and she with him."

Yes. Lauren could see how that could be. The gentle, serene Maria and the robust, virile Ben. They would have complemented each other. He had given her loving protection and she had given him comfort and a son. Happiness. Where one can find it. Was that wrong? A few weeks ago, Lauren would have been scandalized to hear of such a sordid arrangement, but somehow, now . . .

Was this land to rob her of her convictions, too?

"The two sons of Ben Lockett have a deep affection for each other," Gloria said, glancing out the window as the brothers rode away together. "Rudy accepts the fact that he cannot bear the family name, and that he is not the legal heir. Ben loved him and he knew that. Ben's will made it clear that as long as there is a Keypoint, the sons of Rudolfo Mendez will share an equal partnership with the sons of Jared Lockett.

"It's sad isn't it?" she went on when Lauren remained silent, watching the two men on horseback disappear over the horizon. "Maria could not even go to Ben's funeral. Nor could his first son. But Ben came to the ranch just a few days before he died. He spoke of you, Lauren, and promised to bring you to us as soon as possible. That was the last night he spent with Maria. I hope they made love all night long. He had been gone for over a month, so if I know old Ben, they did."

"I . . . I'm sure they did." Lauren said, blushing.

Gloria took her bowed head as a sign of fatigue. "You should have stopped my ramblings. You're probably tired. Why don't you take a nap?"

"I am a little tired," Lauren confessed. "But thank you for telling me the circumstances. I understand things better now." Gloria's face softened and she leaned forward to kiss Lauren lightly on the cheek.

Lauren went into the bedroom that belonged to Jared. It *did* belong to him. His ownership was stamped on everything. As she moved about the room, Lauren could feel his presence like a palpable force. Disrobing slowly, she almost felt as if she were stripping before the man himself.

She stretched out on the bed, having the strangest sensation that Jared was on the bed, too. She moved her hand over the heavy spread and wondered how many nights he had lain in this exact spot. It was an unsettling thought. Her eyes closed and she dropped off into a deep sleep, imagining that amber eyes were watching her.

Chapter 11

Lauren took a bath just before dinner. Gloria told her Ben had piped in water from a cistern several years ago, so the kitchen and two bathrooms had running water. There was, however, no water heater. A small brazier was stationed in a corner of each bathroom, with a large copper kettle kept constantly simmering.

"The only rule," Gloria said smiling, "is that when you empty the kettle, you refill it for the next person. Oh, and Jared asked me to give you this," she added as she handed Lauren a brown bottle.

"What is it?" Lauren asked.

"Liniment," was Gloria's amused reply.

Pepe had arrived earlier and deposited her luggage in the bedroom. Jared's bags stood beside hers. One of them, she noticed, had been opened. What would she do if he followed her into the room tonight? Apparently the Mendezes expected him to. She calmed her nerves, and went into the dining area.

Strangely, and in contrast to the noon meal, everything was quiet. The table was candlelit and set with china and crystal, replacing the pottery which had been used at the earlier meal.

"Where are the children?" Lauren inquired as she brought in a tray laden with serving dishes.

"Bathed and in bed," Gloria sighed. "A quiet dinner is the one luxury Rudy and I allow ourselves."

Jared and Rudy came in from the front porch where they had been enjoying glasses of whiskey. Jared crushed out his cheroot in the nearest ashtray. He was washed and brushed and wearing a clean shirt. He must have taken it out of his suitcase while she was in the bathroom.

Rudy went to Gloria and took her in his arms, kissing her in a thorough manner that stunned Lauren. They murmured to each other privately, oblivious to the other two people in the room.

Jared stood looking out the window, his thumbs hooked in the waistband of his tight pants. Lauren stood in the center of the room feeling self-conscious and nervously fingering the watch on her breast. Seeing Rudy and Gloria be so affectionate made her long for such closeness with Jared. Something inside her wanted to cry out to him, to move toward him.

She was about to take one tentative step in his direction when Maria, who had just entered, said, "What is this? The newlyweds acting like strangers, and the old married people loving like doves!"

"I was about to remark on that myself." Rudy crossed to Lauren and took both her hands in his. "If that sorry husband of yours isn't going to kiss you, I will. Welcome, Lauren, into our family." He kissed her lightly on each cheek.

There was a tense, expectant silence among them. Jared, however, seemed unaffected and went to the table. With a curt nod of his head, he offered Lauren the chair he had pulled out for her. With flaming cheeks, she walked toward it. The others, awkwardly quiet, followed her.

The conversation was easy; the Mendezes were able to talk freely about anything. Some of their topics embarrassed Lauren. Castration, branding, breeding. Sybil would have had vapors for a month.

Lauren and Gloria did the dishes. Gloria adamantly refused Maria's offer to help, but secretly confided to Lauren that she wished she had someone to assist her with the large household and the children.

When they joined the men and Maria in the large living room, Lauren was glad to note that Jared wasn't drinking. His face had lost the hostile arrogance that it usually bore like a shield. He seemed relaxed and . . . yes, happy. He was a different person from the one who lived in that beautiful but cold house in Coronado.

He was stretched lazily in a chair, his long legs extended in front of him. She traveled the length of them with her eyes, much as she had done the first time she had seen him, in the back of the wagon. The bulge at his crotch still intrigued her. She looked away quickly.

Gloria sat down beside Maria on one of the sofas and launched into a tale about one of the children's escapades. The men were talking ranch business. Left to her own devices, Lauren went to one of the bookcases. She took her eyeglasses out of her skirt pocket and put them on, leaning down to inspect the loaded shelves. She found several volumes that were interesting to her and withdrew them, taking a seat in a chair under a lamp.

She soon became engrossed in a book which described the lifestyle of the Comanche as witnessed firsthand by a Texas Ranger. She was vaguely aware of Rudy getting up and going toward the kitchen asking if anyone else wanted more coffee.

She read a few more pages before something compelled her to raise her eyes above the rim of her spectacles. With a jolt, she realized Jared was staring at her through the blue smoke of his cigar. He wasn't wearing his usual cold, implacable expression. He was looking at her almost tenderly, with a slight smile on his lips.

His gaze traveled down to her hand, which was absently fondling her watch. Why did those slim fingers always fuss with that watch? What significance did it hold for her? He really knew very little about her, he realized.

When he had held her against him today on his horse, it had taken every ounce of his willpower to keep from pressing a kiss on the nape of her neck where tendrils of ebony hair lay. He could have ridden for a hundred miles with her on his lap. What sweet agony it had been every time her body had been jostled against his.

The memory of that brief touch to her breast was vivid in his mind. He convinced himself that he hadn't meant to do it. It *was* an accident. But his curiosity had been gratified to feel a firm fullness under his palm. If only he could see . . .

Jared stiffened when it occurred to him where his thoughts were leading. Just remember how she got here, he cautioned himself. She's not the innocent, frail flower she looks with those ridiculous eyeglasses on. She's a scheming little bitch. What I need is a rousing roll in the hay with some obliging whore. A pair of eager, parted thighs and it wouldn't take long to get this preacher's kid out of my mind.

Lauren saw that the soft look had fled his face. Dispiritedly she put the book away and took off her eyeglasses.

"Goodnight everyone." Maria stood as Rudy came back into the room carrying a mug of coffee. "I'm going to bed and leave you young people alone. Lauren," she came and stood in front of the girl, cupping her face between her soft hands, "I'm so glad you are here with us. Ben would have loved to have been here. As a matter of fact, I think he was." She kissed Lauren on the cheek and walked slowly down the hall.

"She'll never get over losing him," Rudy said quietly, as the slender figure moved out of sight.

"Yes," Gloria sighed. "I'm going to bed, too," she said, standing and going to Rudy's chair. She leaned on the arms of it, her gaping blouse giving him an unobstructed view of the generous breasts barely contained within her chemise. They kissed long and hard, his hands resting lightly on her thick waist.

"Get my place warm for me. I'll be a few more minutes," he said when she finally pulled away.

"Don't keep Jared up late. Remember, this is his honeymoon," Gloria teased, rolling her eyes at Jared.

He shifted uneasily in his chair. "That's all right, Gloria. I'm joining a hot poker game over at the bunkhouse. Some of the boys invited me, and you know these things can go all night sometimes." He tried to sound jocular, but failed.

"A poker game!" Gloria exploded. "What in the world—" A sharp look from Rudy halted her. She looked at Lauren, who was standing stiffly in the shadows next to the door.

"Lauren, I'll see that you are settled for the night," Gloria said with commiseration.

"Goodnight, ladies," Rudy said gently.

"Goodnight, Rudy. Goodnight Jared," Lauren whispered hoarsely.

"Goodnight, Lauren," Jared said nonchalantly as he studied a fingernail.

Gloria shot her brother-in-law a murderous look before she went with Lauren down the hall.

Lauren had been tossing on the wide bed for several hours. She had heard Rudy going into the room across the hall and Gloria's welcoming murmur as he closed the door behind him. That had been a long while ago, and the house was silent. The moon was bright, illuminating the bedroom in an ethereal glow.

She started when she heard footsteps stealthily approaching the door to the room. She turned to the far side of the bed and feigned sleep as the door opened.

Her whole body tensed as Jared walked into the room. He picked up one of the bags left standing in the middle of the floor, for she heard the buckle on it jangle. There was a long pause, and then the bag was lowered again to the floor.

He moved on Indian-trained feet to the side of the bed. She could smell the faint aroma of tobacco and the musky scent of leather as he leaned over her. He stood there for torturous minutes, immobile and silent. Lauren was aware of each breath as he inhaled and exhaled rhythmically. She felt a butterfly touch made by strong, lean fingers against her cheekbone. Her throat constricted and her heart pounded as if it would burst. Finally he turned and went back to the bags, picked them up, and then carried them from the room, closing the door softly.

The scents remained to tease her senses.

"Gone?"

"Yes, Lauren. He left before dawn this morning." Gloria looked piteously at her new sister-in-law. Her heart went out to the girl whose husband treated her so abominably. When Rudy had joined her in their room the night before, they had speculated on the strange relationship between Jared and his bride. It appeared to be a marriage of convenience, but Rudy couldn't guess the reasons behind it. He only knew that they must be damned essential to Jared's well-being to have forced him into any marriage.

"Wh-where did he go?" Lauren's heart had plummeted when Gloria told her that Jared had ridden out with enough supplies in his saddlebags to last him several days.

"He went to check out some problems on the far western side of the ranch. There have been reports of marauding bobcats killing our cattle. Don't worry about him, Lauren. He'll be back soon, I'm sure." She didn't tell her that any one of the *vaqueros* who worked at Keypoint could have handled this job.

"Yes, I'm sure he will," Lauren mumbled. A few days ago, she had dreaded the sight of Jared. Now the prospect of not seeing him every few hours seemed dismal. What was the matter with her? She felt rejected, abandoned. This was supposed to be her honeymoon!

The liniment hadn't worked out all the soreness in her legs and hips, but when Rudy asked her if she would like to ride with him that afternoon, she agreed. The ranch life was exhilarating. She wanted to absorb every aspect of it, savor its energy, its vigor. This was Ben's land. Keypoint was his conception. And like him, it was vital and alive. At Keypoint Lauren felt even closer to the man who had brought her here wanting her to become a part of it.

As Jared's absence lengthened, it became her habit to ride with Rudy or some of the *vaqueros* in the afternoons. In the mornings, she played with the Mendez children, who were teaching her

Spanish. They would burst into peals of laughter when she got a word wrong or had trouble pronouncing it. Sometimes she read to them before bedtime. Lauren also loved being with Gloria, and the two women soon shared a deep friendship. Lauren had had so few women friends in her life that she treasured this new relationship.

She relished her visits with Maria Mendez, too. The older woman spent a great deal of time secluded in her room, as had been her inclination ever since Ben's death. Even when she was with the rest of them, she seemed withdrawn, dreamlike, separated from reality. Lauren thought she looked at peace during these times, and rather imagined that she was communicating with Ben on a plane where no one else could intrude.

The first week passed quickly. Lauren's heart raced each time she heard pounding hooves, but she continued to be disappointed. She kept searching the horizon for signs of the large palomino and his mount in the wide-brimmed black hat, but to no avail.

She acclimated to the ranch life so enthusiastically that Gloria and Rudy were amazed. The *vaqueros* would tip their hats to her with a humble, "Good morning, Mrs. Lockett," to which she replied, calling them by name. They all respected and liked her.

One day she was timidly approached by a Mexican cowboy with dark, dancing eyes. "Señora Lockett, I am Carlos Rivas, Elena's husband." He smiled shyly and twisted his sombrero in his hands.

"It's so nice to meet you, Carlos!" Lauren cried. "How is Elena?"

"She thinks the baby come soon."

"Please let me know when it does. Tell her hello for me."

"*Sí, señora.*"

She had also seen the enigmatic Comanche, Thorn. He had never spoken to her, but he tipped his hat whenever they met. His expression never changed, but Lauren felt that his eyes missed nothing. She hoped his assessment of her was favorable. His dark, austere face and long braids intimidated her, though she felt instinctively that he was a friend.

Ten days after his departure, Jared came home. He rode in one evening just before dinnertime, looking tired and dirty as he clumped through the large front door. From his boots to his hat, he was covered with a fine layer of trail dust.

"Well, look what just dragged in." Rudy stood with his hands on his hips eyeing Jared as if he were something distasteful.

"Am I in time for dinner? I've ridden like hell for the past few hours. I'm sick of camp food," he said sheepishly.

"We'll wait for you, Jared. Just go wash up first and turn Charger over to someone in the stable." Gloria spoke to him coolly, and he looked in turn at the faces staring at him reproachfully. Lauren didn't look at him at all. Her dark head was bowed as she stared down into her plate. *He* felt like the outsider.

"I'll be right back," he muttered as he stepped out the door.

Lauren's heart was in her throat. He had barely glanced in her direction, yet she felt his presence in the room as strongly as if he had touched her. Conversation went on around her as everyone waited patiently for Jared to come back.

He returned, having discarded his chaps, leather vest, bandana, and spurs. He wore a clean shirt and his hair was still damp from the recent dunking in the bunkhouse washbowl.

He crossed the room to Maria and kissed her proffered cheek. Her greeting was the only warm one he received. His kiss intended for Gloria's cheek landed somewhere in the air as she turned away quickly, and Rudy shook his hand with none of the usual banter between them. He took his seat beside Lauren and only then did he turn to her. "Hello, Lauren."

"Hello, Jared. Was your . . . trip . . . successful?"

"I shot two bobcats and visited some of the nesters we allow to use our water. It was basically uneventful."

There seemed to be nothing more to say, and everyone commenced eating. The food stuck in Lauren's throat. She was jittery and breathless, and when one of the children called from the bedrooms, she jumped up to go to him, anxious to get away from the dominating individual beside her.

"I don't know what we'll do when Lauren has to go back to Coronado with you, Jared. We have all come to love her so much." Gloria wanted to slap her brother-in-law as he shrugged indifferently. She continued undaunted, "The children adore her and she has been such a help around here, hasn't she, Maria?"

"She's a wonderful girl, Jared. You're lucky that Ben brought her here." Jared growled deep in his throat.

Rudy chuckled. "I know at least a dozen of the hands who would love for you to have a fatal accident, Jared. They'd whisk her away in no time flat."

Jared scowled at him. "When the hell has she been around any *vaqueros?*"

"Every day when she goes out riding. You'd be amazed how eager they've been to answer her questions. She's a fast learner."

"I'll bet," Jared grumbled around the food in his mouth.

Lauren came back and sat down. Rudy stood up for her; Jared stared sullenly at the bowl of chrysanthemums in the center of the table.

"One place Lauren hasn't seen is Pecan Creek. You really should take her up there before the weather turns too cold."

Gloria took her cue from Rudy. "Why don't you go tomorrow? You could take a picnic and enjoy being alone."

"I don't think—" Lauren began.

"Not tomorrow," Jared interrupted. "I've got too much work to do around here."

"Nonsense," Maria interjected. She wasn't going to sit idly by and see one of Ben's best plans thwarted by Jared's obstinacy. "You've been gone for almost two weeks. You deserve a day off. You'll leave first thing in the morning, and I'll supervise packing your lunch. I know just what you like.

"Be sure to take a gunny sack and gather some pecans for me. We'll be needing them for Thanksgiving and Christmas baking. Remember when I used to send you and Rudy there each fall? Ben would give you a penny for each nut you brought back. Those were such happy days," she said wistfully. She cleared her throat. "Yes, you'll go tomorrow."

The matter seemed settled. Jared glared at Rudy with a withering look. Rudy smiled back, the epitome of innocence. Maria and Gloria smiled at each other conspiratorially. Lauren fumbled with her watch, which trembled on her breast.

"Godammit, what do you expect me to do, Rudy? I've tried every argument. They want that power plant and we want a railroad. They've got us by the balls."

"I don't know, but you've got to do something! Ben would have gone to war before letting those sonsofbitches on his land."

The ladies in the main room looked at each other as the voices, raised in frustration and anger, reached them from the front porch where Jared and Rudy had retired after dinner to smoke a cigar. Maria put aside her mending, Gloria paused in stringing some beads she had promised Lucy, and Lauren dropped the book she was reading into her lap. She alone knew what subject had brought such an outburst from the brothers.

The voices outside returned to normal, and the women resumed their activities. Every once in a while, a word or phrase would carry back to them, punctuated in emphasis or urgency.

When Rudy and Jared came back inside, their mouths were set and grim. Each looked immediately toward Lauren, Jared with hostility, Rudy with something akin to pity.

So, Lauren thought, Jared has told his brother the circumstances of our marriage. For a moment, she feared that Rudy's opinion of her would alter, that he would condemn her for the decision she had made. But one look at his face—open, friendly, compassionate—assured her that this wouldn't be the case.

"If we have to go to Pecan Creek tomorrow, be ready early." Jared stalked out the door after addressing Lauren with all the enthusiasm of a prisoner awaiting execution at dawn. No one challenged his sleeping arrangements this time.

Gloria and Rudy went to their room. Lauren placed her book back in the shelf and, taking off her eyeglasses, walked to the window. She saw the tall, lean figure striding toward the bunkhouse with his broad shoulders hunched defensively.

She didn't know that Maria was behind her until the woman placed a reassuring arm around her slender waist. "Ben fought his love for me like a man possessed, Lauren. They are both tough, strong men. Tenderness doesn't come easy to Jared. Or even kindness. Be patient with him."

Lauren couldn't speak for fear of weeping. She turned to Maria and hugged her quickly before seeking the privacy of her room. Jared's room.

Gloria helped Lauren braid her hair in the style now familiar to her. She wore the same suit she had worn on the morning she and Jared left Coronado for Keypoint. The ensemble that had seemed scandalously indecent at the time now felt quite comfortable. She had become accustomed to many changes in her life.

Maria was in the kitchen making good her promise to prepare their lunch. Jared strolled in and without a word handed Lauren a dark blue bandana. She looked at it and then at him with puzzlement.

"It's clean," he said testily. "I borrowed it from one of your many admirers and washed it myself. You may need it today."

She took the scarf and folded it into a triangle. Placing it around her neck, she tried to tie it as the *vaqueros* wore theirs, but her fingers were unaccountably clumsy.

"Here," Jared said in exasperation, batting her hands away. He stepped closer to her and wound the ends of the bandana into a perfect knot. Deft as he was at this, it seemed to take an inordinate amount of time to get it right. He moved closer still, and his fingers found it necessary to brush against the warm, smooth skin of her throat as he adjusted the scarf.

"Thank you," she said when he finally stepped away. He only shrugged in response.

After a hurried breakfast, she and Jared departed. Lauren waved goodbye to Gloria and Maria, who stood framed in the doorway. Flame had now become known as "Mrs. Lockett's mount," and a rapport had developed between Lauren and the mare. Jared was mildly surprised when he spurred Charger into a gallop and Lauren followed suit, keeping pace with him effortlessly. Well, she's learned *something,* he thought grudgingly. She had lost her eastern pallor, too, and her complexion had taken on a healthy, rosy glow.

He wouldn't admit to anyone, even to himself, that he had missed her while he had been away. He wouldn't define the sense of longing that had plagued him from the time he left. Scattered over Lockett land were sheep ranchers and nesters whom he visited, and their daughters always welcomed a pat on the bottom or a stolen kiss. They had all been disappointed this time. Jared spent his time in serious conversation with the menfolk. He hadn't consciously avoided the women. He just wasn't interested, and therefore didn't give them a thought.

At night, rolled up in his blankets, he tossed and turned in an effort to rid himself of disturbing mental images. Lauren in her dressing gown, her hair spilling over her shoulders. Lauren sleeping in his bed at the ranch, moonlight caressing her cheeks. Lauren in deep concentration over a book, her eyeglasses resting on her nose. Lauren. Lauren. Lauren.

He cursed himself for being a fool as his imagination drifted and he pictured himself lifting a stray lock of hair from her shoulder and kissing it. He was caressing her cheek resting against his pillow. He was sliding the spectacles off her nose in order to kiss her soft mouth.

Sleep eluded him night after night. He sat before his dying campfire smoking cheroots and cursing his intense physical discomfort and the conniving wench who had manipulated his father and was now trying to do the same thing to him. Well he'd be damned before he'd let her get to him!

But as he'd approached Keypoint last night, his heartbeat had accelerated as he spurred Charger into a mad gallop. Jared swore that his eagerness to get home had nothing to do with the woman he had left there. Now, as he watched her from under the protection of his hat brim, he wasn't so sure.

They rode in silence for half an hour. Jared slowed Charger to a trot and led the way to the riverbank where cypress roots snaked along the ground, knotted and ropelike. On the other side of the river, a rock formation formed a wall, a backdrop, looming up fifty feet. About midway up, jutting out of the rock wall, was the strangest structure Lauren had ever seen.

It was barely more than a wooden shingle façade a few feet deep. A black metal flue extended a few inches out of the roof, emitting a thin wisp of smoke, The only door, in the center of the structure, was made of rough planks. A square window was on either side of it. Over these had been nailed cowhides, which stirred slightly in the breeze. Various antlers of deer and cattle adorned the exterior walls. The small shelf of rock on which the house was perched was barely wide enough for a man to stand on, but it was littered with all types of utensils; pails and washtubs, bridles and harnesses, rope, plows in sad disrepair, a stack of nondescript pelts, metal objects that Lauren couldn't identify from this distance.

"What is that?" she asked Jared in awe as he reined in and began to dismount.

"Just stay where you are. We'll only be here a minute. Crazy Jack doesn't like company."

"Wh—"

"Just sit still, Lauren," he said crisply.

She watched him as he untied a bundle from behind his saddle and casually walked to the riverbank. He knelt down and scooped several handfuls of the clear water into his mouth. Then he placed the package on a flat-surfaced rock and returned to Charger, mounting with studied nonchalance.

Lauren stifled her curiosity as they rode away from the strange scene in silence. She glanced nervously back over her shoulder to steal a final look at the bizarre sight.

They had covered about a mile before Jared once again led the horses near the Rio Caballo, this time nudging them down to the bank to drink. He handed Lauren a canteen and crossed his leg across his saddle, lighting a cigar.

"What was that house, Jared? Does someone live there?" She couldn't contain her curiosity any longer.

"Yes, someone lives there." His manner was irritatingly casual.

"His name is Jack Turner, though everyone has nicknamed him Crazy Jack. He built a façade over a dry cave for his house. He's a hermit and not at all crazy."

"A hermit!?" she exclaimed. "How long has he lived there? Where did he come from? Is he dangerous?"

With annoying slowness, Jared retrieved his canteen, recapped it, and took a long pull on his cheroot before he replied. "Jack and his brother Bill came to Texas in the late fifties from God knows where and settled in a small deserted cabin. They either didn't have the initiative or the capital to ranch or farm, but they grew staple crops. They did odd jobs when they needed money, otherwise they were pretty reclusive. The German settlers around here were so industrious that they shunned anyone who didn't share their proclivity for work." He shifted in his saddle and drew again on the cigar.

"In 1872, the Comanche went on a rampage and raided the smaller farms. Jack and Bill were both captured, their cabin burned. They were held captive for six months or so, but then Jack was rescued. If they had been the only hostages, no one would have bothered, but some women and children had been taken at the same time, so a rescue party had been formed. Brother Bill had been killed by the Indians. Tortured and killed. Jack was . . . injured . . . and when he came back to civilization he was scorned by all his 'Christian' neighbors."

Jared's lip curled in a derisive sneer. "Jack built his house there in the cave and, though it was on our land, Ben looked the other way. Jack cuts out a couple of beeves each year, but they're never the best ones, and he doesn't waste them. He uses every bit of the carcass. We bring him staples every few months. All he asks is to be left alone. His house is somewhat like a fortress. God knows how he gets in and out of it. You can bet we were sighted in his rifle as soon as we got into range."

Lauren was quiet for a moment as she absorbed the story. "Why was he shunned by everyone? He couldn't help being taken by the Indians." She was immediately sympathetic to the eccentric hermit.

Jared watched her closely as he said slowly, "He'd had his nose and ears cut off. That's what the Indians did to him while they mutilated and killed his brother. He's not too pretty to look at, and people don't like their sensibilities insulted by the sight of him."

Chapter 12

Lauren's hands flew to her mouth. The horrors inflicted on Jack Turner by the Comanche were incomprehensible. But the torture inflicted on him by his own people was even worse. Ben and Jared had treated him kindly. She lowered her eyes as she said softly, "You're very charitable, Jared, to do these things for him."

"It's not charity. We'll find a jar of his home-brewed corn liquor on the front porch in a day or two. It's always left for us after we bring him something. Of course, I wouldn't drink it for the world. It's pure rotgut. But I'd never ignore it, either." Ever since he could remember, Ben had ridden out to take supplies to Crazy Jack. The man must be in his seventies by now. "I wonder if he knows Ben is dead," Jared mused aloud. "He probably does. I think he knows everything that goes on around here." He tossed down his cigar butt and placed his boot back in the stirrup. "Ready?"

Lauren nodded and they took off again. Jared raised his bandana over his nose and indicated that she should do the same. Moving away from the river, the grass became sparse and dry, and their horses kicked up clouds of dust. Lauren was grateful for Jared's thoughtfulness in bringing her the bandana.

A short while later, Jared slowed their horses to a leisurely walk as he entered a pecan grove. The old, massive trees, gradually losing their foliage in the change of seasons, umbrellaed the gently rising hill.

At this point, the river was wide. The bank to which Jared now led her was grassy before becoming littered with pebbles. Those tiny rocks grew into giant limestone boulders that rose like smooth tables out of the river. The swift water rushed over them, crystal-clear and gurgling.

"How lovely!" she cried. In her excitement, she swung her leg off the saddle and dropped to the ground, rushing to the riverbank.

On the opposite side of the river, there was a wall of rock much like the one Crazy Jack had built his house into. With the natural screening of the rock wall and the protective covering of the pecan trees, the setting was intimate and private despite its primitive nature.

She didn't realize Jared had dismounted and come to stand behind her until he spoke. "The water here is fed by underground springs. That's why it's so clear. Come on."

She was surprised when he took her hand and pulled her out onto the rock formations in the river. The leather gloves they both wore did nothing to dilute the warmth of the hand tightly holding hers. They walked together over the white boulders, which had been polished smooth by water washing over them year after year. When they reached the point where the water rushed over the rock, Jared knelt down. Lauren followed suit and took off her glove to place her hand in the water. "Oh! It's so cold," she exclaimed, laughing.

"Until you get used to it," he said with a smile. "When Rudy and I were kids, we came up here to swim. Ben brought us until we were old enough to look out for ourselves. You see, when it rains, this tributary of the Caballo becomes a torrent. Where we're standing now would be covered with water coming down from the hills." They had pulled the bandanas away from their mouths, and she watched the way his chin caressed the soft cloth beneath it as he spoke. "In the spring, this looks completely different. The redbuds bloom and the bluebonnets cover the hills like a carpet."

She listened intently and watched his hands as he gestured. He had said Ben's name without the haunted expression that usually crossed his face whenever his father was mentioned.

She leaned over the water and cupped a handful, bringing it to her mouth. The brackish taste was terrible. She didn't know she had made a face until she heard Jared's chuckle near her ear.

"Tastes bad, doesn't it? The water is pure, but it has to be filtered through charcoal before it tastes good enough to drink," he explained. "See where the water is bubbling up from under that rock?" He pointed and she nodded. "That's one of the springs."

They walked back across the rocks until they regained the riverbank where their mounts were standing docilely, nibbling the grass. As Jared went about the business of unpacking the saddlebags that held their lunch, Lauren walked up the hill to the crest. Her breath caught in her throat: The entire valley opened up beneath her. It was a breathtaking sight.

"Luncheon is served, Madam," Jared called to her and made a sweeping bow over the blanket that served as their table.

Feeling free and uninhibited, she ran down the hill to join him. The fallen pecans and autumn leaves on the ground crunched under her boots.

Maria had packed enough food for an army, but Lauren was relieved to see that for once there were no beans. Thin slices of cold roast beef, potato salad packed in a jar, spiced peaches, fresh bread, *tortillas*, and sugar cookies composed their menu. They ate off tin plates the men used when on the trail. Incongruously, Maria had also packed snowy white linen napkins.

"It's beautiful here, Jared," Lauren said after a long, awkward pause which they filled by concentrating on their food.

"Yeah." He munched on a piece of bread before he said offhandedly, "This is where I want to build a house some day. Right up there on top of the hill." He indicated the place with an inclination of his chin. "I'd have the house facing the valley, and this," he swept his hand in a broad gesture, "would be my backyard. Even if the river overflowed the banks, the house would be high enough to be protected."

"That would be perfect," she enthused. "I'd love living in a setting like this."

The moment the words left her mouth she would have given heaven and earth to bring them back. His head whipped around and his eyes bore into hers, hard and uncompromising. She hadn't meant to imply they would be living together. She had only been speaking rhetorically. Mortified, she lowered her head.

Each was painfully aware of the other and their isolated surroundings. The silence was palpable. Using her best conversational voice, acquired from years of practice entertaining guests in the Prathers' parlor, Lauren asked, "Why didn't you tell me Rudy was your brother, Jared?"

The question took him completely off-guard, and he stopped chewing his mouthful of food. Finally he swallowed, took a long gulp of beer from one of the bottles Maria had packed for him and asked, "Would it have mattered?"

"His illegitimacy?" He looked at her sharply, but saw only understanding in her eyes. "No. That doesn't matter to me, Jared."

"Well it does to a lot of people. That and his being half Mexican," he said bitterly. "No one understands about Ben and Maria."

"I do."

Again she had surprised him, and his eyes studied her briefly before he looked away. He reclined, stretching his long legs in front of him and supporting himself on one elbow. Lauren was reminded of the first time she had seen him and wished he would sit erect. She found it hard to keep her eyes diverted from the body so unabashedly displayed.

To cover her flustered state, she commented, "You always refer to your father by his first name. Why?"

He seemed momentarily irritated by her myriad questions, but then he laughed softly and said, "That's what everyone else called him." Jared shrugged. "He didn't like titles. Didn't need them. I felt the same way when I came back from Cuba and suddenly I was Lieutenant Lockett." His muscles bunched in agitation.

"It must have been terrible there," she offered quietly. "I read that our army fought the climate as much as they did the Spanish."

"That's an understatement," he said. "I never drew a deep breath the whole time I was there. It was godawful. No matter how hard you tried to suck that heavy air into your lungs, you could never get enough. Most of us got a good case of malaria, and we went into battle with the fever and sweating weakening us until it was an effort to crawl. It got to where I didn't care if we took the goddam hill or not."

"There was a girl at home who was married to a soldier, a marine. We prayed for him and were so thankful when he returned with only a slight leg wound." She shifted her gaze away from his belt buckle and plucked at a napkin spread over her thighs.

His eyes, narrowed to slits, traveled from the part in her hair to the toe of her soft boots. "What about you, Lauren? Didn't you pine away for some sweetheart to come home to you?"

She flushed as much from his scrutiny as from his words. "No," she said into her lap. "I had no admirers or . . . anything. Besides, I was too young then."

"Oh. But what about later? Didn't any of the deacon's sons try to steal a kiss behind the church door? No hanky-panky in the choir loft under those voluminous robes?" As he spoke, his hand moved to her chest. His dextrous fingers worked the buttons of her jacket until it fell open. She was dizzy with emotion when she felt him fingering the pearl buttons on her shirt, though he didn't try to undo them.

"Surely someone has made a pass at you." His tone was teasing. He couldn't know that his mockery conjured up abhorrent memories of William Keller. She squeezed her eyes tight and shook her head violently, trying to dispel the hateful recollection.

Jared was alarmed. He had meant to shake her cool reserve, but her reaction was far stronger than he'd expected. His hand stilled, though he didn't withdraw it. She composed herself slowly and finally raised her eyes to meet his. "No," she whispered, "I never had any sweethearts."

Of its own volition, his hand moved up so his fingers could settle lightly on her cheek. It just wasn't possible that anyone could be as innocent as she appeared to be. No one that naive would leave the security of a parsonage for an adventure in Texas with a man, a stranger, as virile as Ben Lockett.

Why *had* she come with Ben? He was on the verge of putting the question to her, but stopped himself. Maybe he didn't want to know the answer. The realization that the truth might hurt caused him to turn his frustration on himself. He looked away from the gray eyes that were now watching him closely. He wasn't going to be a fool over his old man's doxy. He jerked his hand away as though he had reached for something desirable and realized too late that it was decayed and hideous.

Lauren felt his withdrawal immediately. The course their conversation had taken was disturbing, but it *was* conversation, and she hated to give it up. Nevertheless, she was glad he was no longer touching her. His touch, no matter how slight, did strange things to her, set off reactions both alarming and embarrassing.

"We'd better start gathering those damn pecans," he said tersely, and strode toward Charger to get the gunny sack he had brought along for that purpose.

Lauren put their eating implements away after rinsing them in the river. Then she repacked the remaining food. Jared had the sack half-filled with pecans when she bent down to help him.

"I can do it," he said gruffly. "No sense in your getting dirty."

She looked up the length of his body and met the amber eyes glaring down at her. What had she done to make him angry? "I want to help," she said simply.

"Suit yourself," he answered indifferently and turned away, looking for an area that hadn't been harvested.

By the time he came stamping back to her, Lauren had gathered a pile of the nuts. He held the mouth of the sack open while she scooped her hoard into it.

"All done," she said cheerfully, dusting off her hands. Licking her lips quickly, she asked, "Do you think we have enough pecans?"

He didn't answer. He was too intrigued by the tongue which

had raked across incredibly sexy lips and disappeared behind them to hide from him. Then he spun away from her, saying over his shoulder, "Let's go. If I read my weather signs right, we're in for a Norther before long."

They mounted their horses. He spoke only once. "We'll go down the other side. It's not as scenic and we have to go by the charcoal burners' camp, but it's closer. I'm afraid of getting caught out here without warmer clothes."

They followed the springfed tributary that tripped over limestone until, at the bottom of the hill, it flowed into the Rio Caballo.

Lauren sniffed the air and caught the smell of wood smoke. As they rode around a bend, a derelict encampment, like an ugly sore marring the scenery's beauty, came into sight. Tents and dilapidated shacks were scattered around pits from which the dark smoke rose. Ragged children ran among the fires with heart-stopping recklessness. Mangy dogs came running out from under various covers, barking ferociously. Several dirty, bewhiskered men ambled out of the lean-tos to see who the intruders were.

The women, dirty and as ragged as their children, scowled at Lauren as they squatted around campfires stirring pots of foulsmelling stew. One of the dirtiest men separated himself from the rest and shuffled toward them. Lauren suspected his nonchalant swagger was deceptive. His beady, deepset eyes didn't miss anything, and were bright under shaggy brows.

Jared looked at her out of the corner of his eye, never averting his head from the man. "Whatever happens, don't get off your horse." He had barely opened his lips to say the words, rasping them from behind his teeth.

Jared reined in their horses and waited for him to amble toward them. The man was short and stocky with powerful-looking arms that were too long for his body, giving him an apelike physique. He wore dirty, patched overalls, with only his red, faded longjohns under them. Lauren shrank in disgust at the stained and moist armholes of the garment. He had several days' stubble on his face, and his oily black hair was matted to his head when he scooped off a battered hat in feigned humility.

"Well, lookey here. If it ain't Mr. Jared come to pay us a call with his new lady." His teeth were yellow and broken, covered with thick dark scum. Lauren had never seen anyone so repulsive. Or menacing.

"Duncan," Jared said curtly.

"We sure was sorry to hear about yore pa, Mr. Jared. That's a real shame now, ain't it?"

Jared ignored the comment. "How's your business?"

"Well," he whined, "it could always be better. If'n you'd let us clear some of the land where them damned nesters is, we could both be better off."

"You know that land is off-limits to you, and it always will be. You stay on this side of the river, or you're off for good, understand?"

"Now, Mr. Jared, you wouldn't run us off. What with our famblies and all." He paused and split his lips in a sickening parody of a smile. "You couldn't see June no more, either."

Jared swung down from his saddle and stood facing the man, his body as tense as a coiled snake ready to strike. Only common sense and the grim consequences of such a stupid action kept him from grinding his fist into Duncan's insolent face.

The charcoal burner read the hesitation and continued with a leer, "You hadn't forgotten Juney now hadja, Mr. Jared?" He inclined his head and Lauren followed his indication to the cabin where a young woman leaned against the doorjamb. Her expression was as insolent as the man's. She pushed away from the door and sauntered closer to them, her hips swinging suggestively. She was barefoot and her feet were caked with dirt. Her dress barely covered her knees and the bodice was stretched across pendulous breasts. Lauren realized that she was naked under the thin cotton dress and was stunned at the girl's immodesty. Her hair was almost white and her eyes were piercing blue. She might have been pretty, even beautiful, if it weren't for the sullen mouth that drooped at the corners and her lack of personal hygiene.

The slinking walk brought her to within a few inches of Jared. She swayed slightly as she said huskily, "Hello, Jared."

Jared turned on his heels and walked over to Flame and her rider. He raised his voice. "This is my wife." He placed a gloved hand on Lauren's thigh, and if she had not been frightened by this strange camp and the gypsylike people who lived here, she would have wondered why she trembled and felt like melting at his touch. "If anyone from this camp comes near her, I'll kill him. You have been warned." It could have been her imagination that he applied more pressure to her leg just before he released it. He walked around Charger and mounted in one fluid movement.

"Uh . . . Mr. Jared, we was wonderin' what's gonna happen

to all of the goddam nesters and sheepherders when you dam up the river." Duncan stood with his squat legs spread, arms akimbo, his chin thrust out belligerently. Gone was the groveling attitude he had assumed at first.

Jared riveted his amber eyes on the man. "Where in hell did you ever hear that?"

"I don't rightly recall." He scratched his head in mock-puzzlement, and Lauren was nauseated to see startled lice crawling in his hair. "Word just got around, that's all."

"Well, it's only gossip. Understand? I don't want to hear any more about it."

"If'n they was to move on like, could we work that land then?"

"I'm going to say it one more time." Jared's voice was hard and even, as sharp as a rapier. "You work only where I or Rudy tell you you can. Nowhere else. And anything else that happens on Lockett land is none of your business." He rested his hand lightly on his pistol holster.

He nudged Charger with his knees and Lauren did the same to Flame. They rode out of the camp slowly, though she would have liked to gallop, so malevolent were the looks that June had given her. When she had passed close to the girl, Lauren heard her hiss, "Bitch!"

When the camp was well behind them, Jared pulled up and listened for a moment before he spoke. "I think it's all right now."

"What in the world is that place? I was frightened."

"I was, too." He laughed. "That riffraff back there are charcoal burners. Wat Duncan is more or less their leader. Ben made a deal with him years ago that they could cut down the cedar and burn it into charcoal. There's a market for it in San Antonio. They use it to purify the water and make it taste better." Lauren remembered the bitter-tasting water she had drunk from the spring and Jared's explanation that it had to be filtered. "We let them keep all their profits and, in turn, they keep the ranges cleared of excess cedar. The only problem is that they are mean, dishonest, and completely amoral."

Lauren looked away from him as she murmured, "The girl was pretty in a way."

A grin twitched his lips as he studied her. He said, "One day in my reckless youth, Ben caught June and me giving each other a biology lesson. He beat me to within an inch of my life. I never went near her again, especially after he impressed upon me what can befall a young man who fools around with sluts like her. She and Wat must have been insulted, because he never fails to make reference to her when I'm around."

"Are they related?"

"Yes. She's his sister." He paused significantly. "And his mate."

Lauren felt ill as she spurred Flame into a gallop behind Jared's lead.

They were only a few miles from the house when the wind suddenly shifted to northerly and the gusts of cold air stung Lauren's cheeks. Her eyes began to water.

Jared shouted for her to pull her bandana over her nose as he did, and it offered a little protection from the biting wind.

They rode a few more minutes and then he signaled for her to follow him. He led her to a group of boulders and rode into a pocket formed by the enormous rocks.

Lauren was shivering from the cold, but at least now they were out of the fierce wind. Jared came around to Flame's side and offered up his arms to help her down. She placed her hands on his shoulders as he lowered her gently to the ground.

She welcomed the warmth of his arms as they slowly enclosed her in a hesitant embrace. Her hat slipped from her head as she rested her cheek against the hard chest. She looked up, laughing when she realized that she still had the bandana pulled up over the lower half of her face.

Her laughter was choked off as she met Jared's eyes over the top of his scarf. They impaled her with the intensity of their gaze. The brows were dark and the lashes were tipped with gold. The laugh lines at the corners of his eyes were white where his squinting had kept them from tanning like the rest of his face. The brown irises were flecked with gold. Sherry or amber or topaz.

Slowly he reached out and took the bottom of her bandana in his fingers and lowered it. It was a caress. He stroked her lips with his thumb. Only then did he lower his gaze from her eyes to study her lips as his fingers traced their shape, savored their texture, marveled at their softness. They trembled beneath his touch. Leisurely he lowered his own bandana.

She leaned into him as his arms drew her closer. Without conscious thought, her hands went to his waist, then around to meet at his back.

His lips came to hers gently, softly. Barely touching them, he whispered, "Lauren." Then his mouth closed over hers. His lips moved over hers expertly, persuasively. His tongue teased them until they were shyly parted and she met the tip of his tongue with her own. A low moan escaped Jared's throat and his hand went to the small of her back to press her against him. Her fingers splayed over the muscles of his back. Losing all timidity, she opened her mouth to the hungry plea of his.

"Now that *is* a touching sight," Rudy said, laughing.

Chapter 13

Lauren and Jared jumped so violently at the sound of the amused voice that their movement startled their horses.

"Having a nice time?" Rudy queried innocently. He had seen them riding toward the boulders and had followed them into the shelter.

Jared snarled at him. "Lauren was cold and I remembered that I had a poncho in one of my saddlebags. I was getting it out for her." He was infuriated with himself for explaining their kiss like a guilty schoolboy.

"Yeah, you were warming her up all right. Looks like you were getting pretty hot yourself." Rudy would have loved to continue taunting Jared, but Lauren was the greater sufferer. When he saw her distress, he softened. "We'd better get home. Gloria was worried when the Norther blew in and sent me out to check on you."

Jared had extracted an old, worn woolen poncho from his saddlebag and unceremoniously pulled it over Lauren's head. Roughly plopping her hat back onto her head, he remounted Charger. She could tell by the way he sat rigidly on the stallion's back as he rode away that he was angry. Probably with her.

She and Rudy followed him at a distance. Her brother-in-law gave her a reassuring smile.

Jared was seething. It didn't matter to him that Rudy had seen him in a tender embrace. He wasn't shy. He and some of his cronies had even shared whores, cheering each other on. What bothered him was that Rudy had witnessed his susceptibility to Lauren.

She had lured him into kissing her. Those damn captivating eyes, full of tears produced by the cold wind, were hard for any man to resist. The raven tendrils whipping cheeks rosy from the exertion of their ride cried out to be caressed. That body which had tormented him all day with its nearness had been impossible to release once he held it against him.

Above all, he resented her composure. She retained that superior coolness no matter what happened to them. She hadn't panicked at the charcoal burners' camp. She hadn't been violently ill when he told her about the atrocities inflicted on Crazy Jack. Everyone at the ranch adored her. She fit right in.

Damn her!

Dinnertime was subdued. Everyone ate almost silently. Gloria, Maria, and Rudy recognized one of Jared's black moods and spoke to him with the care of one walking on thin ice. He growled his responses.

Lauren was completely withdrawn. She spoke to no one except for an occasional please or thank you. Her head bowed, she stared into her lap as they sat in the living area after dinner. Her fingers would wander to her watch subconsciously and draw comfort from it as she always did in times of stress.

Outside the wind howled, and the fireplace, cheerful though it was with the crackling fire in it, could not lighten the atmosphere of gloom.

"We had visitors today, Jared," Rudy said cautiously.

"Who was that?" Jared appeared completely bored.

"The Vandivers. Father and son."

"Goddammit," he cursed. "What did they want?" Rudy had his undivided attention now.

"They said they were over at the site of their new power plant and just stopped in to say hello."

"Like hell. The power plant will be fifteen miles from here." Jared stood up and crossed to the fireplace. He stared into it for several seconds, then glanced smugly at Lauren. "It's too bad we missed them. Lauren has developed quite an attraction to Kurt." The words were deliberately provoking.

She jerked up her head and met his challenging stare. She was the first to avert her gaze, humiliated and angry with herself for being such a coward and not rebuking him.

There was an embarrassed silence in the room for long minutes. The pendulum clock ticked loudly and the logs in the fireplace shifted, showering Jared's boots with sparks as he maintained his stance on the hearth.

He tossed the remainder of his cigar into the flames and, taking down his shearling coat from the hall tree, muttered a sullen goodnight.

"Jared, it's cold out there. Why don't you stay here in the

house tonight?" Gloria was vexed that her scheme to throw these two stubborn people together for a whole day had not broken down any barriers between them. Instead, it seemed as though more had been raised.

"If I could have my own room back, I would gladly stay. As it is, I don't care to sleep there. If Lauren gets cold, I'm sure one of the *vaqueros* would be delighted to warm her bed."

Lauren bolted out of her chair and flew across the room so quickly that it surprised even her when she stood trembling directly in front of Jared.

She raised her hand as if to strike him, but the arrogant tilt of his chin stopped her. He was daring her to show a bit of temper, and she would not give him the satisfaction. She clenched her fist, but lowered it to her side.

"*Why?*" she asked insistently. "Why do you persist in tormenting me so? I don't like this 'arrangement' any better than you do. But I don't forget my manners."

She turned and marched into the hall leading to the bedrooms. Jared, in spite of his anger, admired the undaunted way she held her head.

Lauren's limbs felt heavy as she climbed onto the wide bed. She was tired from the long ride to Pecan Creek, and mentally fatigued as well. She was weary of trying to adjust herself to Jared's moods, of warding off his verbal attacks. His inconsistency had her totally baffled. He was vindictive and abusive one minute, and tender the next.

She wished she had resisted when he had kissed her. What had she been thinking? Nothing. That was the problem. When his arms went around her, warming her, she had ceased to think. She had allowed her senses to take over, relinquished all control to them. He had been so gentle . . . almost loving.

She buried her face in the pillow—his pillow—and groaned as she recalled the feel of his tongue against hers, the strong hands that had just begun caressing her back when Rudy interrupted them. What would have happened if they had not been seen?

It was no use speculating, for she was still not positive where kissed led. Having been around Gloria and listening to her talk about her relationship with Rudy, Lauren had inferred that whatever it was, it was pleasant. She had fought that mysterious culmination with William. She couldn't quite imagine it being enjoyable.

But if it had been Jared's hands on her back pulling away her clothing, how would she have reacted? She blushed in the darkness. She was restless and physically unsatisfied and her body was transmitting strange, unrelenting impulses to her brain.

Rudy and Jared would leave each morning after breakfast, and return just in time to wash before dinner. The mood in the house cheered somewhat, though Jared and Lauren still treated each other with polite indifference. He asked her permission when he went into his room to retrieve one possession or another. Lauren felt guilty about using the room, but when she suggested that Gloria make a bed for her in one of the children's rooms, the other woman adamantly refused. No argument could convince her, so Lauren dropped the subject.

She continued to play with and read to the children, constantly delighted by them. With Maria, Lauren shared many quiet moments, listening to stories about Ben and about Jared and Rudy as boys. Maria carefully stayed away from the subject of Lauren's marriage. The condition of that union grieved her.

"Jared is so reticent about his early life," Lauren admitted to the older woman one day. "He rarely speaks of his childhood, or schooling, or anything. He won't tell me anything personal," she sighed. "I mentioned Cuba to him once. He was reluctant to talk about it."

Marie shook her small, sleek head sadly. "I'm glad you weren't here when he came home. Ben, I think, was secretly proud of him for joining the army. Olivia was furious and tried to keep Jared from going. She had friends of her family trying to pull strings, but when Ben found out about it, he stopped her. After the war, when the town made Jared a hero, she acted as if the whole idea had been hers." Maria sipped the tea they were enjoying while sitting on the front porch. "She's a very sad, lonely woman, you know," she added quietly.

"Did he catch malaria while he was there?"

"Yes, but his main injury was psychological. He had a friend whose father owns a ranch west of Kerrville. Alex Craven and Jared had been friends since boyhood. They joined at the same time and were in the same batallion. Alex was killed. Jared felt his death was the result of an error in judgment by the company commander, that his friend was sacrificed for no reason. He still has nightmares about that day in battle. Alex's death hurt him deeply, but Jared keeps everything inside. He reveals his true self to no one."

"I'm beginning to think he has no 'true self.' Whenever I think I've figured him out, I discover some new enigmatic facet of his character," Lauren said. Who was this man she had married?

"A very good man is there, Lauren. One day you will know him. I'm certain of that." Maria patted Lauren's hand as she stood up and went into the room she had shared with Ben, closing out the world by shutting her door.

"Oh, no! Look what I've done!" Lauren exclaimed. She was helping Gloria prepare the evening meal. Opening a can of tomatoes, she was about to empty it into a pot of stew when some of the contents splashed onto her sleeve, spreading a dark stain on the fine fabric of her shirtwaist.

"Better go change quickly and let me put that in cold water to soak," Gloria said unperturbedly.

"I'll be right back," Lauren promised as she hurriedly left the kitchen and rushed into her room. No sooner than she had unbuttoned all the buttons down her back and slipped off the blouse than she heard a commotion outside in the hallway. Before she could reach for something to cover herself, the door to the room was flung open and Jared was being pushed inside by Gloria and Rudy.

Lauren forgot her state of deshabille when she saw her husband's torn and blood-smeared shirt. She suppressed a gasp of horror. "What happened?" she asked on a high, anxious note.

Jared was staring at her, too stunned by her appearance to speak. Or was he numbed by pain? It was left to Rudy to answer her. "Jared and I were restringing some fences that had come down. An ornery length of barbed wire backlashed and caught Jared across the chest. It needs to be seen to."

"I told you it's all right," Jared growled as he was shoved from behind into the room.

"Nonsense," said Gloria in the same tone she used to her children. "Get out of that shirt and I'll get the medicine. Lauren, you'd better help him."

A conspiratorial smile was passed from husband to wife as Gloria rushed out to retrieve a bottle of antiseptic and cotton. Lauren shyly walked toward Jared's back and settled her hands on his shoulders. She eased the shirt off his back as he unbuttoned it and painfully pulled it away from the skin on his chest. The drying, congealed blood made the fabric stick, and the wounds reopened and bled profusely.

Gloria virtually threw the medicine at Jared when she returned. Pulling a gawking Rudy out of the room, she said, "Take your time. Maria and I will get dinner. Jared, you should lie down and rest. You've lost a lot of blood."

The door was drawn shut and the two were left alone.

Lauren dropped the bloodsoaked shirt on top of her own soiled blouse. Silently, together, they watched fabric settle against fabric.

Stirred into action, Lauren crossed to the wardrobe, intending to get another blouse and don it quickly when she turned her head slightly over her shoulder and asked, "Does it hurt too much?" She drew her breath in sharply when she saw the oozing puncture marks on Jared's chest and the rivulets of blood that ran through the thick mat of hair. "Oh, Jared," she cried, rushing toward him, suddenly not caring that she was clothed from the waist up in only her sheer, lace-edged chemise. She had taken Elena's advice and stopped wearing a corset every day.

"Here, sit down," she directed, taking his hand and leading him to the small vanity stool Gloria had provided for her. "Let me wash you off so we can see how bad it is."

"It's really nothing," he said again, and she wondered at the low, uneven sound of his voice. Was he in that much pain?

She poured fresh water into her washing bowl and dipped a clean towel into it. Her hand paused over his naked chest. She drew a long, shuddering breath and squeezed her eyes tightly shut. Then she touched him, dabbing at the hairmatted skin with the absorbent towel. "I don't want to hurt you," she murmured.

Jared gritted his teeth, not in pain from his chest wounds, but in agony from having her this close to him. The skin of her creamy white throat was scented with lavender and the fragrance intoxicated him, making him dizzy. Or was that lightheadedness caused by loss of blood? It didn't matter, the result was the same. He could feel her breath, like a cooling balm, fanning his face as she exhaled.

Of their own volition, his eyes lowered to her breasts. His jaw clenched reflexively when he saw them swaying slightly under the soft fabric. It took every ounce of willpower he could garner not to reach out and touch them, peel away the diaphanous cloth and learn the true color of her nipples, which were only vague shadows, elusive and bewitching.

His physical desire was becoming painfully manifested in the tight pants. He diverted his eyes to her hands, which dipped the towel into the washbasin and wrung out the excess water, staining the bowl with his blood. Think about the blood, he commanded himself. Think about the pain you felt when the wire slapped into you. Think about anything but—

"There, I think that will do for now," she was saying. Her voice was soft and low, caressing his ears. "Those punctures are deep. Didn't you have on that cowhide vest you usually wear?"

"No," he answered, glad they were talking. Anything helped. "I took it off because it got too hot. If I had left it on, I probably wouldn't have been cut."

"This is going to hurt, too," she apologized softly as she soaked a piece of cotton with the foul-smelling medicine out of the corked blue bottle.

"I'm tough," he said, and looked up at her with a mischievous smile.

Both were momentarily mesmerized by the other's nearness. Their eyes locked in a silent communication and the message transmitted struck each of them in the heart and was startling in its impact. Lauren tore her eyes away first.

"I'll try not to hurt you any more," she said as she delicately touched one of the wounds. He sharply sucked in air between his teeth, making a whistling sound. Beads of perspiration popped out of his forehead.

"I'm sorry," she said as she quickly dabbed the other punctures. Then, to his agonized delight, she began to blow on the stinging wounds. From the angle at which he looked down at her as she leaned over him, her eyes appeared to be closed. Violet shadows tinted her lids, and her black lashes contrasted with the delicate cheek on which they seemed to rest. He looked along the slender length of her nose to her mouth. The lips were moist, pink, slightly parted, and bow-shaped as her breath passed through them and teased his fevered skin. It stirred the hair on his chest and cooled the burning sensation from the punctures, but ignited a fire in another part of his body.

"Oh, God," he groaned deep in his throat. He stood up abruptly, upsetting the cushioned stool, and clasped her in his arms. He pulled her toward him with such force that the breath whooshed out of her body from the impact. The mouth that took hers was avaricious, parting her surprised lips with a thrusting tongue. Yet when the treasure had been discovered, that plundering invader became gentle and savored what it had found.

His hands slid along the bare skin of her arms, as smooth and cool as satin, and lifted them around his own neck. For a moment, they lay there, unpracticed and still. Jared's breath was expelled in a relieved sigh when he felt her hands lock behind his neck and her fingers plow through his thick, unruly hair. He brought her closer by applying pressure with the hand on the small of her back. His legs straddled hers, molding them into an ageless position as she curved up against him.

Lauren became aware of a foreign hardness spearing into her belly and was both alarmed and intrigued. Responsively she moved against the intruder and felt a melting warmth in the pit of her stomach that rendered the rest of her weak.

Jared's hand moved between their bodies and fear and desire combated in her brain when she realized the direction it was taking. She was wanting something she couldn't name. Did it have anything to do with his hand that hovered near her breast?

He wouldn't touch her there. Would he? No. She didn't want him to. Did she? Yes. Yes, please, she cried silently, not examining where such a wicked thought had originated, but dimly aware that it had something to do with the hard strength of his body pressed against the harmonizing softness of hers.

Jared's mind was reeling. No one felt like this. No mouth had ever tasted this good, he thought as he savored her lips. His hand slid over the soft mound of her breast and pressed gently. It was as firm and full in his palm as he remembered from their brief contact the day he had surprised her in her room. Under the steady, coaxing movements of his fingers, her nipple responded, becoming a firm bud of passion, eager to bloom.

In unguarded and introspective moments, Jared had hoped that somewhere there would be a woman like this. Uniquely his. Different from all others. Hadn't Ben told him—

Ben!

The name screamed through his mind, ricocheting off the walls of his brain with a cacophonous echo. Ben! Had his father held her this way? Had she responded in kind, murmuring that low purr deep in her throat?

He pushed her away from him with such force that she fell across the bed, looking up at him with rapidly blinking and uncomprehending eyes. Her hair tumbled across her shoulders and fell onto the creamy, rose-tipped breasts left partially bare from his caress.

He pointed an accusing finger at her. "I told you to stay away from me!" he shouted. His breathing was a harsh rasp.

"You're beautiful. I'll give you that. And you're softer and taste sweeter . . ." His voice dwindled to an anguished whisper. "God!" He slammed his fist into his palm. The pounding demand in his loins was unbearable. With her sprawled across the bed, looking up at him with such absolute innocence, his organ answered with an excruciating throbbing.

He ought to take her now, conquer her once and for all. He longed to flip up her skirts and see if her thighs were as smooth as he had imagined them to be. Then he would ram himself between them, thrusting until he found release from the desire that had stalked and haunted him for so long.

Had Lauren known his thoughts, she would have been terrified. Instead, as she lay on the bed, watching the misery radiate from every pore of his body, she knew only compassion for her husband. She sat up and timidly extended her hand toward him, an offer to soothe away the pain inflicted by whatever devil tormented him.

He recoiled. "I don't want any part of you," he declared unsteadily. "Do you understand?" He whirled away from her, flung open the wardrobe door, tore a shirt from the hanger, and stamped across the room to the door. It slammed with a resounding crash when he went out.

Lauren fell back and rolled over onto her stomach, burying her face into the mattress of the bed. She sobbed brokenly, her tears absorbed by the bedspread.

Was she crying because he had kissed her so insultingly or because she had responded so wantonly? Because he had stopped kissing her? Or because of his abusive words? Was her biggest fear that he would soon grow tired of the trap he was in, pay her the twenty thousand dollars, and send her packing?

The questions tumbled in her mind. And for none of them did she have an answer.

The next morning, Lauren and Maria were returning from a ride when they heard shouting from one of the corrals. The *vaqueros* were gathered around the fence.

Lauren spotted the tall, lean figure of her husband. She hadn't seen him since the day before when she had tended his wounds. After he had slammed out of the room, she had lain there for a while before restoring herself enough to go in to dinner. The Mendezes were at the table, patiently awaiting her.

Jared didn't appear. After everyone had started eating, Rudy quietly and inconsequentially stated that Jared was needed at the bunkhouse. No one commented, and Lauren had pretended indifference to his absence.

As they dismounted and tied their horses to the hitching rail in front of the house, Lauren said to Maria, "I think I'll stay out for a while." Her curiosity was piqued by the commotion at the corral.

"Very well," Maria said, smiling. "I enjoyed our ride. Ben and I used to ride early in the mornings. I've missed the exercise."

"We'll do it whenever you want." Lauren patted the older woman's arm before Maria climbed the steps to the front door.

Strolling in the direction of the corral, Lauren told herself she wasn't going there to see Jared. As she approached, twenty or so *vaqueros* were driving a bull into a chute.

"What's going on, Rudy?" she asked her brother-in-law as she reached the fence.

He jerked his head around to face her. "It's . . . uh . . . we're going to . . . uh . . . castrate this bull."

"Oh," Lauren replied, red-faced. She turned to go, but was blocked by the sudden appearance of her husband. He put out a restraining arm.

"Why don't you stay and watch? Your being so interested in Keypoint and the ranching business and all, I'm sure you'll enjoy it."

"Jared—" Rudy began.

"No, Rudy. Lauren is dying to learn everything she can about the cattle and the *vaqueros.*"

His words were biting and harsh. Lauren wished desperately that she had followed Maria into the house. Suddenly Jared gripped her shoulders and turned her toward the corral, holding her against him with deceptive gentleness. His hands felt like iron bands around her upper arms.

"Why . . . why do you do that to a particular bull?"

She hoped the question would have a calming effect on him. She really didn't care to know anything about the procedure and certainly didn't want to watch it.

Jared drawled around his cigar, "Well, there could be any number of reasons. Better beef. Or maybe he can't please the cows anymore. It may be only because he's a mean sonofabitch."

"Then maybe that's what we should do to you," Rudy said in a deadly voice. He wasn't about to let Lauren witness the bloody procedure.

Jared spun around and glared at his brother. He tossed his cigar away with a negligent flick of his wrist. "Is that a fact? Well, just who in hell is going to try?"

Without preamble, Rudy lowered his head and charged into Jared's stomach, knocking the younger man down.

Lauren gasped and cowered against the fence as they rolled in the dust, arms and legs thrashing, blood spurting from busted lips and smashed noses. They stood and circled each other warily, then Jared counterattacked and they crashed to the ground again. The *vaqueros* had stopped their work and stood in a wide circle around the fighting brothers. The only sounds were the thuds of landed blows and the grunts of pain and effort.

Gloria came running from the house, skirts flying. A few of the children stood in awe of the spectacle. They had seen their father and Uncle Jared fight before, but it was always playful wrestling. Their young, precocious minds perceived that this was different.

Gloria grabbed the revolver out of one of the cowboy's holsters before he had time to react. Since she knew that the first chamber was always empty, she cocked it twice and then fired into the air.

The two bodies on the ground fell apart and gasped for needed breath. When they had recovered somewhat, they sheepishly wiped away blood from their faces and bodies with dusty, tattered sleeves. The abrasions on Jared's chest had reopened and were staining his shirt with bright red blood. Embarrassed, they looked at each other.

Jared grinned at Rudy, grimacing with the pain of moving his swollen lips. "Just as I thought. You're getting soft and out of shape, old man."

"Like hell. A few more seconds and you would have been begging for mercy."

Jared rose painfully to his feet, swayed until he was not so dizzy, and then extended his hand to Rudy, who took it gratefully and pulled himself up. They supported each other for a few moments and then burst out laughing.

Everyone joined in their laughter, relieved that the fracas had been in fun after all. Only Lauren knew differently.

Without thinking of the consequences, only wanting to put distance between herself and these barbarians, she dashed toward Flame, who was still tied to the rail. Placing her booted foot in the stirrup, she vaulted into the saddle.

She kneed the mare into a gallop and raced past the others,

who were staring at her in temporary stupefaction. Her hat sailed off her head and landed to within inches of Jared's feet.

"What the—" he started.

"You'd better go after her, Jared," Rudy suggested tentatively. "She was upset."

"Why?" Gloria demanded.

"She . . . uh . . . Jared wanted her to watch a castration," Rudy said.

"My God! How could you even have considered such a thing?" Gloria asked angrily. "Go after her. Both of you."

The two men saw the wisdom of her words as they sought the horizon and barely made out the tiny figure of horse and rider as they went over the hill.

"Come on," Jared ordered tersely as he started in the direction of Charger at a lope. Rudy mounted his own horse and soon they were thundering across the plain in the direction Lauren had taken. Gloria muttered imprecations under her breath about the immature behavior of men as she gathered up her children and shooed them into the house.

Lauren's eyes were stinging from the cold wind, but the wind wasn't responsible for the tears that clouded her eyes and ran unchecked down her face. Why had she ever consented to marry Jared Lockett? He was a brute, the most callous, abusive man she had ever met.

Heedlessly, she raced over the rocky ground. Usually, even at a gallop, she handled the obliging mare with gentleness. Today she was too caught up in her own problems to see the prairie dog hole before they were upon it. Flame's hoof caught in the indentation and Lauren heard the fatal snap of the bone a fraction of a second before she went sailing through the air.

Chapter 14

She landed on her back. Lying still a moment, she tried to determine if she were injured. Deciding she wasn't, she sat up gingerly. Nothing appeared to be broken, though she was sure to have bruises the next day.

At Flame's piteous whinnying, Lauren stood up and scrambled toward the mare. Flame's eyes were gaping wide in fright and pain. Lauren saw the awkward angle at which her front leg lay.

"Oh, no," Lauren murmured as she fell to her knees and stroked the mare's neck. "I'm sorry, girl," she sobbed. "I didn't mean to punish you. I'll see that you're fixed. You'll get well. You must." Tears ran down her face and she wiped them away, creating a dirty smear across her cheek.

Dimly she heard approaching horses, but she didn't take her eyes from the mare, who still screamed in pain while Lauren spoke to her in low, soothing tones.

Jared and Rudy reined in and assessed the situation in an instant. Jared didn't want to acknowledge the relief he felt when he saw that Lauren was apparently intact. He and Rudy glanced at each other and nodded in unison. They dismounted together, as though choreographed.

Lauren looked up when she saw their boots close to Flame's head. Bounding to her feet, she ran to her husband, gripping his arms. Her eyes were full of pleading tears. "Jared, it was my fault. She stumbled in a gopher hole. She's . . . It will be all right . . . Help her . . . She'll get well."

With deadly calm, Jared ignored her eyes as his hand sought his pistol in its holster and withdrew it. "No," she rasped. "No!"

"Rudy," was all he said.

Lauren felt herself hauled out of the way as Jared aimed his pistol and fired. The mare's scream ceased immediately, only to be replaced by the echoing of the pistol shot. Then another scream bounced off the surrounding hills, but Lauren didn't recognize it as hers as she flew into Jared.

"You monster! You killed her. Beast! Animal! Killer! Killer, killer." Her small fists pummeled his chest and her feet kicked at his shins. She wanted only to hurt him, to avenge her own pain. He stood passively and took the punishment, not raising a hand to protect himself. "I hate you!" she screamed. "You're vile and savage. Cruel." Her voice began to lose some of its impetus, as did her pounding fists. "I hate you." The words were barely a whisper now and they came out as a sob. She dropped to the ground in a heap, like a wind-up toy which had suddenly wound down. Great racking sobs shook her shoulders.

Rudy squatted down on his haunches and laid a solicitous hand on her shoulder. "He did what he had to do, Lauren. It was hopeless. Jared only shot her to save her pain." His voice became more gentle. "I think you know that."

The crying stopped, but her head remained bowed. Rudy stood up. "I'll get her home," he said quietly. "You see to the horse." He had never felt so impotent in his life. He wasn't sure what had transpired between his brother and his new wife in the past few days. All he knew was that both were suffering, and he was powerless to do anything for either of them.

Jared raised his eyes, which had been riveted on the weeping figure at his feet, to his brother, and spoke resolutely. "No. She's my wife, and no man except me is going to see to her. If she goes home, she goes with me."

Rudy bit off an argument even as he watched Jared lean down and grasp Lauren under her arms, pulling her to her feet. She yanked her arms free and stared up at him defiantly. Then without a word, she walked toward Charger and pushed herself up into the saddle. She sat stiffly as Jared mounted behind her. Rudy watched them until they rode out of sight. He shook his head in puzzlement and despair for these two people whom he loved. Then he set about gathering brush for Flame's funeral pyre.

Lauren held herself rigid on the saddle in front of Jared, who seemed as determined not to touch her as she him. What he was feeling after her attack remained a mystery. When they finally cantered into the compound and up to the front of the ranch house, Jared spoke the first words that had passed between them.

"The honeymoon is over," he said sarcastically. "Congratulations, Lauren. No one has ever been able to come between my brother and me. Before you cause more friction, I want to leave here. In the morning. Be ready early."

"Very well," she replied as she slid to the ground and strode into the house without once glancing back at him.

After the misty-eyed goodbyes and warm farewell embraces from the Mendezes, it was hard for Lauren to return to Olivia's house in Coronado where she knew only disquietude. Had it not been for the arrival of Elena's baby girl, which a beaming Carlos had announced to her a few days ago, leaving Keypoint would have been unbearable.

Upon their unexpected arrival, Olivia pointedly didn't ask about their visit. Lauren now knew why she held such a great deal of contempt for the family who lived at the ranch. Carson Wells politely inquired into Lauren's well-being on their first night back. He was, it now seemed, a regular at dinner.

Jared was defensively sullen and drank steadily throughout the meal. Olivia heaped acclaim on the Vandivers for being successful in securing a trunk of the railroad to Coronado. The date for the groundbreaking was to be announced soon.

"With any kind of luck with the weather, labor, and so on, we should have a railroad by this time next year."

"Swell," Jared mumbled into his glass.

"I should think that would make you happy," Olivia snapped at him.

He pushed his chair back and rose unsteadily to his feet. "I'll tell you what makes me *unhappy*. Those damn Vandivers were snooping around Keypoint the other day. I wasn't there or they wouldn't have gotten anywhere near it. I want them restricted to the area designated for the power plant. Is that clear?" His face was flushed and his amber eyes glowed like animal eyes in the dark.

"Yes, Jared, I'll mention that to them. I'm sure they'll comply," Olivia mollified him.

He only snorted as he refilled his glass, sloshing whiskey over his unsteady hand.

The only joy in the house for Lauren was Elena's baby. Her introduction to Isabela had been made as the baby sucked greedily at her mother's milk-laden breast. Lauren was shocked at Elena's immodesty as she bared her breast, but the new mother wasn't at all embarrassed. Rosa looked on with grandmotherly pride. Isabela's hair was coal-black and her black eyes were lightly fringed with dark lashes.

The baby stayed in the small room off the kitchen that Rosa shared with Elena. When Elena was busy somewhere in the house, Rosa was nearby to answer the demanding cries of her granddaughter. As long as Olivia wasn't disturbed, everything would be fine.

Lauren hated for Carlos to be separated from his family. She intended to talk to Jared about them living together at Keypoint. Surely with another Mendez baby coming, Gloria could use Elena's help.

Lauren was amazed that Elena recovered from her childbirthing so quickly. The new mothers whom she had attended while living in the parsonage had taken weeks to get out of bed, but Elena resumed her duties in the house right away, pausing periodically and only long enough to feed Isabela.

So it was a matter of deep concern to Lauren when she found Elena leaning against the bannister one afternoon, unable to continue upstairs.

"Elena, what's wrong?" she cried as she rushed toward the girl and lent her support.

"I'm just tired, I think." Elena's voice contained none of its usual animation.

"Why don't you go lie down for a while? I'll explain to Olivia."

She took the girl's elbow and steered her toward her room. Her alarm increased even more when Elena didn't argue with her as she was wont to do. Without protest, she lay on her bed and Lauren covered her with a light blanket. The baby was sleeping quietly across the room in her crib. Lauren left them, hoping that Rosa would soon return from her marketing.

After dinner, Lauren surreptitiously slipped into the kitchen while Olivia and Jared discussed some banking business. Rosa was sitting at the work table, her fingers sifting through the beads of her rosary. When the door closed softly behind Lauren, Rosa opened her eyes. "Rosa? What's wrong?" she asked quickly. "Is it Elena?"

The woman clasped large hands over her broad cheeks and bobbed her head up and down in affirmation. Tears pooled in her chocolate eyes.

"*Está enferma*. She has the fever bad."

Lauren tiptoed into the darkened room and knelt down to feel

Elena's forehead. It was burning. Rosa had undressed her and the young woman lay under the blanket clad only in her thin chemise. Lauren turned up the gas light nearest the bed and immediately saw the rash. Red eruptions covered Elena's throat and chest. Lauren unbuttoned her chemise, but knew before she looked that the rash extended down Elena's torso. With an aching heart, she returned to the kitchen.

"Rosa," Lauren said calmly, swallowing the bile that rose in her throat, "did Elena vomit last night or this morning? Did she complain of being chilled?"

"*Sí, señora,*" Rosa answered dismally. The woman's ravaged face confirmed Lauren's suspicions. Rosa knew the gravity of her daughter's illness.

"Her throat is sore?" Rosa only nodded.

Lauren closed her eyes briefly and prayed for strength. The next several days would be a trial for them all. The task facing her was unpleasant, but she would do it. These people were her friends and they needed her. If she didn't help them, no one would.

Her voice showed no trace of the panic she felt as she began issuing instructions. "Brew some tea and keep the kettle on at all times. Move the baby out of that room at once and don't let anyone else near it. Scald all of the kitchen utensils and don't go into the sickroom again. Where has Elena been today?"

"Nowhere, *señora.* She feels too bad to do much. She was in Pueblo a few days ago showing off Isabela." Rosa's voice wavered as she asked, "She has the scarlet fever, *señora?*"

"Yes, she does." Lauren remained calm despite the turbulence inside her as she went again into the dim room.

Scarlet fever. Isabela. She hated to see. Please, God, no. The baby had been sleeping peacefully all day. Unusual. Lauren forced herself to go to the crib. She pulled up the tiny sacque and cried out in anguish as she saw the rapidly rising and falling chest covered with the telltale rash.

"*Madre de Dios,*" Rosa murmured behind her.

"Has the fever been going around in Pueblo?" Lauren asked.

"*Sí, señora.* Many have been sick. Elena didn't think she would catch it. No one in the family had it when she visited."

"Go do what I told you to, Rosa. I'll stay here with her and the baby."

When the woman had retreated to the kitchen to carry out her instructions, Lauren sat down on the edge of the bed and took

Elena's hand. The girl's eyes fluttered open and she offered a weak smile. When she tried to speak, she could only croak.

"Don't try to talk, Elena, I'm here to make you feel better." Lauren pushed back a few strands of lank hair resting on fevered temples.

"Baby?" Elena asked.

"The baby is . . . sleeping. Everything will be all right. You go back to sleep. I'll give you some tea when it's made." Elena closed her eyes apathetically and her breathing was soon even if somewhat shallow.

Lauren left the room, went through the kitchen, and walked in slow, measured steps into the parlor where Olivia and Carson were playing cards. Jared was slumped in a chair, a whiskey decanter near his hand.

Not quite believing her temerity, she asked for their attention, and when the three had turned startled eyes toward her, she told them about Elena and the baby.

"You can't be serious!" Olivia exploded when Lauren made clear her intention to nurse them.

"I'm quite serious, Olivia," she said levelly. "They need constant care and, since I have no other responsibilities, I'm the one to do it. I only came to tell you that you might want to have food catered in, as the kitchen is so close to the sickroom. And keep everyone out of the house. Go nowhere that isn't absolutely necessary. We should quarantine ourselves for the sake of others."

She spoke with such authority that the other three were momentarily stilled. But the respite was brief. Olivia unleashed her fury in full force.

"If you think I'm going to let a Mexican girl and her brat lie sick and possibly die in my house, contaminating the rest of us, you are very much mistaken. Get Pepe to remove them at once, Jared. Let them take care of their own."

Lauren turned to Jared, who had sobered considerably and was watching her closely through clear eyes. "Jared, if they go, I do, too. Would you have it said that Jared Lockett banished his wife to Pueblo?" she challenged.

He glanced toward his mother and said uneasily, "Lauren, those people are accustomed to epidemics. They die by the hundreds in San Antonio every few years from yellow fever. Pueblo doesn't have proper sanitation to protect them from these diseases, and once one gets started, it runs rampant."

"Then someone who has a lot of money and power should improve their sanitation system, shouldn't he?" Her voice was an accusation. She wondered why these Locketts had ever intimidated her. Right now, she felt very strong.

Jared tried another tack. "It's highly contagious, Lauren. Did you think of that? What's to prevent you from catching it?"

She looked at him steadily. "I had it. When I was ten years old. I was ignored by a father terrified of disease and by a house-keeper angry with me for causing her so much extra work. It's a wonder that I lived. I have not forgotten the misery and fear. I won't let Elena suffer that way. Now am I to nurse her here or somewhere else?"

Olivia opened her mouth to speak, but Jared ordered, "Shut up, Mother." His eyes never left Lauren's face. They stared at each other long and hard. Her hand found its way to his arm and rested there as she gazed up at him suppliantly.

"All right," he said finally. "Is there anything I can do?"

"No. Stay away from the rooms in the back of the house. I'll have Rosa scrub everything with disinfectant as soon as possible. Thank you." It was only when she tried to pull away that either of them became aware of his strong fingers trapping hers against his arm. Slowly, regretfully, they were released.

She didn't look at Olivia or Carson as she moved out of the parlor. At the portiere, she turned and looked back at her husband. "I don't think the baby will live." He saw tears shining in the luminous eyes.

The days and nights blended together in a montage of pain, suffering, exhaustion, and despair. Isabela died the afternoon of the second day. Lauren tried valiantly to spoon sweetened tea through the tiny lips, but the swollen, red tongue and obstructed throat strangled on it, and the baby couldn't get the fluids essential for her life.

Lauren watched the tiny chest as it shuddered one final time and, without so much as a cry, Isabela ended her short sojourn on earth. Lauren wanted to grieve the loss, but she needed to focus her attention on saving Elena.

Lauren spooned gallons of tea into her patient despite Elena's unwillingness to accept it. Her tongue was covered with painful red blisters that made it look like a strawberry. Her fever rose drastically each night. Rosa and Lauren would strip her and bathe her body with cool water. They didn't tell her about Isabela, and she was too delirious to ask.

Pepe made a tiny coffin, and the infant's grandmother laid her out for burial. Carlos was summoned, but he remained in the stables in compliance with Lauren's orders. It was not only for his protection, but also for those she loved at Keypoint. Pepe ran messages back and forth to the anxious young man who mourned the death of his daughter and feared for the life of his wife.

Lauren never left the sickroom. She sent Rosa to her room for fresh clothing, but barely had time to change into it during her vigil over the sufferer. At night, after they managed to keep Elena's fever from rising further, she would sleep fitfully in a chair near the bed. She prayed constantly for the life of her friend and for continued strength. She prayed, too, that Jared would not contract the disease. The words had formed on her lips, coming straight from her soul before she gave them conscious thought.

The fever literally burned the skin off of Elena's palms and fingers and the soles of her feet. While the girl slept, Lauren gently peeled it away so Elena would not be frightened if she should see the dead tissue hanging like cobwebs from her hands.

Five days after Lauren had gone into the stifling room, she woke from a cramped position in the chair to hear regular breathing instead of the labored, shallow respiration she had listened to for long days and nights. She hurried to Elena's bed and put her hand on a cool forehead. Forcing apart the relaxed lips, she saw that the tongue was less swollen and the blisters had all but disappeared. The rash was fading. She could have laughed aloud. Instead, she sank back into the chair and offered a prayer of thanksgiving.

The next morning, when she told Rosa the news, the old woman wept openly. For the rest of that day, they allowed Elena to sleep a healing sleep. They changed her linens and, at noon, spoonfed her some beef broth until she slipped once again into slumber. Lauren stayed with her to make sure the fever wasn't going to return.

She was exhausted but happy and relieved when she stumbled into the kitchen late that evening. She was surprised to find Jared standing at the back door, staring out over the yard through the window. Rosa had informed him of Elena's recovery earlier.

He turned when he heard her enter. "Lauren, this has gone on long enough," he said without preamble. "I will not let you quarantine yourself in that room one more minute without some rest."

"I'm fine, really I am," Lauren sighed. "I don't think Elena needs me anymore, though. Only plenty of liquids and sleep. I'll let Carlos see her in the morning."

"Si, señora." Rosa came to Lauren and took both of her hands in hers, kissing them in turn. "Señor Jared, she is an angel."

"Yeah, she's an angel all right, but she looks like hell right now," he said grimly.

Through her fatigue-muddled mind Lauren noted absently that he didn't look all that wonderful himself. Stubble covered his chin and upper lip. His cheeks were gaunt and sunken under red-rimmed eyes.

Rosa could have told her that for days he had paced, cursed, threatened, and pleaded. He was like a wild man in his worry. His only source of nourishment was a shot of whiskey taken at regular intervals.

Lauren tried to focus her eyes, but images began to blur, recede infinitesimally, then loom hugely. The kitchen was spinning crazily. "Jared—" she cried hoarsely before she collapsed into the strong arms reaching out for her.

"She's unconscious," he said. "And hungry, from the feel of her. I'll bet she's lost ten pounds. First thing in the morning, Rosa, fix her a big breakfast and serve it to her in her room. Stay with her until she eats every bite. I think she needs rest first."

He swept the inert figure into his arms and carried her upstairs to her room, kicking the door shut behind him. He stood for a moment, allowing his eyes to grow accustomed to the darkness, then moved toward the bed. There was just enough light coming in through the windows for him to see without lighting the lamp.

Lauren murmured unintelligibly as he put her feet back on the floor, supporting her with his body. She leaned heavily against him and he muttered imprecations at her foolishness for totally exhausting herself like this. He tried to keep his mind off the body pressed close to his. How could she stay in a sickroom for a week and come out smelling like lavender? He didn't know that Lauren had asked Rosa to fetch a bottle of cologne from her room which she added to the water she washed with each day.

Well, I can't just dump her on the bed, Jared reasoned. With trembling fingers, he began unfastening the buttons on the back of her shirtwaist. Her head lolled against his chest. It took a long time for him to get to the last button because he used only one hand, supporting her with the other. His trembling fingers lacked their usual dexterity.

He pulled the blouse out of the waistband of her skirt and then began undoing the fastener. He untied the ribbons of several petticoats, cursing as they knotted in his fingers. Why do women wear so damned many clothes anyway? he thought. Finally he was able to push the skirt and petticoats down over her hips and they fell to the floor in a ruffled froth at her ankles.

He paused, drawing deep breaths in an effort to supply oxygen to his brain, which was whirling like a maelstrom. If she woke up now, he thought ruefully, she would probably scream the house down.

With meticulous care, he supported her against one of his arms and, leaning her back, slowly pulled the shirtwaist from her shoulders and slid the sleeves down her arms.

It was off. She still slept. He was perspiring and trembling. He pressed her against him, postponing the moment when he would look at her, savoring the anticipation.

He reached up and began hunting for the pins that held her hair, removing them gently as he found them among the thick tresses. Her hair tumbled down her back and over her shoulders, spilling into his hands. Then, as he had wanted to do ever since he had first seen her, he ran his hands through the black silk, caressing each strand, rubbing the smooth curls between his fingers, delighting in the feel of them the way a miser loves the feel of gold. He buried his face in her hair and whispered accolades to its glory.

Jared lowered her gently onto the bed, slipping the skirt and petticoats from around her ankles. She lay on the pillow and sighed contentedly, her hair fanning out behind her on the snowy linen.

Jared sat on the side of the bed, easing himself down in order not to wake her. God! She was exquisite. Even the lines of fatigue around her mouth and the hollows in her cheeks added to her beauty. Long black lashes rested on alabaster cheeks. He followed the column of her neck to the base of her throat, where he saw the flutter of her pulse. Her shoulders were white and sloped into a flawless bosom.

He hesitated, but his fingers moved of their own volition and reached out to the top of her camisole. He untied the blue satin ribbon that was threaded through the eyelet lace and slowly, leisurely unbuttoned the first few buttons. Again he wanted to prolong the anticipation.

His eyes traveled down to her waist, which was wasp-thin, then to the slight flair of her hips. He usually preferred more voluptuous curves, but she was perfectly proportioned, he noticed as he took in the long, slender thighs and shapely calves.

Damn! He had forgotten the shoes. The tedious buttons were almost impossible to handle in the dark, but he finally succeeded in undoing them all.

When he had slipped her shoes off silk-encased feet, he returned his gaze to her face as his fingers slowly parted the camisole. She didn't stir. His eyes wandered aimlessly, until he rewarded his patience and looked down at her.

He had imagined how she would look, but the fantasies were inadequate and he wasn't prepared for the vision that greeted his eyes. Two perfectly shaped breasts, round, high, and firm, were displayed. Her skin was as creamy and white as a magnolia blossom. The nipples that crowned each soft mound were virginally pink. Botticelli would have adored her. Her ethereal beauty was definitely *quattrocento*. Rosa wasn't far from wrong. In her naked loveliness, she appeared to be an angel.

But Jared was mortal, and he wanted her as he had never wanted a woman before. He carefully lowered his head and kissed the pulse in her throat. Then his lips traveled with a blissful laziness over her breasts, nibbling and licking lightly so she wouldn't ever know that he had worshiped at this temple of her body. She was forbidden to him. It was a self-imposed denial, but that made it even more binding.

But now, now . . .

He raised his head and touched one rosy nipple. Gently rolling it between his fingers, he watched in fascination as it responded to his touch and became pointed and inviting. Unable to resist, his mouth opened around it. It melted against his tongue like a piece of sugar candy, and tasted even sweeter.

His eyes lifted once again to the face that lay in peaceful repose in the cape of black hair. "Lauren, forgive me," he whispered as he lowered his mouth once again.

When Lauren awakened not long before noon, she couldn't remember the events of the past few days or why she was sleeping so late and wearing her underwear and stockings. She stretched cramped muscles as she pieced together the fragments flashing through her memory.

Elena! She recalled the girl's illness and jumped out of bed, throwing back the single blanket that covered her. Why was she sleeping on top of the bedspread? Disoriented, she stood in the middle of her room, her hands on either side of her head, trying to banish the yellow spots that danced against the black curtain which seemed to have fallen over her eyes. She reeled dizzily. She had stood up too fast for the blood to flow into her head. Lack of proper food for the past six days had rendered her weak.

Rosa bustled in as Lauren was feeling her way back to the edge of the bed.

"Señora Lauren, you are awake! You have been sleeping like a baby."

"How is Elena?" she asked quickly. The radiant look on Rosa's face dispelled any fears.

"She is weak and sleepy, but she ate some toast this morning and talked to Carlos." The happy features drooped a little. "We had to tell her about the *niña,* and she is very sad. But seeing Carlos made her feel better. She is grateful to you *señora.* I thank you, too." Her lip began to tremble.

"I'm glad I could help Elena. I only wish we could have saved the baby, though after the high fever, Isabela might never have been completely healthy."

"*Sí,* her little soul is in heaven and she is well now. If I know Elena and Carlos, they will make another *niño* soon." She grinned broadly. "I brought your breakfast." She stepped out to the hall and retrieved a tray she had left on a hall table. The delicious aromas emanating from the dishes made Lauren's mouth water. When had she last eaten a complete meal?

"Señor Jared told me to see that you stayed in bed and ate everything on the tray."

"Is he . . . I mean, are the rest of the family healthy? I haven't seen them for almost a week."

"You saw Señor Jared last night, *señora.* Don't you remember? You fainted in the kitchen. He brought you up to bed. Carried you in his arms."

The room was spinning again and in her ears was a great roaring. She sipped the scalding tea and tried to keep her hand from shaking as she placed the cup back on the saucer.

"No . . . no, I . . . uh . . . don't remember that. I know I was very tired."

"He was angry I think for you to be so tired. You would like a bath, *señora, sí?*" Without waiting for an answer, Rosa waddled into the bathroom, gathering up the discarded clothes lying on the floor beside the bed.

Her clothes! Jared had put her to bed. Jared had undressed her!

She had dreamed of him during her deep sleep. She recalled the dreams vividly now. Jared was leaning over her and looking at her tenderly. His head was resting against her flesh. If only her arms hadn't been so heavy, she could have reached up and run her fingers through the sun-bleached hair that tickled her throat. In one dream, Jared was whispering Spanish words against her ear. In another, he had been doing something with his mouth that spread a delicious warmth through her.

She finished eating slowly, distracted by the memory of her disturbing dreams. When she began undressing, she noticed the ribbon from her camisole was missing. She would have to tell Rosa to be more careful when laundering her underwear.

She stepped into the bathtub and welcomed the soothing warmth of the water. It had been days since she had enjoyed the luxury of a bath. Cupping her hands and ladling a handful of suds over herself, she was shocked when the soapy water caused a stinging sensation on her flesh. Involuntarily she gasped. Examining herself self-consciously, she noticed her nipples were slightly sore, though when she touched them, they tingled and a thrilling shiver coursed through her body. Her breasts were chafed, as if abraded by something scratchy. Whatever could have—

Her eyes dilated with the horror of the thought. Trembling fingers crammed against tight, compressed lips gone white with shock.

No! No! That could not be. Her dreams and this actuality had nothing to do with each other. It was unthinkable. Still, she quaked at the possibility. Jared, unshaven, seeing her, touching her, kissing...

Hastily she got out of the tub, dried quickly, and wrapped a robe around her before returning to the bedroom. "Where is Jared?" she asked Rosa timidly as she prepared to go downstairs and visit Elena. She wanted to avoid him. Meeting him face to face with her speculations vividly intact would be too humiliating.

"He went to Austin this morning. He say he may be gone several weeks. Something to do with business. He left a package for you." She bustled out the door and returned immediately with a small box. "He say you need this next time you go to Keypoint."

Lauren untied the ribbon around the box, lifted the lid, and saw a blue silk scarf nestled in the tissue paper. A bandana. He had remembered that she needed one. Tears misted her eyes, but aware of Rosa's keen perception, she shoved the scarf into one of her lingerie drawers with feigned indifference.

"I must remember to thank him when he comes home." She walked out her door leaving Rosa shaking her head, baffled and disgusted.

Chapter 15

"Have you heard from Jared, Olivia?" Carson asked one night at dinner. "Seems he's been in Austin an uncommon length of time."

"Come, Carson," Olivia said with a laugh, "you know why Jared is 'detained' in Austin. I'm amazed that he abstained as long as he did. Having a wife of convenience drives a man to find some release from his physical needs, doesn't it, Lauren?"

Lauren's fork clattered to her plate. How dare the woman be so blatantly crude! "Since it's Jared's 'physical needs' you're referring to, you should save that question for him," she retorted angrily. But underlying her anger was heartsickness. Her mother-in-law was most probably right. Why else would Jared extend his stay in Austin? She hadn't guessed she could miss him so much. The longer he was gone, the more the tension mounted in the house.

The daily routine in Coronado was different from that at Keypoint, but was routine nonetheless. Elena gained strength each day. If the weather permitted, she would walk with Lauren in the gardens, which boasted only a few chrysanthemum blooms. The wind, when it whistled in unpredictably from the north, was biting and bitter, and there were a few days in early November when it rained incessantly and Lauren thought she would go mad at the tedium of her life in the large house.

She longed for the hectic days at Keypoint with Rudy and Gloria, their loving banter, and the children with their pranks. She missed her quiet talks with Maria, too. A few months ago, Lauren would have been scandalized by a woman living with someone else's husband, but she now condoned Maria's life with Ben. Their love had been pure. Lauren's uncharacteristic broadmindedness was due in part to her knowledge of the kind of life Ben must have had with Olivia.

Olivia went to the bank most days, and when she stayed at home, Carson telephoned often from his office. He was always at the house for dinner, and Lauren was grateful for his kindly presence. She could not have borne being alone with Olivia. The woman looked at her with such hostility that it startled Lauren each time she caught Olivia's emerald glare on her.

Carson continued to be obsequious to Olivia. They talked constantly about the railroad and the plans for the power plant. Apparently any hesitation Olivia had once had about forming an alliance with the Vandivers no longer existed. She commended their decisiveness and ability to manipulate others to achieve their goals. Olivia mentioned Kurt often, and always with a sly look in Lauren's direction, which made her feel distinctly uncomfortable.

One evening at dinner, Olivia observed her daughter-in-law balefully through a forest of lowered lashes. She would never forgive her for convincing Jared to allow that sick Mexican and her baby to remain under her roof. The fact that Lauren gave shelter to an ailing Mexican was bad enough, but her real transgression was that she had triumphed over Olivia in an argument with Jared. More threatening than that, she had forced Jared to make a decision. That could be dangerous to Olivia's plans. If Lauren gained any control over him, it could jeopardize everything.

Olivia also resented that, for appearance's sake, she had to act the doting mother-in-law. God! Friends pressed her for news of approaching grandchildren. They simpered over their teacups about how handsome Jared and Lauren looked together, and ladies coming into the bank stopped to remark how wonderful it was that Jared, after having waited so long, had finally found the perfect mate. Olivia bore it all with a stiff smile and the proper responses. She dutifully attended church with Lauren every Sunday. The young woman insisted on going, and Olivia knew it would never do for Jared's wife to be seen there alone.

It was evident that Lauren had formed quite an attachment to the family at Keypoint. Whenever Carson drew her into conversation, she ended up relating some anecdote that had happened at the ranch. She never mentioned names, though Olivia knew each character in these narratives intimately. When you hate someone for as long as she had hated Maria Mendez, her son, and his brood, you come to know them quite well. She had made it an obsession to learn all she could about them.

Unable to punish the Mendezes just yet for the humiliation they had caused her, she found a perfect scapegoat in Lauren. She had been raised to honor her elders, to respect family, and to bear persecution with forebearance and forgiveness.

Olivia was quite sure that the marriage between Jared and Lauren had not been consummated, though she was well aware of her son's strong sexual appetite. Her lips tightened into a bitter line when she equated it with her late husband's.

She was certain Jared's fierce pride would have kept him from loving any woman chosen for him by his father. Still, the girl had a look, a way about her that Olivia knew was irresistible to men. That gentleness, that vulnerability shook them to their very core. She herself had never had that quality, and she loathed it in other women.

In every glance, gesture, and spoken word, Olivia tormented Lauren. She must keep Jared and his wife at odds with each other. To think that they might reverse her whole scheme and form a lasting affection was an abhorrent possibility.

It wasn't jealousy, Olivia assured herself. Jealousy was such a petty emotion, and far beneath her dignity. All she demanded in any relationship was absolute loyalty. Ben had betrayed her love with disloyalty. Olivia was determined that Jared would not.

"How is Elena, Lauren? All well by now, I hope." Dinner was over and Carson had followed the ladies into the parlor for coffee. Lauren knew that Olivia's question didn't stem from concern. It was merely to remind her again that she had gone against Olivia's commands.

"Yes, she's recovered. The death of her baby was a blow she'll not soon get over, but that is to be expected."

"Most unfortunate that the child couldn't live, Lauren. You did a miraculous job of pulling the young woman out of it."

"Thank you, Carson, but I had self-interested motives. Scarlet fever nearly cost me my life. This was my only opportunity to fight back."

"It's a shame those Mexicans in Pueblo can't keep their community clean and sanitary." Olivia's face was ugly.

"I'm sure they do their best. I don't think they choose for their children to die," Lauren said quietly but with conviction.

"Nonsense. You haven't been here long enough to know how dirty those people are. They're vile."

"How can you say that Rosa is vile and then eat the meals she prepares? She's the cleanest person I've ever met," Lauren said heatedly.

Olivia tossed her head in anger. Her green eyes were brilliant and her slender fingers gripped the arms of the chair like talons. "It won't be long until we will be able to relieve some of their worries in Pueblo. I can't wait—"

"Olivia!" Carson interrupted abruptly. "I don't think we should discuss this any further. I can see that it upsets you." He gave her a telling look.

Olivia drew herself up sharply, then let her breath out slowly. She had almost made a blunder and was grateful that she had been stopped. "You are quite right, Carson, it does upset me. More coffee?"

Lauren excused herself and went upstairs. Unable to stop herself, she paused outside the door of Jared's room, staring at it intently. What did she expect to see? Would the door dissolve and reveal him sitting in a chair smoking one of his inevitable cheroots? Would he materialize before her as he did in her dreams night after night?

No. He wasn't here. He was in Austin on "business." Surmising what kind of business he was involved in brought a heavy pain to her heart. Was he with another woman? Women? Why should she care? Yet she did.

Her hand went instinctively to the watch pinned on her breast. Without conscious thought, her fingers lowered and lightly brushed her nipple through the soft cotton of her blouse. Her whole body flushed hotly and she caught her breath at the sensations that assailed her.

Did you really touch me here, Jared? she asked the darkness. She didn't want to know, didn't want to care, but couldn't refrain from adding, What did you think of me?

Anguish and loneliness accompanied her into her room.

Jared came home the day before Thanksgiving. Lauren was in her room reading. Her heart leaped in her chest when she heard the familiar clump of boots and the ring of spurs in the hallway. She gripped the book tightly and held it against her. The door to his room opened and closed quietly, and she heard the thump of valises on the floor. He moved around the room a while, then the bed creaked as his weight was lowered onto it. All became quiet.

Try as she might, Lauren couldn't regain her interest in the book.

She took a great deal of care in dressing for dinner, donning a flattering dress and soft kid slippers. Her hair had been washed and brushed. She had a wild impulse to leave it hanging loose but, of course, that would be unseemly. Instead, she let Elena arrange it in a glossy pompador.

She heard Jared leave his room and go downstairs, and followed a few minutes later. She was incredibly nervous. How could she face him after he had taken her to her room, undressed her, and put her to bed? And if he had . . .

She walked into the parlor and her heart turned over when she saw his tall, broad back leaning over the sideboard as he poured a drink.

"Lauren, you make the evening glow. How are you, my dear?" Carson came to her and kissed her cheek.

She watched Jared over Carson's shoulder. His back stiffened and he took a long gulp of whiskey before he turned around. He is so handsome, she thought mournfully. She could bear his indifference and cruelty, his desertion, if he were ugly or repellent to her. But from the first she had felt a strange chemical attraction to this man.

He met her eyes over Carson's pudgy form and lifted his glass in a mocking salute.

"Jared, would you pour Lauren a sherry, please, and I'll have another." Lauren noticed that Olivia's eyes were especially brilliant. The news that Jared had brought from Austin must have pleased her.

"I'm so glad the Vandivers are coming for Thanksgiving tomorrow. Thank you for delivering my invitation, Jared." Olivia watched closely as Jared handed Lauren her glass of sherry.

"You're welcome," he replied. He looked down at Lauren from his towering height as she took the drink. Their fingers touched briefly. The contact was electrifying and she thought she heard his breath rush past his teeth in a soft gasp. But as her eyes traveled up the long body to meet his glowing eyes, she saw them frost over immediately.

"I knew Lauren would want to see Kurt again. It's been such a long time." The slurring words were said low and for her hearing only. Why was he doing this again? He was as arrogant and hateful as the first night she had seen him in this room.

All her excitement at seeing him drained away as dinner dragged on interminably. Jared drank more than he ate. What had happened to the healthy appetite that couldn't be appeased at Keypoint? Maria and Gloria were always teasing him about his hollow leg.

159

He was sullen and erratic. One minute he was strenuously criticizing the Railroad Commission and their ineptitude, and the next minute, he was muttering into his glass.

Lauren went into the library to read by the fire after dinner. She had stood all the tension she could in one evening. The others retired to the office to discuss the results of Jared's trip to the capital.

Hours later, Lauren was still in the library, seated in an overstuffed chair with her shoes lying on the hearth and her feet curled up under her legs.

She didn't know how long he had been there before she noticed Jared standing in the doorway. When she looked up at him, he stumbled wearily into the room and collapsed into the twin chair beside hers. His head fell back against the plump cushions and he closed his eyes. Lauren sat still. As the minutes ticked by, she thought that he must have fallen asleep, but eventually he opened his eyes, though he didn't move his head or body.

"It's awfully late, Lauren. Why are you still up?" He sounded exhausted.

"I got absorbed in my book. Sometimes I can read well into the night if a book is particularly interesting." *Or if I can't get you off my mind*, she added to herself.

She looked like a vision in the firelight. Its shimmer caught on the black hair and seemed to ignite each strand. Her dress was a soft rose wool with pearl buttons at the neck. With the firelight, it enhanced the enticing blush on her cheeks, which he knew were velvet-soft. Behind her eyeglasses, her eyes were wide and deep and clear.

Jared cleared his throat, rousing himself from his perusal. "What do you read? You are quite a bookworm, you know," he teased softly.

"Everything," she said lightly, indulging his need for small talk. "Books were my best friends when I was growing up. Other children didn't want to play with the minister's daughter. It made them uncomfortable, you see. My mother died when I was three." He noticed her reach up and touch her watch. "So my friends were the characters I found in print. I read the classics, history, and philosophy. But for fun, I like Dickens, the Brontës, and Jane Austen."

His eyes were closed again and it surprised her when he picked up the conversation. "When I was a boy, I was enthralled with

Poe. Ben used to rile me about reading such 'rubbish,' as he called it. 'If you want to hear ghost stories, have Thorn tell you some.' Thorn's were pretty good, too." He laughed. "He used to raise the hair on my neck telling me about Indian legends, taboos, and secret rites." He stared reflectively into the fire, the flames dancing in his amber eyes. Putting his thumb and middle finger against his lids, he rubbed them in fatigue. "I don't have time to read anymore."

She hesitated only a moment before asking gently, "Was your trip a taxing one?"

He sighed heavily. "Yes. Some of the men in public office are frighteningly stupid. I'm sick to death of having to pander to them. I want . . ."

When he didn't continue, she urged him softly. "Yes. You want . . . ?"

It was the only prodding he needed to voice his innermost thoughts. "I want the railroad because it's the only way we can operate a successful, profitable ranch in the twentieth century. Ben wanted it so bad he could taste it, but I hate having to go through so much red tape and catering to idiots in order to get it." He leaned forward and clasped his hands between his knees.

Lauren remained quiet. This was a time for listening.

"I want to live on Keypoint and ride the fences like any other *vaquero* and let someone else do all of this politicking."

Lauren swallowed her caution, stood, and went to him timorously. She placed her hands lightly on his shoulders and massaged the knotted, tense muscles. "Maybe when the railroad is finished, you can do that, Jared. I hope so, for your sake."

He leaned back in the chair again, noticeably relaxing under the magic touch of her fingers. After a few moments, she said, "Thank you for the scarf. It's lovely."

He looked up at her standing behind him. Hie eyes were tired and bloodshot, but he read the encouragement and compassion in hers as she smiled down at him. He covered one small hand on his shoulder with his, then grasped it and squeezed tightly. He brought it up to his face and pressed her palm against his hard cheek.

"Your hands are beautiful, Lauren. I noticed—" He broke off, feeling that he was probably making a fool of himself, but then went on, "I noticed them that first night we were at dinner together." His fingers smoothed down her slender counterparts.

"If they are, it's from hours at the piano, I suppose. My father once told me my hands were like my mother's. She played, too."

"Do you miss it?"

"Yes," she admitted readily. "I suppose my music is for me what riding the line is for you."

He studied the hand in his with the appreciation of an art connoisseur for a masterpiece. Bringing it back to his mouth, his tongue brushed each fingertip. Lauren's eyes closed.

His lips moved to her wrist, and when her ruffled cuff obstructed him, his thumb slipped between the buttons and buttonholes and laid bare her translucent skin.

"You're so soft," he murmured as his lips caressed her wrist. "You make everything seem so uncomplicated, so . . ." His words trailed off as he buried his lips in the soft cushion of her palm. Her heart fluttered erratically when she felt the moist warmth of his tongue sliding sensuously over her flesh.

He raised his hand and trailed a finger down her cheek as his eyes traveled her face beseechingly. "Lauren, I—"

"Jared." Whatever he was going to say was arrested by Olivia's imperious interruption. "Carson is waiting to go over that last group of figures before we call it a night. Lauren, dear, there's no need for you to wait up."

Jared's mouth tensed into a thin, hard line and the muscles of his face became rigid as he pushed himself out of the chair and strode from the room.

Lauren retrieved her shoes and her book and, after turning off the lamp, faced the door. Olivia's tall figure was still silhouetted in the doorway. As Lauren came closer, she saw that one of Olivia's black eyebrows was raised speculatively.

"Goodnight, Lauren," she said coldly.

"Goodnight." As she mounted the stairs, Lauren could feel her mother-in-law's piercing eyes boring into her back.

Lauren went down to the kitchen the following morning to ask if she could help Rosa with her preparations for the Thanksgiving meal. She was assured that things were well underway. Elena was sorting laundry at a work table. When Lauren was about to leave the kitchen, she offered to take her things upstairs and save the girl the steps.

"I'll take Jared's things, too," she offered as Elena piled her arms with fresh-smelling clothes. The stiff, starched white dress

162

shirts and the soft-colored ones Jared wore on the trail were added to Lauren's load.

She went up the stairs quickly and tapped on Jared's door. There was no response. She was about to call out to him, when she heard splashing sounds coming from one of the bathrooms down the hallway. To her knowledge, he had never used the bathroom that connected their rooms.

Indecisively she stood outside his slightly opened door. What could it hurt? she asked herself as she eased the door ajar far enough for her to slip inside.

The room was simply furnished. A bed with a tall oak headboard occupied one wall. A massive wardrobe filled another. A bureau, complete with shaving mirror, washbowl, and pitcher, stood in the corner. The only other piece of furniture was a tall wing chair.

The brown striped curtains at the window had been pushed aside to let in the sunlight. The bed had been neatly made with a spread that matched the curtains. There was no sign of disorder around her as she crossed the decidedly masculine room toward the bureau. She carefully lowered the stack of shirts onto its glossy surface and was turning to leave when something caught her eye.

Apparently Jared had emptied his pockets onto the top of the bureau the night before. She studied the items curiously. A tortoiseshell pocket comb. Did he ever use it? she asked herself with a fond smile. Coins of every denomination. A roll of bills. She recognized his pocket watch with its gold chain. Three pieces of paper, doubtless receipts of some kind, each folded neatly in two. A key ring with six brass keys. A tiny box of matches. And—

Her heart stopped for a moment. When it started again, it beat so rapidly that she covered it with her hand, enfolding her watch in trembling fingers.

There, winding its way through the other items, glaringly out of place, was a slender, blue satin ribbon. A ribbon much like the ones which laced through the chemises that Mrs. Gibbons had made for her before her wedding. Much like the one she had lost only a few weeks ago, the night Jared had undressed her and put her to bed.

She didn't know she had spoken his name until the soft, wondering whisper vibrated through the still room and jarred her out of her stupor. Just as well it did, for she heard the bathroom door down the hall opening. Spinning around, she stared at the door through which he would walk any moment. She mustn't let him see her!

She dashed toward the door opening into the bathroom connecting to her room and pulled it open. She just had closed it after her when she heard him enter his room. He was humming softly, quite unaware that he had caused an emotional avalanche in the breast of his young wife.

Chapter 16

"Olivia, your bountiful table never ceases to amaze me," beamed Parker Vandiver. He had eaten several helpings of traditional Thanksgiving food, and was enjoying one last glass of wine.

They were sitting at the table in the same arrangement as on the first occasion the Vandivers had taken a meal with the Locketts. Olivia and Carson sat at either end, Parker and Jared on one side, Lauren and Kurt on the other.

"Yes," Kurt chimed in. "Everything was delicious, made even more enjoyable by the beautiful company."

The hand wrapped around Jared's wineglass clenched, the knuckles turned white, and Lauren was amazed that the glass didn't shatter under the pressure.

She moved away from Kurt, his presence at her side becoming more unbearable each minute. Since they had taken their chairs at the table, his thick, heavy thigh had pressed against hers, and he used every opportunity to lean toward her, touching her in some way.

She hadn't lost her aversion for the Vandivers. Both father and son repelled her with the brutal strength apparent in each move of their husky bodies. Their polite conversation and demeanor, she was sure, stemmed from some secret ulterior motive.

She was grateful to Carson when he suggested they retire to the parlor for coffee, thereby relieving her of sitting next to Kurt.

"We were sorry we missed you when we visited Keypoint, Mrs. Lockett," Kurt said as everyone was seated in the formal room. Lauren had taken a chair next to the fireplace, forsaking the couches for fear that Kurt would sit beside her.

Lauren didn't want to lie and say she was sorry she had missed seeing them, too. Not knowing what else to say, she replied truthfully, "Jared and I went on an outing that day."

No one noticed Olivia's shocked face, for Jared was saying caustically, "It was our honeymoon, remember?"

Kurt maintained his poise. "Yes, so it was. Did you like life on the ranch, Mrs. Lockett?"

"It was a different experience for me, Mr. Vandiver. I enjoyed the uniqueness of it." While she responded to Kurt's question, she was remembering the night before with a pang of wistfulness. She had felt so close to her husband for the first time. What had happened since then to make him cold and unapproachable? Because it was a holiday, she had worn a new dress in a violet-gray shade of georgette, knowing that the color highlighted her eyes. If Jared had taken note of her appearance, he hadn't deigned to comment.

"You obviously like ranching, Jared." Parker studied him shrewdly.

"Yes," Jared retorted shortly and went to the sideboard. He poured a large glass of whiskey and walked to the wide windows, staring outside, his attitude one of total indifference to the rest of them. Yet all through dinner, his mood had been one of constrained violence, and Lauren was apprehensive.

"I've never had the time to learn the ins and outs of ranching. Maybe you could teach me all about it sometime, Jared."

Jared took a swallow of his drink. "I've never had time for the ins and outs of schoolteaching, Mr. Vandiver. If you want to learn about ranching, I suggest you learn the way everyone else does—by trial and error. That's the way Ben did, and it seemed to work for him." He turned on his heels and fixed Parker with a menacing stare. "And learn to ranch some place other than Keypoint," he warned.

"Jared, how rude!" Olivia chided him. "We're business partners with the Vandivers now." She smiled reassuringly at Parker.

"Not in ranching we're not." Jared tossed down the last of the whiskey and turned to the window, putting his back to them again.

An awkward silence descended over the room. Olivia fidgeted with her coffee cup. Carson covered a pretend yawn. Lauren looked bleakly at Jared. She knew he felt that Keypoint, his true love, was threatened by these unscrupulous men.

"I, for one, am looking forward to the groundbreaking ceremonies," Carson interjected heartily. "We've arranged festivities for the entire population to enjoy. It should be quite a celebration."

"That's the spirit, Carson," Parker agreed. "We want the townspeople to know that this railroad is something they can all be proud of."

"Will you be going to the ceremonies, Mrs. Lockett?" Kurt asked.

Lauren floundered. "Well, I suppose so." Then she added, "With my husband, of course."

No one had a rejoinder to that, so silence descended again.

"I would love a game of bridge. Would anyone else be interested?" Olivia's green eyes sparkled, and she looked younger and gayer than Lauren had ever seen her. She must have stopped the heart of many a New Orleans blade when she turned on the charm.

"That would be wonderful. Lauren, would you be my partner?" Kurt walked over to her and extended his beefy hand. Loath to touch it, Lauren shrank from him. And when had he started calling her by her first name?

With a broad yawn, Carson said, "Go ahead, Lauren. Olivia will play with Parker. I dislike bridge myself." He walked toward the door, saying over his shoulder, "I'm going into the library for a nap. Wake me when the game is over."

Lauren looked helplessly toward Jared as he stormed out of the room without speaking to anyone.

Olivia smiled to herself. She hated to admit to a flash of concern when Lauren had mentioned their "outing." Surely Jared was smart enough not to get involved with the chit any more than necessary. But if he wasn't, Olivia planned to make such an involvement difficult, if not entirely impossible.

They gathered around the game table in the corner of the room and the rubber was soon started. Lauren was able to go through the motions without concentrating too hard. Her mind was on Jared and his whereabouts. She didn't think he had left the house. What was he doing?

The rubber went on for hours. Carson eventually joined them and, diplomatically, cheered first one team and then the other.

When Rosa announced a cold buffet had been laid out in the dining room, everyone protested but strolled into the room and began filling their plates with leftover turkey, salad, and relishes. Olivia asked Rosa to fetch Jared.

They moved back into the parlor toting their plates. Lauren sat on one of the small couches in the shadows of the room. Realizing her mistake too late to move, she saw Kurt striding over to her.

"You didn't get much to eat, Lauren," he said as he sat close beside her.

She murmured, "I'm not very hungry." His looming closeness would have taken away any appetite she might have had.

"You didn't get any of the pickled peppers. Here, try one." He lifted one of the peppers from his plate and offered it to her.

She remembered vividly the first night she spent in Coronado and the innocent-looking tomatoes garnishing the beans. "No, thank you. I don't like them." She shook her head.

"This isn't one of the hot variety. It's very mild. Look." He bit into the pepper and chewed it slowly and deliberately to show her that he suffered no ill effects. "Come on, Lauren."

Hoping he would go away if she complied, she leaned forward and took a tiny bite between her teeth. She sat up and pulled away from him as he smiled down at her.

When she looked away from that victorious smile, she saw Jared standing under the portiere watching them.

His fists were clenched at his sides, the muscles of his jaw working furiously. His eyes held a demonic gleam as he took in the scene. She realized how intimate she and Kurt must look to him, sitting together on a couch in the shadows.

"Jared." Her voice was a strangled whisper.

Kurt whipped his head around, following her gaze. He spotted Jared and noted his fury. Turning back to Lauren, he chucked her under the chin playfully. "See, it didn't hurt a bit."

She practically pushed him from her as she stood and hurriedly followed Jared, who had spun on his heels and stalked out of the room.

She caught up with him in the hall and reached out a hand to restrain him. "Jared." She cleared her throat. "Jared, I—"

"Shut up!" he barked at her and jerked his arm away. His face was contorted with rage. She wanted to shout at him, plead with him, and strike him all at the same time. Anything to erase the angry, accusing look on his face.

Rosa was cowering against the wall wishing she could escape unseen. Lauren saw her and, knowing that conciliation was hopeless, went to her. "Rosa, I'm going up to my room. I have a headache. Would you please extend my apologies to our guests?"

"*Sí, señora,*" Rosa whispered, hoping that Jared wouldn't say anything.

He didn't, but only glared at his wife as she retreated.

* * *

Jared lit another cigar and fanned out the match as he stood at the window of his upstairs room. He watched Lauren as she walked slowly along the fence that encircled the front yard. Wasn't she cold out there? Yes, she was, he concluded when he saw her shiver slightly. What in hell was she doing walking around in the front yard in the middle of the night?

The Vandivers had finally departed. It had taken every ounce of self-control Jared possessed not to kill Kurt Vandiver with his bare hands. He didn't remember ever being so consumed with anger and hatred just at the mere sight of a person.

As he left, Kurt had turned to Jared and said, "I'll look forward to seeing you at the groundbreaking. I hope Lauren is feeling better by then. I would hate for her not to be there." His smile was mocking, and Jared's fists clenched at his sides to keep from smashing them into that smirking face.

After that, he had spent several hours getting progressively drunker. The sound of Lauren's slippers tapping on the floor of the hall had penetrated his alcohol-befuddled mind, and he listened, following their progress.

It surprised him when he heard the front door opening and closing. From his front window, he saw her step from the porch and walk toward the iron gate. She was wearing the dressing gown he had seen before, her hair trailing down her back. She folded her arms tightly to ward off the chill November air.

Bitch! he thought vindictively. She was playing it so cozy with that Vandiver buffoon. He had been right about her all along. She was a schemer, an opportunist, a whore who teased and tormented but never came across.

Well, I don't give a damn, he swore. But he did. That was what rankled. He did care, and it ate at his gut every time he saw that Vandiver bastard go anywhere near her.

Jared watched her now with the moonlight shining silver on her hair. She leaned wearily on the gate and bowed her head, some of her hair falling forward over her cheeks. Her slender back was outlined by the trim, snug fit of the dressing gown, and with a growing ache in his groin, Jared remembered how her body looked partially clothed. He gulped the whiskey in his glass.

If he had to have a wife of convenience, why couldn't she be ugly? Why did she have to be Lauren?

His sexual exploits were well known in the capital city, and in others as well. Whores vied for the chance to offer him their services. His ardent lovemaking was followed by a nonchalant, take-it-or-leave-it attitude that challenged every woman's innate feminine instincts. Perversely they loved him for it.

But when he had been in Austin, he had had no desire to frequent any of his usual haunts. Lauren's image was constantly in his mind, leaving no room for others. Her body was the one he saw in his fantasies, the one he craved.

Furious with the monklike existence he was leading, he had finally forced himself to go to one of the most exclusive "clubs" in the city. He was greeted enthusiastically. Everyone had missed him. Had marriage spoiled Jared Lockett? they asked.

He had drunk whiskey. He had gambled. But when it came time to choose a woman and retire with her upstairs, he was tired of pretending to enjoy himself.

Striving for objectivity, he surveyed the women displayed provocatively before him. This one was too heavy. That one's hair was too brassy. Another one was too coarse. And so it went.

Finally, disgusted with the place and more so with himself, he mumbled some lame excuse and returned to his hotel room. Lying alone on the bed, the hard throbbing between his thighs painfully demanded assuagement. He resorted to a means that had been unnecessary since early adolescence.

Afterward, as he was drifting off to sleep, he convinced himself that it was purely an accident that it had been Lauren's name he had cried into his pillow when the tumult came.

I ought to leave right now. If I did, I could tumble several good whores before morning. But he didn't want anyone else. No, he decided. What I ought to do is act like a man and tumble my own wife.

Lauren was walking slowly back toward the house. Why not? he thought. She *is* my wife, isn't she? She flirts with everyone from the lowliest *vaquero* at Keypoint to Kurt Vandiver, and God knows how many others when I'm not around.

Why not?

He took one last long swallow of the liquor before he staggered out into the hall.

Lauren had been miserable when she retired to her room pleading a headache. She threw herself across her bed and cried as she had not done in a long time. The tears were bitter, angry ones, and had no healing properties. She had drenched her handkerchief and the pillowcase before the tears ran out and then she cried in dry sobs.

Elena had knocked and inquired about her, but Lauren sent her away with reassurances that she was feeling better, and only needed a good night's sleep.

She heard Jared when he came upstairs and went into his room. The house had been quiet for some time when she undressed and climbed into bed. Sleep eluded her. Every time she closed her eyes, Jared's angry face rose up before her. The lips that had curled in contempt were so different from those that had kissed her. The eyes that had looked at her with such enmity were not the same ones that had looked at her tenderly over the top of his red bandana.

Seeking respite from the agonizing images, she donned her robe and crept downstairs and outside to get some fresh air. The night was quiet and beautiful. Everything was bathed in silver moonlight. The stars were brilliant and close.

Lauren was never sure when the thought took form and solidified in her mind, but all of a sudden it was there. I am in love with Jared Lockett. I love Jared.

Never before had she known the meaning of the word in all its scope. Never had she experienced this all-consuming passion.

Every thought related to Jared. Each word she spoke was weighed against what he would think of it. With everything she did, no matter how trivial, she secretly sought his approval. He dominated her mind. She wanted to share his torments as well as his joys. Was this love? Did it always bring so much pain?

She loved Jared. Smiling to herself, she basked in her secret knowledge as she went back into the house and climbed the stairs.

Jared was standing behind the door in her room, so she didn't see him until she shut it. She stifled a startled scream. "Jared, you scared me out of my wits," she gasped, holding a hand against her thumping heart. "What do you want?"

He was balanced on the balls of his feet as if about to pounce. She noticed for the first time that he reeked of whiskey and his golden eyes shone maniacally. His shirt was opened and the shirt-tail hung around his hips.

"Jared?" she said tremulously, and took a step backward.

"What do you think I want, Mrs. Lockett?" His voice was raspy and harsh, the inflection on her name ugly. He lunged at her, cornering her against the wall.

His lips swooped down on hers in a brutal kiss that tore her lips apart. A rapacious tongue plunged into her mouth as he pressed his hard body against hers. The buckle on his belt gouged her stomach. His knee plowed between her thighs, thrusting them apart.

Lauren had been so stunned at first that she hadn't reacted. Now she panicked. She fought him ineffectually with her fists, beating him about his head and shoulders.

She twisted her face free, sobbing, "No, Jared. Please, no!"

"No? Why not?" he growled through clenched teeth. "You are my wife, Mrs. Lockett. So do your duty by me. You've given it away to everyone else, and I won't be denied any longer."

She recognized the illogical reasoning induced by alcohol, but part of what he said was the truth. She was his wife. His words reverberated in her head like an echo. She was his wife.

She stopped struggling immediately, and he almost lost his balance. She made no effort to stop him as he jerked open her robe and ripped the sheer nightgown from neck to waist. He feasted his fevered eyes on her breasts, covering them roughly with his hands and squeezing with the intention of hurting her. Expecting a reaction and getting none, it finally registered with him that she wasn't fighting. He looked into her eyes.

She returned his gaze steadily, levelly, without fear. It was the look of a small animal that offers up the jugular to its predator when it admits that struggling is futile.

If she had poured cold water on him, she couldn't have extinguished the fires of passion more thoroughly. He stood motionless before her, breathing heavily. After long moments rife with suppressed emotion, he ran his hand through his hair, making a valiant effort to regain a modicum of dignity.

He leaned against her, but not with the lust of a moment before. His head rested against the wall above hers and he rolled his forehead from one side to another as if in agony. She felt his hands at her breasts, but realized he was pulling together the front of her dressing gown to hide her nakedness.

When his breathing had returned to normal, he backed away, holding a lock of her hair between his fingers. As he moved backward, he kept the strand in his hand until it was extended its full length, and then he let it fall from his fingers a little at a time. He watched every hair as it filtered through his fingers, falling to lie against her shoulder. Then he turned and left the room, closing the door softly behind him.

Lauren slumped to the floor and muffled her sobs with the fabric of her gown.

Jared was gone the next morning. He had returned to Austin. A week later, Lauren accepted the delivery of a brand new, baby grand piano. It had been purchased for her by one Mr. Jared Lockett.

Chapter 17

The date of the groundbreaking ceremony for the new railroad was set for December fifteenth. Everyone hoped that the Texas weather would cooperate. The collective spirit of the townspeople was soaring with excitement and anticipation. The municipal band gathered for joint rehearsals with the high school band. Speechmakers wrote and rewrote their speeches. Games were organized and yards of bunting were taken out of storage to be used in decorating the platform that was being erected in the center of the park.

Lauren had spent considerable time alone while Jared was away. She hadn't yet recovered from the shock of his attack Thanksgiving night. Again he had shown her that side of his character that was violent and frightening. She knew that most of his anger that night had been brought on by the Vandivers' presence in his house. Compound that with him seeing her with Kurt, and then by the alcohol he had consumed, and the results weren't too surprising.

Lauren still trembled as she recalled his face as he lowered it to hers in a parody of romantic passion. He had intended to punish her physically, but had wounded her spirit instead. If she could hate him, things would be easier. But loving him, his insults hurt even more.

The tender way he had touched her hair before he left that night had almost been her undoing. The anguish and suffering she had read in his eyes were more than she could bear. Had he wanted to apologize? Did masculine pride prevent him from expressing his regret?

When the piano was being unloaded from the wagon sent to deliver it, she had cried. Was this supposed to be a substitute for his respect and affection? It was a generous, beautiful gift, but she would have preferred one kind, gentle, caring word from Jared's lips.

After she had thought about it for a long while, she realized that Jared didn't know how to ask her forgiveness. She, more than anyone, had come to know how fierce his pride was. He would never verbalize an apology, so he had sent her the expensive piano as his peace offering.

Lauren played the instrument every day. Having not played for months, her fingers had become stiff and her touch lacked the fluidity that she had been capable of before. She practiced for a week before she felt she had regained some semblance of her former talent.

She was playing on the afternoon Jared rode into the yard on Charger. He slowed his horse when he first heart the music. He slipped from the saddle and nodded absently as Pepe came running from the stable.

He relinquished care of the animal to Pepe and walked on light footsteps up the steps to the front door. He didn't want to disturb her playing, and he was anxious as to what her attitude toward him would be. He had never had to resort to rape in his life. And then to try to rape his own wife! Godalmighty! He was brimming with self-loathing and disgust. What would she do when she saw him? Probably clutch her clothes to her body and flee in terror. He couldn't blame her.

Slipping quietly into the hall and shutting the front door, he crept on tiptoe toward the parlor, raising his heels high off the floor to keep his spurs from jingling.

Lauren saw him the instant he stood under the portiere. He looked much as he had when he had invaded her bedroom that first time. The clothes, hat, holster, boots, everything was the same except for his demeanor. Then he had been sardonic and arrogant. Today he looked like a shy little boy. He melted her heart, banished her fearful reserve.

"Jared!" she cried. Her face was wreathed in smiles as she stood quickly and went to him. "Thank you for the piano. I can't tell you how much I love it. Thank you." She stood on her toes and kissed his cheeks in turn, lightly.

He was so taken aback by her reception that he stood mute, staring into the sparkling gray eyes. They held no accusation, no anger, no revulsion. He was completely baffled.

Her hands still rested lightly on his shoulders. The fragrance he had come to associate with her wafted up to him. Her complexion looked warm and rosy. Her lips were softly parted, inviting, expectant. It was all too much.

When he drew her to him, it was with extreme caution, as

though she might rebuff his embrace. He moaned with gratitude when, all too willingly, she fit her body along his. His arms went around her carefully as he buried his face in the rich glossiness of her hair. When his lips met hers, they were suppliant. At her immediate, sweet, acquiescent response, he grew bolder and traced her lower lip with the tip of his tongue.

"Jared," she breathed, before his invading tongue prohibited speech. He kissed her frantically, like a man who had been doomed to die and then had been granted a reprieve. Thirstily he drank of her mouth. Finally they drew apart, regretfully.

"Why don't you take off your hat and stay a while?" she asked shakily. She reached up and pulled the hat from his head, clutching it quickly and tightly to her bosom before handing it back to him. "Would you like something to drink?"

"N-no, thank you, Lauren. I'm not . . . not thirsty."

"Would you like to hear me play something? Maybe you don't think my talents warrant such a magnificent piano."

"I heard you from outside. It was . . . You play very well."

"Sit down and relax," she invited gently as she returned to the piano.

He sat on the edge of the sofa, aware of his dusty clothes. He felt gauche and awkward. What the hell was the matter with him? She played several selections, and he stared in fascination at her hands as they flitted over the ivory keys. Her back was straight, her head tilted, tendrils of black curls had escaped the confines of her chignon during their kiss and were resting on her cheeks and neck.

For just a moment, Jared felt a hard lump forming in his throat. He was going to make a damn fool of himself if he didn't get out of here. He stood abruptly and said, "It's beautiful, Lauren. You play better than anyone I've ever heard. I've got to go upstairs now. Clean up and all." He fled the room.

Lauren's fingers were poised over the keys where they had halted when he took his hasty exit. Thoughtfully she began to play again. The music followed Jared upstairs and into his room.

One adage Lauren had heard often since she had come to Texas was that if there was anything predictable about Texas weather, it was that it was unpredictable. No one would have bet that a December day in Coronado would have dawned clear and crisp, perfect for the activities planned for that auspicious day. For Carson Wells's sake, Lauren was glad this was so. He had worried, worked, and planned until she thought he would explode before the day of the groundbreaking ceremonies finally arrived.

The Locketts and Carson gathered in the dining room to share an enormous breakfast before they left for the site of the new depot. Jared looked dashing in black britches tucked into his high, black boots, black coat over a white shirt, and butter-colored leather vest. His black hat had been brushed and hung on the hall tree. Olivia murmured that she wished he had worn dress clothes. He ignored her.

Lauren wore a wool suit of deep burgundy with a cream lace blouse underneath. The skirt had a high waistband that came to a point in the center just under her breasts. Jared found it hard to keep from staring at the spot and wished she could leave off the jacket to the suit.

Carson was nervous and kept clattering his china and cutlery until Olivia berated him and said that he was driving her to distraction. He humbly apologized and settled down somewhat.

Lauren pinned on her veiled hat. There was a flurry of gathering up gloves, extra coats in case a Norther should blow in, blankets, flasks, and, at Rosa's insistence, a basket of sandwiches. At last, they departed.

Jared handed Lauren and his mother up into the buggy, while Carson climbed in with them. Jared mounted Charger, whose golden coat gleamed from the brisk brushing Pepe had given him that morning at Jared's instructions.

"Why don't you ride with us, Jared?"

"And let Charger miss all the fun today? No, thank you, Mother."

Lauren looked at him and he met her gaze. She understood his purpose. He was showing everyone that despite the new business undertaking, Jared Lockett, like his father, was first and foremost a rancher.

Pepe guided their buggy through the traffic. There was already a large gathering of people at the groundbreaking site but they moved aside and deferentially made room for the prominent family who had made the dream of a railroad a reality.

Lauren was aware of curious stares. She felt self-conscious as Jared came around to her side of the buggy and lifted her down, taking her hand lightly as he led her to where Carson and Olivia had joined the other dignitaries. The mayor of Coronado was there, a county judge, the state representative from the district, several clergymen, and the Vandivers.

Jared held Lauren's hand throughout the mayor's speech, and released it only when it was his turn to spade a shovelful of dirt.

Lauren was proud to be standing next to him. He was playing his part well, she thought ruefully. If she was aware that the townsfolk watched every move of their favorite son and his new wife, she was certain that he was cognizant of it, too. He treated her with respectful politeness, but there was new warmth in the amber eyes that glanced at her with embarrassing frequency. She stifled a soft gasp when his elbow pressed against her breast as he held her hand under his arm. He looked down at her quickly, but he made no effort to remove his arm.

Moving en masse to the park, they filed onto the platform that had been erected in the center of it for the official proceedings. The state representative introduced Parker Vandiver, who stepped forward to deliver a flowery speech which extolled the advantages of a community committed to growth and expansion. Coronado, he proclaimed, was such a community.

"This railroad will pave the way for more commerce, more opportunity, more profits for all the citizens of this great city. We are proud to have a small part in bringing this about. We will watch with eager interest to see the progress you make. We want each one of you to realize the potential this offers you, your business, your family. We will be even more pleased when we can return to announce the completion of the track." There was a smattering of applause and a chuckle or two.

"There is a man not with us today who I'm sure would have shared in this celebration. Mr. Ben Lockett made strides for years to bring this railroad to his community."

Lauren risked a quick glance at Jared, whose face had turned as hard as stone. She prayed he could restrain himself.

"Ben Lockett would have been proud to have stood here today and seen the fruits of all his labors. We grieve his passing and are grateful to his widow and son, who endorse this venture whole-heartedly."

There was a burst of applause and cheers from the crowd for Ben Lockett and his family.

After a few more minutes of overblown oratory, Parker Vandiver took his seat. The mayor graciously offered the podium to Jared. He politely refused. The audience was disappointed, but some remembered when he had been honored after the war. He had refused to speak then out of sorrow for those not fortunate enough to come home. There were murmurs of approval and nods of understanding. They had been worried over some of his wild escapades, but anyone with eyes could see that he had married a real lady and was devoted to her. Marriage had settled him down. No doubt about it.

It was a good thing that the attention of the crowd was riveted on Jared and his wife, for had they been watching Olivia, they would have seen the perturbed expression on her face. She was angry with her son for not publicly commending the Vandivers and the railroad venture.

The formalities were out of the way, and everyone was ready to have a good time. Barrels of iced-down beer were heaved onto wagon beds, relay races were organized, the band assembled in the bandstand and began playing their limited repertoire.

As Jared was helping Lauren off the platform, one of the local youths came rushing up to him. The boy's freckled face was flushed, and his carrot-red hair radiated from his head like a burnished halo.

"Jared, Jared, there's gonna be a shootin' contest and they sent me to fetch you. Come on. They're waitin'."

Jared smiled at the boy's exuberance. "Lauren, may I present Billy Holt. Billy, Mrs. Lockett." The boy gave her a perfunctory nod. "Shooting contest, huh?" Jared continued. "Why did they send you after me, Billy?"

"Ah, hellfire and damnation! You know—" Realizing what he'd said, Billy turned scarlet cheeks toward Lauren. "Oh, pardon me, Miz Lockett," he gulped. Not able to meet her eyes, he turned back to Jared. "Hell, Jared, you know you're the best goddam shot anywhere around. It won't be no kinda contest atall if you ain't in it." He was so excited that the other expletives escaped unnoticed.

"Lauren, what do you think? Would you like to see a shooting contest?"

She smiled up at Jared. "It sounds as though everyone will be disappointed if you don't enter it."

"I'll do it only if you'll go with me and watch."

Billy was hopping first on one foot and then the other, barely able to contain his enthusiasm. "Please, Miz Lockett?"

"Yes! Lead the way." She laughed.

Billy leapt into the air and whooped, then raced off to let the others know that the star attraction was on his way.

Jared yelled for Pepe to bring his holster and pistol from the back of the buggy.

Lauren looked up at him in feigned exasperation. "You knew all along there would be a contest, didn't you? And you planned to enter it."

"Well, it's nice to be begged every once in a while." He grinned engagingly. "I just hope I don't humiliate myself. Obviously I have a reputation to maintain."

They strolled over to the men who were gathering for the contest. Some were checking out their revolvers and others were placing bets on the outcome of the match. The odds were strongly in Jared's favor.

Billy and some of his cohorts had assembled bottles and cans for targets, and were lining them up on a fence rail about thirty yards away from the large oak tree that served as the base.

Jared took off his coat and handed it to Lauren as Pepe brought him his holster. He checked the Colt pistol, twirling the chambers and nodding in satisfaction. Lauren remembered being told that *vaqueros* loaded only five of the chambers in the Colts which most of them toted. The first chamber was always kept empty, preventing excited cowboys from shooting their own knees, toes, or friends in a stressful situation.

The ground rules were laid down by Carson whom, it appeared, was the accepted referee. "Each man takes three shots. One miss and he's disqualified," he intoned.

The ten men entering the contest lined up. Jared was last in line to shoot. He caught a glimpse of Kurt Vandiver leaning negligently against a tree. He wasn't watching the contest. He was watching Lauren. Jared looked toward her and she gave him an encouraging smile. He turned his attention back to the contest.

It became boring as all of the gunmen proved to be expert marksmen. But slowly, one by one, they began to miss shots. There were three entries left, Jared among them, when someone suggested that they "fan" their hammers and try to hit three of the targets.

The first man stepped to the line that had been drawn on the ground and, when given the signal, fired rapidly while fanning the hammer of his pistol. He hit three of the targets. The second man only hit two of the bottles.

Jared stepped to the line. He picked a cheroot out of his breast pocket, nonchalantly struck a match, and lit the cigar, drawing on

it for several seconds while everyone stood stock-still in anticipation and awe at his insouciance. His pistol was in his holster,
though Lauren had seen him loading it while the others were
shooting.

"Call it when you're ready, Carson," he said over his shoulder.

"You're going to draw?" Carson asked in amazement.

"Yes. Call it." He spoke calmly, though Lauren could sense
his excitement.

Carson shrugged and gave the call. "Draw!"

With the speed of lightning, Jared whipped his pistol from the
holster and loud retorts spewed from the barrel so fast that they
sounded like one continuous blast. When the smoke cleared, the
witnesses saw only one bottle left on the fence. He had hit five
out of six!

A great roar went up from the onlookers and other contestants.
Billy was turning somersaults in the winter grass. Lauren clapped
her hands in delight. Jared took all of the slaps on his back with
casual aplomb.

"Goddam shootin' machine, that's what."

"Quicker'n a mad rattler."

"Heard that Rudy Mendez is just as fast. You can tell that
sonofabitchin' Ben taught them boys how to shoot."

Lauren was so wrapped up in the commotion that she didn't
notice Kurt standing near her.

"It's a pity he can't control his drinking as well as he can that
Colt."

She whirled on him, furious. But Jared's approach prevented
her from snapping a rejoinder to Kurt's petty observation. Instead
of wasting thought on him, she congratulated Jared as she helped
him put on his coat. "Jared, you were brilliant."

Undaunted, Kurt interrupted any response Jared might have
made. "Lauren, I have a surprise for you. Come over here. I want
to show you something."

"Jared?" Lauren looked up at him. She didn't know how to
rebuff Kurt without making a scene for everyone in town to see.

"It's all right, Lauren. I'd like to see this surprise, too." Jared
took her arm possessively and followed Kurt's stocky figure as
he plowed his way through the throng. There was a small cluster
of people gathered around something, and only when Kurt rudely
shoved them aside did Lauren see it was a motorcar.

She had seen them in North Carolina, particularly on her trips to Raleigh, but she had never seen one in Coronado. Apparently no one else had either, because the automobile was causing quite a stir.

"It's an Oldsmobile. One of the gasoline-powered models," Kurt boasted. "I want to take you for a ride in it, Lauren."

The automobile was beautiful. The sides and motor casing were glossy black, trimmed in red. The tires had white sides, and the hubs of the wheels were red. The upholstery was black leather. There were two brass lanterns mounted on the front of the car, and brass accents shone on the steering stick and a mounted horn.

"I . . . uh—"

"I'm sure your *husband,*" he stressed the word, "won't mind. Would you, Jared?"

Aware of the people standing by listening to every word, Jared smiled expansively and said, "I think Lauren would enjoy that very much. Here, dear, let me help you." She saw the tight lines around his mouth as he lifted her carefully into the vehicle. She wanted to protest, but knew she couldn't.

Kurt went to the front of the car and made a big show of cranking the motor. It churned to life with a terrific racket. Running around to the driver's side, he vaulted into the seat beside Lauren. Unconsciously she moved her skirt away from his heavy thigh. The gears were engaged and the automobile moved forward. Lauren cast an anxious look back at Jared, but he was staring at Kurt's back with a threatening scowl.

Kurt took the road that led down to the river and followed near its banks. They crossed a narrow bridge and continued on the road to the opposite side. They were virtually out of sight, hidden by the trees that grew along the riverbank on both sides. Under other circumstances, she would have enjoyed the ride, but the ominous presence of Kurt made Lauren terribly uncomfortable.

"Are you having a good time?" he asked close to her ear.

"It's very pleasant."

She shifted farther away from him on the narrow seat. He continued to maneuver the car along the rough road, and Lauren was relieved that he didn't try to engage her in conversation.

"I'd like to go back now," she said. "Jared will be worrying about me."

He laughed humorlessly. "I'm not fooled by this so-called marriage, Lauren. Separate bedrooms, isn't it?"

"My married life is none of your business, Mr. Vandiver." Her voice was hard and cold, but her cheeks flushed hotly. His swift, derisive look told her he was not convinced. He did, however, turn the automobile around, recross the bridge, and retrace their way back to where they had started. The crowd was still there. Jared was leaning against a tree, casually smoking a cigar. Only his flashing eyes indicated his anger.

In his haste to get out and help Lauren down, Kurt didn't take time to cut the motor. Jared strolled to the car with studied leisure, then jumped onto the seat vacated by Kurt.

"You call that a ride, Vandiver?" He rammed the car into gear. Lauren clutched the seat as the car lurched, almost running over Kurt, who scrambled out of the way just in time. It had all happened so quickly that he was stunned as his Oldsmobile sped away at a speed he would never have dared to push it. The crowd went wild with hysterical laughter at his expense.

Jared handled the steering stick like a magic wand, turning corners at breakneck speed, managing to hit every chuckhole in the road. They drove around the square in the middle of town several times, until Lauren's head was spinning. She clung to Jared's arm for fear of being thrown off the seat as the car bounced over the streets. Finally they left the center of town, taking one of the lanes that led away from the city.

The wind lashed her face, and her bonnet blew back, painfully pulling against the pins that held it on. She would have reached up to take it off, but dared not release her grip on Jared.

He was laughing uproariously, like a naughty child who had pulled off a tremendously funny joke on his schoolteacher.

"Did you see his face, Lauren? Did you? That sonofabitch! I'll show him how to drive a car." His hat had blown off, and his hair tumbled around his head. His face was flushed and his eyes glittered in delight over his own devilry.

Before she realized it, Lauren was joining his laughter. They were like two children let loose from restrictions for the first time. Jared risked looking at her when he heard her laugh. He realized his error when his eyes returned to the road. It had curved and they were headed for the ditch. "Hold on!" he shouted as he applied the brakes. They slowed then, but the automobile was going too fast. The wheels locked and the car spun crazily until it slid off the road and the front wheel on the driver's side sank up to the hub in the soft ground. Jared cut the chugging, choking motor.

They were gasping for breath, momentarily shaken over their

narrow escape from death or severe injury. The car sat at a perilous angle and Lauren had been thrown against Jared. He looked down at her and asked, "Are you all right?"

She took stock of herself. "Yes, I'm fine," she answered breathlessly. "I'm not so sure about Kurt's Oldsmobile."

Then they burst into spontaneous laughter. They laughed so hard that tears gathered in their eyes. It was the first time they had ever laughed together. There had been times when one of the Mendez children had reduced the family to laughter with an antic, but this was different. This was a personal moment that they were sharing.

Lauren dabbed at her eyes with her gloved hands and drew the long, lethal-looking hatpins from her hair. The hat came off and her heavy bun drooped almost to her shoulders; strands of hair escaped it completely.

Jared's merriment subsided and, of its own volition, his hand touched the knot of hair resting against her neck. She raised her eyes to his and they held only briefly before she was in his arms. It happened quietly, naturally, instinctively. He held her to him and whispered her name repeatedly against her ear, his breath sending shivers of pleasure down her spine.

He drew back and searched her eyes fro some sign of rejection, but saw only invitation. His mouth took hers in a telling kiss. Their lips sought and found and celebrated each other. The kiss was tender, but held promise of restrained passion. It was committing, but left room for reservation, for caution. It was a kiss for the moment. For now. Only now.

Jared pulled away from her and studied her face, startled by the intensity of his feelings. They stared at each other in a silent communication. Then Jared rasped, "Lauren, kiss me again. Kiss me—"

"Lauren, are you injured?" Kurt was galloping toward them pell-mell. He reined up before his car and dismounted, running to Lauren's side and offering his hands up to her. Before she could assure him she didn't want to be rescued from Jared's embrace, his beefy hands gripped her around the waist and swung her down to the ground. "Lauren, are you all right? That idiot could have killed—"

The breath gushed out of Kurt's body when Jared's fist landed squarely in his stomach after first spinning him around. Kurt landed on his back in the ditch and, before he could regain his breath,

Jared had straddled his chest and pushed the barrel of his pistol against Kurt's nose.

"If you ever, *ever*, touch my wife again, I'll kill you, Vandiver." His face was an inch from Kurt's and the words were strained through his teeth. "If you even look like you're thinking of touching her, I'll kill you. Do you understand me?"

"Get that goddam gun out of my face," Kurt said with misplaced bravery. "It's not loaded. You emptied it on that last round." He struggled but couldn't budge Jared.

The clicking sound of metal on metal as Jared cocked the pistol arrested Kurt's futile movements. "Are you so sure it's empty, Vandiver?" Jared taunted.

Kurt laughed nervously. "There's no way in hell you could have kept from firing that sixth shot as fast as you were fanning."

"You forgot that there was one target left," Jared said smoothly.

"Even so," Kurt persisted, though his voice was beginning to waver and he was perspiring profusely, "everyone knows cowboys leave the first chamber empty."

Jared shrugged negligently. "Some do. Those not confident in their abilities. In all humility, I'm not one of those."

"The damn gun isn't loaded!" Kurt screamed as Jared shoved the barrel further into his fleshy nose.

"Wanna bet?" Jared drawled.

With the merest movement, he turned his hand and fired the pistol only inches from Kurt's head. The bullet embedded itself in one of the rubber tires of the car.

The blood drained from Kurt's face and he began making a whimpering sound.

"I could have hit that last target, Vandiver, but no fool carries around an unloaded pistol." With disdain, Jared stood up and stepped over the groveling, inert form.

"Señor Jared!" Pepe came riding up on Charger with several other riders trailing him. "Are you all right? Is the *señora* all right?"

He reined in the palomino stallion and slid off his back, running up to them.

"Yes, yes, we're fine," Jared assured him. "Had a helluva good time, too. Can't say much for the car." Lauren knew that he was speaking for the benefit of the curiosity seekers who had followed them. "I don't think it'll ever be as thrilling as galloping on

Charger. And he sure as hell has better sense than to go off in a ditch."

All of them laughed, relieved that no one was hurt. Mr. Vandiver looked a little peaked, but he was just worried about his car, they thought.

"Lauren." Jared extended his hand and she took it. He led her to Charger and lifted her to the saddle. He mounted behind her, putting his arms firmly around her.

"Pepe, can you ride with someone back to the park?"

"Sí, Señor Jared."

"Fine. Gentlemen." He tipped his hat, which Pepe had retrieved for him, turned Charger around, and headed for town at a slow trot.

Chapter 18

Their escapade had created quite a commotion. They were asked hundreds of times about their well-being, despite their continued assurances to everyone that they were fine.

Sitting at a picnic table with Olivia and Carson, they ate the sandwiches that Rosa had packed for them. Jared drank locally brewed beer with the men gathered around the barrels. Lauren watched him from her place near Olivia, and was thrilled when he glanced her way and smiled. She tried hard to keep her mind on the conversations going on around her and to give the proper answers to the myriad questions being asked by the ladies of Coronado about how she liked her new life in Texas. But her mind was on Jared's mouth, how warm it was against hers. His hands, strong, demanding, yet gentle.

While the band played a Christmas concert to mark the conclusion of the festivities, Jared sat close beside her on the blanket he had spread on the grass. His breath was on her cheek. She could smell the aroma of his cheroots, the leather of his vest. If only we could stay like this forever, she thought.

Olivia hadn't missed the looks and the "accidental" touches between them after the madcap drive in the car. After the Vandivers had left, pleading that they had commitments in Austin, she focusd all her attention on Jared and his wife. She didn't like what she saw. Something was simmering, and it must be cooled before it came to a boil. It was dangerous to all of her plans. It must not happen!

They left late in the afternoon. Rosa had chili and cornbread waiting for them when they got home. They ate tiredly, but two of the people at the table were too exhilarated to have much of an appetite.

Carson left directly afterward, and Olivia pleaded fatigue and suggested they retire early. Lauren and Olivia walked up the stairs together, leaving Jared in the library with a nightcap.

* * *

Sometime during the night, Lauren awoke with a start. It took a moment for her to get her bearings. She listened. The house was still. She lay back down and, just as she did, she heard a groan. When a sharp cry followed it, she jumped out of bed, alarmed.

The sound came from Jared's room. Without even pausing to put on a robe, she crept through the bathroom and tentatively knocked on the connecting door. He didn't answer, but again she heard the rasping cry and louder moans. What if he were ill? Should she go in? She paused only an instant before she opened the door a crack and peered into the room.

Jared was thrashing on his bed, twisting and tossing in the agony of a nightmare. Lauren quickly crossed to the bed and saw his bare chest heaving, his face beaded with perspiration. The words coming out of his mouth were unintelligible, but conveyed a terrible torment. He murmured the name Alex over and over. "Jared, wake up." Reaching out a cautious hand, she touched his shoulder and shook him slightly. "Jared, please wake up. You're having a nightmare."

He only became more violent. He thrashed his arms and tossed his head on the pillow, his teeth bared as he gnashed them. Lauren dodged the flailing arms, but managed to capture both wrists and, leaning over, pinioned them on either side of his head.

He struggled for release, but somehow she was able to hold him. "Jared, wake up."

He opened his eyes and, as if hinged at the waist, bolted upright. The sheet fell around his middle. Oh, my Lord, he's naked! Lauren realized. He gulped in great amounts of air and shook his head in an effort to clear it of the tormenting dream. Shaky fingers raked through damp, tousled hair before covering his face.

Lauren slipped through the darkness to his shaving mirror on the bureau and poured fresh water from a pitcher into the basin. She moistened a towel and brought it back to the bed.

"Jared, you were having a nightmare," she said softly, comfortingly. "Are you all right now?"

He nodded dumbly as she sponged his forehead with the cool cloth. When he lowered his hands, she bathed the rest of his face and neck.

"Thank you, Lauren. I'm fine now." He moved away from her hands.

"Were you dreaming about Cuba? Alex?"

He looked at her sharply, then away. "Yes," he said hoarsely. Was he trembling?

"Would you like to talk about it?" Her voice was a faint whisper. Until her fingers touched the sun-bleached curls on his head, she hadn't realized she had reached for them.

"No," he answered gruffly. Then, desperately, "Yes. Lauren?" His arms went around her waist in a viselike clasp, and he drew her to him, burying his face between her breasts. Her knees bumped against the bed frame.

She hesitated only a moment before cradling his head in her arms. His ragged breath was warm and moist on her skin through the thin batiste nightgown. She was grateful to the darkness for lending her a modicum of modesty. Murmuring words of comfort, she stroked his head, weaving the coarse curls through her fingers. His hands moved over her back, tracing her spine with sensitive fingers.

Long minutes passed, and still he didn't release her. Almost imperceptibly, he moved his head between her breasts, and began nuzzling her with his nose and mouth, pressing small, hot kisses on her flesh.

A longing deeper and more potent than any emotion she had felt in her life pierced her to the core. A warm flush washed over her skin as her heartbeat accelerated.

Her limbs seemed to have turned to water, but with surprising strength, she drew his head closer yet. A soft, ecstatic cry escaped her open lips when he took her nipple into his mouth. He tugged on it gently with a sweet warmth before his tongue swept across it, wetting the fabric of her gown.

Lauren's body was swimming with sensations and she almost melted to the floor when the strong support of his arms was suddenly withdrawn. Jared sat with his knees raised, his head hanging between them, his face in his hands.

"Leave me, Lauren," he grated. His voice was so low that she could barely hear the words.

"Jared, I—"

"Leave me, please," he repeated with a groan.

"Why? Why must I leave you . . . now?" She was on the verge of tears. Her emotions were running so high, her voice cracked under the pressure.

"Because, dammit," he swore vehemently, "I can't stand having you this close, this willing, this . . . naked . . . and not . . . Just go back to your room, please."

"No, Jared," she breathed.

He looked up then. "No?"

She swallowed hard. "I . . . I want to be a real wife to you, Jared." She couldn't help the tears that spilled down her cheeks. "I want to stay with you."

"Lauren," he said, shaking his head. His voice was sympathetic, like an adult speaking to a child. "You don't know what you're saying."

"I realize that! I don't know anything about . . . this. But I want to know. I want to be a wife like Gloria is to Rudy. Like Maria was to Ben." Neither of them noticed the incongruity of that statement. "Please let me stay with you tonight."

He looked at her. Tears were rolling down her flawless cheeks, her hair was tumbling over her shoulders onto the breasts he longed to caress again, her slim figure was outlined under the sheer nightgown, and the pounding of his heart thundered through his head. His body was on fire with desire for her, and his manhood stood proudly, painfully.

He didn't dare move when she raised one knee onto the bed and sat down close to him. She leaned forward and, resting timid hands on his shoulders, placed her lips against his.

He moaned in helplessness as he clasped her to him and fell back against the pillows on the wide bed. Drawing her beneath him, he kissed her with a searing fervor, thrusting his tongue into her mouth and exploring it with unleashed passion.

Frantically he fumbled with the buttons of her nightgown. Lauren didn't have time to be embarrassed by her nakedness as he flung the offending garment over her head, and quickly covered her body with his.

Difficult as it was, he forced himself to practice self-control. This wasn't a whore. This was Lauren. His wife. He must go slowly, mustn't frighten her.

Lauren felt the long, hard body against hers relax somewhat as Jared kissed her again, leisurely this time, as if memorizing her lips and tongue and teeth. He traced kisses over her cheeks, and nibbled at her earlobe until she felt her own body turning languorous and pliant beneath him.

One large, tanned hand moved over the tops of her breasts. He cupped one gently. Her nipple became hard as the palm moved in slow, easy circles over it. He took the swollen bud between his fingers and caressed it tenderly until Lauren wanted to cry out from the pleasure he brought her, pleasure she had never known existed.

Then he enfolded her nipple in his wet, warm mouth, and drew on her with exquisite tenderness. As he moved to the other breast, his beard stubble scraped against her smoothness, heightening her awareness of their physical differences. He gave the same attention to her other breast as his hands moved to her abdomen, stroking, caressing, arousing.

It was a sensation like warm liquid being poured over her as he lowered his head and kissed her naval with an ardent, hungry mouth. His palm rested lightly on the tight nest of raven curls at the top of her legs and she wondered why she wasn't repulsed or afraid. The feelings were so . . . what? She had nothing to compare this to.

His hand moved between her thighs, and Lauren was alarmed when he encountered a moistness. Apparently he found that strange wetness gratifying. He sighed and whispered, "God, Lauren, you're ready for me. Oh how sweet you are." The movement of Jared's hand then took away all conscious thought. The delicious explorations of his fingers released a primitive instinct and she rotated her hips against his powerful body. When I think of this later, I'll be so ashamed, she thought, but now, I can't help it.

He was kissing her mouth again, tenderly, deeply, murmuring against her lips a mixture of English and Spanish. He moved on top of her and she welcomed the crushing weight by wrapping her arms around the breadth of his back. His knees gently urged her thighs apart as he settled himself between them. She felt his masculine strength as he probed the opening of her body.

A flash of panic seized her, and he was instantly aware of it. He raised his head and looked into her wide, fearful eyes, searching for the answer he hoped was there. "It's true then? You've never been with a man?" His inflection was one of awe and carried with it a need to know. And she knew why her reply would be so important to him. Ben. She didn't speak, but her lips formed the word *no* as she shook her head. "Lauren." Every trace of emotion that made up the spirit of Jared Lockett went into that speaking of her name. He kissed her quickly, hotly, passionately. Then he beseeched her, "Forgive me. I'm going to hurt you, Lauren. I'm sorry." He thrust himself inside her and she would have screamed if he hadn't held her head protectively against the hollow of his shoulder.

The burning pain was ripping her apart, searing her insides. "I'm sorry, my darling. Relax as much as you can."

The words were husky against her ear, and she forced muscles she didn't know she had to relax into acceptance. The pain abated, but how long did this last?

Jared hadn't moved. She heard his breath rushing in her ear like a strong wind. She shifted under him, seeking a more comfortable position, and heard his sharp intake of breath. "Oh, God, you feel so good," he ground out, pressing his face into the pillow. "So tight. Perfect, perfect."

Slowly he began to move inside her. The pain came back in rhythmic waves to match his thrusts, but somewhere amidst the pain was a promise of pleasure. Jared's murmurings in her ear were indiscernible, but their meaning was clear.

Jared was inside her! It was a thrilling thought—his body and hers fused together in the most intimate and unifying way. Without her knowing it, her body had taken control and she was responding to his thrusts with answering movements. Suddenly his whole body tensed and she felt a shower of life flowing into her. Instinctively she squeezed her knees against his hips.

He lay spent on top of her until his breathing returned to normal. She ran her hands over his broad back, marveling at the contour of muscles, bone, and skin. Eventually he raised himself onto his elbows and looked into her eyes.

"My God, Lauren," he whispered in wonder. "What did you do to me?"

He rolled off her and drew her to him, nestling her against his chest. They lay for a long while without speaking. His hands traveled lazily over her back, hips, and legs. The place between her thighs was still on fire, but she was content. She sighed. Placing a finger under her chin, he lifted her face to him.

"My little virgin. Did it hurt too much?"

"No," she lied.

He tried to keep from smiling, couldn't, and even laughed quietly. "Like hell. You are a lady to the bitter end, aren't you?" He lowered his head and kissed her sweetly, almost chastely.

He swung his long legs over the side of the bed and walked unabashedly across the room to the dresser. Lauren studied his physique. No artist could have captured the sensual grace of Jared's walk or the texture of his skin covered lightly with soft, tawny hair. He was a beautiful male animal and, in spite of her new awareness, she blushed.

He came back to the bed carrying a damp cloth. Kneeling

beside her, he moved to open her legs. She shrank back instinctively.

"I'm not going to hurt you," he said gently. "This may make you feel more comfortable."

His voice was so soothing and his hands so tender that she allowed him to separate her legs and press the cloth to her. Avoiding his eyes, she stared up at the ceiling, astonished that these things were transpiring. Never in her uneducated fantasies had she imagined that such familiarity could exist between a man and a woman. Or maybe such things only happened with Jared. She risked a glance at her husband. He was gazing at her as though he could read her mind and knew each personal thought.

"I promise, Lauren, that it will never hurt as much again." He smiled slightly. "You may even learn to enjoy it."

The cooling cloth had reduced the stinging considerably, and she whispered, "Thank you," as he took it back to the dresser.

She sat up, clutching the twisted sheet to her, and reached for her nightgown lying at the foot of the bed. "What are you doing?" he asked as he crawled back beside her.

"I thought—"

"You thought what?" he interrupted, taking the garment away from her and tossing it out of her reach. He began nibbling at her shoulder as he drew her back onto the pillows. "What did you think, Lauren?" he asked thickly. His lips were at her breasts now, and she couldn't think at all.

"I thought . . . uh . . ." Oh, Lord.

He chuckled softly. "Go to sleep." Laying his head close to hers on the same pillow, he closed his eyes. His arm rested heavily on her stomach. His hand cupped her breast lightly.

Sleep? Not tonight. She had too much to think about. She and Jared, who had fought, argued, ignored each other, and hurt each other, were lying here side by side completely naked in his bed after experiencing the most splendid coupling, and he wanted her to sleep. Impossible.

She would never be able to sleep.

But she did.

"Good morning."

"Hmm?"

"I said 'good morning,' Mrs. Lockett."

Lauren sleepily opened one eye and saw her husband's smiling face close to hers. The room was still wrapped in dark gray shadows. "Jared," she mumbled in complaint, "it's not morning. It's still the middle of the night." She buried her face against his hairy chest and yawned broadly.

"I love getting up first thing in the morning." He laughed at his own double-entendre, but Lauren looked up at him with naive eyes. He realized again just how innocent she was. Still. "Lauren." He stroked her cheek and leaned down to kiss her softly on the lips.

She snuggled against his warmth as he pulled a blanket higher over them. He caressed the hair that spilled across his chest. As his eyes roamed the soft form cuddled against him, he laughed ruefully to himself. Who would have thought this of Jared Lockett? That he had spent the entire night with a woman was unusual in itself. As soon as he had satisfied his initial lust, he was always anxious to leave any woman he had been with before. Last night he had wanted to stay. With this woman.

Never had he lost himself so completely with a female as he had with Lauren. He always enjoyed the act, certainly. But his thoughts were often elsewhere: on a card game, business, another woman.

Last night, however, he had been aware only of the woman beneath him, responding with only a trace of virginal shyness. The feel of her, the scent, the texture, the taste had all combined to totally capture his senses. His absorption had been so tremendous that he hadn't wanted it to end.

In a million years, he would never admit that last night had been a first for him, too. It was her initiation into the rites of loving. She had been a virgin. And it was the first time Jared Lockett had ever been with a virgin. It was a gift he had never expected to receive and one he didn't feel he deserved, yet she had given herself to him.

Why? After the abuse he had heaped on her, why had she come to him, offering herself? He bent his head and brushed his lips across her forehead as the question continued to haunt him.

Her fingertips smoothed the crease between his thick, brown brows. They'll be shaggy like Ben's when he gets older, she thought. Twenty-four hours ago, she hadn't even known that it was possible to be as intimate with another human body as they had been. Now they were lying with arms and legs entwined, and she felt no shyness or modesty or guilt. What had happened to all her rigid scruples? No matter. She didn't want them back. Even now, she wanted to discover what further delights his body could offer hers.

"Jared, when? . . . I mean, how long? . . . Does it? . . ."

He smiled. In answer to the question she couldn't quite bring herself to ask, his mouth sought hers. That first real kiss since the night before generated the same stirrings, the same exciting anticipation of things to follow. She allowed him unlimited access to her body. He found her secret places and caressed or kissed, eliciting moans of pleasure from them both.

Shyly at first, then encouraged by his soft groans of ecstasy, her fingers traversed the forested chest. Lightly she fanned the crinkly hair. His skin was warm and stretched tautly over contoured muscles which she massaged with fingers suddenly grown talented in the art. Air hissed through his teeth when she encountered the turgid brown nipples. She withdrew quickly, but his hand went to the back of her head and brought her back. Nuzzling her face in his neck, she traced it with her tongue. As she leaned over him, his strong fingers splayed over her hips and pressed her against him to meet his virile force.

"I want you again, Lauren. But I don't want to hurt you," he said, anguished.

"You won't, you won't."

Strands of her hair were still wound around his neck as he almost fiercely rolled her to her back. Poised above her, he sought her eyes and demanded, "Say my name, Lauren. Let me see my name on your lips. Say my name, please."

Reaching up, her fingertips played upon his cheekbones as she whispered, "Jared. Jared. Jared." The last syllable was a plea.

When he entered her, it was slowly and deliberately. There was a remnant of soreness, but none of the burning pain she had experienced before. Jared moved against her like a well-trained machine whose only purpose was to bring sensuous pleasure.

His hands gently kneaded the fullness of her hips as he lifted her up and forward to meet his sublime invasion. He plunged more deeply than ever before, stroking the walls of her femininity, the gate of her womb, withdrawing to tease and tantalize the portal, only to bury himself within her again.

Lauren felt her spirit rising, floating above the surface of the bed, climbing higher and higher toward some pinnacle still nebulous and mysterious but desirable. It frightened her, this abyss she hovered over. She squeezed her eyes shut.

"No. Lauren, come with me," he urged breathlessly. "Come . . .

with . . . me. . . ." He held her tight as his passion, beyond the point of restraint, emptied inside her, laving her with living fire.

He rested only a moment. Then, with a hand on the small of her back, he eased them to their sides. Still entrapped within that honeyed cave, Jared stirred himself arousingly.

"Can you feel me, Lauren?"

"Yes," she whispered. "Yes."

"Do I hurt you?" He moved inside her again.

Oh, Lord. "No, it's . . . it feels nice."

"Then why did you stop?" he asked in a solicitous whisper. "You were on the brink of incredible joy. Are you afraid of it?"

Unable to meet his probing eyes, she nodded into his shoulder.

"I see," he said quietly. Confident of his own abilities, he knew he could bring her to completion even now, but decided she wasn't ready to accept it. He eased himself away from her, aware that, in spite of her denial, she must feel bruised and battered.

He brushed the hair away from her temples and kissed her forehead and eyelids. "Let's take another nap." Turning her away from him, he drew her back against his chest.

He fell asleep breathing in the perfume of her hair.

Chapter 19

Olivia knew immediately upon seeing Jared and Lauren together at lunch that her worst fear had come about. The household staff was buzzing about something, but she had never taken it upon herself to learn Spanish. She didn't understand their excited whispers.

At the meal, however, the secret smiles, the oblivion to everything around them, and the dark smudges under their eyes testified to her how Jared and Lauren had spent the night.

Damn! How could her son succumb to that hothouse flower? He always preferred boisterous, blowsy girls, girls with scandalous reputations. What did he see in this fragile, ladylike paragon of virtue? Well, it didn't matter if he slept with the chit as long as he didn't form a lasting affection. Or—God forbid—if she should conceive a child. Hopefully, Jared was smart enough to prevent this from happening.

She watched them as they excused themselves and started upstairs for a "nap."

"Jared, could I have a word with you?" she asked quickly, folding her napkin beside her plate as she stood. "Yesterday Parker and I talked over some plans amidst all that insanity at the groundbreaking, and I think you should be kept apprised of the developments."

Jared looked wistfully toward Lauren, but begrudgingly complied. "All right, Mother. I'll see you later, Lauren."

After her daughter-in-law left the dining room, Olivia suggested that Jared follow her into the office. When he was relaxed and seated in a deep leather chair and smoking a cigar, she told him their new scheme.

"Really, Jared, I think you overreacted this afternoon."

They were at dinner, and Olivia was speaking in well-modulated tones that belied the underlying turbulence in the room.

"I'd rather not discuss business now, Mother." Jared's voice was clipped and terse. Lauren had been dismayed to find that all his lightheartedness of the morning had disappeared after the meeting with his mother. They had been sequestered in the office for over an hour and, when Jared had returned upstairs, he made no effort to see her. He had gone straight to his room and then later left the house. He had returned just before dinner. She hadn't seen him alone since before lunch.

"We certainly have no secrets from Lauren, do we?" Olivia asked sweetly, glancing at her daughter-in-law. "After all, she is your wife, Jared."

Lauren blushed and looked unseeingly at her plate. Did Olivia know about last night? How would she react to the consummation of their marriage?

"Do you think some of our plans will shock her?" Olivia asked her son coolly.

"Dammit, Mother!" The lines around Jared's mouth seemed to be carved of granite.

"You see, Lauren," Olivia continued, undisturbed by Jared's anger, "the Vandivers and I have reconsidered the optimum location for the power plant. The new site will require damming up the river above Pueblo instead of below it. Naturally this will greatly affect the community. We fear an outcry of public disapproval, since the community's source of water will be cut off. Therefore, we have taken measures to assure that Pueblo's destruction be seen as a blessing."

Lauren had placed her fork on her plate and was staring from mother to son with blank, uncomprehending eyes. Olivia returned her stare levelly. Jared wouldn't look at her.

"I don't think I understand." Lauren licked her lips. *"What* measures are you taking?" She didn't want to know. But she had to know.

"Lauren, stay out of this. It's none of your concern," Jared barked.

"Of course it concerns her, Jared. My dear," Olivia said, addressing her again in that pleasant, conversational voice, "we are going to round up a gang of desperadoes, mercenaries, whatever name you choose to call them. I think you get the idea. They will go into Pueblo and, posing as citizens, cause a ruckus. They will be instructed to burn, loot, injure, anything they deem necessary to bring about a riot. The ghetto will destroy itself. Our mercenaries will help it along by igniting some well-set fires. I thought it up, of course. Parker thinks it's a brilliant idea. He's asked Jared to come to Austin to organize the men. Jared frequents places where such characters might be found."

Lauren's face had drained of color. She couldn't believe what she was hearing. When she spoke, her voice was barely more than a hoarse croak. "But people could get killed! And think of all the homes that would be destroyed."

Olivia shrugged. "I suppose they will, but it will be no great loss, will it?"

"But it's unnecessary! Why can't the power plant be built where originally planned?"

"It could. It's just that I don't wish it there."

"Then it *is* unnecessary. You would have a whole town destroyed on a whim. Why?" She slumped back in her chair and stared at the woman across the table from her with perplexity. Olivia's face was hard and ugly, filled with hate. Suddenly Lauren understood. "Revenge," she wheezed. "You're taking out your hate of one woman on a whole people."

Olivia glared at her. "I don't know what you're babbling about, Lauren," she said.

"Of course you do. Maria Mendez. You can't bear it that Ben loved—"

"Shut up!" Olivia screamed and thumped her fists on the table. Glassware and china clattered.

"No, I will not shut up. You would have let Elena and Isabela die in the streets before caring for them. At the time, I thought it was the epitome of heartlessness and cruelty, but now you surpass even that. Perhaps I can see why you would feel the way you do about Maria, but to unnecessarily—"

"It's necessary if I say it is," Olivia broke in. Her chest was heaving with emotion. "I don't have to justify myself to you, or to anyone else on earth."

Lauren was struck then by the passion in the woman. She was driven to hate, to destroy. It was useless to try to reason with someone so obsessed. "No, you don't have to justify yourself to anyone on *earth*," Lauren said, stressing the last word. She knew then that she would never fear Olivia again. Distrust her, dislike her, but never fear her. Olivia was a lost cause, but there was still hope for Jared.

During the heated exchange between his wife and his mother,

he had continued to stare into the candle flame lighting the dining table.

Lauren turned toward him. "Jared? Jared, you can't endorse such a horrendous scheme?" The words came out as an incredulous question.

"I told you to stay out of it, Lauren," he growled. "You don't understand these things."

"I understand everything!" she shouted. "I understand that what you propose is heinous and criminal and—"

Jared jumped from his chair, knocking it over and upsetting a glass of red wine onto the table. "Goddammit, get off my back." He strode toward the door leading into the hall, but Lauren was right behind him. She stepped in front of him, placing both hands on his chest, searching his eyes.

"Tell me that you will have no part in this. Please tell me that." When he didn't move, she went on, "Jared, *think*. There are families there who will be hurt. Elena, Rosa, and Gloria have friends and relatives who live there. Surely you would not condone anything that would harm them?"

On top of what his mother had ordered him to do, he didn't need this. He didn't need Lauren looking up at him with an expression that was both pleading and accusing.

Last night he had wanted her with a passion that surpassed anything he had ever experienced before, and the culmination had been earthmoving. Memories of the hours they had spent in his bed still stirred him.

He didn't need that, either. He didn't want her to be special. To feel the way he was coming to feel toward her would be dangerous with any woman, but with her, it was insanity. She had come to Texas for Ben Lockett, not his son. And she had only married him for the twenty thousand dollars; no doubt she'd leave as soon as she got the money. His face became an ugly sneer and he threw off her hands, sending her reeling backward.

"Who the hell are you to tell me anything about it? Have you lived here all your life? Have you ever been down to see the way those people live? It's a cesspool, Lauren. The dregs of society. Whores and gamblers and thieves. You don't know what you're talking about when you plead with me to save it."

"I'm sure that element of society is there. But there are innocent people who will suffer needlessly." To emphasize her words, she gripped his upper arms again.

"Don't presume to interfere in my life," he hissed and impatiently flung off her hands. His gesture carried more impetus with it than he had intended and he watched in bitter remorse when his hand flew up and caught her in the lip, cutting the tender flesh on her teeth and drawing blood.

They were held suspended in surprise, stunned by what had happened.

Jared was the first to rouse himself. He reached into his breast pocket and withdrew a handkerchief, extending it toward her. "I'm sorry, Lauren. Here—" He reached to blot up the thread of blood.

"Don't touch me!" She jerked away from him and slapped his hand away. The handkerchief fluttered to the floor. "I don't want anything from you. You're just like the rest of them. Leave me alone."

Animosity lay between them like a great gulf. Her gray eyes, stormy and hostile, met his hard and unyielding gaze. "So be it," he said after a long silence. "You won't be bothered with my touching you ever again."

She fled the room and rushed for the stairs. She was halfway up when Jared halted her. "I'm going to Austin tomorrow. I don't know when I'll be back."

She looked down at him. In spite of her disillusionment, she loved him. During their argument, his hair had become mussed and hung over his forehead, shadowing his eyes, making their expression indiscernible. His booted foot was resting on the bottom step, his arm draped over the bannister. His dishevelment only added to his handsomeness. Her heart cried, "Jared, I love you!"

But she said nothing. Not even goodbye.

"I'm leaving for Keypoint tomorrow and I'm taking Elena with me." Lauren faced Olivia across the wide expanse of Ben's desk. She had made a decision and was now daring Olivia to protest her action. "I think Gloria will need all the help she can get with her new baby coming. Elena and Carlos need to live together, like the family they are. I shall ask Rudy to give them one of the cabins on the ranch."

"The *foreman* doesn't make decisions for Keypoint, Lauren." Olivia was seething. How dare she mention that bastard and his brood to her? Lauren was deliberately provoking her as she had done for the past several days.

The morning Jared left, Lauren had launched her campaign.

Before Olivia was privy to her intentions, Lauren had organized a church committee strictly for the purpose of aiding and abetting the community of Pueblo.

Lauren's head wasn't in the clouds. She realized that if the citizenry of Coronado had really been concerned about their Mexican counterparts, they would have done something long before now. She used her new last name to its full extent. Sweetly she asked for help as Jared Lockett's wife on a project they had conceived. Her victims were powerless to refuse.

She had coaxed a reluctant Pepe to drive her through the streets of the town and she had been appalled at what she saw. In the bright sunlight, all of Pueblo's ugliness and deprivation were displayed like open wounds. Lauren had been shocked at the lack of sanitation, the poverty, the sickness, the squalor.

Under Lauren's direction, the church ladies commissioned other social groups to start charitable projects of their own. Old clothing was collected and distributed. Lumber—albeit used— was donated for construction projects. And Lauren wrote to the university in Austin, asking them if medical students would consider establishing clinics for the treatment of the sick and to teach basic lessons on hygiene.

When Olivia heard about Lauren's efforts from a guileless bank customer, she barely made it home before her temper erupted with the impetus of a volcano.

She began the interview in the office with, "You will desist from your ridiculous project immediately."

Lauren didn't pretend to misunderstand. She had come into the office well armed for combat. "I will not sit here and discuss anything with you until the drapes behind the desk are drawn." Whether Olivia was shocked by Lauren's bravery or too stunned by anger to object, she sat silently while Lauren calmly went to the windows and drew the drapes. When she returned to the chair opposite the desk she said, "Now, Olivia, I believe you have an opinion on my activities in Pueblo."

"Your interference in that community is sheer lunacy!" Olivia fairly screamed. "Whatever 'committees' you have organized will die a sudden death, starting now. Am I understood?"

"You are, but no, none of the projects I've started will be stopped."

"I'll see to it that they are," she threatened with a tone of voice that would have intimidated many a brawny man.

Lauren didn't even blink. "I don't think you will," she stated calmly. "What would everyone think if my 'noble' efforts were halted by my own mother-in-law?"

"No one would know," Olivia said with a trace of amusement. Was the girl simple?

"Yes they would. I'd tell them."

"Oh, I see. It's your intention to disgrace me?"

"Since when is it a disgrace to aid one's fellow man?" Lauren considered the interview over then, and left Olivia alone with her hatred.

If Olivia planned to stymie Lauren's actions, she found herself ill-equipped and ill-trained to do so. This was the type of work Lauren had done all her life. She was a good administrator. It was a rare talent to be able to talk someone into doing an unpleasant task and leave them thinking that it had been their idea in the first place.

Everyone was enamored with the courageous Mrs. Lauren Lockett. Olivia's subtle, tentative suggestions that her daughter-in-law might be a bit ambitious met only high praise and enthusiasm for the projects.

When all her committees were in full swing and Pueblo already showed signs of improvement, Lauren decided to return to Key-point. For the present, she had done all she could do. The cold hostility in the house in Coronado had become untenable. Now, as she faced Olivia purposefully, unafraid of the woman's imposing mien, she said, "I spoke to Jared about Elena and Carlos, and he agreed." That was the first time that Lauren Holbrook Lockett had told a lie, but she felt that she would be forgiven. "Besides, with both Jared and me away, I'm sure you can spare her. Pepe can escort us to Keypoint and bring the wagon back. He should be able to return the day after tomorrow."

"You have it all planned, I see. What do you hope to accomplish with this little escapade? Do you intend to tell certain persons our plans in hopes that they will be aborted?" Olivia's green eyes were daggers as she glared at Lauren.

"If I told Rudy," she paused after emphasizing his name, "it could endanger him and his family. I wouldn't do anything to jeopardize their safety."

"How thoughtful."

Lauren ignored the sarcasm and continued, "I don't think your barbarous plans will ever see fruition, Olivia. I don't think Jared will take part. I've come to know him, and it would be against his nature to do such a despicable thing. It's your soul I fear for, Olivia, not Jared's."

Olivia laughed with genuine pleasure. "What a fool you are. You think you have redeemed my son. I warrant that he would be a challenge for any missionary to try to save." Then all amusement left her cold, beautiful face. "Don't count on Jared. He belongs to me and will always do as I tell him to."

Lauren rose gracefully from her chair and, totally composed, left the room.

The next morning dawned cold, rainy, and dreary, in perfect harmony with Lauren's mood. Rosa bid a tearful goodbye to Elena, but the younger girl was jubilant. When Lauren had told her about taking her to Keypoint so she could live with Carlos, Elena had been overcome with gratitude. She couldn't believe that it was really going to come about. Despite the dreadful weather, she was chattering merrily when they left.

The trip took longer than usual because of the rain and the muddy roads. Lauren sat on the seat of the wagon with Pepe, while Elena sat huddled under a tarp in the wagon bed.

They were cold and tired and hungry when they finally reached the ranch house late in the afternoon. Gloria ran out to meet them and hugged Lauren to her in a sisterly embrace.

"We've missed you so much. It's good to see you. Where is Jared? Is he coming later?"

The mention of his name brought a lump to Lauren's throat, but she answered calmly enough, "I don't think he's coming out this time. He has business in Austin."

Gloria would have said more, but Lauren's obvious reluctance to talk about her husband stifled any questions she would have asked. Would these two never get their differences settled?

"Gloria, this is Elena, Carlos Rivas's wife and my friend. I've brought her with me to help you here in the house. I hope Rudy can arrange for them to live in one of the cabins. Do you think that's possible?"

"We'll make it possible. Welcome, Elena," Gloria said, taking both of the girl's hands in her own. "We think a lot of Carlos and I'm happy to finally meet you. We were sorry to hear about your baby. Will you help me take care of my children? They are more than I can handle."

Gloria was reacting just as Lauren knew she would. Elena would be happy here. Lauren sighed and went into the house to greet the children and Maria. As each child was hugged, he or she had a special story to relate to Aunt Lauren. She listened to them avidly, jealous of their carefree innocence. They were full of questions about their hero, Uncle Jared, and she told them about his winning the shooting contest. They listened with wide, round eyes to the entire episode with the automobile.

Gloria shooed them into their rooms and Maria stepped forward to embrace Lauren, who welcomed the succor she found in those slender arms. Maria pulled away from her and looked deeply into the sad gray eyes. "I think you are unhappy, Lauren, no?" Lauren hung her head and nodded miserably. "We'll talk later." Maria patted her arm and turned to welcome Elena.

When he came in that evening, Rudy gave her a hearty kiss. At a signal from Gloria, he refrained from asking too many questions about Jared or the situation in Coronado.

Pleading exhaustion, Lauren retired early to her room. It was painfully reminiscent of Jared—his things, his clothes, his scent. Everything was a grim reminder of their parting.

She knew he hadn't meant to strike her. That had been an accident. What she considered to be his betrayal was the harsh, angry words he had flung at her. Could those words have come from the same mouth that had kissed her with such tenderness? Kisses that even now as she remembered them made her body tremble?

It was futile to deny the sensations that rocketed through her whenever she recalled his lovemaking. Her body became as malleable as melting butter when she recalled his hands and lips and how they had aroused and pleased her. The intricacies of her body and his had been revealed to her under Jared's practiced touch, yet she longed to know more. She wanted to feel again that sublime ecstacy that had encompassed her the moment his masculinity filled her and made her complete.

Love words he had chanted in her ear came back to haunt and mock her as she tossed restlessly on her pillow, which was already damp with tears.

Rudy gave the use of a cabin about a mile away from the large house to Carlos and Elena. He even permitted Carlos to take a day off to set up housekeeping. Very little got accomplished, but

Elena was radiant the next morning when Carlos dropped her off at the ranch house before he reported to work. She fell right in with the routine in the kitchen and herded the children around with the patience of an experienced schoolmarm. The children adored her and minded her far better than they did either their mother or their indulgent Aunt Lauren or their grandmother, whom they manipulated unmercifully.

Lauren wasn't in the Christmas spirit, but the holiday came nonetheless. On Christmas morning, James and John were delighted with a new pair of suspenders and play guns with holsters. The girls squealed when they found new petticoats and hair ribbons in their boxes from Aunt Lauren.

There was so much confusion amidst the packages and presents that Santa Claus had left behind, that no one noticed when Lauren slipped back into her bedroom and shut the door.

Some compulsion she couldn't name moved her toward the closet and she opened it slowly. She looked at Jared's clothes hanging there, an old pair of boots flung negligently onto the floor, a leather vest hanging on a nail inside the door.

"Jared," she groaned, and pressed her face into one of the shirts that, even though it had been laundered, still retained his scent, the aroma of his tobacco and the faint smell of leather. She sobbed for several minutes into the cloth until she felt gentle hands on her shoulders.

"Lauren, are you ready to talk about it now? I'll listen if you are."

"Oh, Maria, I don't want to burden anyone with my problems, especially not you, when Ben's death is so heavy on your mind."

Maria led her to the bed and they both sat down. The children's exuberant exclamations came from the next room. Maria patted Lauren's hand, giving her time to assemble her thoughts.

"I . . . this . . . my marriage is a farce," she blurted out. Unevenly, brokenly, she told the whole story from the time she had met Ben to William Keller's attempted rape and the Prathers' censurous acceptance of his lies. She was ashamed to tell Maria about the terms of her deal with Olivia, but she related them dispassionately, omitting any mention of the Vandivers. "You probably think I'm terrible to sell myself that way."

"I'm in no position to pass judgment on anyone, Lauren. But under the same circumstances, I would have done the same thing. Sometimes our choices in life are between the lesser of two evils.

You did what you hoped would be the right thing. No one can condemn you for that. Besides, I think your motivations included something besides Ben's wishes and the money, didn't they?"

This was the question that Lauren had asked herself time and again. Had she been in love with Jared even then? Was that why she had gone along with this outlandish scheme? Nothing was clear to her anymore.

"You fell in love with Jared, didn't you?" Maria asked softly. Lauren nodded and Maria continued, "And this marriage of convenience has become something else, hasn't it? You've . . . been with Jared?"

Lauren covered her face with her hands and sobbed, "Yes, oh, yes. Not until just a few days ago and . . . oh, I don't know, Maria. All my life I've been conditioned to believe that men did 'bad' things to women and that ladies protected themselves from that debasement. Even though we're married, I know that Jared doesn't love me. Is it sinful for me to feel what I do? To find pleasure in . . ."

"Did you think it was 'bad'?"

"No," Lauren answered vehemently, and Maria suppressed a smile. "When I first came to Ben, I was young and unsure, too. I tried to deny the joy he could bring me. But when I saw that I was giving him great happiness, I could share it without guilt or shame. I, too, was brought up to think that the woman should expect nothing but pain and degradation from lovemaking. God, not Man, created sex, Lauren. And even though Man perverts it and misuses it, it is still a gift to two people who love each other."

"But Jared doesn't love me. I'm terrified of the day he'll grow tired of this farcical marriage and send me away."

"I think Jared is fighting his own battle of feelings, Lauren. I don't believe he could have been coerced into marrying anyone, no matter how high the stakes, if he hadn't been attracted to her. He's far too headstrong. And I think sending you away is the last thing he wants to do." She looked at the tearful young woman and her heart went out to her. Ben had wanted them to be happy. He'd had such high hopes that their relationship would bloom into love.

"Lauren," she said gently, "don't be afraid of loving Jared. If I hadn't loved Ben, think of the useless life I would have had. Think of the misery he would have had to bear alone. I don't think you will regret loving your Lockett any more than I do having loved mine. The only regret I ever had was not being able to give Ben more children."

Lauren sniffed and dabbed at her eyes with a lace-edged handkerchief Maria had extended her. "Thank you, Maria. You go on and join your . . . our . . . family. I'll be out later." She smiled tremulously.

Maria stroked the tear-stained cheek and then left Lauren alone to wonder where Jared was spending Christmas.

Chapter 20

Two weeks after Christmas, the residents of Keypoint enjoyed a few days of unseasonably mild weather. The old-timers predicted that the worst of the winter wasn't over if the weather was this warm in January, but everyone was glad to see a respite from the howling winds that sometimes brought icy rains and sleet.

One morning, Lauren rode out by herself. Maria had a cold and she hadn't wanted to bother Rudy or one of the *vaqueros*. It was amazing how much she missed Flame. But any recollection of the mare reminded her, too, of Jared. A Jared vicious and violent. She pushed those thoughts from her mind.

Never losing sight of the compound and judging her direction by the Rio Caballo, she cantered up and down several hills, grateful for the exercise. She had been gone about an hour and was on her way back to the house when she noticed her mount's ears pull back sharply. About the same time, Lauren heard a mumbled curse followed by a moan. She reined in the gelding and listened. The moan was repeated, coming from the direction of a clump of cedars. She nudged the horse nearer. When she was a few feet from the grove, she could barely make out a form lying on the ground.

She dismounted cautiously and took a tentative step forward.

"Stay right where you're at." She heard the unmistakable click of a rifle being cocked and she froze, her heart jumping to her throat.

"Don'tcha come no closer." The voice was sinister, but clipped as if the effort to speak was painful.

"Are you hurt? I heard you moaning." Lauren was quaking on the inside, but she felt this person needed help.

"You Jared Lockett's woman?"

"Yes, I'm Mrs. Lockett. Who are you?" She took one more step forward.

"I said don't come no closer." The last word raised an octave as the sentence dissolved into a long, heart-constricting wail.

Throwing caution aside, Lauren ran into the thicket. She pulled up sharply and covered her mouth to stifle the scream that rose from her throat.

The man was ragged and dirty, his ankle caught grotesquely in a trap of some kind, blood oozing out around the steel teeth that were biting into his flesh.

His face was a hideous nightmare. This was Crazy Jack, the hermit. It was a death mask this poor creature wore instead of a face. Red ugly scars adorned the sides of his head where his ears should have been. Two open holes that gaped eerily served as his nose.

Lauren swallowed the bile that flooded into her mouth. "Mr. Turner, let me help you." She crept closer to him.

What was left of his face was contorted in pain. His lips were pulled back in agony over a scarcity of teeth, and his eyes were squeezed shut. Lauren noted that the fingers which had held the rifle were now clenched around the injured leg. The firearm had been abandoned on the ground.

"Don't want no help," he hissed.

"You may not want it, but I think you should have some." The firmness in her voice surprised him. He opened his eyes and looked at her suspiciously, searching for some threat. He saw none.

"Can you get this goddam contraption off my leg?"

"I . . . I don't know." She looked at the ominous thing and shuddered. "I can try."

"Well, quit jawin' then and do it afore I bleed to death," he grumbled. "Take aholt on either side and pull as hard as you can."

"Won't it hurt when I lift up your foot?" she asked timorously.

"Yes, goddammit, but it's hurtin' like hell now, and I got to git it off, ain't I?"

"Very well," said Lauren decisively, removing her gloves. Obviously the man was determined to be rude.

Her heart was thudding as she knelt down beside the disfigured hermit and gently closed her fingers around his shin above where the trap had sprung on his ankle. He gasped even at this slight pressure and she looked at him with pity. "I'm sorry, I know it's excruciating."

"Go on and git it over with," he rasped.

She placed her fingers on either side of the trap, finding as good a hold as she could on the blood-slick metal. Tentatively she tried to pull the trap apart. It didn't budge and Crazy Jack's breath sucked into the vacuum of his mouth as the pain increased. "Harder, lady."

Lauren tried again, exerting tremendous pressure. Just as she was about to give up, she felt the metal beneath her fingers give way a fraction. The muscles of her arms ached with the effort she was demanding of them. Finally the sides of the trap sprang apart, tearing into the poor victim's flesh before coming free of it.

Jack screamed. The trap's teeth had left deep puncture wounds around his ankle. They were bleeding profusely. Lauren went to her saddlebags and retrieved a canteen of water. She knelt down again beside him and poured the liquid onto the wounds. Jack actually laughed at her.

"Water won't do no good, Missy. Get that canteen off my horse. He's around here somewheres." She looked around until she saw a mangy animal nibbling on the short grass under the trees. She approached him timidly, afraid that he might be as shy of people as his owner, but he stood docilely as she lifted the canteen from where it hung around the saddlehorn. She uncapped it and the unmistakable odor of whiskey assailed her nostrils. This must be the rotgut that Jared had told her the old recluse distilled.

She paused only an instant before generously bathing the punctures with the liquor. Jack winced and his eyes began to water, but he didn't scream again. He gestured for her to take the scarf from his neck and wrap it around his leg. It was grimy and dark with grease.

"Why . . . why don't I use mine? It's . . ." she suppressed the word cleaner and substituted, "larger."

"Ain't takin' no charity—"

"No, no, nothing like that." She didn't give him time to protest further as she whipped her bandana from around her neck. She formed a silent, selfish prayer of thanksgiving that she wasn't wearing the blue silk one Jared had given her, but one of cotton print she had bought for herself in Coronado. Not allowing herself to think of the pain she must be causing the poor man, she hastily tied the scarf around his oozing wounds.

"There. That should hold you until we can get you back to Keypoint and summon the doctor. Can you ride?"

"Hold on just a goddam minute, Missy. I ain't agoin' nowhere but to my house, and no stinkin' sawbones is goin' to touch any part of Jack Turner."

"But, Mr. Turner, those wounds are serious. Your ankle may

be broken." She couldn't let him return to that cave he lived in without medical attention. "Please, if you don't want to go to Keypoint, let me get Rudy, you know Rudy Men—"

"Hell, yes, I know who Rudy Mendez is, and he or no one else is goin' to take care of this ankle ceptin' me. I've had more broken bones than you've had years."

"But you may need to be sutured."

He raised his scornful eyes to her then and cursed imaginatively. "Who you think sewed up my face when them Injuns did this to it, huh?" He didn't expect an answer and Lauren was too mortified to make one. "Now get outa' my way."

Jack struggled to his feet and shrugged off her attempts to help him. He leaned down and picked up his trap, condemning it for being empty. He damned as well his own clumsiness at having stepped on it. He limped to his horse and took a long pull on the canteen before he hoisted himself into the saddle.

"Would you like for me to follow you and see you home? You may need *some* help."

"No ma'am. You seen more of Jack Turner than any other human has in twenty years or so. I'd be obliged if you was to forget what you seen." He looked away shyly and said, "You seem like a real decent sort of woman, Miz Lockett."

Lauren knew that he would resent the pity she felt inclined to show him, so she said, "Thank you. It has been a pleasure to meet you, Mr. Turner."

He tipped his hat to her and rode away. She didn't follow him so as not to invade the privacy he coveted. She waited until he was out of sight before she mounted her horse and rode back to the ranch house, after stopping once at the river to wash the blood from her hands.

She went into the kitchen and gathered up a basket of food, then returned swiftly to the riverbank across from the house growing out of the rock wall. She left the basket on the flat rock as she had seen Jared do. She didn't tarry, but rode away without looking back.

As Gloria's delivery date drew near, the women sewed and knitted, talking over names, deciding first on one and then discarding it for another. Elena happily announced one morning that she, too, was pregnant again. She radiated good health and energy, while Carlos wore a perpetually sappy grin. Lauren was touched by their obvious happiness with each other and their new home.

The Mendez baby chose the twenty-third day of January to make its appearance. Gloria had been listless since getting up that morning. She, Lauren, and Maria were sitting in the large living room near the fire enjoying a cup of midmorning tea when she clutched the arms of her chair.

"I think I'm going into labor. That's about the third pain, and it's the strongest."

Lauren nearly dropped her cup, but Maria went to her daughter-in-law and supported her as they walked into the bedroom she shared with Rudy.

"Lauren, will you come help Gloria into bed, please?"

Lauren jumped in alarm, but she followed the other two into the room. At Maria's instructions, Lauren turned down the spread and covers on the bed, and Maria eased Gloria down onto the sheet.

"I'll undress her, Lauren, if you'll go tell Elena to take care of the children for the rest of the day," Maria said placidly. "Send word to Rudy by one of the *vaqueros*. They'll know where he is. Then come back. I'm sure we can use another pair of hands."

Lauren sped out of the room, grateful for any task that took her away from the birthing bed. She didn't relish witnessing that secret rite which had killed her own mother.

Elena was elated, and assured Lauren that she would take care of the house and the children and would stand by if needed for anything else. Rudy came bounding into the house a few minutes later, looking gray under his dark features.

"Rudy," Lauren cried. "I was counting on you to calm my nerves. I thought you'd be used to this by now. You look like a *new* father."

He grinned abashedly. "I guess every time is like the first time. Is she all right? Can I go see her?"

"Well, I suppose so." Lauren wasn't sure what etiquette dictated in this instance. "Let me check."

She crept into the dim room to find Gloria propped up primly in the middle of the bed talking amiably to Maria. Lauren hadn't expected that. She thought she would find her writhing in pain. "Is it all right if Rudy comes in to see you?"

Gloria laughed. "It's his fault I'm in this predicament, so I guess that entitles him."

Rudy entered after Lauren bade him to and crossed to the bed in three long strides. He sat down close to Gloria and put both of his large hands on her abdomen.

"So by nightfall we'll have another mouth to feed, hey?"

"I'll be the only one feeding it for a while, remember?"

"I'm sure you can handle it." He grinned and cupped her swollen breasts in his hands.

She swatted them away playfully. "Rudy Mendez, even at a time like this you're a lecher. And in front of your mother!"

"She knows I take after my father." He laughed. Then he leaned down and kissed his wife tenderly on the forehead. "I'll be outside if you need me. I love you."

Gloria kissed both his hands before he got up and left the room. Lauren's eyes filled with tears and a lump in her throat prevented her from replying as Maria asked her to stoke the fire in the grate.

The afternoon dragged by. Gloria's pains became more insistent, and Lauren watched in horror as the bed was flooded with water tinged pink with blood. She thought something was dreadfully wrong until Maria assured her that this was normal, and that the baby would be coming soon.

About an hour later, Gloria's face twisted in pain, but with Maria's gentle urging to push harder, she was delivered of a baby boy. Lauren watched as Maria drew him from his mother's body and cut the cord that had bound them together. Her mother must have suffered in the same way to deliver her and the little brother whose birth had killed her. She felt a great loneliness for the woman she had never known. She wished she could remember telling her mother that she loved her. Surely she had.

Maria was wrapping the squirming, squealing baby in a warm blanket when Gloria cried out, "I don't think that's all!"

Maria and Lauren rushed back to her and saw another dark head emerging from the opening between her legs.

"Lauren, help her," Maria commanded as she held the infant boy closer, trying to muffle his loud cries.

Lauren turned pale and started to object, but Gloria moaned again. She looked back to see the baby's shoulders trying to push their way into the world. Trembling, Lauren took the child's head in her hands as she had seen Maria do and gently pulled. The baby didn't move, but it set up a howl even with mucus still clogging its small throat. Lauren was perspiring and shaking as she pulled more firmly on the slippery head. The baby almost popped out into her waiting hands. It was a girl.

She was laughing and crying all at once as she announced, "It's a girl," to the anxious mother whose face then relaxed into peaceful repose.

"Here, Lauren, you take this one and I'll cut the cord." Lauren laid the baby girl on the sheet as Maria shoved the other one at her before cutting the cord for his sister.

"Gloria, you have twins. One of each." Maria was giggling like a young girl.

"Tell Rudy," Gloria whispered weakly from the pillows.

Lauren turned and left the room, still carrying the new boy who was making his presence known.

"Rudy, it's twins! A boy and a girl!"

Rudy came to her quickly and looked down at his new son. "Twins?" he asked stupidly.

"Yes, come and see." She led him back into the room where Maria held up the baby girl.

"Twins!" He laughed, then whooped so loudly that the babies started screaming even louder.

"Now see what you've done," scolded Maria as she laid the baby girl on Gloria's shoulder. Rudy took his son from Lauren and sat down on the bed next to his wife. They oohed and aahed over the babies even while Maria was tending to Gloria between her raised knees. Lauren felt like an interloper, and left the room.

She didn't realize how tired she was. It was late in the evening and she had spent most of the day in the room with Gloria and Maria. She hadn't eaten since breakfast, but the emptiness she felt inside wasn't hunger.

Crossing to the wardrobe, she opened the door. She took one of Jared's shirts from its hanger and held it close to her. It had been over a month since she had seen her husband. She longed to share the experience of the birth with him, the wonder of it.

She lay down on the bed and pulled the shirt over her. Closing her eyes, she could see Jared's face just as it was when he had gazed down at her in awe after he had made love to her. There had been no cynicism or bitterness on his face then. Only tenderness. Where are you now, Jared? What are you doing? Do you ever think of me?

She pulled off her shirtwaist and skirt and slipped Jared's shirt over her head. Pulling a pillow against her, she fell asleep.

For the next few days, the arrival of the twins upset the normal routine of the household. The other children were continually underfoot trying to get glimpses of their new brother and sister. Lauren was amazed at the patience that Gloria exhibited. She listened to their chatter and managed to have a private time with each of them every day. Lauren knew she was fatigued after the birth and from the necessity of feeding two healthy infants, yet she didn't neglect her other children.

Benjamin was the name given to the baby boy, in honor of his paternal grandfather, and Lauren was deeply moved when they named the girl after her.

"After all, you brought her into the world. And I hope she will grow up to be a lady like you." Gloria had hugged her sister-in-law and ignored the tears rolling down her cheeks. She was quick to cry these days.

Young Benjamin and Lauren were one week old when something greatly disturbing happened. Rudy was in the house for the noon meal when one of the *vaqueros* came to the door and told him someone outside wanted to see him. The ranch hand shifted his eyes uneasily and looked ready to stand behind Rudy if support was needed.

Lauren followed Rudy out to the porch and saw the charcoal burner Wat Duncan and his sister June sitting on a derelict horse which was almost as dirty as his riders.

Duncan dismounted and strode toward them. "Howdee do, Seeñor Mendez. Heerd you had a new set of twins." Duncan smiled his insolent smile. He had not changed clothes since Lauren had first seen him, only added layers in deference to the cold.

"What are you doing here, Duncan? You know only certain areas of Keypoint are open to you, and this is definitely not one of them." Rudy's voice was firm and cold.

"Well, I jes' came to give you my congrajulashuns. It 'pears your babies is the only younguns that'll be born in the Lockett fambly. Seein' as how Jared deserted his purty bride an' all." He grinned sardonically at Lauren and she shivered under his lascivious scrutiny. She averted her gaze to June, whose shapely legs, bare and seemingly impervious to the cold wind, straddled her mount.

June was staring at Lauren spitefully and licked her dry, chapped lips when she met the other's eye. "Reckon Jared had to go to Austin to find a warm bed for the winter," she drawled.

"My brother's business is none of your concern," Rudy snapped, after a furtive glance at Lauren. It worried him that they knew so much about the happenings at Keypoint and Jared's whereabouts. "He is engaged in important business with the railroad, but keeps in constant contact with us. Now, you'll state your business and leave."

Wat Duncan assumed an obsequious attitude. "Now don'tcha go gettin' all riled up, Rudy. I come in good faith. Vandiver and some of his heavies been snoopin' around and axin' a lot of questions. I don't give a good goddam what happens to them Mexies— no offense intended. I jes' don't want nothin' to happen to my deal with Lockett. Y'all understand. It's my bisness I'm worried about."

The muscles of Rudy's jaw had hardened to granite and Lauren saw him stroke the holster that held his six-shooter. "Get out of here, Duncan. Don't ever come near this house again, or I'll personally kill you. As for your *business*, it's intact as long as Jared and I say so. Vandiver has nothing to do with it. Now get off this property."

"Awright. I'm agoin'. Jes' tryin' to be neighborly like." He sauntered to the mangy horse and mounted in front of his sister. She hooked her thumbs into his belt. Her fingers brushed the front of his trousers as she cooed, "Who's Rudy been sleepin' with, Miz Lockett, now that his wife is laid up havin' babies?"

Rudy reached for his gun, but Lauren put out a restraining arm. "No, Rudy," she whispered, for she had seen Duncan's hand moving to the far side of the horse where a shotgun was strapped. She was grateful to see that the word had spread among the *vaqueros* that the disreputable pair were there and that many of them were moving into place, virtually surrounding the miscreants.

The girl tossed her long white hair and laughed, confident that Rudy wouldn't draw on her brother. "Tell Jared I come axin' about him. I'd like to see him when he gets back." She looked at Lauren and snorted. Duncan pulled the reins of the horse around and they clopped out of the yard, obviously in no hurry to leave.

The *vaqueros* and Rudy watched until they were out of sight, then Rudy commissioned two hands to follow them and make sure that they returned to their camp.

When he came back into the large room, Lauren was sitting staring into the fire. He crossed to her and took both of her cold hands into his as he squatted down in front of her. "Lauren, Jared has never had anything to do with that dirty slut."

Lauren smiled at his kind, sympathetic face. "I know that. He has no affection for me," she confessed wryly, "but I know his taste in women would be more discriminating than that." Maria and Gloria had moved over to them and were listening anxiously to the conversation. "What worries me," Lauren continued, "is what Duncan said about Vandiver and his heavies being in Pueblo."

"Yes, that bothers me, too, but not as much as his knowing about everything that is going on in this house. He is trouble and no doubt about it. Ben would have had him shot on sight if he had come here before, and I may regret that I didn't. How did he know you?"

Lauren told them about the day she and Jared had gone to Pecan Creek and passed through the charcoal burners' camp on their way home.

"Rudy, I'm frightened," Gloria said.

He stood and put his arm around his wife, who had been up out of bed only one day. "I'm sure he's just testing our authority now that Ben's gone. There's no need to worry. Jared and I'll talk it over and decide what's to be done about them. I don't like having that scum anywhere on Keypoint."

The lines around his mouth were grim and he stayed near the house for the rest of the day, though he tried not to appear nervous. Lauren noticed that for the next few days, three or four *vaqueros* were posted around the house. Despite his reassurances, Rudy was still worried about Wat Duncan.

Holding true to the dire predictions, the unseasonably mild weather of January gave way to blindingly cold storms in February. There was little that could be done on the ranch in such weather, and Lauren felt sorry for the *vaqueros* whose turn it was to ride out and check on the vast acreage of Keypoint. They always took plenty of provisions, planning to spend days at a time in one of the line cabins built for just that purpose.

Those in the house confined themselves to entertaining the children, caring for the demanding twins, and sewing and baking for the family and the idle cowboys in the bunkhouse.

It was on one such late evening excursion to the bunkhouse to deliver a batch of cookies that Thorn approached Lauren. The basket had been gratefully received by the *vaqueros* and she was scurrying back across the compound toward the house when the Comanche loomed out of the deep shadows to stand directly in front of her.

She managed to stifle a startled scream by covering her lips with her hand.

Without preamble or apology, he said, "Mrs. Lockett, I found this on the gate this morning."

She hadn't known what to expect his voice to sound like, but it was low and deep, almost cultured. She found herself staring up into the implacable mask of his face. Then she looked down at the crude package he had extended to her.

The bundle was wrapped in brown paper and tied with a string. On it had been childishly scrawled *Miz Lokit*. "What . . . ?" she said, looking into Thorn's face again.

"I believe it's something that belongs to you."

She slipped the string away and opened the paper. The kerchief she had wrapped around Crazy Jack's ankle was caught by the cold wind and nearly ripped from her hand. When she had grabbed it back, she saw that it had been washed and folded. All traces of blood were gone. Her lips tilted into a secret smile. Who would have expected the old hermit to meticulously launder her scarf? Had he chanced being seen to return it to her? He must have.

Lauren was suddenly aware that Thorn was staring at her closely. "I . . . I must have lost this somewhere," she stuttered. "I guess someone found it and . . . returned it. Thank you."

The Indian's eyes didn't waver, and she sensed that he knew more than that stoic face revealed. He didn't speak again, but acknowledged her thanks by a quick jerk of his chin. Lauren didn't realize he had moved away from her until his form was swallowed up by the descending darkness.

The third week of February, they saw the first snowfall. It had threatened for about a week with fierce north winds bringing rain, freezing drizzle, and enough sleet to coat the ground.

As the storm increased its fury after nightfall, Rudy, Gloria, Maria, and Lauren sat around the fireplace enjoying the peace and quiet that descended as soon as the children were put to bed. Gloria had nursed little Lauren and handed her to her namesake. Lauren held the baby on her chest, stroking the small, dark head under her chin. Gloria was appeasing Benjamin's hearty appetite while Rudy and Maria looked on lovingly.

They all jumped in startled reaction when they heard heavy boots thudding across the porch. Still edgy about the charcoal burners, Rudy reached for his holster, which was hanging over the mantel, pulled out the Colt, and had almost reached the door when it was flung open, accompanied by a gust of snow-laden wind.

Chapter 21

The looming figure entered, closing the door quickly behind him. He turned slowly and Lauren gasped when she recognized her husband under his heavy clothing. He followed the sound of her reaction and almost repeated it as he saw her sitting in the glow of the fire, hair tumbled around her shoulders and down her back, holding the baby at her breast. He stood as if struck dumb.

"Good Godalmighty, Jared, aren't you full of surprises!" Rudy clapped his brother on the back. "You almost got shot, you stupid sonofabitch. Why did you plan your homecoming on the night we have the season's only blizzard?"

Jared shook his head as if to clear it. "I . . . I didn't know it was going to get so bad until I got halfway here."

"We're glad you made it safely, Jared." Maria looked at him fondly and he returned her affectionate smile.

"I think it was a crazy thing to do, but I'm glad to see you anyway." Gloria went to him with her arms extended. She was still piqued at his abandoning Lauren, but her natural fondness for him temporarily overcame it.

"Well, look at you, Sister. You've got your figure back. I'd better hug you before Rudy pumps you up again." He took her in his arms in a bear hug despite her protestations.

"Come see what we've done," she said, extricating herself from his embrace.

She had laid Benjamin in one of the two cradles set near the fire where the babies slept during the day when their brothers and sisters permitted it. Jared bent over the cradle and hesitantly stroked the baby's cheek. "Who is this?" he whispered.

"That is Benjamin," Maria said proudly.

"And this is Lauren," Gloria said, turning Jared toward the twin still held by his wife.

Lauren hadn't been able to move or speak, his presence in the room stunning her into silence. She couldn't take all of him in at once and was glad to have had time while the others greeted him to look at him closely. He untied the bandana that held on his hat and ran his hands through the long, unruly hair still damp with snow before shrugging out of the shearling coat as he crossed to the cradle to view Benjamin. He looked gaunt and tired. The stubble on his face was twenty-four hours old at least.

But he was Jared. And he was here.

He dropped down to his haunches in front of her chair. He met her swimming eyes over the top of the baby's head. A silent communication more puissant than words passed between them.

"Lauren delivered her, so we named her after her aunt," Maria said.

"You delivered the baby?" Jared asked softly, incredulously.

Lauren nodded as she turned the small bundle toward him. He took the tiny fist in his and smiled as the baby made a sucking motion with her mouth.

He looked closely at Lauren once more before he straightened to his full height. He eyed his brother derisively, spread his arms wide, looked heavenward, and pleaded, "Is there no end? Twins!" Then he broke into a broad grin and slapped Rudy on the back as he congratulated him. "Does this entitle me to a drink?"

"You bet. I haven't even celebrated properly. I've been waiting for you to get here."

"Are you hungry, Jared?" Maria asked him.

"Yeah, but let me warm up a little first. It's cold enough to freeze your . . . it's cold out there," he finished lamely, and everyone laughed.

He and Rudy shared a couple of glasses of whiskey while they caught up on general ranching business.

Gloria and Lauren took the babies into the bedroom that they shared with their parents for the time being. Maria kissed Rudy and Jared in turn and excused herself for the night.

A short while later, Gloria said, "Jared, please forgive me, but you have no idea how exhausting twins can be. I'll see you in the morning and you can tell me everything that's going on in Austin." She leaned over him and kissed his cheek. He smacked her bottom soundly with the palm of his hand. "Jared Lockett, my husband is sitting right there," she said indignantly.

"Yeah! Let's do something that will make him really jealous."

"You! You're incorrigible."

"Yes, but you love me." He grinned winningly.

"A little bit," she conceded, suppressing a laugh. "Coming, Rudy?"

"In a minute." He ignored her exasperation as she stalked out of the room.

"I'm hungry, Lauren. Could you get me something to eat?" Jared's voice was curt, and Lauren felt that she had been summarily dismissed. Rather than make a scene in front of Rudy, she nodded just as curtly and went into the kitchen.

She warmed the soup that was still on the stove, cut thick slices of bread baked that afternoon, poured a steaming cup of coffee and, almost as an afterthought, added a large slice of apple pie that she had baked to the tray.

The men were talking low with their heads close together when she came back, and stopped abruptly when they saw her. A knowing glance passed between them. She read it to mean that they would continue their conversation later.

"Rudy." The plaintive cry came from the direction of his bedroom. "Please come to bed. I'm cold."

Rudy stood and tossed his cigar into the fireplace. He stretched his long frame and gave an exaggerated yawn. "The babies are just barely three weeks old and already that woman can't keep her hands off me." He shrugged in feigned helplessness and sighed, "What's a guy to do?" He winked at Jared and swaggered into the hall toward his waiting wife.

Jared chuckled as he turned his attention to the tray. Lauren had practically dropped it onto the low table in front of the easy chair by the fire. If he had noticed the loud, angry clatter of dishes, he didn't show it. He took several bites of the scalding soup, ignoring her completely. Angered by his calculated indifference, she whirled around and headed toward the hallway.

"Lauren."

It was hard for her to face him, but she forced herself to stifle her anger and pivoted toward him. "Yes?"

He studied her a moment as she stood framed against the darkness of the hall. She was poised for an attack, but her militant stance was belied by the vulnerability she conveyed in her white woolen robe and slippers. No warrior Jared had ever seen had hair that cascaded in a riot of thick waves and curls.

"How have you been?"

She folded her arms across her chest and laughed mirthlessly. "I don't believe for one moment that you care about my well-being, but as was taught me, I'll answer politely. I've been well, and you?"

He raised one eyebrow in quizzical surprise at her tone. "I've been fine. But please refrain from doing my thinking for me. I *do* care about . . . about you."

"Then I can only surmise that all your messages and letters were diverted." She loathed the sarcasm in her voice, but she was angry, had a right to be, and he deserved this. "I assume your business in Austin went well."

He glanced back down at the tray quickly. "Some of it, yes," he replied in clipped tones. His own anger wasn't far from the surface.

"No doubt you're pleased. I think I'll go to bed now. We took the children out in the snow today, and I'm tired."

"Yes, go on. I'll clear this up when I'm finished."

"I'm sure Gloria will appreciate that. Goodnight."

He didn't look at her as he mumbled a response. He seemed dejected, the hollows of his cheeks and the lines around his mouth and eyes emphasized by the shadows the firelight cast on his face. Lauren steeled herself against the temptation to go to him. Instead, she walked down the dark hall to the bedroom.

She had just warmed a spot under the covers where her body huddled when she heard the bedroom door open. Jared came in, closing the door behind him.

She sat up quickly, pulling the blankets up to her chin. "What do you think you're doing?" she demanded.

He didn't even look toward her as he sat down on the ottoman and began tugging off his boots. "If I recall correctly, this is *my* bedroom in *my* house. It is a very cold night out, and I have no inclination to seek another place to sleep. If it offends your sensibilities to sleep with me—and I stress *sleep*—then I suggest you find yourself another bed. This one belongs to me."

He had pulled off his socks, shirt, and the top of his underwear, and was working on his belt buckle. The firelight picked up golden tints on the hair that furred his chest.

Lauren flounced back against the pillows and scooted to the far side of the bed, putting her back to him. She heard his pants drop to the floor followed by the soft swish of his underwear. No! He couldn't sleep like that on such a cold night! He padded across the floor and tossed a few more logs onto the fire in the fireplace, then went to the trunk at the foot of the bed. He raised the lid, which squeaked slightly, and took something out. She dared not look. He flung whatever it was over the bed.

"Thorn made this for me. It'll keep us warm as toast."

She opened her eyes to slits and saw that it was some sort of fur blanket. She closed her eyes quickly when the cold air rushed in under the raised covers as the bed sagged with his weight.

"Goodnight, Lauren," he said. She lay perfectly still and didn't answer. He laughed and turned away from her, settling himself in the warm cocoon of the bed. It wasn't too many minutes before she heard the even breathing of his sleep.

She didn't sleep for a long while.

At some point during the night, they turned to each other. Whether it was for warmth or something Lauren didn't want to name, she awoke to find herself lying against Jared's chest, his heavy arm imprisoning her, their legs wrapped together.

She lay still, savoring the nearness of the body next to hers. The hairs tickled her nose as his chest rose and fell gently beneath her head. She could feel his breath on the top of her head. The dull thudding of his heart echoed in her ear.

Afraid to move for fear she would wake him, her eyes wandered as far as they could and delighted in their perusal. The fire in the grate had all but burned itself out, but one small log caught and flickered in the dark room, illuminating it briefly. Lauren saw Jared's broad chest under her head, the hair fanning out at his throat and tapering to a slender, silken column on his stomach.

Hesitating only a moment, she lifted her hand and, placing it against him, began slowly tracing the pattern of hair on his muscular chest, down the corded, flat stomach, until she felt it grow thick and coarse on his abdomen. She rested her hand on the wiry mat, unable to bring herself to explore further. Only then did she notice that the breathing above her head was no longer steady and the heartbeat beneath her ear was more rapid. She raised her head quickly and met the amber eyes glowing in the fading firelight.

"Ah, Lauren, Lauren." Her name was half-sigh, half-groan before his mouth melted into hers. He kissed her hungrily, wildly, while his hands sought the hem of her nightgown and raised it past her waist, her quivering breasts, over her head, and flung it away.

Raising his head, he looked deeply into her bright eyes as he lifted her hand. He kissed the palm ardently, teasing it with his tongue. Without taking his eyes away from hers, he drew her hand beneath the covers and placed it over his awakened manhood. He studied her reaction, fearing that she would be repelled. Jealously he watched the tip of her tongue disappear between her lips after nervously wetting them.

Don't be afraid of loving this man, Maria had told her. Don't be afraid. Her slender fingers closed around the warm shaft with its velvet skin stretched smooth. Gently her fingers played over him, curious, wondering fingers, fingers made exultant by their discoveries.

Reflexively Jared arched his back. His head went back in a gesture of exquisite feeling. Then his chin lowered and he was searching her face again. His golden eyes shone bright with emotion. "Touch me, Lauren. Touch me until I die from the pleasure of it. Know all of me." His voice was breathy and uneven.

Emboldened by his impassioned plea, she stroked and caressed until she found the smooth spearhead lubricated with the precious nectar of his desire. "Oh, God," he groaned as he lowered himself over her and took her mouth under his. His hands found her breasts and massaged them in rhythm to her own caresses. He squeezed the soft mounds gently while his thumbs appreciated the aroused centers.

For Lauren, every vestige of reluctance, doubt, and mistrust disappeared as she thrilled to the mysteries of her husband's body. Instinct instructed her in the best ways to show her admiration, and she was rewarded with his urgent, whispered words of praise and encouragement. Her hands glided over the firm muscles of his buttocks, down the hard thighs, up the sinewy back. She touched him unafraid. Imitating him, she kissed him passionately, using her mouth and tongue to explore his thoroughly.

His mouth and fingers were gentle stimulants that tormented her mercilessly. Relentlessly they trailed her neck, chest, breasts, and stomach, until she was making small whimpering sounds that surprised him as much as they shocked her.

"Put your hands around my neck," he instructed as he rose above her. His fingers found her feminine threshhold moist and pliant and trembling. She tightened around his fingers like warm, closing petals as they entered that haven. He withdrew a fraction and stroked her lightly, but the mere touch struck her like a lightning bolt.

Her eyes opened wide in astonishment as she began to writhe uncontrollably. "Jared—" she gasped.

He replaced the seeking fingers with his tumescent shaft. Guided by his own hand, it rubbed against her, that magic spot, until she didn't think she could bear the pleasure any longer. She felt herself swelling, reaching out to him, opening, squeezing, dying brief little deaths to know his magnificence fully.

Jared, who before now had boasted of his sexual prowess, learned from the woman moving with him in such perfect tempo that he had known nothing of lovemaking. Not until he saw her face radiant with joy as she reached the peak of fulfillment under his manipulation did he realize the immense satisfaction of giving. Then he filled her completely, giving her all of himself, leaving no room for the frustration and fear that had come between them.

She clung to him tenaciously, matching his ardor, his fervent kisses that deepened even as he delved into her. In one shattering instant, they met on a plane where joy replaced sorrow, trust reduced uncertainty to insignificance, unity conquered loneliness, and indecision became commitment.

After the tumult, they held each other tightly, still unable to comprehend the upheaval of emotions that continued to race through them. Jared looked into her face and smoothed the ebony tendrils from her temples. Satiated, he slid down her body to cushion his head on her breasts. He kissed them lightly in turn, flicking his tongue over the rosy nipples, swollen and agitated with their recent lovemaking. "Beautiful, beautiful woman," he sighed.

He laid his head on that welcoming pillow. He was almost asleep, drugged by the fragrance of her dewy skin, when he heard her voice coming from far away and whispering, "Jared, I love you."

It continued to snow until noon the next day. The accumulation was in excess of six inches, which was unusual for that part of Texas. The world, from the view of those in the ranch house at Keypoint, appeared to be covered by a vast blanket, white, clean, pristine, and soft.

The bedroom occupied by Lauren and Jared was off-limits to the other occupants of the house. When the two failed to come to breakfast, and Gloria noted that Jared's coat still hung on the bracket by the door—evidence that he had not gone out to the bunkhouse the night before—she was thrilled. She forbade Rudy or any of the children to go anywhere near the bedroom. Rudy was amused by her protectiveness, but at the same time glad that his brother was finally sleeping with his beautiful, neglected wife. He would tease him later, away from Gloria's hearing.

The two people in the closed bedroom were totally unconcerned about any of the others in the house. In fact, they had not given them a conscious thought, so absorbed were they in each other. After sleeping for a while, they talked long hours about themselves. Lauren told him of her lonely childhood with a remote, undemonstrative father. Jared, in turn, reminisced about Ben, and about his slain friend Alex.

In the months they had known each other, they had never discussed personal things, except for that one brief conversation in the library in Coronado. Now they talked of trivialities—food preferences, favorite things, aversions and fears, birthdays—revealing the bits and pieces of themselves that made them what they were.

Early in the afternoon, there was a light tap on the door. The entwined figures on the wide bed moved but slightly, resentful of anything that separated them by more than inches. Jared muttered to himself as he crept out of the covers and crossed to the door. He was quite unashamed of his nakedness, and Lauren gloried in his physique with equally unashamed interest.

"What is it?" he asked through the heavy door.

There was no answer. He opened the door a crack and peeped around it. No one was there. Then he began to chuckle.

Lauren sat up, puzzled by his amusement. He knelt down and picked up a tray laden with food and drink. He closed the door with his foot before bearing the repast to the bed.

Lauren saw a platter of light, fluffy eggs, thick slices of ham, biscuits and *tortillas* dripping with butter, a pot of coffee, and even a decanter of whiskey, along with plates, napkins, cutlery, and glasses.

"Remind me to thank Gloria later," Jared said as he bit into a *tortilla*. They ate until they were filled, and he removed the tray from the bed. They had opened the drapes earlier to enjoy the sight of the snow-covered hills. Now he went to the windows and closed the drapes, dimming the room.

He stretched like a lazy mountain cat and yawned broadly.

"Am I boring you?" Lauren asked mischievously as she twirled a curl around her finger then dropped it precariously close to a pouting nipple.

His footsteps, hurried because of the cold, slowed as he came closer to the bed. He placed one knee on the mattress, eyed her provocatively, and drawled, "Could be. What are you going to do about it?"

Lauren's flushed face became impish as she retorted, "Nothing!" and flopped to the opposite side of the bed, providing him an unrestricted view of her smooth back, tapering to the gentle swell of her hips.

He laughed before falling down beside her and grabbing a handful of hair. He wound it around his fist, pulling on it inexorably until she was forced to roll against him. Not quite sure how it came about, she discovered herself atop his chest, her legs straddling him.

"Jared!" she exclaimed, trying to disengage herself from the arms that clamped across her back. Her struggles only widened his grin. He risked taking one arm away from her back to cup her head in his hand and force her face down to receive his burning kiss.

At last, she pulled away from him and sat up. He was dazzled by the breasts that were enticingly suspended in front of him. With an index finger, he skimmed across the tops of her breasts, circled them leisurely, then teased the tips. He watched her immediate response in awe, intrigued and bewitched.

"Jared, I . . . oh . . . what do I . . . please . . ."

"Do whatever feels right," he said before he lifted his head and raked his tongue over her distended nipples.

"I—"

"Whatever feels right, Lauren," he breathed as his hands slid down her ribs to settle on her hips. His thumbs met at the dark nest in the center of her abdomen and impressed hypnotic circles onto it. Impossible to ignore, the hard shaft pressed up into her. His hands stroked her thighs as she rose to her knees, poised over him, then impaled herself on his strength.

"My God," he hissed through gritted teeth. His head tossed on the pillow. She rocked upon him, moving up and down, reveling in the feel of him inside her. She combed her fingers through the mat of hair on his chest, teasing the hard brown nipples. When she grew tired, she lay upon his chest. Her lips sought out the sensitive areas of his face and neck, nibbling, caressing them with light kisses.

His hands clasped the backs of her thighs even as his fingers stroked the moist folds between them. Neither could stand any more, and the eruption came. He filled her with the lava of his loins, which seemed to flow into her veins and scorch each nerve ending until it exploded under the onslaught.

Afterward, she knelt beside him, bathing the residue of their lovemaking from his body with a warm, damp towel.

He yawned again as she dropped the towel to the floor. Laughing as she brushed her lips across his, she asked, "Bored again?"

He smiled. "No, I'm sleepy," he confessed. "Come here." He pulled her down deep into the covers and snuggled against her. The hair on his chest tickled her back and his arm weighed on her waist. She moved closer still. He kissed her shoulder before they both slipped into dreamless sleep. Dreams had ceased to be necessary.

Jared knelt in front of the fireplace coaxing the dying embers into a red glow, adding small logs until they flared and ignited. He had wrapped the fur blanket around him to ward off the chill. Lauren could see no light seeping in around the edges of the drapes. It was after nightfall.

She took up her discarded dressing gown and slipped into it as she stepped from the bed. Her bare feet touched the cold floor and she scurried to the hearth and squatted down beside Jared.

"Hey, you're going to freeze. Why didn't you stay in bed?" He ran his hands briskly up and down her arms to warm her.

"Because you weren't there," she replied honestly, her eyes reflecting the glowing fire. Impulsively she kissed him on the lips.

He wrapped his arms around her and drew her down on the rug in front of the hearth. Staring into the flames, neither spoke for a moment. He stroked the length of her hair absently while his chin rested on the crown of her head.

"Jared?"

"Hm?"

"You can't imagine how terrified I was of you the first time I saw you."

He pulled his head back. "Terrified of *me?*" he asked with mock-dismay. There was a glint of mischief in his eyes.

"You were sprawled out, unconscious, in the back of that wagon. I had never been near a man who was so . . . virile . . . threatening . . . I don't know. You intrigued me, though. And that day you sneaked into my room, I was afraid I was going to faint."

He laughed quietly. "I was intrigued by you, too, though up until then I hadn't even seen you. Pepe told me later how I fell against you most ignominiously." He chuckled and hugged her tight. "I wanted to put you on the defensive. You were just as threatening to me."

"I? Threatening? How?" She stared at him incredulously.

Jared reached up to the small table where he had emptied his pockets the night before and picked up a cigar. He struck a match against the stones of the fireplace and lit the cheroot, drawing on it slowly and blowing the smoke over their heads.

Now was the time. She had to know.

"I resented you like hell, Lauren. Not you specifically, but any woman suddenly thrust upon me the way you were. The night Ben died, we had a fierce argument. I don't think he intended to tell me his plan for our marriage at first. He started the lecture by reminding me of my responsibilities and warning me that my indiscretions would eventually catch up with me. 'You're a man now, Jared. It's time you settled down and started behaving like an adult and not some wild bronco bent on destroying yourself and everything I'm leaving you as a legacy.'"

Jared drew once more on the cigar and flicked the gray ash at its tip into the fireplace. Lauren didn't speak. She wanted to know what had transpired that night, why Jared had hated her for so long.

"Mostly out of belligerence, I countered every point he made, until he lost his temper and hit me with both barrels. Our houseguest, whom I had been commissioned to fetch off the train in Austin, was the woman he had selected for me to marry. Since I had dragged my heels, he had taken matters into his own hands, and provided me with a wife. He stressed the fact that you knew nothing of this when I referred to you as an opportunist, along with some very ungentlemanly epithets."

He tore his eyes away from the dancing flames and looked at her closely. His hand cradled the back of her neck as his thumb stroked along her jaw. "You see, Lauren, my whole life, my parents had used me as a pawn to hurt each other. If I did something to please one, it infuriated the other. If I came to Keypoint, which I loved, my mother would be on a rampage for weeks after I returned to Coronado. My childhood and adolescence were one big battle to see who had the most influence over me. The older I got, I just didn't give a damn anymore. I sought to please myself and to hell with everyone else. I didn't relish having a wife chosen for me, especially when I wasn't sure what kind of relationship she had had with my father."

Lauren was suffused with love and pity for this complex man who was her husband. No wonder he had reacted to her intrusion with hate and resentment. "I think I see how confused you must have been by my coming here." Then, with an insight that surprised him, she said quietly, "You want to know why I followed Ben here. Is that it?" He didn't answer, but she sensed by his silence that this was the crux of the matter.

She sighed and stared at her hands as they pleated the skirt of her robe. "Jared, there was never anything illicit between your father and me. You couldn't be more wrong if you think there was. I was attracted to him because he was dashing and exciting and interesting. To someone raised in a parsonage, living with a sweet, but naive couple interested only in their small world, he was like a character out of one of my books. Of course, accepting his invitation to come to Texas to visit was unthinkable, and I never would have done it except for something that happened within days of Ben's departure."

Her lips trembled slightly as she remembered William's attack. Quickly, nervously, she said, "Believe me, it . . . those reasons for my leaving were justified."

He cupped her chin in his fist and asked, "What happened to make you want to leave your home?"

She tried to turn away, but he was adamant. He didn't release her chin, but forced her to meet his probing eyes. "It . . . I . . . Does it matter so much?" she asked piteously.

"Yes."

Again she tried to lower her eyes, and again he held her fast. "Please," she begged in a whisper. Slowly he eased the pressure of his fingers and his hand fell away. She turned her back on him to stare into the fire.

"There was a man," she said. "His name was William Keller. He . . . the Prathers thought that we should marry. I told them countless times that I couldn't abide him, but . . ." Her voice trailed away to nothingness and she breathed in deeply. Dare she tell Jared the rest of it? Would he turn away from her in disgust, blame her as her guardians had done? "Go on," he said from behind her.

Haltingly, she related the full tale of William's attack, his deception of the Prathers, her inability to persuade her guardians that the minister was lying. "After that, I had to leave," she finished hoarsely.

For at least a full minute, a heavy silence hung over them. She had raised her knees and rested her forehead against them. She didn't want to know what Jared thought. Yet she had had to tell him the truth.

His movement was so sudden that she started when he bounded

to his feet. Whipping her head around, she saw him reach for his hat and clamp it on his head. Then, as she watched in stupefaction, he grabbed his gunbelt with the deadly pistol safely ensconced in it and strapped it around his hip.

"Jared? What . . . what are you doing?" she sputtered.

He had reached the door by now and his hand gripped the knob. Glancing over his shoulder, she could see the rigid planes of his face set with determination. His amber eyes shone with resolve. "I'm going after that sonofabitch to kill him."

Despite the severity of his pronouncement, a smile twitched Lauren's lips and then burst forth in delighted laughter. "Like that?" she asked, her eyes shining with new love. He cared! He wasn't angry at her, but at William.

Stunned by her laughter enough to shake him out of his fury, Jared suddenly realized the picture he must present. He glanced down at himself. The gunbelt was his only garment. He smiled at her sheepishly from the shadows under his hat. "You reckon he's worth going out buck naked in a snowstorm for?"

Her eyes still twinkled, but she answered seriously, "He's not worth going after at all."

He rid himself of the ludicrous attire and, before she realized, was beside her, gathering her into his arms. "I'll kill anyone who touches you again. I swear it." He spoke in a low rumble in her ear as he pressed her head against his chest.

His mouth descended and captured hers in a blazing kiss that branded her as his own. Their mouths fused together hotly. Tongues sought, found, took, gave.

Lauren's fingers tangled in the curls lying in wild disarray around his head and pulled her mouth free. "Jared, you must believe that my attraction to Ben was not sexual. To me, he represented the affectionate father I never had. Since that day I saw you framed in the doorway of my room, looking like the meanest desperado ever to roam the plains of Texas, you have dominated my thoughts. Until you kissed me in the office that morning Olivia said we were to marry, I had no idea how a woman was supposed to feel toward a man."

He took her head between his strong, lean hands, sliding his fingers under her hair and drawing her mouth back to his. The kiss was tender, soft, and her lips yielded to the slight pressure of his. But, as all their kisses had done in the past intimate hours, the tenderness turned to passion, and when he lowered her to the fur blanket covering the floor, she was more than ready to comply. Her hair spread out like a dark fan behind her head.

He slid his hands into the opening of her robe and separated the folds, revealing her breasts. His hands closed over them, gently, but with no question of his possession. His mouth gave them the high praise he thought them worthy of. First his lips closed around each crest, then his tongue paid them homage until they glistened wetly in the firelight.

Lauren moaned ecstatically under his adoration while her own hands smoothed over the bunched muscles of his shoulders and back.

His lips left a fiery path across her breasts, down her ribs, back onto her stomach and then lower to her abdomen. He kissed her navel and then lower still until—

"Jared—" She covered the dark thatch his lips had just reached with the palm of her hand.

He raised passion-clouded eyes to hers, opened wide in alarm. "Lauren," he said huskily, "you must know that I would never do anything to hurt you. Trust me." When she remained silent, staring at him with fearful, pleading eyes, he repeated, "Trust me."

Slowly she nodded her head, and didn't resist when he leaned down and kissed the back of her hand where it lay. His lips were warm. Pleasure-giving. In spite of her modest wariness, she felt her muscles surrendering to the diplomacy of his mouth.

Without haste, he lifted her hand and pressed a kiss into the palm. Then he kissed her where it had lain on the dark delta. An intense heat washed over her and a cry of joy bubbled out of her throat. His mouth brought her a pleasure so exquisite that she was helpless to think of anything except his lips and tongue as they moved lower to explore, probe, and please.

The storm mounted and ebbed as he alternately teased and demanded. The pressure within her increased, and when it crashed around her, she called to him plaintively and was gratified when his body covered hers to protect her from the assault of emotions and senses. Still, she wasn't satisfied until he was inside her, deep, hard, fulfilling, touching her womb with the essence of himself.

Her fingers dug into the flesh of his hips as his own passion peaked. His face was buried in her neck and her skin felt his rapid, moist breath as he chanted her name.

He didn't leave her. He couldn't forsake the paradise just yet. Nestled within her body, he raised himself on his elbows and looked down at her. Tenderly he kissed each feature of her face.

"Is this possible?" she breathed, referring to the enormity of her rapture.

"Yes, yes," he murmured against her lips.

He raised his head and his eyes searched her face once again. His expression was difficult to define, but it closely resembled love.

Chapter 22

The next morning, everyone looked up in surprise as Jared and Lauren strolled arm in arm into the dining alcove for breakfast. Lauren flushed in embarrassment under the curious stares, but Jared assumed his casual, aloof attitude and questioned why there were no place-settings in front of their chairs. Gloria immediately ran toward the kitchen.

Jared held the chair for his wife as Rudy asked him teasingly, "Hey, Brother, why did you risk a snowstorm to get here when all you've done is spend the entire time closeted in your room?"

He took the plate from Gloria, filled it to his satisfaction, and only then answered, "Well, I'd been away a long time. When I got to Coronado and saw that Laur . . . I . . . uh . . . just figured that it was time for me to get back out here to check on things. I was worried about Keypoint."

"Your concern is touching," Rudy teased. His black eyes flashed wickedly as he said, "It couldn't be because you were, uh, restless, and wanted to see Lauren, could it?"

"Rudy! You're going to embarrass Lauren," Gloria scolded.

Jared laid his fork in his plate. "You know something? I think you might be right." He grabbed Lauren and leaned her backward over his supporting arm so quickly that she didn't have time to protest. He kissed her full on the mouth with exaggerated passion. The children began squealing with laughter and were soon joined by their initially startled parents and a delighted Maria, who smiled on them fondly.

Breathlessly Jared released Lauren and they joined the laughter. Eventually Gloria resettled the children and everyone resumed eating.

A few minutes later, Jared caught Lauren's eye, winked at her and, finding her knee under the table, squeezed it.

* * *

The snow melted quickly under a crystal-blue Texas sky. The brothers rode out each day to check on various sections of the ranch. The snow had been heavy and wet, and some of their fences had suffered damage. *Vaqueros*, restless for something to do, were sent out to repair them and to keep an eye out for animals that had not survived the storm.

Lauren rode out with them one afternoon. They were only a mile or so from the main house when they came upon the carcass of one of the finest Lockett beeves. It had been mutilated. A few chunks of meat had been carved out. The rest had been left to rot in the warming temperatures.

"Goddammit!" Jared cursed. "Who in hell did this?"

"It couldn't have been Crazy Jack. He never wastes any part of a carcass," Rudy said.

"No. Mr. Turner wouldn't do this," Lauren said quietly.

The men looked at her in surprise and she told about meeting the hermit. Humbly she recounted how she had taken the trap off his foot when he had been injured. "Fortunately I took him some food, too, before the weather got so inclement. But he was in no shape to do a thing like this even if he had been so inclined."

"You mean you actually saw him? Had a conversation with him?" Rudy asked in astonishment. He had never seen the hermit, only traces of him.

"Yes."

"I've learned that my wife has a great capacity to get involved with people, usually the desperate and helpless." Jared spoke teasingly, but there was respect in his eyes. During his brief stop in Coronado, Olivia had filled his ears with a tirade against Lauren's charity work in Pueblo. Little did she know that she was making her son all the more lonesome for his wife. He had been shocked and disappointed to learn that Lauren had gone to Keypoint. His eyes warmed as he looked at her now and said, "If anyone could worm their way into Jack Turner's life, it would be Lauren."

"That still doesn't answer who killed our cow," reflected Rudy.

"It was probably one of Duncan's gang," Jared said bitterly. "It looks like something they'd do."

"Did Lauren tell you about the visit they paid us a while back?" Rudy asked hesitantly.

"What?!" Jared exploded.

Rudy related the conversation he'd had with Duncan. Lauren was relieved that he wisely omitted the slur that June and her brother had made to her. She feared Jared would seek Duncan out immediately. Hadn't he been ready to charge naked out of their bedroom in search of William Keller? She smiled at the memory, but his loud, angry voice brought her back to the present.

"Why didn't you tell me about this sooner?" Jared demanded.

"Because I knew you'd react exactly as you're reacting," Rudy replied calmly. "I think we should exercise caution and keep an eye on them, but I don't want to provoke them into any more meanness."

"Okay," Jared said grudgingly. "But by the end of next summer, I want them off of our property. When the railroad is finished, the *vaqueros* won't have to be driving the cattle to Austin. They can assume more duties toward maintaining the ranch. One of those duties can be clearing the cedar. We won't need that scum anymore." He gave one more disgusted glance to the carcass, then spun Charger around and spurred him to a gallop.

When Wat Duncan struck again, it was swift and sure and deadly. To say the least, it got the attention of the Locketts and Mendezes and proved to them what a powerful enemy the man and his gang were.

Lauren and Maria had arranged the night before to meet in the stables the following morning for a sunrise ride. They had grown accustomed to riding together at that time of day.

Lauren crossed the yard and strolled toward the stable. She was wearing a black suede riding skirt and coat. Her boots were soft black leather, as were her gloves. The ensemble had been a belated Christmas present from Jared. She had wrapped her head in a long, woolen *serape* loaned to her by Gloria and, of course, she was wearing the blue silk bandana. The vapor of her breath hung in the cold morning air. The door to the stable was closed.

Strange, she thought to herself. Maybe it was so cold that Maria had chosen to leave the door shut against the wind. But it wasn't windy, Lauren argued with herself.

The door was heavy, and she had to tug hard several times before it came open. The interior of the stable was dark. It was quiet except for the restlessness of the horses.

"Maria?" A sinister chill, having nothing to do with the weather, crept up Lauren's spine, and she was suddenly afraid to enter the building. Glancing over her shoulder, she saw that no one was stirring in the house. She had left Jared asleep under the covers of their bed. Elena hadn't yet arrived with Carlos to begin her day's duties.

"Maria?" Lauren called again, praying for the sound of Maria's soft voice. Swallowing a lump of fear, she stepped into the stable. She didn't need to go far.

Maria's body was sprawled out in front of her. Even in the darkness, Lauren could see the pool of bright blood forming beneath her.

Her scream ripped through the morning air. Fists clenched at her sides, then rose to cover her mouth, but didn't stifle the screams of terror that kept coming. She was vaguely aware of cursing and nonsensical mutterings as the doors to the bunkhouse were thrown open and the *vaqueros* stumbled out in various stages of undress, their eyes bleary from sleep. Running footsteps came pounding across the yard.

Her screams had dwindled to faint whimpers as she heard someone say, *"Madre de Dios!"*

Rudy pushed her aside and moved cautiously toward his mother, disbelieving his eyes. Strong arms gripped her shoulders. "Don't look, Lauren," Jared said in her ear as Rudy knelt down to turn Maria's body over. Jared's warning came too late. She saw the gaping windpipe with its gurgling fountain of blood where Maria's throat had been neatly sliced. She screamed again, but the sound was muffled against Jared's bare chest as he held her head against him, supporting her wilting body with his.

He led her out of the stable so she wouldn't have to witness Rudy's grief. They could hear his deep, soul-piercing animal wail. Lauren sobbed drily as they walked past the *vaqueros* standing awkwardly, their eyes averted, instinctively knowing what had happened.

Gloria and the sleepy-eyed children were huddled together on the front porch. Gloria's lips were white, her eyes questioning.

"Maria," Jared said tersely. Gloria squeezed her eyes shut, intuitively understanding as she heard her husband's racking sobs.

"Come into the house, children." To Jared, she said, "I'll get some coffee."

He only nodded as he ushered Lauren into the house. She stood mutely just inside the door as he went into the bedroom to pull on pants and a shirt. When he came back, he knelt down on the hearth and began rekindling the fire.

It came as a great surprise to Lauren when Rudy's shadow blocked the dawn light coming in through the door that had been left open.

There were no tears. Instead, his eyes were hard and cold, devoid of any emotion except bitter hatred. He tossed something onto the floor and Lauren jumped back from it, staring in horrified comprehension. Jared looked at the object, too. There was no mistaking the battered, greasy hat that was usually worn on Wat Duncan's head.

"You going with me?" Rudy asked his brother.

"I'm going," Jared said quietly.

Without another word between them, they went through the hall toward their bedrooms. Gloria came out of the kitchen carrying a coffee pot and three tin cups. When her eyes lit on the hat on the floor, she set the coffee on the dining table and went to the gunrack.

While Lauren watched in stupefied astonishment, Gloria methodically took down the rifles, checked them, loaded them, and set them aside.

When they were dressed, Jared and Rudy joined her and, like well-trained soldiers preparing for battle, they moved without wasting words or motions.

When all was ready, Rudy drew Gloria to him and held her tightly. "One of the *vaqueros* will bring her in after we've left. See to her." He kissed his wife quickly on the lips and strode from the room.

Lauren was spun around from behind. Jared kissed her fiercely, almost angrily, before he released her and followed his brother out the door. She rushed after him.

The *vaqueros* had formed a semicircle in the yard. Thorn, his hawklike features fearsome, stood holding the reins of the waiting mounts. Charger pawed the hard-packed earth beneath his hooves. Rudy and Jared mounted in unison. Disdaining the stirrups of his own saddle, the Comanche vaulted astride his horse. Rudy nodded briefly to his small army and then jerked hard on the reins of his horse, turned him, and galloped out the gate, Thorn and Jared on either side, his men behind him.

Lauren whirled around and faced Gloria, who had come out onto the porch. "Gloria, you're not going to let—"

"It's something they have to do, Lauren," she said with quiet assurance. "Come. We have things to do, too."

The hours ticked by with a slow monotony. To Lauren, the horror of seeing Maria lying in her own fresh blood had been dimmed by the realization that Jared might never come back. The brothers had left seeking revenge and she knew the battle would be bloody. No, God, no, she prayed as she mechanically went through the tasks Gloria assigned her.

Maria's body had been carried in by one of the older hands. She was laid on the bed she had shared with Ben. Gloria prepared her for burial. Lauren didn't think she could have looked at the body again, but felt that Gloria would be offended if she didn't accompany the children into the room to pay their last respects to their grandmother.

Lauren was shocked. She didn't know how Gloria had managed it, but Maria's wound didn't show under the high collar of her dress. Her hair was smoothed back in its usual bun. Her face was unlined and her lips were relaxed into a semblance of a smile. Her hands, beautiful, gentle hands, rested on her breast with a rosary entwined in the slender fingers.

The same cowboy who had carried Maria inside constructed the coffin. Lauren took the children out of the room when he came in to lift Maria into the wooden box.

For the rest of the afternoon, Lauren and Elena, who had come to the house upon learning of the tragedy, tried to keep the children quiet while Gloria tended to the twins. Even after the children were all abed, and the twins were sleeping peacefully in their cribs, the women kept vigil, waiting tensely for their men to return.

Finally, long after sundown, they heard the thunder of horses and raced to the porch. The figures were too small to distinguish at first in the fading light, but each woman sighed relief when she saw her man among those returning.

Rudy and Jared rode up into the yard and tiredly got off their horses, turning the reins over to the *vaquero* who would care for their exhausted mounts.

Gloria didn't say a word, only went down the steps to greet her husband by wrapping her arms around him. He held her close, as if to absorb her strength. When she raised her head and looked into his weary face, he said, "Not a trace. Nothing."

They all went into the house and the men collapsed at the dining table. Gloria and Lauren scurried to set the food, which had been simmering on the stove, on the table. Elena had seen to it that the tired *vaqueros* had a pot of the savory stew delivered to the bunkhouse before she left with Carlos.

When his plate was empty, Rudy wiped his mouth with a napkin and scooted his chair back. Jared pulled Lauren down onto his lap and rested his head against her breasts as Rudy began to speak.

"We went to their camp first. Deserted. Not a sign except for the rubbish they left behind. We combed the hills all day, looking in every nook and cranny, and didn't see a trace of any of them." He paused to take a drink of the whiskey Gloria had poured for him. "We found one old nester, about half-crazy. He said he'd seen Duncan and a few others at the river just above the Fredericksburg Road. Day before yesterday, he thought. Duncan was talking to a 'fancy man.'"

"Vandiver?" Gloria asked. Lauren gasped.

"Probably," Jared answered.

They all became quiet then, each lost in his own thoughts. Rudy broke the silence. "I'll find him," he said. "Murdering son-ofabitch. I'll find him." The level tone of his voice was frightening to hear. He raised his eyes to Gloria. "Where is she?"

"In her room."

He nodded and stared at the flame of the gas lamp on the table in front of him. "One of the hands offered to ride into Pueblo and bring a priest back in the morning. We'll bury her then." He paused, then said, "I was thinking today that she would never have gotten over losing Ben. Ever since he died, she's been unhappy. Maybe . . . maybe this was . . . She'll be happy. . . ." His voice broke and Gloria rushed to his side. He came to his feet under her support and they left the room.

"Jared, that's impossible! Even if you could pull off such a thing, do you realize the lives that could be lost? The property that would be destroyed? How could you suggest such a . . . harebrained scheme?"

"What choices do I have? Try to understand this from my point of view."

Lauren heard the voices raised in heated argument coming from the front porch. Dinner was over and the brothers had gone outside. Gloria was caring for the twins. Lauren had been reading in front of the fire in the large living room when she heard Rudy's harsh words.

It had been a week since Maria's burial in a cottonwood grove overlooking the Rio Caballo. Each morning, Rudy and Jared rode out with their men to search for Wat Duncan. Each evening, they returned disappointed in not having seen a trace of their quarry. Maria's death had affected them all, Jared included. But even before that, since the night of his arrival during the blizzard, he hadn't been the sarcastic, angry man he was in Coronado. The man she slept with every night made tender, passionate love to

241

her on the wide bed that had been his since childhood. He told her of his plans to build a house of his own at Pecan Creek. He related to her the circumstances surrounding the death of his friend Alex, in Cuba, and clung to her, tormented by visions of the atrocities of war even as he related them. She had come to love Jared in a new dimension. She loved him fiercely, passionately, and protectively. Strong as he was, virile, stubborn and proud, she had discerned a shred of vulnerability. She loved that most of all.

Lauren longed to share with her husband the rewarding news coming out of Pueblo. Pepe, whenever the weather permitted, brought her news of the projects she had initiated. All were going well. A clinic had been set up two days a week. Remedial construction on public buildings was underway and more was planned for the spring. Warm clothes were being distributed to those who needed them the most. Pepe left with a detailed list of instructions for the committee chairwomen and a personal note of gratitude and praise from Lauren.

She wished to tell Jared about all of this, but she remained silent. She wanted to do or say nothing that would remind him of the events taking place in Austin and Coronado. For that reason, she had not broached the subject of the railroad and the Vandivers. It seemed that Rudy had.

"I know you feel that you have to go through with this, but there has to be some alternative, Jared," he argued.

"I don't see any other way. I've gone over every single aspect of it, and unless I carry out this plan, everything will go up in smoke."

"Everything will go up in smoke if you do. Literally," Rudy countered.

They were silent for a while. Lauren didn't move. Jared was still planning to bring on a riot in Pueblo. He was selling out to the Vandivers and his mother for the railroad.

"At least promise me this." Rudy spoke quietly. "Don't do anything until you've given me some warning. Let me see what can be done from this angle."

"All right, Rudy. I promise. But I don't know how long I can hold them off. They're ready to go. Just be forewarned. When they do it, I'll have to be there. You understand that."

Rudy hesitated for just a moment. "Yes," was the curt reply.

Lauren was crushed. How could he? Maybe he wouldn't. Maybe he could convince them not to destroy the community. She heard their boots shuffling toward the front door and forced her face into a smile before they could see the distress on it.

Jared came to stand in front of her and said quietly, "Lauren, I must leave for Coronado in the morning. You're to stay here until I can come back and get you."

"No. I want to be with you." Her voice trembled, but she didn't give in to the tears she felt gathering in her eyes. He was running away from her again!

"I . . . I'm going to be very busy with the railroad and you'd be bored in town. Here you have Gloria and the kids to keep you busy."

Her eyes beseeched Rudy for support, but he was concentrating on lighting a cigar and wouldn't meet her eyes. She turned back toward Jared. "I'm going back with you, Jared. I don't care how busy you are. If you don't take me with you, I'll just follow on my own." She raised her chin a fraction, and he saw the resolve in her steady, blue-gray gaze.

"Dammit!" he cursed, and slammed his fist into his palm. He turned toward his brother as if seeking an ally. Rudy had become even more fascinated by his cheroot. Jared muttered sourly, "All right. Get packed tonight."

Besides Rosa, Pepe, and her piano, Lauren was not happy about seeing anything in the house in Coronado. It was truly one of the most beautiful houses she had ever been in, but her mother-in-law cast such a cold foreboding on the atmosphere that it could never be considered a comfortable home.

Olivia's greeting had been polite, if not exactly warm. Carson complimented Lauren on the healthy bloom in her cheeks. Lauren met Olivia's green eyes over his shoulder as he hugged her, and wondered if Olivia knew the reason for the glow she had taken on. She reasoned that the older woman did. It was after Jared's first night with her that Olivia had provoked the argument between them that culminated in their separation.

Lauren recognized the subtlety Olivia had used to drive the wedge between her and her husband. She was capable of anything to ensure that her own greedy plans come to fruition. She would even jeopardize the happiness of her son. Perhaps she did love him. But it was a jealous, self-gratifying love. Olivia Lockett had to be in control. Wasn't that the reason her marriage to Ben had been so disastrous? Ben was not a man who could be controlled.

Olivia was learning that Jared wasn't so easily manipulated, either. Not like Carson Wells.

"Carson, thank you. I can always rely on you to make me feel beautiful even when I'm covered with trail dust." Lauren laughed and hugged the plump man again. He evoked her pity, and she couldn't quite decide why.

The next few weeks went by smoothly and uneventfully. Olivia went to the bank every day. Jared went out on pursuits of his own, sometimes riding out to check on the progress of the railroad. The track moved closer to Coronado daily. If the spring weather held and there wasn't too much rainfall, it would probably be completed sometime in the early fall.

Lauren spent long hours at the piano.

She missed Elena more than she could have imagined. There were no laughing children to break the staid atmosphere of this house. There were no disruptive calamities that reduced everyone to a state of mirth. There wasn't the serene presence of Maria . . . Maria. Her friend. Ben's love. Perhaps Rudy was right. Maybe her death had mercifully brought them together again.

There was no more discussion of the Pueblo riot. Lauren could almost imagine that she had dreamed the whole ugly episode. Was it even possible that Olivia had changed her mind?

One afternoon in early March, Lauren sat at a small table in Ben's office composing a letter of commendation to the Ladies of Texas Freedom who had so generously donated fifty pounds of cornmeal to be distributed to the needier citizens of Pueblo.

She heard Jared's spurs jingling on the parquet floor in the hall just before he stood framed in the doorway. The sight of him never failed to accelerate her heartbeat. Never had anyone loved as much as she did. Of that she was positive.

He was wearing his cowboy garb and looked much as he had the first time she saw him. She put her fountain pen down and started to get up and go to him.

"No, stay there." Puzzled by his words, she sat back down and watched him close and lock the door.

"Jared?" She laughed a bit nervously. His expression was so intent it was almost frightening. "What are you doing?"

"Do you know how many times I've fantasized about you looking just the way you do now? You nearly drive me crazy with that prim and proper countenance, the eyeglasses perched on your nose, back straight as you bent over some damn thing or another. It's become a driving ambition of mine to ruffle those calm feathers."

He advanced into the room, pausing only to fling his black hat into a chair. He strode purposefully to the large picture windows and pulled the drawcord on the heavy drapes, plunging the room into deep shadows.

As though stalking prey, he came toward her chair with measured steps and drew her out of it. He sat down where she had been and pulled her onto his lap facing away from him.

"Can your feathers be ruffled, Mrs. Lockett? Since that day I sneaked into your room and spied on you, I've wanted to do this." He placed his lips against the nape of her neck and traced a path of warm kisses from there to her earlobe, tantalizing it with a capricious tongue.

"And this." Her watch pin was covered by a hand that came around her and pressed against her breast. His hands slid over her breasts and met at her waist where he began to pull her blouse from the high waistband of her skirt.

"Then I was going to do this." His hands moved slowly to her back and began unbuttoning the bottom buttons on her shirtwaist. He only released about half of them before his hands slipped under the blouse and moved to her front. Brushing past eager, quivering breasts, he untied the decorative bow at the top of her chemise. Feeling his way, he unbuttoned the tiny buttons, pulling the diaphanous garment down with agonizing slowness until her breasts spilled into his hands.

Lauren had not spoken, but leaned back against his hard chest and purred pleasurably as his fingers caressed her, bringing her nipples to hard peaks by rotating his thumbs over them.

"Tell me when you lose all composure," he whispered challengingly. His breath became uneven. The lips that nibbled at her neck became more impassioned, the tongue more adventuresome.

Hands, too, ceased to be teasing and became imploring. "You feel so good, Lauren," he rasped as he stroked her. "Silk . . . no, satin. Cool. Warm. God, I don't know," he groaned, as he gently rolled the dusky pink crests of her breasts between his fingers.

A fumbling, clumsy hand finally waded through the material of her skirt and petticoats, over a silk stocking and a lacy garter, to find her linen-covered thigh. The skin beneath the sheer covering trembled as the searching fingers smoothed up the length of her thigh until, even through the light fabric, he discovered her prepared for his love. "Oh, God," he groaned.

One hand left her to unfasten the remaining buttons on her back and slip the blouse from her shoulders. Then he pulled the pins from her heavy hair and buried his face in its cascading waves, drinking in the lavender-water fragrance of it.

Turning her slowly toward him, he rested her shoulder against his chest and looked down at her disheveled state. "Just as I imagined. You're ravishing," he whispered huskily.

She suddenly realized she was seeing him through the lenses of her eyeglasses and raised a hand to take them off. He trapped her hand in his and said, "Uh-uh. They're part of the fantasy."

His fingers followed her collarbone and moved down her chest, adoring the tips of her breasts, tormenting her by not touching what she craved to be touched. She arched her back at the same time she tangled her fingers in his thick hair and drew his head to her.

He cupped one of her breasts, brought it up to his descending face, and nuzzled it with his nose and beard-roughened chin before closing his lips around the center bud and raking it lightly with his tongue. When she moaned into his hair, he raised his head and smiled in devilish satisfaction before melting her lips with an ardent kiss.

He pulled back in shock as he felt her slender fingers working with the buttons of his shirt. Playful lips and a darting tongue tormented his nipples until they were turgid. Then her mouth followed the path down his chest and stomach that her fingers charted. She snuggled down his body until she dropped to her knees between his thighs. Staring up at him boldly, she peeled away the chemise and slipped her arms free, completely baring her breasts for his avid inspection. Her raven hair cloaked his thighs as she rested her cheek against his lap.

"I've had some fantasies of my own, Mr. Lockett," she whispered as her fingers deftly unfastened his pants.

She said something else as her hand closed around the swollen shaft, but he couldn't hear her over the pounding of his heart. And when the love-moistened tip of his sex felt the sweet brush of her tongue, his ragged breathing drowned out every other sound.

Much later, they lay on the rug before the fireplace where Jared had struck a match to the logs already stacked there. He lay on his back, hands folded under his head, a cheroot clenched in his teeth, brazenly unconcerned by his nakedness.

Lauren was curled up on her side, staring into the fire, her cheek resting on folded hands. He had covered her with his shirt, long ago discarded along with the rest of their clothes.

"You're very quiet, Lauren. Is something wrong?"

She was glad that he was sensitive to her mood, but reluctant to disclose the worry niggling at the back of her mind. She felt him turn on his side toward her, felt his eyes on her, though she didn't look at him. "What is it? Tell me."

He could barely hear her, she spoke so softly. "I enjoy . . . the things we do, Jared. I . . . it's wonderful, but . . ." She stopped speaking, closed her eyes in embarrassment, and continued, "I don't think ladies are supposed to . . . to participate. I'm afraid you'll think me wanton if I do . . . if I . . ."

His laughter boomed in her ear as he drew her around to face him. Between guffaws, he covered her face with light kisses. When his amusement subsided, he said tenderly, "Lauren, you'll always be a lady. You couldn't be anything but a lady. And no matter how *often* we make love, or *how* we make love, or how *much* you enjoy it, you'll still retain that aura of innocence that first attracted me. It set you apart from any other woman I'd ever met."

He traced her high cheekbone with a gentle finger. "Wanton? I'm surprised you even know the meaning of the word." He chuckled again before his mouth claimed hers.

The kiss was deep and telling, and when it ended, his lips remained on hers as he said, "However . . ." The shirt was moved aside. His index finger began at the base of her throat and traveled down the length of her torso, between her lush breasts, over the smooth skin of her stomach, past her navel and mons to disappear between her thighs. "As long as we're on the subject of wantonness . . ." He touched her knowingly and was rewarded by her ready response.

She sighed in mock-despair. "I'm no better than a common prostitute."

He smiled even as he kissed her. "Yes, you are. Much better."

She wanted to admonish him for his impudence, but his swift and certain possession robbed her of the initiative.

Chapter 23

They came out of the office arm in arm into the wide hall. There they met Olivia. She looked at their wrinkled clothing and mussed hair and assessed the situation correctly.

"I heard you had come home early today, Jared."

"Yes, Mother. You might say I took the afternoon off."

She chose to ignore his bantering tone as she did his holding Lauren close to him with an arm firmly around her waist. She could feel her control over him slipping and it both angered and terrified her. "You have some mail, Lauren," she said tightly.

Lauren looked at her with questioning eyes and took the white envelope that was extended to her. A tiny gasp escaped her lips when she read the return address. "It's from the Prathers," she said. "My guardians," she clarified to Jared, who was looking curiously over her shoulder at the letter. She glanced up at him significantly. He knew the story behind her leaving North Carolina, knew why she would be surprised to receive the letter.

"Open it," he said gently.

She inserted her finger under the flap and withdrew the two sheets of white paper. Lauren had read enough of Abel's sermons to recognize his neat, careful handwriting. Eagerly, somewhat apprehensively, her eyes scanned the page.

"They don't know of Ben's death. They send him their regards." Her eyes roved lower on the page. "Oh!" she exclaimed. Her hand flew to her throat. "William Keller is dead!"

"Good. How did he die?" Jared asked harshly.

Stammeringly she explained as she read, "A big scandal. He was murdered . . . a woman's husband shot him . . . she confessed to their being lovers." She paused in her recitation to read more. The words blurred on the page, seen through a lake of tears. "He . . . they are sorry now for not believing me." She folded the paper and looked up at Jared. "They beg my forgiveness and say that I have a home with them if I ever want to come back."

Jared was looking at her, but he was thinking of the fate of William Keller and not the sentiments of the couple who had condemned Lauren. "That bastard! I wish I had killed him."

"Someone from Lauren's past?" cooed Olivia, who had watched the whole scene with growing interest. She was ignored.

Lauren grabbed Jared's sleeve and shook him slightly. "Don't say that, please."

At her touch and remonstration, he snapped out of his temper. His gaze was warm and compelling as he looked down at her. "In a way, I guess I have Mr. Keller to thank, don't I?"

She smiled, understanding his meaning. Shyly she murmured, "I guess maybe I do, too."

Lauren would remember that afternoon and evening in the weeks that followed. She treasured those hours with Jared in the seclusion of the office. For after that day, everything changed.

The next night was the first time the men came to the house. Jared had left early that morning and didn't come in until after Olivia and Lauren had shared a silent and tense meal.

Jared's mood was surly and rude. He ate little of the food Rosa had kept warm for him, but drank incessantly. When the men began to arrive, Olivia suggested that Lauren might be more comfortable in her room upstairs. Lauren took the hint. She looked toward Jared, expecting him to intercede, but his back was to her as he poured himself another drink at the sideboard.

She watched from the front windows of her bedroom as more and more men arrived. They came in groups of twos or threes, but they all had the same characteristics. They looked mean, disreputable, and vexatious. These were the mercenaries who had been hired to excite trouble in Pueblo, trouble that would be blamed on the inhabitants of that community.

Loud, ribald talking and laughter came from the rooms below. Lauren saw Parker and Kurt Vandiver when they arrived, and a cheer rose to greet them as they entered the parlor.

That was the only occasion when the mercenaries all came at once. As the weeks went by, a few of them would come to the door almost nightly asking for Jared. He would leave with them and Lauren would hear him return to his room in the early morning hours. Sometimes he would ride out alone late at night and be gone for hours before she heard Charger galloping up to the stables at the back of the house. Was he holding meetings to plan the attack on Pueblo?

To help relieve her anxiety and alleviate her boredom, Lauren took a more visible role in the projects abetting Pueblo. Her frequent trips to that community filled her committee workers with renewed zeal. The townspeople soon grew accustomed to seeing Pepe drive her down their dusty streets in a buggy. Some of the less shy even presented her with handmade gifts. She accepted each one graciously and with a gratitude disproportionate to its value. If Olivia or Jared knew of or cared about her work in the Mexican settlement, neither said so.

Just as dawn was breaking one morning, Lauren awakened to the heavy thumping of Jared's boots in the hallway. Excitement welled in her breast when the footsteps neared her door. There they stopped. Expectantly she sat up in bed. Long moments passed. Once she even thought the doorknob rattled slightly. But she was crushed with disappointment as Jared's tread retreated toward his room.

Flinging the covers aside, she flew out of bed, grabbed her wrapper, and dashed to her door. Opening it, she called faintly, "Jared."

The large silhouette halted abruptly. Dejection and weariness were etched along every angle on his body. He turned toward her slowly. "I'm sorry I awakened you, Lauren. Go back to sleep."

She clung to her door frame, her knuckles white with anxiety. "D . . . did you want, need, anything?" She hated the pleading sound of her voice, but she longed for that closeness they had shared for even a brief time.

"No," he said harshly. "Go back to bed." He took a step away from her.

"Jared," she said with more force. "Tell me what you're doing, where you're going. Tell me you're not having anything to do with—"

"Lauren," he barked, cutting her off. His voice echoed through the still house. In agitation, he whipped off his hat and slapped it against his thigh as he stared at the floor. Finally he raised his head. His tone was softer, almost apologetic. "You're my wife, but don't expect me to account to you for everything I do. Some things you'll either have to overlook or . . . or accept on trust. Do you understand?"

Trust? Could she trust him? She wanted to. Never had she thought Jared could carry through with Olivia's plot. She wanted to believe that still. "Yes," she answered softly. "I understand." Silently she begged *come to me*.

"Then we won't speak of this again," Jared dismissed her, entering his room alone.

From then on, Jared avoided Lauren completely. If they should chance to meet each other, he inquired politely about her well-being. That was all. He never came to her room. She never went to his. It was as if the intimacies that had been established between them only existed in her vivid imaginings. His indifference was as hard for her to accept as the reason for it.

Olivia sparkled radiantly during these weeks. Her smooth cheeks were flushed and her eyes glittered with excitement. She looked far younger than her years. The tight lines on her face relaxed. She was in her element.

Carson was at the house constantly. He was extremely nervous.

Lauren found the presence of the Vandivers the hardest cross to bear. Three or more times a week, they had dinner with the Locketts and Carson. For Lauren, the meals were an ordeal. Jared sat picking at his food, drinking too much, snarling if Kurt so much as spoke to her, answering anyone brave enough to speak to him in monosyllables.

Kurt, as if sensing Jared's animosity, provoked it at every opportunity. He was unctuously courteous to Lauren. Each time his hand closed around her elbow to lead her into another room or seat her in a chair, it took all her control to keep from snatching her arm away. She worried, too, that Jared might make good his threat to kill the man one day. Nor had Kurt forgotten Jared's pistol being pointed into his face.

For all his bravado, Lauren knew that Kurt was afraid of Jared. Her husband's malevolent looks were too blackly threatening to be taken lightly.

One evening, Jared was called away for one of his "secret meetings," as Lauren termed them to herself. Olivia had just suggested that she and her guests take their coffee in the parlor. Lauren watched forlornly as Jared went out the front door without so much as a nod in her direction. Instead of following the others, she excused herself and went into the library. She loved that room of the house and often sought refuge there, for no one else used it much.

She had been reading in one of the overstuffed easy chairs for about twenty minutes when she heard the door open and close quietly. She turned to see Kurt standing just inside the room. His thick, bulky body was repugnant to her, as was the insinuating expression on his ruddy face.

"Lauren, I missed your piano playing this evening. You deprive us of your company. Why? Are my father and I so offensive?"

She knew he was deliberately bating her and she refused to rise to it.

"Of course not, Mr. Vandiver. I was overly tired tonight and knew that I would not be very good company."

"I'm sorry you are unwell." He approached her and took the chair closest to hers, his knees inches from her own. She pulled back quickly and the action wasn't wasted on Kurt. He was not at all perturbed. Rather, he seemed to enjoy her uneasiness. Again she felt that there were undercurrents of cruelty in this man.

"Your husband shouldn't neglect you this way. You're far too tempting to be left alone for long."

"Jared will be home shortly," she said hurriedly, furious with herself for showing him her nervousness.

He laughed. "I happen to know that he'll be gone most of the night, Lauren." He fixed her with a sinister stare that caused her to jump from her chair.

"If you'll excuse me, Mr. Vandiver, I'll—"

She all but ran past him, but he reached out and grabbed her arm, spinning her around and pulling her against him.

"You're not being very friendly, Lauren, with your husband's business partner. Haven't you learned anything from your mother-in-law? She has always been *nice* to Carson, Ben's partner."

He laughed and it was an ugly sound. By now, Lauren had figured out for herself the relationship between Carson and Olivia. It would have taken a fool not to see it. Kurt's snide comment maligned Ben and she wanted to slap his face in Ben's defense. But he held her arms painfully just above her elbows.

"Of course, Ben had Maria Mendez. It's a shame what happened to her, isn't it?" he asked in a lilting voice that suggested he didn't think it was a shame at all.

Lauren's struggles ceased abruptly as she stared open-mouthed into his cold, blue eyes. "Wh-what do you know about Maria? How did you know—"

"I make it my business to know everything about the Locketts. Did you learn anything from Maria's unfortunate demise? Hmm?" he went on smoothly. "See what happens to whores who sell themselves cheaply to the first bidder?"

"Let me go," she grated, and renewed her efforts to escape his grasp.

"Be nice to me, Mrs. Lockett, and I'll take care of you. You won't end up like that Mexican slut."

His thick lips were inches from hers and she was near screaming when Parker's voice thundered down the hallway. "Kurt! Let's go. I'm tired and need to get to bed early."

Kurt cursed under his breath and the hands on Lauren's arms increased their pain-inducing pressure. "I promise you, Lauren, there will be a time when I won't be interrupted by your cowboy husband or anyone else. I won't be disappointed again."

"Kurt!"

"Coming," Kurt called back. Then, lowering his voice again, he whispered near her face, "You won't be disappointed, either, because you've never seen one as big as mine. It's going to rip into you like a battering ram. And when it's finished, you'll be begging for more." To emphasize his vulgar promise, he ground his hips against her middle.

"Kurt!" the voice down the hallway boomed out.

Cursing expansively, Kurt released her and was gone. Lauren leaned weakly against the back of one of the chairs, her head spinning, her knees trembling and threatening to buckle beneath her.

When she heard the front door closing after Olivia and Carson had bade the Vandivers goodbye, she crept upstairs to the sanctuary of her room. She was violently ill in the bathroom.

Lauren hung her head over the basin in the bathroom and retched dryly, her stomach having been emptied the night before. The muscles in her throat constricted and painfully urged something to come up and relieve the racking nausea. When the spasms finally subsided, she fell weakly back into her bed.

She thought the illness which had overcome her the night before had been the direct result of her encounter with Kurt. That her nausea had carried over to the morning must mean that she had a minor ailment of the stomach. In fact, she hadn't felt well for several days, she realized now.

Each morning, an uncharacteristic lethargy accompanied her out of bed. It pressed upon her head and grew heavier as it shrouded the length of her entire body. The simple chores of arising and dressing seemed insurmountable burdens. The weight of her hairbrush as she drew it through her hair caused her arms to fall weakly to her sides. When she brushed her teeth each morning, bile rose up in the back of her throat, and the smell of breakfast wasn't at all appetizing. Though she ate sparingly, her stomach felt full and bloated and continued to feel like that even when she was hungry.

Lauren's spirit was ill because of the rift that had come between her and Jared. The idea that soon the heinous plan dreamed up by Olivia and seconded by Parker Vandiver would be put into action was sickening, and she decided that her physical ailments must be manifestations of her mental upheaval.

Rosa's smooth brown face gazed down at Lauren with concern. "The *señora* is not well this morning?" She brushed a few stray tendrils of hair away from Lauren's pale cheek as she lay back on her pillows.

"No, I don't feel very well. I don't know what's wrong with me. I have no energy, food makes me sick, even the thought of it makes me sick. I feel so puffy and . . ." Her voice trailed off, lacking the energy to continue.

Rosa scrutinized her mistress pensively. "When did you last bleed?" she asked softly.

Lauren blushed furiously, but she tried to remember. The process of thinking seemed not worth the effort it required. "I . . . I don't recall. I was still at Keypoint. It was sometime in late January. I remember because Gloria had just had the babies and she and I—"

"*Señora*, don't you see?" Rosa interrupted her excitedly, "It's been two months. You are going to have a baby."

The words fell like stones on her ears, rolled to her aching stomach and almost caused it to revolt again. A baby! That was impossible. She tried to sit up, as if negating her weakness, ignoring the symptoms, could eliminate the malady.

"No, Rosa. I couldn't be with child. It's something else, I'm certain."

As she looked at her friend for confirmation, she saw only the beaming smile, the gladness at their discovery. Yet Lauren felt an inexplicable wave of sadness for she knew one day she would have to leave Jared. To Rosa's consternation, she burst into tears and buried her face in the cook's plump bosom, weeping uncontrollably.

It was a long time before the tears stopped and, when they did, Lauren was embarrassed by her sudden show of emotion.

"I'm sorry, Rosa. I couldn't help it."

"It is another symptom of women in your condition, *Señora*. The tears will make you feel better. Would you like some tea?"

"Yes, that sounds nice," Lauren mumbled absently as she rose from the bed and walked to the window. Rosa was shuffling out of the room to fetch the tea when Lauren called her back. She didn't turn around and her voice was soft as she requested, "Rosa, don't tell anyone about the . . . the baby . . . just yet. Please."

"I understand, Señora Lauren." Rosa closed the door behind her.

Lauren kept her secret, though she longed to talk to Gloria. She took long walks around the gardens outside even when she didn't feel like it, but her face remained pale and wan. Dark shadows circled her eyes. If Jared noticed her listlessness and lack of appetite when he saw her in brief snatches, he didn't mention it. Olivia acted as if she weren't there.

When Lauren saw Jared for the first time after she had learned of her pregnancy, her heart warmed with love for a few moments before the chill of gloom settled over it again. She had given little thought to their "arrangement" since the marriage had been consummated. Now, she was forced to think about it.

Jared had said that the railroad would be completed by the end of the summer or early fall. The baby would come, if she calculated correctly, around the first of November. She couldn't hide her pregnancy until the railroad was finished and then leave according to the bargain. What would happen to her baby? She would take him with her, of course, but finding work to support herself would be harder to do with a baby. She could live for several years on the twenty thousand dollars Olivia had promised her if she were frugal, but what then?

The Prathers had urged her in their letter to return to them. She had written back telling them of Ben's death, her marriage to Jared—omitting the details—of her family and friends at Keypoint. The missive had been warm and loving, but she knew she could never return to their staid, dull life. Where could she live with her baby?

The one thought that plagued her was that she would never be able to take her baby with her. She might well be providing the next Lockett heir. Try as she might, she couldn't decide how Jared and Olivia would feel about her child. Of one thing she was sure—nothing and no one would separate her from her baby. She already loved it, was protective of it, and it was probably the only part of Jared she would have after her usefulness to the Locketts' enterprise had ended.

A small glimmer of hope refused to dim on the horizon of her mind. While Jared had never spoken of love, she had read tenderness in his eyes, seen an affection there as he watched her. Surely he felt some fondness for her. It wasn't much to go on, but it was all she had.

But as she met his closed, remote face at each of their fleeting encounters, that hope began to diminish.

The tension in the house mounted. The chasm between Jared and his wife grew wider. His midnight rides became a nightly ritual. The muscles of his face, the nervous darting eyes, and the continual clenching of his fists indicated a restrained violence that had to erupt soon or destroy the man from within. His abrupt, curt attitude toward Lauren forbade her to approach him. He'd asked for her trust. Now, in the dawn light, that appeal seemed unreal. His behavior certainly didn't inspire trust.

She ventured into the stables one morning and was alarmed to see boxes of guns and ammunition stacked against one wall. It was an arsenal of immense proportions. Her heart quaked. Before, she had been concerned about other people getting hurt. Now she realized there was a very real possibility that her own husband could be injured or killed. She prayed fervently that something would happen to prevent this entire fiasco.

Nothing did.

Unable to tolerate her own passivity, Lauren decided that if she couldn't keep the tragedy from happening, she could at least erect obstacles for the perpetrators. Late one evening after Jared had left the house, she let herself quietly out the front door and ran to the stable. Pepe was working by lantern light mending a bridle.

"Señora Lockett," he said in surprise as Lauren swiftly shut the door behind her.

"Pepe, do you know what is in those boxes? What they're for?"

He licked his lips nervously and looked away quickly. "*Sí*, but Señor Jared told me not to tell."

"Well, we're not going to let it happen, Pepe. You and I are going to do something to slow them down."

"But, Señora Lockett, he—"

"How can you keep a gun from firing, Pepe?" she asked, ignoring his discomposure.

"Señora, the guns—"

"You're right. We'd never be able to handle all of the guns without them noticing. What can we do?" she wailed, twisting her hands. Then her eyes lighted on the boxes of shells. "The bullets! That's it. Without a bullet, a gun is useless, isn't it?" She was talking rapidly, musing aloud. "We'll hide them. Of course, they might bring their own on the night of the raid, but at least they won't have these."

"You want to hide the bullets?" Pepe's voice had risen an octave as he stared at her incredulously. His dark eyes were wide and his mouth hung agape.

She placed a comforting hand on his arm. "Don't worry, Pepe. I'll take full responsibility if Jared or anyone else should ever find out." Then her gentling tone changed and became brisk and businesslike. "Now, where are the shovels? We'll bury the boxes out there," she said, pointing to the back of the building. "Please hurry. I may be missed any minute."

"Señora—"

"Please, Pepe," she said impatiently. "Don't be afraid of reprisals. Don't you want to help your own people?"

He turned away from her, muttering to himself in Spanish and shaking his head, but he did as he was instructed. By the time they hauled the heavy boxes to the rear of the stable, dug the holes, and buried them to her satisfaction, Lauren was dirty and tired and her back ached abominably.

"If I can, I'll try to get word to you when the raid is going to take place. Can you warn the people of Pueblo?"

"*Si,*" he said with the weary attitude of one who is ready to agree to anything.

"If I can't get word to you, take it upon yourself. Ride into Pueblo and alert as many as you can. Tell them to take cover. Anything to protect themselves."

"I will, Señora Lockett."

"Thank you, Pepe. You've been a tremendous help. You'll be a hero to your people." She smiled at him before leaving the stable. Undetected, she made her way upstairs, where she washed away the damp soil clinging to her hands and clothes. When she fell into bed, her limbs were as heavy and sore as her spirit.

It was fortunate that she and Pepe had done their work the night before, because the next day it began to rain and it rained for several days. Large, heavy pellets of water fell relentlessly from the sky. The air was close and stifling, adding to Lauren's pregnancy-related discomfort.

Confined to the house, Lauren paced back and forth in her

room between the bed and the windows, unable to read or sew, or to concentrate on anything except her unforeseeable future and that of her child.

Then the rain stopped. The clouds hung low in the sky and the air was still thick with humidity, but the rain ceased.

And at dusk one evening, the mercenaries converged on the house.

Lauren heard the first clump of boots as she sat at the dinner table with Olivia, Jared, Carson, and the Vandivers. She toyed with her food, every now and then putting a bite into her mouth and forcing herself to swallow it, praying that it would stay down.

She was deathly afraid of Kurt Vandiver now. Since he had accosted her and made his lewd threats, the sight of him sickened her and made her tremble in fear.

When the sound of the heavy treads was heard on the porch, the others at the table started, glancing at each other quickly and tensely. Kurt rose from the table and rushed out of the room to the front door even before the knock echoed through the still rooms.

Lauren heard the low mumblings of several voices before Kurt closed the door and returned to his place at the table.

"I told them to wait in the stable. They'll gather in there and . . . ready themselves."

Parker nodded, satisfied. His cold blue eyes flashed in anticipation. His look was predatory. Lauren shivered despite the warm, muggy air.

She looked at her husband, unable to continue the pretence of eating. He was dressed like a *vaquero*. The red scarf he had been wearing the day he kissed her in the shelter of the boulders was tied negligently around his throat. He usually wore formal attire for dinner in Coronado, but she had been too absorbed in her own thoughts to notice this incongruity before now. She knew he felt her eyes on him, but he refused to meet them.

Carson's normally hearty appetite had waned and he sat sipping his wine. Olivia ate calmly, as though the interruption had never happened. Kurt leaned back in his chair indolently, studying Lauren. He seemed unaffected by the tension around the table.

"How . . . how long before we know something, Jared? I mean, how long will it take?" Carson asked nervously.

Jared shrugged and took a long swallow of whiskey.

"You have a big night ahead of you, Jared. I'd lay off the whiskey if I were you," Parker said.

Jared fixed a golden stare on him, then tipped the glass to his lips once again. Parker's face flooded with anger, which purpled the veins in his nose and cheeks.

"Send us word when the plan has gone into effect. Carson and I will be eager to know what is happening." Olivia's face was shining. She might well have been talking about a Mardi Gras ball. To Lauren, her eagerness to destroy was obscene.

"Well, never put off until tomorrow what you can do today, or something to that effect," Kurt said lightly, rising from the table and going to the window. "Looks like they're all here. It's a good thing you don't live in the center of town, Lockett. People might wonder what the hell was going on."

Parker, Olivia, and Carson stood, pushing their chairs back and moving toward the door. Except for Lauren, Jared was the last one to rise. He did so slowly, deliberately. His Colt, in its holster, lay against his hip. A leather cord tied around his thigh held it secure. He wasn't entering a harmless shooting match. His gun was loaded and primed for a deadly purpose.

Lauren was out of the chair in a flash, her former sluggishness forgotten. She placed herself between Jared and the door, grabbing his forearms with her slender fingers.

Breathlessly but incisively, she said, "Jared, I beg you, don't be a part of this thing. Please." His face was cold, implacable, his eyes impenetrable. When he didn't speak, she went on, "Think, Jared! Think of Rudy and his family."

"Rudy is a fool," he lashed out. "He wants to solve things peacefully. He thinks everything Ben ever said is chiseled in stone, but I've learned that Ben could be wrong. He was certainly wrong about you and me and this 'grand love' between us."

The barb hit home and she floundered, aware of the others listening to their dialogue. She tightened her grip on him. "I believe in you, Jared. Once, just a few weeks ago, you asked me to trust you—"

"You heard only what you wanted to hear. I also strongly hinted that you'd do well to accept things as they are and to keep your moralistic opinions to yourself. Apparently you don't take hints too well. I don't give a damn whether you *trust* or approve of me. I do as I please."

She wanted to scream in frustration. "Do you realize how this might jeopardize your future . . . our future?"

His eyes darted to the interested witnesses behind her, then came back to her face. His lips curled mockingly. *"Our* future?

259

We have no future, Lauren. You know what your future with us is. When you have fulfilled your part of the bargain, you're gone. A lot richer, but gone. Do you now regret selling yourself so cheaply? What do you want? More money?"

Lauren swallowed the congestion in her throat. She stuttered as she tried to speak. "At . . . at Keypoint, you . . . we . . . it was . . . different."

He laughed at her mirthlessly, his face ugly in its contempt. "Do you think because I've slept with you that things have changed between us? That I've developed an 'attachment' to you?" He snorted derisively. "You were a pretty good lover once you learned how. And you were handy. What did you expect me to do? You were the only warm body available in a snowstorm. If you place any more importance on my bedding you than that, you're even more stupid than I thought."

Her disillusionment turned to pain, then to anger. "Not too stupid to see you for what you really are. I placed far too much faith in you, Jared Lockett. I thought you were growing up, becoming the kind of son your father deserved, the kind of husband I wanted." She paused and gulped for air. "Now I see that you're as avaricious, as cruel as they are. Jared, I—" She wanted to tell him that she loved him, to beg him not to do this thing. Instead, she said, "I curse you to perdition if you do this thing."

"Then to hell I shall go." He laughed again as he shoved her away from him and shouted, "Let's go," to Kurt and Parker.

His words struck her like physical blows. The breath had literally been knocked out of her. She heard the shouts and thudding of horses' hooves as a score of men mounted and rode out of the stableyard. She stood rooted to the spot, oblivious to everything except the constricting pain around her heart.

Carson came up behind her and touched her shoulder solicitously. "Jared's a little keyed up, Lauren. He spouts off things he doesn't really mean."

His kindness penetrated the protective shell she had drawn around herself. It was strange, but she wasn't humiliated or embarrassed that they had heard what Jared said to her. Her wounds went too deep to be bothered by superficial lacerations.

She felt only the desolate loss. They had shared something beautiful and the product of that sharing lay sleeping in her womb. She touched her stomach as if to reassure herself that his words hadn't ripped the seed out of her body. Scalding tears rolled down her cheeks as she was ravaged by despair.

Passing Olivia on her way out of the room, she met the smug, triumphant face of her mother-in-law fully. Lauren wondered at the hate that so consumed her that she sought to destroy those she supposedly loved. Maria had once said that Olivia was a sad, lonely woman. Lauren thought she was most likely right. In spite of her aversion, she felt a moment of pity for Olivia. The woman was incapable of real love. Her destructive selfishness wouldn't permit it.

Olivia must have perceived her thought, for her emerald eyes narrowed with loathing. Lauren knew then that she had scored a small victory over this domineering woman. That knowledge emboldened her as she swept past Olivia and went up the stairs.

The hours passed with interminable slowness. Once Rosa had finished clearing the dinner things away, a tangible silence settled over the house. Carson and Olivia sat in the office, she in her usual place behind the large desk, he in a nearby chair. They talked little.

Had Jared noticed the missing ammunition? Surely. It hadn't stopped them. Had Pepe gotten away with his warning in time? The questions came at Lauren out of a dark void which provided no answers.

She lay on her bed wondering how she would survive this nightmare. Visions of Jared wounded and bleeding crowded those of him with the mocking sneer on his face, his eyes cold and hard, resembling those of his mother. Dimly she saw him tender and loving. But only dimly.

The pounding hooves were heard from far off, so quiet was the house. Lauren held her breath as she heard the single horse being reined in just outside the fence-enclosed yard. When she heard the rapid knocking on the front door, she rolled off her bed and fled to the top of the stairs where she could see Carson hurrying to open the door. Kurt Vandiver lunged into the hall.

"Jared's been shot!"

Chapter 24

"It looks bad," Kurt told the startled Carson. "Where is Lauren?" Just then he spotted her at the top of the stairs, gripping the bannister so hard her knuckles were as white as her face.

He stepped quickly to the bottom of the staircase and looked up at her. "Can you get into some riding clothes? He's asking for you."

She didn't even answer him, but whirled away and ran toward her room.

Olivia was standing next to Carson when Kurt turned back to them. "The bastards were waiting for us. Somehow they were tipped off. There was a lot of shooting. I don't know how many of our men were killed or wounded. None of the fires we planned really got started because of the damp weather. It's raining now."

"Are Jared's wounds serious, Kurt?" Carson asked anxiously.

Kurt's eyes darted to Olivia, then he answered slowly, "It's hard to tell just yet, Carson. I thought his wife ought to be with him."

Olivia's features remained calm. She asked no unnecessary questions. Carson had always respected her stoicism in the face of trouble. He patted her arm reassuringly.

Lauren came racing down the stairs. She had donned one of her split riding skirts and boots, but left on the lace-trimmed shirtwaist she had been wearing. She had raided the bathroom for first-aid implements and stuffed them into a small cloth bag.

"I'm ready." She hurried out the front door, never even glancing at the others.

Kurt glanced hastily at Olivia before he followed Lauren swiftly out the door. "I told your man in the stable to saddle up a horse. I'll get it," he called to her.

His stocky legs carried him quickly across the yard and he

turned down the side of the house toward the stable. Lauren was unmindful of the rain that fell gently around her. She saw lightning flash and light up the sky to the west in the direction of Keypoint, but it was far away. She clasped her hands in front of her and prayed silently for the life of her husband. Don't let him die. Please, God, don't let him die.

She had changed her clothes with trembling fingers, shaken to the depths of her being at Kurt's news. Judd brought the gelding around and offered to give her a boost up. She hesitated only an instant. Would it hurt the baby for her to ride? But she had to get to Jared. She mounted quickly.

"Where is he? Jared. Where did you take him?"

Kurt shouted over the crunching sound of the horses' hooves as they sped down the lane, "He was shot up pretty bad. We took him to a cave one of the men knew about. I think they were going to try to fetch a doctor. They were afraid to move him anymore. He was bleeding pretty bad."

Lauren clung to the reins and shut her eyes momentarily. Shot up pretty bad. What did that mean? Bleeding. Oh, God!

Carson never ceased to be amazed at Olivia's composure. She sat with her eyes closed, her head leaning against the high back of the leather chair behind the desk. It had been an hour since Kurt had ridden in with the news of Jared's injury and the terrible turn of events in Pueblo. Soon after that, Parker had arrived and stormed into the office in a rage.

"The whole goddam thing blew up in our faces. I tell you, they were like animals hiding in the buildings where we couldn't even see to shoot them. They picked off our men one by one. They knew we were coming. They knew!"

"Parker, please calm down. There's nothing we can do now." Olivia's voice was dispassionate. "In a way, we can turn it to our advantage. We can say that the degenerate citizens of Pueblo went on a shooting spree and shot a few cowboys who drifted into town after dark. We'll think of something."

"Well, it better be damned good. I'm getting tired of all of this muck." The Teutonic features were congested and contorted.

"We'll work it out, Parker," Carson said with more assurance than he felt.

"You'd goddam better. I could call off this whole thing just like that." He snapped his pink, sausage fingers loudly and then turned his bulky body and strode out the door.

Even after that altercation, Olivia had remained tranquil. Carson paced the rug in front of the desk as if hypnotized by the pattern woven into it.

Suddenly they heard hurried footsteps and jingling spurs coming across the porch and through the front door.

"Maybe that's word of Jared," Carson said hopefully and rushed into the hall. He was struck dumb.

Jared was striding purposefully toward the office. He wasn't wounded at all. In fact, Carson had rarely seen him so exhilarated. Behind him was Rudy Mendez, his white teeth flashing against the dark complexion of his face, his black eyes dancing. Carson was shocked as always by their resemblance. Standing in the doorway but not coming into the house was Thorn, the taciturn Comanche who had been the boys' childhood friend and their father's before them.

"What—" Carson started before Jared interrupted him.

"Carson, you look as if you've seen a ghost," Jared said heartily. "I believe you know my brother and Thorn." Jared pushed past the flabbergasted man and tramped to the desk, confronting his mother.

"It didn't work, Mother. Your friends from Austin ran off with their tails between their legs. It's all over."

Olivia had fastened her eyes on Rudy and her face had paled significantly. "What is he doing in my house?" she gasped. Her voice rose a note or two on the last words. Her agitation was apparent. "Get that bastard out of my sight."

"Rudy is my brother," Jared said levelly. "He stays in my house if I say so." His eyes never wavered from her face, daring her to challenge him.

She looked at him closely then, the truth dawning on her. "It was *you*, wasn't it? *You* were the traitor. You ruined everything for us."

"No, Mother, I didn't ruin anything. Hopefully, I helped to save a lot of property and lives."

"You sound just like your father," she spat. "Always so full of goodwill and nobility. You were against me all along. Don't you see, Jared, that you've probably set us back for years by this insane high-mindedness?"

Jared shook his head. "No. No, I didn't. We'll get our railroad, but not through exploitation and violence. And without the help of Vandiver and his lot." Jared turned to the stunned man standing behind him. "Carson, you see why I had to go against you, don't you? We were being manipulated. I had to take matters in my own hands. I think I did what Ben would have done."

Carson looked deflated and tired and old. He smiled kindly at the young men before him. They were both good men. Honorable. Strong. Ben's sons. He was proud of them for their absent father, his best friend. "Yes, Jared, I think you did the right thing," he said, clamping him on the shoulder. The two men stared long at each other. Finally the younger man turned away in embarrassed humility. It was an emotion completely new to him and he covered it quickly.

"Rudy, wait here just a minute. I'll go tell Lauren the news and then we'll bed you and Thorn down for the night. I know you're both exhausted." Jared was already headed for the door when Olivia halted him in mid-stride with her level, quiet words. "Lauren's not here, Jared."

For some reason, her tone and the calm manner in which she spoke set off an alarm buzzing in his head. A great foreboding squeezed his chest.

He turned back slowly and faced his mother. "Not here? Where is she?" His voice was low. Lethal.

"She's with Kurt Vandiver. They left on horseback about an hour ago."

"She wouldn't go anywhere with Vandiver. What the hell are you talking about?" His anger was building.

Olivia smiled sweetly at her son. "Jared, have you forgotten your first impressions of Miss Lauren Holbrook? You thought she was a trollop, an adventuress. I think your hunch has proved to be correct."

Carson butted in, sputtering, "Olivia, tell the boy why she left. Tell him!" He stared incredulously at the woman whom he had worshiped for over a score of years, as if he were now seeing her for the first time.

"This is none of your concern, Carson," she declared sharply.

Jared faced Carson, his whole body tense. "Where is she?" he asked hoarsely.

"I don't know, Jared," Carson answered honestly, baffled by this twist of circumstances. "Kurt came in here hellbent for leather about an hour ago. He said that you were hurt critically, and that Lauren should go with him. He hinted that if she didn't, she might never again see you alive." He left Jared and walked over to where Olivia sat with her hands folded on the desk. "You knew that Jared wasn't hurt." It wasn't a question. It was a statement.

Jared pushed Carson out of the way and spread his hands wide on the desk as he leaned over it, his face a few inches from his mother's. "Why did you let her go off with that sonofabitch? Why, goddam you?" He slapped the desk with his palms and the sound exploded like a shot in the air already fraught with tension.

When she answered, it was with the same even tones she had used before. "Lauren has served her purpose. It was expedient for her to be a victim of tonight. That way, no one could blame us if anything went wrong. As it did." She looked malevolently at Rudy. "Who could blame us if one of our own had been kidnapped and . . . hurt as a result of the fracas?"

Jared was trying hard to keep the coldness in his stomach from spreading to his entire body and freezing him on the spot. His teeth were clenched as he rasped, "Where did he take her?"

"I don't know."

"Where?!" he screamed.

"I don't know!" she screamed back.

Rudy hadn't spoken once since entering the house. Now he grabbed Jared by the sleeve. "Come on. We're wasting precious time here. Thorn can track them, but they've got an hour's head-start in the rain. We'd better hurry."

Jared still stared at his mother, thinking all sorts of crude insults to fling at her. But she wasn't worth it. She was defeated and she knew it. Bitter disappointment that this woman who had given him life could never give him love filled his lungs, drowning him. The innumerable times in his life he had been hurt and rejected by her flashed through his mind in kaleidoscopic fashion. All his efforts at attempting to please her had been scorned and for naught. He never quite met her expectations. That rejection had been the crux of his bitterness, his contempt, his anger at the world. If he wasn't loved, then, by God, he wasn't going to love anyone!

But it hadn't worked. He had loved Ben. Yes. He admitted it now. He loved his father and had been devastated by his death. And in spite of Ben's ill health, Jared was still haunted by the argument that had precipitated the final seizure. He had loved Ben. He loved Rudy and Gloria. And Maria. And he loved Lauren.

Lauren! It had only taken a few seconds for these soul-rending admissions to pass through his mind. Rudy's hand was still on his arm. He gave his mother one last regretful look and then turned on his heels and fled the room.

"Thorn, we need to track two horses that left here an hour ago.

Vandiver's got my wife." He shouted all of this as the three men dashed out to the yard and mounted their horses.

"We'll have to hurry. The trail could be washed away soon," Thorn said matter-of-factly as they picked up the faint trace of horseshoes impressed in the soft mud.

Lauren clung to the pommel of her saddle with stiff, cold fingers, trying to navigate her horse up the slippery, muddy incline. The rain that had started as a fine drizzle had now increased to a steady downpour. She had not taken the time to put on her hat after Kurt had informed them of Jared's injury, nor had she put on a jacket or any kind of protective covering. The hard raindrops fell like lead balls on the top of her head. Her hair, even heavier with the weight of the rain in it, had pulled loose from its pins and hung down her back, making her neck ache. She was soaked through to the skin and shivered with cold.

Vivid flashes of lightning had spooked their horses several times and the thunder rolled over the plains and off the shallow hills like giant bowling balls striking a stone wall.

Cold, wet, and miserable as she was, one thought kept reverberating through her head like the thunder: Please, God, let Jared be alive.

It seemed to her that it was taking an inordinate amount of time to reach their destination. They had ridden off in the opposite direction from Pueblo and had been riding for what she calculated to be a couple of hours. But they may not have been riding anywhere near that long. Time had stood still for her when she heard that her husband's life was in danger.

She questioned Kurt about Jared's condition when the trail had widened enough to allow them to ride abreast. "Where did they take him, Kurt? We've come miles from Pueblo and you said they were afraid to let him travel too far."

He avoided her eyes. "Well, one of the men knew about this cave. They wanted to get Jared away from the scene of the trouble for his own safety, so this cave seemed ideal. Not too many people know about it."

His words didn't make much sense to her, but she didn't argue. She only wanted to get to Jared as quickly as possible.

She had been hearing a loud roaring for the past several minutes, and when the sky was illuminated by a lightning flash, she saw that the river was about fifty feet ahead of them. The Rio Caballo, which was usually so placid even as it formed small rapids over the limestone that lined its bed, was raging and boiling out of its banks.

Kurt rode toward it and cursed loudly as he saw their predicament. "We have to cross it, Lauren," he shouted over the roaring of the river and the crashes of thunder. In daylight, the prospect would have been grim, but in this darkness, with stinging rain in their faces, it seemed suicidal.

"Isn't there another way?" Her throat hurt in the effort to make herself heard over the din. "The horses can't swim this. Even if they could, look at all the debris."

There were large trees, barrels, wagon wheels, lumber, and sundry other objects being carried by the swift, churning water. Lauren didn't think they could make it to the other side without seriously injuring either themselves or their mounts.

"Do you want to get to Jared or not?" Kurt demanded, frustrated by her caution.

"They couldn't have brought him this way and gotten him across the river with it flooded like this," she argued.

"It's been hours since they must have crossed it. I'm sure it didn't flood until it started raining hard again."

He was right and she knew it. With all the rainfall of the past few days, the possibility of a flash flood was great. When the new rain had begun to fall, the saturated ground at the top of the hills had refused to hold any more, causing it to funnel downstream into the river. It wouldn't have taken long for the river to rise to these proportions.

She nodded at Kurt as she gripped the pommel more firmly.

"You go first, and I'll be right behind you," he shouted. "If the horse won't swim, just try to ride the current until you get a chance to make it to the other side. Okay?"

She nodded again, dumbly, her heart pounding, and nudged the horse's flanks. The gelding shied away from the water, tossing his head, and for a moment, Lauren thought he would refuse to go into it. Obedience won out, however, and he stepped into the boiling river. He had just gotten all four feet into the water, when he was almost immediately swept into the middle of the river by the swift current.

Lauren held on for dear life, thinking suddenly that if she died, her and Jared's baby would die, too. Why didn't I tell him I carried his child? She berated herself. She tightened her knees, gripping the sides of the horse. She risked looking back to see if she could spot Kurt and saw him urging his horse away from the bank into the water.

Darkness and rain surrounded them, but when the lightning flashed again, she saw the tree being swept toward her with alarming impetus. Oh, God, no! her mind screamed, and she braced herself for the impact.

The main trunk of the tree floated in front of them, but apparently a branch that was under the surface struck her horse in the forelegs, for he suddenly buckled and Lauren was all but thrown from his back. She gripped the pommel tighter, her fingers slipping on the muddy water that had doused the saddle. The horse was screaming in pain, and Lauren knew his legs must have been broken. The tree had not flowed past them, but was circling wildly as if seeking direction. In his agony, the gelding thrashed violently and, this time, Lauren couldn't maintain her hold.

She was hurled into the dark murky waters of the raging river. The current lifted her up long enough for her to gasp a breath before once again she was sucked under. Beneath the surface, she struggled to propel herself upward. She could feel herself growing lighter, knowing that the surface and the much-needed oxygen were near, when her head struck something above her, and a blinding pain shot through her body. She floundered helplessly, felt the drawstring of the cloth bag with the medical supplies slip from her wrist and began to sink into the deep oblivion of unconsciousness.

Then her head was stung with a million needles as she was lifted by her hair out of the river. She swallowed the brackish water in her mouth and began sucking in great mouthfuls of precious air. Kurt held her under the chin as she clutched his saddle trying desperately not to lose her hold on either it or consciousness.

Somehow, miraculously, Kurt's horse was able to make it to the other side of the bank. He dropped Lauren gently onto the ground, where she lay choking and spitting. Kurt dismounted and lifted her limp form against him. He shook her slightly as he asked, "Are you all right?"

It took her a few moments to regain enough strength to answer, "Y-yes. I think so."

"Come on, it's not far now. Just at the top of the hill there." He lifted her onto the horse, and she would have fallen forward if he hadn't mounted quickly behind her and supported her with his sturdy arms.

She must have slipped out of consciousness then, because when she came to, they had stopped and Kurt was dragging her off the horse. He steered her toward what appeared to be a solid wall of rock. As they got nearer, she saw that there was a small opening practically hidden by a clump of bushes. Kurt drew them aside and pushed her into the cave. She had to bend from the waist in order to get through the low opening. She walked in the crouched position with dread of the unseen terrors lurking in the walls of the cavern.

Finally she saw light ahead and, knowing that she would soon see Jared, she quickened her pace. The pale light came from a small lantern hanging on the wall within the cave. She stepped into it and stood upright. She was looking directly into the hooded, reptilian eyes of Wat Duncan!

Behind him stood June, her pale hair forming a halo around her head as the light from the lantern reflected on it. Lauren's eyes darted swiftly to all corners of the room, and nowhere did she see Jared.

Myriad horrors flashed through her mind, so quickly that her brain couldn't catalogue them. She felt Kurt behind her as he stepped into the room.

"Well, well, Miz Lockett. I see you made it to our little party. Not a very nice night for a swim, though." Duncan grinned indolently and his eyes roved her body.

Lauren whirled on Kurt. "Where is my husband? You said you were bringing me to my husband!" She clenched her fists and pounded his bulky chest ineffectually. Grabbing her wrists, he held her away from him.

"I had to tell you something to get you here. And it worked."

Stunned, she stammered, "B-But why? You planned all of this? Why?" She was too shocked at the situation she found herself in to be frightened. That would come later. Now she was angry and puzzled.

"I don't think I have to tell you *why*, Lauren. Surely you can guess my motivation." His eyes moved from her face to her chest and all the way down her body, taking in every detail. Lauren shivered, but not from the cold. She looked down at the dripping garments that were molded to her and revealed every secret of her body.

"We done just what you axed us to, Mr. Vandiver. I got the lantern and brung some food. It's all ready for you." Duncan's tone was sycophantic, and Lauren knew he must have been promised money for his generosity.

"Everything is fine, but what's she doing here?" questioned Kurt, indicating June, who as yet had not spoken.

"June and me, we got a lot in common, and one of them common interests, you might say, is bringing down Mr. Jared Lockett." At the mention of his name, Lauren started and June looked at her smugly, haughtily. "So she begged me to bring her along. 'Sides, she kinda took a shine to you, Mr. Vandiver. She wanted to see you again."

Kurt smiled seductively and looked through half-closed eyes at the girl who stood with her feet planted far apart, hands on her hips, displaying her body shamelessly in the thin, low-cut dress. Lauren looked away in disgust as June's tongue slid slowly across her bottom lip, making promises to Kurt with her eyes.

"You're not bad, Miss June." Kurt walked further into the cave and stood directly in front of her. "Yes, not bad at all. I may have you for seconds." Then he turned to Lauren. "After I've satisfied Mrs. Lockett."

June shot Lauren a look full of jealous hatred and resentment, but Lauren didn't see it. June posed no threat at all compared to Kurt Vandiver.

"Why did you do it, Olivia? It wasn't necessary. Why did you endanger that girl?" Carson had not quite recovered himself after having faced the fact that Olivia had betrayed her own son. He still couldn't believe that she was capable of such treachery.

Jared and his brother, along with Thorn, had ridden out of the yard only minutes ago. Carson hoped they would find Lauren before any harm could come to her at the hands of Vandiver. Carson stood over the woman he had loved for years and stared down at her black hair. The silver strands fanned through it, away from her aristocratic brow. He had always thought her hair was beautiful.

Olivia appeared not at all unnerved either by the events that had happened earlier or by Carson's close scrutiny.

"Answer me, please, Olivia. Why did you do this?" His voice was raised and held more censure than she had heard since she had known him.

"Carson, really, I find this sudden streak of conscience in you surprising and tiresome. You, of all people, should know that sometimes in business we must do things that are not always appealing."

"I have done things, yes, to manipulate people. As far as I

know, however, I have never sacrificed an innocent young woman, who has done nothing to hurt me, to someone as ruthless as Vandiver."

"Innocent? Ha! You men, you're all alike," she accused. "And I wouldn't exactly call the way she turned Jared against us doing *nothing*. That was no small feat."

"Lauren isn't responsible for Jared's convictions, and you know it. He has mistrusted the Vandivers from the beginning. He felt that his whole legacy from Ben was threatened by them. He protected it as he saw fit. Lauren has been good for him, I think. She has made him take a real hard look at himself."

Olivia slammed her hands down on the desk much the way Jared had done earlier. "I don't want to hear any more about Lauren and her virtues. I'm sick to death of everyone showering her with accolades."

Carson considered her closely. Her green eyes were flashing fire and her nostrils flared with the heavy breaths she took. Then he understood. "You're jealous of the girl, aren't you, Olivia? She came between you and Jared. I showed her some paternal affection. And Ben—"

She pounced on the name. "Yes, Ben! He had humiliated me for years with that whore of his. People laughed behind my back because my husband preferred that Mexican bitch to me. He loved her son as much as he did mine. His liaison with her was a continual insult to me. *Me!*" She punctuated the pronoun by pointing to her chest. "The belle of New Orleans society. Me, from one of the most respected, affluent, influential families in the history of that city. He brought me to this barbaric, godforsaken country and expected me to live like one of his Mexican peons." Tears were streaming down her cheeks. In all the years he had known her, Carson had never seen Olivia cry.

"And he didn't love me," she added miserably, pitifully. "He didn't love me." She was still for a moment and then she tilted her chin in that autocratic way she had. "But I wasn't going to stand by and let him deposit his latest doxy here in my own house. I'd be damned first!"

Carson spoke softly, "Olivia, you know that Ben brought Lauren here in hopes that she and Jared—"

Once again, she interrupted. "That's what he *said*. But you heard the way he talked about her. Lauren was so beautiful. She was so kind, so innocent, so sweet, so polished." She buried her

272

face in her hands as her elbows supported them on the desk. "Why didn't he love me? *Why?*"

The words tore at Carson's heart. He didn't want to ask, but he did. "You've loved Ben all this time, haven't you?"

"No!" she cried. "I hated him. I hated him!" She pounded on the desktop with her fists.

"No," he said quietly. "You loved him."

Olivia looked up at him suddenly as if remembering that he was still there. Her eyes were bright with tears, the lashes spiky and black. "You!" she snarled with contempt. "Don't you see that you were used as a means to hurt Ben? I carried on a shabby affair all these years with his best friend and business partner as revenge for all the humiliation he had heaped on me." She laughed a bitter laugh. "But he just turned his back and forced me to tolerate *you* all these years. I look so forward to the day when the railroad is completed, Vandiver is satisfied, and I can throw you out of my house, my life, and never have to look at you again. Didn't you ever ask yourself why any woman would want a short, fat, balding man who made love like a sloppy adolescent when she was married to a hard, virile stallion like Ben Lockett? You are a fool."

The words really didn't have any meaning for Carson. He had already been shattered to learn that he had given the prime of his life to a selfish, shallow woman. He had given up having a wife, and children, and the respect of his best friend for a chimera, an illusion. Worst of all, he had sacrificed his self-esteem. He looked at himself now and found himself wanting in every facet of his being. He was a shell of a man. Olivia's words had not hurt him. He was too empty to hurt anymore.

Olivia sat staring straight ahead, her eyes glazed. She didn't see Carson remove the derringer from his inside breast pocket. He moved the gun close to her head, and when at last she saw it in her peripheral vision, she looked up at him and laughed.

Her mouth was wide, her eyes streaming tears, and her head was thrown back in laughter as he pulled the trigger. He watched sadly as her head fell forward and thudded onto the desk. She was so beautiful. So beautiful.

He was still looking at her as he raised the pistol to his own temple.

Chapter 25

The heavy rainfall wasn't making the tracking any easier. Had it not been for Thorn's innate ability, Jared would have been even more desperate than he already was. Thorn had taught him and Rudy in their youth to track with precision but, though they were keen pupils, they still wouldn't have been able to follow this mud-obscured trail. The darkness and the blinding rain made it nearly impossible to find.

They had been riding for an hour and a half when the tall Indian pulled the reins of his horse. "They're headed toward the river."

Jared heard him over the loud rumble of thunder and said, "Well, let's get on with it." He was puzzled by Thorn's hesitation.

Rudy intervened. "Jared, do you know what the Rio Caballo will look like? It will be raging. I don't think they could have crossed it, and even if they did, we couldn't pick up the trail until morning. Shouldn't we go on to Keypoint and wait out this storm? We can start again at dawn."

"Hell, no!" Jared's roar challenged the thunder. "If you aren't coming with me, I'll go by myself. No telling what that bastard has in mind for her. And she's afraid of him. I know it."

He wore the determined look he had inherited from two very forceful personalities. Rudy and Thorn exchanged looks. Rudy's was exasperated. Thorn's was totally noncommittal, as if it were of supreme indifference to him that he was riding around the countryside in the middle of the night in a fierce spring thunderstorm. Without speaking, he turned his horse toward the river and focused on the rapidly dissolving hoof prints.

"I don't know how we'll cross that damned river when we get there," Rudy muttered. He was surprised when Jared answered, thinking he couldn't have heard him over the sounds of the storm.

"I don't know either, but we have to go on. I've got to find her. We'll proceed with Thorn's plan—it's our only hope."

The trio rode on in silence.

The dull throbbing in Lauren's head had increased to excruciating proportions. She suspected that when she was seeking the surface of the water and banged her head on the tree branch, she had been hurt more seriously than she had first thought. Waves of nausea threatened to make her vomit, and she struggled not to give in to them. She wanted to keep the focus of attention off herself. The other three in the confines of the cave with her were entertaining themselves with a bottle of whiskey. She had time to think.

Lauren's main concern was for the baby she carried. She was still somewhat ignorant about pregnancy, but she was sure that an exhausting horseback ride, falling into a raging river, and receiving a severe blow to her head were not good for the embryo in her womb. She prayed fervently that it had not been injured.

What was going to happen to her at the hands of Kurt and Wat Duncan? Had she not been in such pain, she would have been more afraid. As it was, she more or less accepted her fate with a passive resignation. She couldn't fight them. She lacked the strength and the ability. She couldn't escape them. Where would she go in the middle of the night in a fearsome storm without anyone to guide her over the rough terrain? Just don't hurt my baby, was her only lucid thought. That and the slim possibility that Jared might rescue her.

Kurt hadn't mentioned him, and she was afraid to ask. He hadn't been shot. At least, he hadn't been brought here as Kurt had told her. He could have been wounded or . . . killed. No! She wouldn't even think that. He might—just might—be alive and searching for her. He might not be motivated by any grand passion for her. He had made his feelings clear earlier this evening. But he might be motivated by pride. He wouldn't let Kurt Vandiver take away anything belonging to him. Lauren grabbed onto that thought and clung to it.

Too much thinking had caused her head to ache even more, so she held that one thought and kept repeating it to herself as though to will it into a reality.

Wat Duncan and Kurt Vandiver were having an argument and, as their voices rose, Lauren raised her head and looked across the cave floor from where she sat on an old blanket toward the two men. It was hard to focus on their figures no matter how she squinted.

"I tell you, we got sumpum' comin' outa this too, Mr. Vandiver." Duncan was standing a few inches from Kurt and looking defiantly up into the taller and more powerfully built man's face. "Juney and me, we been waitin' a long time to bring Jared Lockett down. And you owe us for heppin' you these past weeks. Ain't we done everythin' you axed us to? Didn't we do right by you with that Mendez woman?" He thrust his face even closer to Kurt's.

Kurt spoke softly. "I don't care what you do to her after I've had mine, but right now you're not touching her. Now the two of you get lost. When I need you again, I'll let you know." His superiority and carelessness was a mistake. He underestimated the Duncans' feral instincts.

At a small, quick signal from Wat, June threw her arms around Kurt's neck and toppled him to the ground. He landed face-down in the soft earth of the cave, June lying on his back, pinioning him on the ground with surprising strength.

Duncan laughed bitterly. "That'll teach you to cross a Duncan, Mr. Vandiver." He all but spat the name. "You hold him, Juney, while I service Miz Lockett here. Vandiver, you watch. You may pick up a few pointers."

June laughed into Kurt's ear, a soft, seductive laugh, and ground her hips against Kurt's buttocks. Kurt lay perfectly still, chagrined that he had let this lowlife get the best of him.

"Now, Missy, I'm gonna show you what a real man is like."

Lauren watched with terror-glazed eyes as Wat Duncan approached her. His lips were pulled back in a lubricious grin, revealing putrid teeth. His black eyes raked her body and she shrank back against the damp stone wall. He licked his lips as he knelt down in front of her and reached out to the top of her shirtwaist and began unbuttoning it.

Lauren's hands tried to push his away, but they seemed capable of only useless flutterings. His efforts grew more frantic as he ripped her chemise and laid bare her breasts, made fuller by pregnancy.

"Lookee here, Juney," he whistled. "Did you ever see any tits purtier than these? Soon's I'm done, you can play with 'em ifn' you've a mind to."

Lauren hadn't intended to do it, but she opened her mouth and a scream that originated in her deepest self propelled its way out of her throat and pierced the dim enclosure.

June jumped involuntarily at the startling cry and Kurt used that split-second to roll from under her and unsheathe his gun from its holster. He couldn't imagine why Duncan and his sister had overlooked it. He pointed the Colt directly at the center of Duncan's back and pulled the trigger. Lauren felt the thudding impact as the bullet entered Duncan's body. If a bone hadn't stopped it, it could have exited his body and entered hers.

He fell heavily against her, a puzzled expression on his ugly face. Blood bubbled out of his mouth. Lauren screamed again, fighting frantically to push his weight from her. She managed to lift him enough for her to slide from beneath him, and almost fainted when she saw his blood soaking into her clothes.

June stared transfixed at the body of her brother, emptying its blood onto the earth. She growled a savage sound as she attacked Kurt, who was still lying on the ground. They rolled together, punching wildly, thrashing arms and legs. June's thighs flashed whitely in the lantern-lit cave as she struggled for possession of Kurt's gun. Then another shot blasted through the cave. Lauren watched breathlessly as the two forms locked in combat lay still.

Finally Kurt moved, extricating himself from June's death grip on the front of his shirt. He slung her limp arms from his impatiently, pulling his legs from their entanglement with the dead girl's. He practically crawled to the heap of supplies that Duncan had gathered for him. Finding another bottle of whiskey, he uncorked it and tilted it to his lips, watching Lauren all the while.

He drank deeply, then lowered the bottle and wiped his mouth with the back of his hand. Several bloody scratches ribboned down his cheeks. June had managed to inflict her own brand of pain before she had died at the hands of this ruthless man.

Lauren was encapsulated in a mild stupor, viewing the atrocities happening before her apathetically. Her head was pounding with a cadence that was deafening to her ears and agonizing in its intensity. The walls of the cave were slowly tipping first one way and then another, and her eyes refused to focus on any one thing.

"You goddam well better be worth it," Kurt snarled at her as he stood above her. As she tried to focus her eyes, his form swayed in a sickening rhythm. He reached down to her and, with hands magnified to the size of hams by Lauren's distorted vision, grabbed her shoulders and hauled her suddenly to her feet. She closed her eyes as pain shot through her head. Dizzily she tried to stand upright.

"I've been waiting a long time for this," grunted Kurt as he feasted his eyes on her. He seemed unaware that her eyes were glazed and, if not for his support, she would have collapsed. One of the large hands closed over a tender breast and squeezed her nipple roughly, while with the other hand, he worked feverishly with the fastenings of his pants.

Lauren recoiled, and for the first time began to struggle against him. "That's right, Lauren, fight me a little. I don't want you completely docile."

She saw the swinging movement out of the corner of her eye just an instant before the rifle butt cracked into Kurt's skull. His eyes rolled back into his head before he fell heavily to the ground. He dropped Lauren in his fall and she collapsed beside him.

"Miz Lockett!? Is that you?" Crazy Jack Turner knelt down beside her cautiously. She focused on his hideous face, but never had anyone looked so beautiful to her. "What in hell is goin' on here? Where's your husband?" Lauren had a fleeting impulse to laugh. Of all things to ask at a time like this!

"Mr. Turner," she croaked. It was difficult to get her thick tongue to form any words. "Help me. Where are we?"

"You're in the back of my house, that's where. I thought no one else on earth knew about the rear door to my cave, ceptin' me. I heard the screamin' and shootin' and came through the tunnel to see what in hell the racket was all about."

He surveyed the bodies lying sprawled on the cave's floor. "Whoever shot those two should be decorated," he said without emotion.

Lauren realized that this must be an alternate entrance to Crazy Jack's house that jutted out of the rock wall above the river. The mutilated face gazed down at her with kindness in the eyes. He looked away, embarrassed, as she vainly tried to cover herself with the bloody remnants of her chemise. She tried to talk, but the words would not come. Her brain seemed incapable of forming a coherent thought. He sensed this and leaned over her. "Let's get out of here before that—"

He was interrupted when his breath was expelled in a great *whoosh* as Kurt's booted foot caught him in the stomach. Crazy Jack fell backward and rolled to his side, reaching for the rifle he had set down on the ground as he knelt over Lauren. Kurt was quick to note the action, raised his pistol, and fired. Lauren's scream was stifled by shock as Jack's body jerked when the bullet struck it. She looked at the prone figure. He was bleeding from a hole in his chest. "Oh God," she groaned. When does this nightmare end? She wondered.

Kurt kicked the sole of Jack's boot. "Godalmighty! Have you ever seen anything so ugly? I'd heard of this crazy old hermit, but thought he was only a legend that mothers used to scare naughty children. Surely, my dear, you don't prefer his company to mine?" he questioned as he noticed her whimpering and edging away from him. "Come—"

"If you touch her, you're dead." The words came out of the shadows on the other side of the cave near the entrance.

Lauren knew Jared's voice immediately. He had spoken, but she was as confused as Kurt, who whirled toward the voice and then stood stock-still, frightened and bewildered.

Two figures stood side-by-side. Both had on the clothes of *vaqueros,* their hats pulled down low and dripping raindrops from the brims. Both had pulled their pistols from their holsters and the barrels glinted in the light of the lantern. Both guns were aimed with deadly accuracy on Kurt's chest.

But what was so startling was that the figures were mirror images of each other. Bandanas were pulled up over their noses. They were of the same size and build and, in the dim light of the cave, their hair appeared to be the same dark color. In the shadows cast on their faces by the faint light, their eye-color was indiscernible.

Kurt's heart pounded and rose to his throat as he stared at what seemed to be twin apparitions, a figment of drunkenness, when everything seen is doubled. Slowly sanity returned, and he knew he was facing Jared and his half-breed brother. But they looked so much alike he couldn't tell which was which.

"Move away from her slowly, or by God, I'll kill you, Vandiver." Even as Jared spoke, it was impossible to tell which figure the voice belonged to. It was so controlled that the bandana over his mouth didn't move with the expulsion of his breath. "You've only got three shots left, unless you've used one we don't know about, which makes your position even more precarious. We have twelve shots between us. No matter how you add it up, you die. Move away from Lauren." There was steel in the level voice.

Lauren was finding it hard enough to focus, and now she was seeing four Jareds instead of two. His voice sounded faraway and indistinct, but somewhere in the back of her mind, it registered that he was here. Regardless of what he had said in the past, or what he had done, he was here to save her from Kurt Vandiver. When Jared spoke her name, she reacted by jumping slightly, and this drew Kurt's attention. With uncanny speed, he turned his gun onto the figure crouching at his feet.

"You aren't going to shoot anybody, Lockett, unless you want your bride to die. Even if you got me, I would kill her, too, before I died. No way I could miss. I suggest that you and that bastard brother of yours put down your guns and stop playing masquerade games." He laughed as he saw them glance at each other out of the corner of their eyes. "Now!" he commanded.

Reluctantly the men let their pistols drop from their hands. Kurt moved with cautious steps closer to the brothers, but even at a distance of a few feet, he couldn't make out which was which. He kicked the Colts dropped in front of their boots out of their reach, and stepped back hurriedly. He wanted to yank the bandanas from their faces, but he wasn't quite that brave. The dangerous stance of their bodies and the fierce hatred glowing out of their eyes were identical.

"Which one of you *hombres* is Jared?" Neither so much as blinked. "Which one is Jared?" Kurt's suddenly soprano voice betrayed his frayed nerves. The two figures could have been statues. "Then I guess I'll have to kill both of you. I can't very well rape this woman with one of you breathing down my neck, can I? And I'm in a great hurry to do just that." He paused, hoping that the threat would goad Lauren's husband into revealing himself, but both remained motionless, knowing well his intention. They knew, too, that Thorn was waiting . . .

Kurt Vandiver took advantage of having the mighty sons of Ben Lockett held at gunpoint. Since he was going to kill them, he might as well have some fun first. "I wonder if she's as hot as that Mendez woman? Took quite a bitch to keep a stallion like Ben satisfied all those years. I think Duncan was planning on getting a piece of that himself, but Lauren came out of the house too soon. Was that slice across her throat as clean as he bragged it was?"

A vile-tasting fluid filled Lauren's mouth and she almost gagged. The two men appeared unaffected by Kurt's taunts.

"All right then," he said. "I gave you both a chance to stand up like men." He took careful aim at one of them. Lauren held her breath. She thought that Kurt was only bluffing. He would never kill a Lockett for fear of the reprisals. He was basically a coward.

Refuting her supposition, the pistol shot exploded in the room of the cave. She watched both men, her hands covering her mouth, trapping her scream and terror inside. For long moments, neither of them moved: then, as a dark stain began to spread on one's shirtfront, he fell backward against the rock wall and slumped to the ground.

Her husband or her brother-in-law had just been murdered. It was too much to grasp. Her head was pounding and the rock room was spinning, dancing crazily in front of her. It couldn't be Jared over there bleeding, motionless and unconscious . . . dead.

Something tapped against her knee and she flicked it away. She didn't want to look, didn't want anything to interrupt her grief, her disbelief, at what she had just witnessed. Finally she forced her eyes away from the inert body across the cave and looked down at the persistent nudging. It was the barrel of a rifle.

Her befuddled mind couldn't imagine how the weapon was moving of its own volition. Her eyes painfully focused and traveled down the length until she saw the gnarled hands of Jack Turner holding it by the butt, moving it just enough to poke against her knee and get her attention.

Crazy Jack wasn't dead! He looked at her through eyes glazed with pain, and tried to communicate a silent message to her. She glanced at Kurt's bulky silhouette, his back to her, as he threw disparaging remarks at either Rudy or Jared, whichever it was who remained alive.

Lauren knew what Jack wanted her to do. But she knew she couldn't do it. Everything she had ever been taught, every principle she held, forbade the action Jack was urging her to take. Even if she had the physical strength and the mental capacity to do it, she knew she could not. It wasn't right. Nothing justified it. Nothing.

Jared? Her baby? At what point did wrong become right?

Why didn't this dark, moist, dreary room cut out of rock stop moving? Her head throbbed. She couldn't swallow. Her stomach wasn't going to hold what was in it much longer. Splattered blood was drying on her skin.

Has my baby survived this? Yes, please, God, she prayed. And my husband? Is that him lying over there with his blood flowing onto the ground? No! Jared! she screamed, but made no sound. She was stunned, dazed, weak.

Metal clicked on metal as Kurt cocked his pistol again.

God, please don't ask this of me, she begged. What if I miss Kurt and hit someone I love instead? I don't know how to fire a gun. God, please, let there be another way.

It was too late. Kurt was taking careful aim. Of their own volition, her hands reached out for the rifle. The dizziness and blurred vision vanished. With heightened clarity, she pointed the barrel at the broad back and pulled the trigger even as she heard the blast from Kurt's pistol.

The rifle butt slammed into her chest with unbelievable force. The echo of the rifle shot joined that of the pistol and bounced off the stone walls, filling the small, dank chamber with a deafening racket.

Then there was another explosion. This one was in Lauren's head. It was louder and more terrifying than the ones preceding it, and reverberated in her mind, blocking out conscious thought. Bright yellow flashes burst in her brain with the rhythm of heartbeats. Then all went black as she surrendered to blissful oblivion.

Chapter 26

Peace. Serenity. Silence. All welcome.

Dreams.

The Prathers' parlor. Lauren was sitting at the piano playing, though no notes sounded. Her dress was lacy and white, startling in its brightness.

Maria stood beside a smiling Ben. He was bigger than life and twice as robust as she had remembered. He glanced down at Maria and patted her arm fondly. Carson Wells was there, smiling at Lauren in his kind, sad way. What were these people doing in the Prathers' parlor?

She searched for another face, missing the notes she was trying to play. She tried vainly to spot a dark, lean face among the others. Whom was she looking for? She didn't remember. She only knew that she wanted to see that face more than any other. It was important to her, but why? Why? The vision vanished into a nebulous whirl around her and she was alone again.

Later, she was flying down a long corridor. There were pillars lining the sides of the hallway. Her hair was long, so long that if she flew between the pillars, it wound around them like a bolt of fine cloth. It trailed for miles behind her as she continued down the corridor, weaving in and out of the columns. At the end of the hall, she saw a figure dressed in a wedding gown. The face framed in the lace veil was like hers, but not hers. It was her mother.

Mother! she cried silently. Mother, I'm coming. She drew closer and closer to the apparition and gazed at the beautiful face that was almost transparent and yet real. Eyes exactly like Lauren's gazed back at her with apparent love, and she was suffused with joy. The lovely lips smiled and opened to speak. Though no sound came from them, Lauren understood what her mother was saying.

"Lauren, I'm so proud of the woman you have become. I loved you when you were a baby. I would come into your room at night while you were sleeping and watch you, kiss you, and touch you, marveling at your delicacy and praying for a brilliant future for you. You were such a sweet child. You never caused me any trouble. I'm sorry I had to leave you. I wanted to stay and see you grow up, but I was in such pain, Lauren. Please understand why I had to go when I did."

"Mother, Mother, I loved you. Did I ever tell you that I did? Did I?"

"Of course you did, darling. Over and over sometimes. I knew that you loved me."

"I wear your watch over my heart, Mother. Every day. And I look at the picture of you and Father on your wedding day." She spoke rapidly, trying to cover years in moments. Even as she spoke, her mother began to move away from her, and she wanted to reach out and take hold of her and never let her go away again.

"Mother, don't leave me, *please*. I need you."

"No, Lauren, you have someone else to take care of you now. We'll have time much later to talk. I'll be waiting for you, but now I must go." The image of the woman moved farther and farther away. She couldn't let her go. She had waited so long to see her, talk to her.

Her arms reached out for her mother, but something held them down. She struggled, but she couldn't shake off the force that held her back. "Mother!" she screamed as the beautiful lady vanished.

Once she tried to open her eyes, but the pain prevented her. She could hear muffled voices, but she didn't know what they were saying. It was so hard to concentrate.

Someone held her hand in both of his. Cool lips brushed her forehead lightly. A thumb caressed her palm. None of this was unpleasant, but she didn't want to cope with it yet. She slipped back into the region of dreams.

But the dreams were no longer pleasant. She recognized and knew Jared immediately, though he was strange and transformed. He stood in a blinding light, his whole body looking golden, shiny. He was naked except for sandals whose leather thongs wound around his muscular calves up to his knees. He carried a sword and a small, round shield. He looked like a Spartan warrior. His face was chiseled, hard. His sex stood erect and was the only part of him that was pulsing with life. He stood motionless. She approached him timidly, almost frightened by his stern countenance.

He was so handsome. She reached out to touch him, then recoiled in horror. He wasn't real, not human. He was made of stone, a beautiful carving reflecting the bright light around him.

Behind her came a ghastly laugh that made the hair on her neck rise and crawl. She turned and saw Olivia, her hair radiating from her head like Medusa's snakes. Her face was ugly and cruel. Lauren screamed, but Olivia only laughed harder, opening her mouth wide.

Lauren screamed again and again, thrashing her arms in an effort to escape those that reached for her. She turned her head wildly from side to side, trying not to look at the beast that stood before her.

Then, again, black oblivion.

The climb up was hard, but once she started, she couldn't stop. There, on the other side of the door, was the life she had left on the floor of the cave. She remembered it all now. She had only to open the door, and she would have to face all that she wished to forget. It wasn't possible. She wasn't strong enough yet. But she had to come back sometime. Now. She opened the door.

Her eyes took in the ceiling of Jared's room at Keypoint. The familiar window was there, but the drapes were drawn against bright sunlight she saw around the edges fo them. The large wardrobe stood against the opposite wall. Slowly she turned her head. Reclining in the chair at her bedside was Jared.

He wasn't dead! He was alive. She wanted to shout with joy. She felt a momentary pang of guilt at her happiness, knowing that Rudy must have been the one shot in the cave. Gloria! The children!

But she couldn't help staring in wonder and love at the man to whom she was married. He was asleep, his hands dangling off the arms of the chair. Lauren remembered seeing one of those hands hanging outside the buggy that carried him to his father's funeral. It had looked just like that, casual, negligent, yet bespeaking strength. That was so long ago. She looked up at his face and was instantly alarmed. He looked haggard and worn. His cheeks were sunken. Deep lines furrowed across his forehead and down the sides of his sensuous mouth. His lashes rested on dark shadows under his eyes. Several days' growth of beard stood out from his chin and his clothes were rumpled and stained. What had happened to him? She wanted to smooth the blond-streaked curls away from his brow where they lay limply.

The door to the bedroom opened slowly, and Gloria came through it carrying a tray with a teapot on it. She closed the door behind her and stopped with a small cry when she saw that Lauren's eyes were open. *"Gracias a Dios!* Lauren, you are awake."

Jared bolted out of the chair, trying to assimilate his surroundings after being startled out of an exhausted sleep. He stumbled to the bed and fell to his knees beside it, searching Lauren's face for signs of pain or delirium.

"Jared?" she sighed.

"Darling." He held both her hands tightly, as if he would never let them go. "How do you feel?"

Darling? Had he called her "darling"? Maybe she was still dreaming.

"How do you think she feels?" questioned Gloria with amusement, trying to ease the tension she felt building in the room. "She's hungry and weak, and probably still has a headache."

Lauren looked from one of them to another. "Rudy?" she asked with a trembling lip. A tear escaped her lid and trailed down her pale cheek.

"He's not near as nice an invalid as you are," Gloria said cheerfully. "He doesn't sleep all the time like you. Instead, he whines and complains and tries to sneak out of bed."

"He's alive?" Lauren was confused. Had she dreamed the incidents in the cave? Her head ached abominably.

Jared answered her quietly, smoothing back tendrils of hair from her cheek. "Yes, he's alive. It would take more than a wound in the shoulder to kill him."

"But I saw him die." She began crying in earnest as memory of all that had happened came flooding back.

Jared gathered her into his arms and shushed her. "It's all right, now, Lauren. It's all over. Don't cry. We're all safe. Shhhhh."

She rested against his strong chest, letting his strength flow into her. Then a terrifying thought occurred to her. The baby! She pushed herself away from him and looked into his eyes. "My baby? Is it all right?"

Jared looked puzzled and then smiled a gentle, patient smile. "Darling, you've been delirious for days and had some very confused dreams. That must have been one of them."

"No it wasn't." Gloria watched this tender scene with tear-blurred eyes. "Dr. Graham told me she was pregnant after he examined her. I . . . I thought you had enough to worry about, Jared, so I didn't tell you. Lauren, your baby is fine."

Jared stared at his sister-in-law stupidly before turning once again to Lauren. "You're going to have a baby? A baby?" he asked incredulously. "Why didn't you tell me?"

Lauren's lip began to quiver with emotion again and tears rolled down her cheeks as she remembered the last few weeks before that fateful night. Even now she could hear Jared's harsh voice and see his cold face as he denounced her in front of Olivia and the Vandivers.

When he saw the hurt so blatantly apparent on her face, he had a hard time keeping tears out of his own eyes. He cupped her face between his hands and whispered, "Why, indeed?" He wiped away her tears with his thumbs and looked deeply into the gray pools so full of disillusionment. "Can you ever forgive me for the hell I've put you through? Can you, Lauren?" His voice cracked with distress. His plea was desperate. Gloria didn't wait to hear any more. She crept out of the room and shut the door on the two who had so much to discuss.

Jared came out of the room about an hour later. He glanced over his shoulder at the bed one more time, assuring himself that Lauren was still there though he had just left her side. She was no longer in danger, but he wasn't taking any chances.

He found Gloria in the bedroom with her husband, trying to keep him in bed one more day. Rudy's shoulder was swathed in bandages, but it seemed to be mending properly. They looked up expectantly when Jared entered.

"She's sleeping again, but peacefully," he answered the question he read in their eyes. "God, but I'm tired." He collapsed into the nearest chair and buried his face in his hands, rubbing his eyes with the heels of his palms.

"She's been through a lot, Jared. We still don't know what happened to her before we got there. She's the only one who can tie up the loose ends, but we can't press her on it. It will take time for her mental injuries to heal." Rudy knew his brother had suffered since they had brought Lauren out of the cave.

Rudy had regained consciousness just in time to see Kurt Vandiver pitch forward after the rifle blast. Pandemonium broke loose. Jared leapt across the cave to Lauren's side, bending over her and shouting her name with a strangled cry. Thorn came in as stoic as ever. As had been arranged, he was waiting just beyond the room in the tunnel leading to the outside. It was his idea that the brothers go in looking like identical reproductions of each other. His Indian blood put a lot of stock in the psychological breakdown of one's enemy. Anything that would be unnerving to one's opponent was considered a weapon. He was to wait outside and make sure Kurt died if anything happened to Rudy or Jared. He understood and didn't question Jared's need to seek his own vengeance.

Thorn had come into the cave and assessed the situation quickly. He bent over Rudy and gave him a perfunctory examination. Fortunately it was a superficial wound. He hid the fact that an inch lower and the bullet could have punctured his friend's lung. Then he stood and walked to the bodies of Wat and June Duncan, giving them no more than a glance. As he knelt beside Crazy Jack and ascertained that the hermit was still alive, Thorn immediately began giving him first aid, because his wound was more serious than Rudy's.

Jared sighed and closed his eyes as he began to speak. "I filled her in on what happened. About how we left the cave with her and me on Charger and Cr . . . Jack riding with Thorn. She didn't think it was near as funny as I did that you fainted and nearly fell off your horse when we crossed the river."

A grin split his tired features and Rudy scowled at him. "Yeah, well, just let me get well and we'll see how funny you think it was." Rudy knew his brother was only teasing him, and they looked at each other with mutual love.

"Lauren's worried because Thorn didn't take out the bullet in Jack's chest," Jared continued. "But I told her it was too deep, too close to vital organs."

"I think he'll be all right," Gloria said. "Especially since Thorn's taking care of the wound."

"That's what I told Lauren," Jared said. "She's glad we left him with Elena." Elena had taken the old man under her wing as would a loving mother. With black eyes flashing and braids dancing as she tossed her head, she said, "He'll never go back to live in that old cave. I promise that on my daughter's grave!" Lauren had laughed when Jared told her about Elena's pledge.

He didn't tell her about the misery he had suffered. When they had brought her battered body back to Keypoint, he had been beside himself.

Her torn clothing and the blood splattered on her torso and face could only hint at the horrors she had been through. She had shown no outward signs of injury, but kept vomiting even in her unconscious state. Dr. Graham was dispatched, but it wasn't until noon that he finally arrived. He had diagnosed a concussion and showed them the lump on her scalp underneath her dark hair. He had also discovered that the lady was pregnant, but confided this information only to Gloria after taking one look at Jared's haunted face. Besides, the news about his mother would also be devastating to this young man. He feared for Jared's sanity.

But Jared surprised them all and received the news of his mother's death with grim resignation. The shock of seeing Lauren near death so absorbed him that it cushioned all other blows.

Dr. Graham followed Jared back to Keypoint after the expedient and private funeral for Olivia and Carson in Coronado. He was disturbed to find that Lauren hadn't yet regained consciousness, but said that he had done all he could.

"She'll have to come out of this by herself and in her own good time. I just hope she's . . . well, she received quite a blow on the head."

He left them with those grim words. That had been five days ago. Jared had barely left the room since then, pacing back and forth like a caged animal and snapping at anyone who even suggested that he rest.

Now, as he sat with his head hanging low over his knees, Gloria and Rudy felt compassion for him. He had come so close to losing the woman he had only recently realized that he loved.

He spoke in a low voice. "She remembered shooting Kurt, and it was horrible for her. She feels so damned guilty." He couldn't meet their eyes. "She said that he didn't . . . uh . . . do anything to her except . . . touch her. And Duncan . . . God! Will she ever be normal again?" He threw his head back and clenched his bared teeth, tormented by thoughts of the way Lauren had been mistreated. By everyone. By him.

"Did you tell her about Olivia and Carson?" Gloria asked.

Jared sighed wearily. "Yes. I wanted to spare her the details, but she wouldn't let me." He was still amazed that even in her own pain, she had consoled him for his mother's death. She had reached out pale, thin fingers and placed them against his lips as he told her about the grisly sight that Rosa had found in the office.

"Do you know what she said?" he asked them rhetorically. "She said that Mother was to be pitied. How can she be so generous after everything Mother said and did to her?" He shook his head in wonder. His voice was choked when he added, "She said that Mother had loved me in the only way she could, that it wasn't in her nature to love sacrificially."

Gloria was touched by his desire to believe that. "I think Lauren is probably right, Jared," she said.

"Yeah, well," he cleared his throat and sat up straighter, trying to control the emotions that were so near the surface. "She was shocked to hear about Parker leaving Austin when he found out about Kurt's death. Then I explained about the shady deals he was pulling off with some of his railroad buddies, getting kickbacks and so forth. She didn't know that all these months I've been skirting Vandiver and his yes-men and going to the top executives of the TransPlains Railroad and working out my own deals with them. Vandiver barely crossed the state line into Oklahoma Territory before he could be caught. I haven't finished with him yet."

"What about the railroad?" Gloria asked.

"Oh, we'll get it. On schedule, too." He smiled. "I told Lauren the bank would be subsidizing Kendrick and helping him expand his power plant's operation without jeopardizing anyone's water supply. I even promised to initiate some more community improvements in Pueblo." He laughed. "I feel like the Salvation Army."

"Jared, you jackass. Why did you let her think you were in cahoots with Vandiver?" Rudy was thoroughly disgusted at his brother's lack of openness with his wife.

"Because if we became too close, Mother and the Vandivers would have become suspicious. After I fell . . ." He blushed uncharacteristically. "After I fell in love with Lauren, I had to turn my back on her. Otherwise, they would have known I wasn't on their side and I would have been powerless to fight them. She had heard our conversation on the porch that night, Rudy, and thought I was talking about their plan to raid Pueblo."

"She didn't know you were planning to take a virtual army of *vaqueros* and ranchers and storm the Vandiver office complex in Austin. Thank God I was able to talk you out of that!"

"She thought all these midnight rides of mine were for meetings with the toughs that Vandiver had hired and not the men we had gathered up to ambush that gang when they rode into Pueblo." His lips curled into a half-smile. "She even had poor Pepe bury boxes of ammunition, thinking it was for the mercenaries. Pepe, of course, was sworn to secrecy about my organizing Pueblo's defense. As soon as she went back to the house, he had to dig the bullets up again." He laughed softly, then stared at the floor and shook his head. "I just hope we'll be able to reconcile our differences after all that's happened."

"Lauren is strong, Jared. She has shown a lot of fortitude by putting up with you for so long." Gloria went to her brother-in-law and hugged him. "Go on now, and *please* take a bath. And rest. I'll wake you later."

He looked down at her and then at his brother propped up on pillows in the wide bed. He smiled boyishly as he asked, "Does Rudy know about the baby?"

His brother winked at him broadly. "Yes, I told him," Gloria said and patted Jared on the back as he slumped out of the room.

Gloria was true to her word and awakened Jared when she had seen to Lauren's needs. But by the time Jared had dressed and gone into the bedroom, she was asleep again. He didn't have the heart to awaken her, but sat quietly in the chair beside the bed and watched her as she slept.

The next morning, Lauren awoke feeling much improved. Her brain wasn't fuzzy, even though she now realized the full weight of the past events. She felt stronger and had a much more active appetite.

"Well that's no surprise," said Gloria when Lauren mentioned it. "You have lived on sweetened tea for almost a week now."

Rudy came in to visit her. She was so happy to see him alive, she felt tears gathering in her eyes. Embarrassed by her emotion, he made light of his injury, not wanting to remind her of the horrors of Crazy Jack's cave.

In the course of the day, everyone came to see her but Jared. Pride kept her from asking about him. She knew she shouldn't have expected him. He always deserted her. She should be accustomed to it by now.

Gloria was furious with her brother-in-law for riding out that morning before anyone else was up and about. She tried to ignore the hurt she read in Lauren's eyes.

Something quite unexpected did cheer her, however. The clear notes of her piano were instantly recognizable, no matter how discordantly the keys were being pounded upon by the children.

"My piano!" she exclaimed.

"Yes," Gloria said. "Jared had it brought out here. He's closed up the house in Coronado for a while. He knew you'd want it. Rosa is with Elena, helping her care for Jack. The stables are now under Pepe's supervision. Jared also has another surprise for you, but I'll let him tell you about it."

Lauren's eyes closed and Gloria asked softly, "How do you really feel?"

"I'm all right. Truly. But I'm worried about my baby."

"I've told you a thousand times, the doctor assured me that it was fine. He wants to see you in a couple of weeks to make sure that the baby is growing, but you didn't lose it. Please believe me. I wouldn't lie to you."

Lauren took Gloria's hand. "I know you wouldn't. I was just so afraid." She plucked at the bedspread with her other hand. "The baby may be all I have left," she mumbled.

Jared returned late. He took Charger to the stables and commissioned Pepe to take care of him. Then he went into the bunkhouse and washed and changed clothes. He had been riding all day and felt grimy.

When he was clean and brushed, he went into the house. With a fleeting hello to Rudy and Gloria, who sat in the living room surrounded by their children, he went directly to his bedroom.

The room was dim; only one lamp on the vanity across from the bed had been lit. In the shadows, he saw Lauren leaning against the fresh linens that Gloria had put on the bed.

Her hair had been brushed until it shone like the wings of a raven. She wore a snowy nightgown, the scooped neckline molding to the gentle rise of her breast. Her skin, dusted by talc after a sponge bath, shone with the iridescence of a pearl.

Jared closed the door quietly behind him and walked toward the bed, thinking she might be asleep. But as he drew nearer, he saw that her eyes were open and that she was watching him.

"Hello, Jared." An emotional whisper was all she could manage.

"Lauren." He asked her permission to sit down by raising his eyebrows and she accommodated him by sliding over toward the middle of the bed. He lowered himself next to her and studied her face, taking in every lovely detail. Lauren had never seen such a tender expression on his face. Even during moments of passion, she had never captured so much . . . love . . . in his eyes.

"Today I rode out to Pecan Creek and looked over the place where I want to build the house. The way Rudy's family keeps multiplying. I think they will squeeze us out before too long." He took her hand. "I'm not sure if we can have the house completed by the time the baby comes, but we'll be able to provide our son— or daughter—with some kind of roof. I paced off a few of the rooms, so we can start construction right away." She looked so surprised that he said hurriedly, "If you like the site and the house plans, that is."

She stuttered, "I . . . I know I will, but are you sure you want me to stay?"

"Want you to stay?" he asked, genuinely puzzled. "What the hell are you talking about?"

"Well, you never . . . The marriage agreement and all . . ."

"Lauren, darling, when I thought I might lose you, I went crazy. I had never told you how much I love you. If you had died without knowing what you mean to my life, I . . ." He shrugged helplessly. Tracing her cheekbone lightly with his finger, he said, grinning, "Of course, you're twenty thousand dollars poorer than you could be. Am I worth it?"

"I'll reserve judgment. But it may take me forty or fifty years to decide."

He pinched her earlobe lightly. "I think I started loving you when you marched so proudly out of the house wearing that ridiculous riding getup." She too, laughed, at her own foolishness. "But you were haunting me even before then. I've no doubt that if Mother hadn't speeded up the process, I would have married you just to get you into my bed. Exactly as Ben had expected me to. He knew me pretty well." He smiled.

"Then you loved me just for my body."

"Well, it was a start," he said mischievously, his eyes glowing topaz. He kissed her then, sweetly and gently, on her mouth.

"Thank you for bringing out my piano," she said softly as she caressed his eyebrows with her finger.

"You're quite welcome."

"What's my other present?" she asked slyly.

He quirked one of the eyebrows so recently smoothed. "I can see that Gloria is great at keeping secrets." Lauren laughed. "How would you like a palomino mare for your very own? She's the color of honey and has a white mane and tail. Big brown eyes. Charger's hotter'n hell." He chuckled. "Come to think of it, I'm not sure I should entrust you with another horse."

Lauren was stricken. "Oh, Jared—"

Her distress was obvious and he was immediately sorry for his tactlessness. "I was only teasing. Truly. The accidents weren't your fault." He outlined the veins on the back of her hand with his thumb. "About Flame, Lauren, I—"

"No need." She covered his mouth with her fingers. "I understand you now."

"I almost died that night I slapped you. It was an accident. I—"

"I know all of that, Jared."

Silently they stared at each other, each dangerously close to tears.

"You're beautiful," he murmured. He hooked his thumbs under the straps of her nightgown and pulled it down over her breasts and lower until it bunched around her hips. He noticed the changes in her breasts brought on by motherhood and marveled at them. Her waist was still trim. He encircled it with his hands, his thumbs caressing her navel. Then he lowered his head and laid it on her stomach. His hair tickled, but she didn't move. She ran her fingers through the unruly waves.

"My baby," he whispered, and kissed her abdomen with an emotion deeper than passion.

"I love you, Jared," she vowed.

He raised his eyes to hers and smiled ruefully. "You said that to me months ago, and I more or less ignored it." His voice became gruff. "I'm listening now."

"Then come to me."

He seemed surprised. "You're sure? Duncan and Vandiver in the cave . . ."

"Was something else entirely. I want you."

He rose and undressed quickly. When he was settled under the blankets, he pulled her close and kissed her deeply. His hands traveled over her body, reacquainting themselves with the curves and textures he had missed for so long.

While still capable of rational thought, Lauren placed a cautious hand on the thick mat of hair covering his chest. "Jared, will it hurt the baby? Should we wait—"

"There's no way. No way," he said as he pressed her down deeper into the pillows, trying to capture her evasive lips.

"Jared," she said with more emphasis.

Patiently he raised his head and sighed. "Didn't I tell you once before that I would never do anything to hurt you? Would I lie about something as important as my own baby?"

She smiled teasingly. "Forgive me for thinking that at this moment your judgment might be somewhat clouded."

Her hands locked behind his neck as his mouth melded with hers. Her fingers moved over his back and ended up stroking his shoulders as he lowered himself to fondle and kiss her breasts.

"You taste so good," he murmured as his tongue flicked over

her aroused nipples. "Our baby is going to be the fattest one around." He stayed at her breasts to tell her of his loneliness of the past few weeks. "I wanted you so badly, Lauren. But I had to stay away from you for your own protection." He raised his head and she saw the sincerity in his eyes. "Tell me you know that."

In answer, she took him in her hand and guided him to the gate of her womanhood. Bathing the pulsating tip with the moistness of her own loins, she led him further into the welcoming folds of her body.

He stretched himself along her length, covering her completely. "Hold me tight, Jared," she breathed.

"Entrap me, Lauren. Surround me."

The sweeping tide of loving was carrying them away when she heard the soft, husky cry which was most precious to her. "Lauren, thank you for loving me."

About the Author

Laura Jordan is a pseudonym of the popular romance author Rachel Ryan, who is also Erin St. Clair. *Hidden Fires* is the first historical novel for this busy author who has had eight books published in the span of one year.

Her father was a journalist, so she may have been destined to write from the beginning. However, she took several detours before sitting down at her typewriter on a steady basis. She has done weather reports on television, as well as commercials, and she had her own talk show which was aired in Tyler and Dallas, Texas. That isn't all, though. She has also managed a cosmetic studio and still models.

Laura Jordan's favorite time to write is on a rainy day. Then, she burns logs in the fireplace she designed herself and lights some candles. It sets just the right mood for developing a romance story. Her next one, which will be released soon, is a moving contemporary novel.